When It
Rains . . .

Also by Angie Daniels

LOVE UNCOVERED

WHEN I FIRST SAW YOU

IN THE COMPANY OF MY SISTAHS

TROUBLE LOVES COMPANY

CAREFUL OF THE COMPANY YOU KEEP

Published by Kensington Publishing Corporation

When It Rains . . .

Angie Daniels

KENSINGTON PUBLISHING CORP.
http://www.kensingtonbooks.com

DAFINA BOOKS are published by

Kensington Publishing Corp.
119 West 40th Street
New York, NY 10018

All Kensington Titles, Imprints, and Distributed Lines are available at special quantity discounts for bulk purchases for sales promotions, premiums, fund-raising, and educational or institutional use. Special book excerpts or customized printings can also be created to fit specific needs. For details, write or phone the office of the Kensington special sales manager: Kensington Publishing Corp., 119 West 40th Street, New York, NY 10018, attn: Special Sales Department, Phone: 1-800-221-2647.

Dafina Books and the Dafina logo Reg. U.S. Pat. & TM Off.

ISBN-13: 978-0-7582-0742-5
ISBN-10: 0-7582-0742-5

First trade paperback printing: February 2005
First mass market printing: December 2009

10 9 8 7 6 5 4 3 2 1

Printed in the United States of America

ACKNOWLEDGMENTS

To my Lord and Savior for giving me the ability to tell stories that have touched the hearts of so many.

I'd like to thank Arlene Robinson for editing the original manuscript and making it just right.

To my siblings, Dennis and Arlynda Daniels, for over thirty years of unconditional love. To Terrence, Nichole, and Tanisha Moore for your love and support.

To the Daniels clan: my aunts Sylvia and Cynthia, my grandmother Eleanor, and of course my father, Dennis Daniels. Words couldn't begin to describe the love and gratitude I feel for everything you have all done for me.

To my mother, Kathleen Anderson, and my grand-mother Willie Mae "Mommae" Rogers, for always being there when I needed you most.

To my aunt Elizabeth Moore and all of her support and to her daughters April, Melanie, and Chiquita. Thanks for opening up your homes and your hearts. I love you guys.

To my best friends Tonya Hill and Novia Mearidy for your unconditional friendship. Also to my girls Kim Ashcraft and Norma Rhodes and my sister-in-law Ja'Net. When are we goin' back to Jamaica, mon?

To my gurl Beverly Palmers for taking the time to read everything I have written and catching the mistakes I missed. To my gurl Sherrie Branch for a friendship that has survived the distance.

To my extended family at Stylistic Hair Design. Special thanks to Tony for hookin' up a sista's eyebrows, and to my homey Tyrone Hollingsworth, a helluva poet who is gonna send me to an early grave if he doesn't put his talent to use.

To my Delaware bookclub family, In the Company of My Sisters, for all of your support. Thanks Melissa, Pam, Latasha, Sharon, and the rest of the bunch for making our weekends together loaded with calories!

To my fellow authors Doreen Rainey, Toni Staton Harris, Tanya T. Henderson, JM Jeffries, Seressia Glass, Natalie Dunbar, and Wanda Thomas. Thanks for your friendships, unlimited support, and words of encouragement.

To my new friends Maureen Hunter and Pam Robinson for reading everything I have written and loving it.

To my husband, Kenneth Darryl Hills, for all of your love and support 'cause I know I am not the easiest woman to get along with. Thanks for sticking by me all these years. To my children, Mark, Ashlie and Evan. I love you all. Thanks for making my job as your mother easy.

To all of the fans that have supported me and have asked for this book. I hope it is everything you have been waiting for.

To my new editor, Karen Thomas, for making this dream possible. I so look forward to years of working together.

Prologue

As he braced himself against the front door, Jay Andrews's eyes traveled frantically from the unmistakable swell of her abdomen back to the satisfied smirk on her round mocha face. While her announcement reeled through his mind, shock sucked the air from his lungs until he found the breath to gasp, "You've got to be fuckin' kidding!"

Kendra Johnson found his behavior rude; her mouth thinned with displeasure as she quickly concluded that Jay had no intention of inviting her inside, out of the chilly January wind. She brushed him aside and entered his masculine dwelling. With obvious familiarity, she traveled to his large mahogany dining room table and seated herself heavily on one of the accompanying soft chairs. Only then did she raise her chestnut-colored eyes to analyze his reaction. His panic-stricken expression was quite amusing. With smug delight, Kendra responded, "Docs *this* look like I'm kidding?" She shifted uncomfortably in the chair, her long wool coat

parting as she belligerently placed her palms on her inflated belly.

The blood raced to his head, which pounded with
disbelief. *This can't possibly be happening.* Within
seconds his mind traveled back almost seven months,
returning to the exact moment the only woman he had
ever wanted rejected him. It was also the same night,
that in a drunken stupor, he'd fallen into the bed of another woman—the same woman who now sat before
him, claiming to be pregnant with his child.

After shutting the door to his condominium, Jay
slowly crossed the living room, feeling the weight of
the world on his shoulders as he eliminated the distance between them. Perching a lean hip against the
edge of the table, he looked down at Kendra. Although
his temples pulsed, his face gave away no trace of the
dread that filled him. With a calm voice, trying to mask
his resentment that she had waited seven months to inform him he was going to be a father, he asked, "Why
the hell didn't you tell me?"

Kendra peered at the towering figure for several seconds, pretending not to understand his exasperation.
Then, inexplicably, she turned away to reach for an apple
sitting in a ceramic fruit bowl at the center of the table.
After several noisy bites, she allowed her eyes to settle on
his long face, responding to his question as if the answer
was obvious. "Because I didn't need for you to know."

Hands stuffed deep inside the front pockets of his
jeans, Jay pushed away from the table and paced a
small path on the chocolate carpet. Puzzled by her behavior, he asked himself if Kendra was trying to get
back at his black ass for something he'd unconsciously
done.

It was Thanksgiving Day two years ago when Jay

had found himself in agony with a toothache. With a long holiday weekend ahead, the chances of finding a dentist willing to be called away from a turkey dinner with all the trimmings was next to fuckin' impossible. Natalia Bonaparte, a good friend, came to the rescue by calling upon her former college roommate for a long overdue favor, and Kendra was happy to oblige. Not only did she alleviate his pain and repair his tooth, Kendra invited him to her home for a holiday dinner with pussy for dessert. Jay found himself instantly attracted to the Creole beauty, and while thinking with the wrong head, quickly fell into a sexual relationship with her.

Jay made it perfectly clear from the beginning that he wasn't looking for commitment. Even though he found Kendra buck wild in the bedroom, and she could suck a dick as if it were a damn lollipop, it was going to take more than a bomb-ass pussy to tie him down. However, Kendra had her own agenda. She began reviewing his caller ID and checking his pockets for phone numbers. The nail in the coffin was when she started dropping hints pertaining to love and marriage. True to his word, Jay had severed the smothering relationship. Now watching the smug expression on Kendra's face, Jay realized she hadn't taken the rejection well.

He stopped his pacing and stood only inches away from her chair, legs planted wide apart. In a coolly guarded tone he asked, "What the hell do you mean you didn't need for me to know?"

Kendra took another bite and chewed for several seconds before bringing her thumb to her lips to catch a drop of juice running along the side of her mouth. Sighing, she replied, "I was dating a surgeon who couldn't have children. He was intent on marrying me and raising this child as his own." Her eyes shone with momentary delight and she paused briefly, remembering the excitement of being engaged to Dr. Lawrence Hill, one of the country's most recognized heart surgeons. "I was willing to do whatever he wanted," she said. Then her smile faded, and she dropped her eyes and looked away from his steady gaze. "But, shit . . . since then, things have changed."

Immune to her theatrics, Jay narrowed his eyes and asked, "Changed like what?"

Kendra relaxed and transferred her gaze back to his well-defined face, blinking her eyes several times as if trying to get her emotions in order. "I mean . . . we aren't together anymore." She again bit into the fruit, allowing Jay a few moments to get used to the idea that she was back in his life and this time he couldn't do shit about it, then turned toward the table, where she found a magazine of sudden interest.

While she flipped through the pages, Jay studied her profile. He wondered what he'd ever found attractive about the conniving bitch. There was no denying Kendra was a beautiful woman. Even now, she looked *fine* as hell. Pregnancy had obviously been good to her sensitive skin; it was clear and smooth as butter. It had also added several attractive pounds to her usually thin figure. However, beneath the eye-catching package, Kendra was still the same selfish, manipulative bitch who had maneuvered herself in and out of his life for over two years. Although he couldn't excuse his own actions, Kendra had clearly lured him into her bed and taken advantage of his drunken state. It wasn't until after they'd spent that night together that he finally saw her with abrupt clarity.

Jay snorted at the memory. The following morning he had awakened with a fuckin' hangover and Kendra's naked ass pillowed against the curve of his body. He'd remembered their night only vaguely, but Kendra quickly filled him in with elaborate details. When he rejected her desire to resume their relationship, she lashed out with the rage of a damn lunatic. It was no wonder the doctor had changed his mind about marrying her. Kendra Johnson was like that crazy bitch with the split personalities named Sybil.

Jay waited, but Kendra was apparently in no rush to explain, which only pissed him off even more. Clearing his throat several times, he said in a formal voice, "I'd appreciate it, Kendra, if you'd get to the point."

As she looked up at him, Jay thought he saw two deep lines of worry appear between her eyes, then vanish so quickly he thought he had imagined them. He was further bewildered when her face suddenly creased into a smile.

Kendra crossed her swollen ankles, then purred, "Now that Lawrence and I are no longer together, I believe it's time we get back together and raise this baby . . . as husband and wife."

Fortunately his throat tightened, because Jay didn't know if he was going to laugh or cry. Never in his wildest dreams could he imagine doing anything permanent with Kendra's crazy ass. If the child she was carrying was his, he'd take care of his responsibilities as a father. But marriage? Shhiiit! That wasn't even an option.

Gazing down at Kendra's face, he noticed a shadow of uncertainty there, and it tugged at his heart. He didn't want to hurt her, but what little they once had had ended long ago. Her persistence and his feelings for someone else had closed that door.

Angie Daniels

Jay moved to rest his frame against the taupe wall, facing her. "Girl, you're trippin'. A baby's not gonna bring us together."

Kendra's heart sank at the sight of his grim face, but she stubbornly refused to believe it was over. She knew that with a little persuasion, Jay would do the right thing. However, from what she saw of his sour expression, she knew his decision wasn't going to be instantaneous. Disappointed, she realized it was going to take much longer than she had anticipated. Jay would fight her. Kendra nibbled on her lip impatiently. Shit! She didn't have the time to wait! Where was the joy? Send out the mothafuckin' champagne. Her voice low and wounded, she said, "Damn, Jay. I guess I don't mean shit to you."

Jay stood across from her, silent, his arms folded tight across his chest, waiting for her to continue.

Let his ass wait. However, the realization of his resistance, coupled with his silence, caused something inside Kendra to snap and turn cold. Following several eye-blinking seconds, she retaliated. "Without you, this baby's a waste of my time."

Jay had to sink his teeth into his lower lip to stop the heated words from falling from his tongue. What the fuck did she think a child was, a toy? Frustrated, he took a deep breath and tried to remain calm. "Can't you for once think about someone other than Kendra?"

Kendra closed the magazine and pushed it away. A note of irritation had spilled into his voice. *Who the hell does he think he is?* Jay was a man who liked to control every mothafuckin' thing. He was the one who had decided how often they would spend time with one another, and when the opportune moment came for his weekly booty call. And it was Jay who decided when it was finally time to go cold turkey on her ass. Well, this was one situation he would neither control nor dictate. *You've come too far to punk out now.*

Kendra lifted her shoulders, and her confidence rose. For once in her life, she knew who had the upper hand. She had an agenda, and damn if she wasn't going to stick to it. Setting the apple core on the table, she raised her eyes and met his probing gaze.

Jay's eyes were calm, but he shifted uneasily.

"Okay, let's get down to business," she said with straight attitude. "I don't want this baby."

Jay swept an agitated hand through his short wavy hair in irritation and dismay. In a thunderous voice that no longer tried to hide that he was pissed off, he bellowed, "Girl, what's up with you? A few minutes ago you wanted to get married. Now you're ready to give up your own child!" He pointed to her midsection. "How the hell do you expect me to react to somethin' you should've told me about months ago?" He forced himself to pause; getting angry wasn't going to get him anywhere. "Damn, Kendra," he said, his voice softer now, "if this really is my child I should have some kind of say."

"If this is *really your* child?" Kendra mocked, then rolled her eyes. "Fuck you, Jay! I never wanted you or this baby in the first damn place. I was doing it for Lawrence. Now it is too late for me to do shit about it." She took a moment to catch her breath, and her lips curled into a slow, challenging grin. "And as a matter of fact, you *do* have a say in the matter. Yes . . . or no?"

Jay stepped forward, his brow elevated in confusion. "Yes or no what?"

"Yes or no on whether you want to be a part of your child's life or not." She'd spoken in a low voice, but now she chuckled, and her next words rushed out. "As my husband, of course."

Not waiting for an answer, Kendra latched on to the edge of the table and attempted to rise out of the chair. Jay stepped to her aid but she held up a hand, refusing his assistance, and struggled into a standing position as she mumbled, "Don't touch me."

Jay was at a loss for words. The seriousness of their situation slowly sank in as he watched Kendra button her coat and waddle toward the front door. It wasn't until she reached for the doorknob that she pivoted sharply on her heels to face him. What he saw chilled his bones. Her expression was cold, her eyes glowing with hatred.

"I'll be damned if I'm gonna raise a child alone, especially when I never wanted it in the first place." Her eyes flashed a stern warning. "You've got six weeks to make up your fuckin' mind. After that, I'm putting *your* child up for adoption."

With that she was gone, leaving both the door and Jay's mouth wide open.

One

"What do you think?" Honey asked, studying her handiwork.

Wrapping long manicured fingernails around a hand-held mirror, Mrs. Doyle tilted her head from one side to the other, admiring her reflection, and said, "Sweetie, you've done it again."

Honey Love watched her customer run her palm along the upward sweep of her gray hair, held tight in a sophisticated French roll. She was pleased to see Mrs. Doyle finally looking forward to her fortieth class reunion tomorrow night.

Mrs. Doyle set the mirror down on the vanity, then reached into her billfold and removed several crisp bills that included a substantial tip. "I'll see you in two weeks." She clasped Honey's hands in gratitude before she rose from her seat and practically skipped to the coatrack in the corner.

"You make sure you call me," Honey called after her in a warm, maternal tone. "I want *all* the details."

Slipping her arms inside her navy blue wool coat, Mrs. Doyle nodded happily as she exited the salon.

Honey grinned as she watched the older woman walk out to her car with more pep than she'd had in years. Mrs. Doyle was a faithful customer, and it warmed her heart to know she'd done something to uplift the grieving woman's life. Since her husband's death, Mrs. Doyle had become increasingly self-conscious, and Honey had done everything in her power to try and boost the woman's self-esteem.

Honey moved to the front window, where her warm breath lightly fogged the frosted glass, and watched her customer climb into a silver Cadillac. She was certain the new hairdo and the smashing two-piece outfit Mrs. Doyle had brought in for her to see would definitely give the lovely woman the self-confidence she deserved.

As the car pulled out of the parking lot, Honey turned to her efficient, twenty-something receptionist who was just finishing up a call. "Candy, please pencil in Mrs. Doyle's two-week appointment."

"Sure," Candy chirped, eyes shining with enthusiasm as she bobbed her head. The action sent her microbraids swinging in several different directions as she reached for the large leather-bound appointment book on the corner of her desk.

Even though Honey had only just completed her first appointment of the morning, the salon already smelled of hair care products. After quickly straightening her workstation, she untied her smock and placed it on the counter. "I'll be in my office if you need me," she called over her shoulder, then headed to the back of the shop, stopping along the way to retrieve a cup of freshly brewed coffee.

Once inside her private quarters, Honey leaned back

in her chair and brought the mug to her lips, savoring the Colombian blend Candy always prepared to perfection. Her receptionist was a lifesaver. Although young, Candy was outgoing and extremely eager to learn, which was just what the salon needed as its first level of contact.

Tuesdays were slow at the shop. Her staff typically didn't schedule appointments until early afternoon, but Honey took care of the majority of her customers in the morning, allowing ample time to catch up on paperwork and prepare weekly checks for her employees. Peering over the rim of her mug, she looked down at the totals for the previous month and smiled. Love Your Hair had done well since she'd opened its doors four years ago.

Love Your Hair was an upscale salon in the heart of St. Louis that Honey had designed to make her customers feel right at home. The décor was pink, with burgundy carpeting in the waiting room that held four conversationally arranged love seats. There was a stereo for her customers' listening pleasure, and a large console television fully equipped with cable. At the back of the salon, across the pink and white tiles, were six workstations occupied by some of the best hairstylists in the city. While Honey also had a chair on the floor, it was booked by appointment only; the majority of her day was spent in her private office.

She was proud of her establishment. In fact, the shop had been doing so well she had an appointment at her bank next week to inquire about purchasing the vacant suite next door. She wanted to expand her business by adding six additional workstations and a kitchen.

Flipping through her schedule for the week, Honey realized she still needed to order a cake for a baby shower she was hosting over the weekend. She removed the yellow pages from her lower desk drawer and hummed while thumbing through the bakery section. Her best friend, Sasha Andrews, was scheduled to give birth to her first child in March.

Honey was thrilled to become a godmother, and was especially pleased that her longtime friend had finally found happiness. She leaned back in her chair and sipped her coffee, remembering the day Terraine Andrews walked into Sasha's life.

Sasha, a fashion model, had met the CEO of Diva Designs with the hope that if she modeled his designs, she could persuade him to purchase several of her own unique creations. Honey chuckled and shook her head as she remembered the power struggle between the two—Terraine's pursuit, and Sasha's denial of her feelings. Eventually Sasha had followed her heart and given in.

Tapping her knuckles on the desk, Honey felt a twinge of sadness as she remembered Terraine's brother, Jay. She hadn't seen him since the wedding, where she had served as Sasha's maid of honor and Jay was the best man. She remembered how *fine* he'd looked in a tuxedo tailor-made to fit his rugged body. Honey had hoped that maybe they'd have a chance to talk. But as he took her arm and they proceeded down the aisle, Jay's actions had been extremely formal, his responses monosyllabic; no one would have ever guessed they had once shared a powerful bond.

Honey sighed, remembering the way things had been. Once, Jay had been her close friend. Her ace. Her confidant. Staring up at the floral wallpaper bordering her office, she knew why he'd behaved as he did. *You brought that shit on yourself.* As much as she wished things could be different, she knew in her heart they couldn't be.

Her private line rang, intruding upon her thoughts. She reached for the receiver and brought it to her ear. In a professional voice she answered, "Honey speaking."

"Hey, baby, what's up?" the familiar masculine voice greeted her.

Closing her eyes as his words churned her stomach, Honey realized the time had come. Damn! Had it been two weeks? Where the hell had the time gone? "Hello, Lavell."

Lavell didn't miss the disappointed tone of her voice. "You don't sound too happy to hear from me."

Honey quickly tried to correct the mistake of allowing her feelings to surface. This time when she spoke, her voice was friendly as she blurted, "Oh no, you just caught me deep in thought."

Pleased to hear the thaw in her voice, Lavell let out a hearty breath. "Good. I was starting to think you didn't want to see me anymore."

Honey said, "No, not at all," then pressed her lips together. Lavell was the son of one of her many faithful customers. After he'd brought his grandmother to several appointments, and initiating idle chatter, Honey had agreed to have dinner with him. During the past two weeks, Lavell had done everything under the sun to sweep her off her feet: more dinners, movies, flowers, and chocolate. Tired of her family constantly on her back about bringing a date, Honey had even taken him to her mother's house for dinner last Sunday.

The problem hadn't arisen until that evening after Lavell had dropped her off at home. Instead of accepting her usual brief kiss on the cheek, he'd pulled her into his arms and kissed her with passion, parting her lips and seeking her with his tongue before whispering against her flushed cheek, "I want to make love to you."

Once upon a time, those words would have caused her to fall apart, but now, as she was learning to come to terms with her past, she had managed to remain calm. She hadn't called him since.

"How about a quiet candlelit dinner at my house to-morrow night?" he suggested in a deep seductive voice that came out as a very bad imitation of Barry White.

Panic rose in Honey's chest. Visiting a man's home was a dangerous game, one where there were no rules. This was a game she wasn't about to play. "I can't," she began, then quickly added, "I already have plans."

"How about Saturday night?"

"No, I don't think so."

After a brief silence Lavell said, "Then you tell me when."

How about never? she thought, but didn't feel nearly brave enough to say the words aloud. It already had been two weeks. She never dated anyone longer than that. And damn if she was going to start now.

Honey sighed inwardly and imagined a picture of Lavell sitting at the law firm where he was a partner. He probably had both feet propped up on the end of his executive desk. Sporting twists, Lavell was rawboned, with a handful of freckles the same color as his amber eyes, sprinkled across a broad nose. More than likely he was wearing one of his numerous psychedelic ties that looked as if they were cutting off his damn air sup-ply. He was preppy, clean-cut, and so damned profes-sional. When Honey once suggested a game of *NBA*

Jams on her PlayStation, he'd looked at her as if she had lost her damn mind. Talk about a fuckin' bore!

She sighed with regret. Their brief relationship had finally come full circle. There was no point in putting it off any longer; it was time to part ways. Honey closed her eyes and took a deep breath. *Here goes nothing.* "Lavell, it's been a wonderful two weeks, but I think things are moving too fast."

His laugh was indulgent. "I don't think we could possibly move any slower."

She rolled her eyes at his comical remark and tried again. "I'm not lookin' for a man in my life."

"Honey, I didn't ask you to marry me," he said with a chuckle. "I just want to get to know you better."

Her fingers tightened around the telephone. "I don't want to rush into anything."

Lavell gave a frustrated sigh at that. "Okay, I can deal with that. But what's that got to do with dinner at my place?"

She groaned inwardly, then asked herself why she continued to subject herself to the same ole' bullshit. "I'm not ready for sex," she said. "And that's where we're heading."

There was a long silence before he said, "I'm not gonna lie. I'm feelin' you. Nothing would please me more than to lick your sexy body from head to toe." He paused a moment, as though contemplating his next question, then asked, "Be straight-up with me, Honey. Am I wasting my time and money?"

Ain't that a bitch! Just like a man to remind a woman of all that he'd done for her so she'd feel obligated to do something for him. All the men she encountered did it, and for the same reason. To get some ass. "I guess you're wasting your time," she admitted, biting back a note of resentment. A strained silence fell between them. For her it was fuckin' déjà vu, repeatedly reliving the same scenario. From past experience, she was familiar with how awkward the situation was for a man when he was being rejected.

With a note of irritation, Lavell asked, "So what are you saying?"

"Can't we just be friends?" Honey asked, knowing the answer to that question.

She heard him click his tongue, then say, "I want to be more than friends. I want to make you my woman. Hopefully more."

Honey was quiet as she tried to think of an answer that would soften the blow, but failed.

Breaking the prolonged silence, Lavell cleared his throat, then said, "Yeah, whatever. I'll be in touch."

"Lavell, I'm sorry—" But all she heard was a dial tone.

Honey replaced the phone on the cradle, then dropped her chin to her palm and pressed her lips together. When was this shit going to end? Why, when it rained in her life, did it have to be a damn thunderstorm? Why couldn't it drizzle every now and then? She was drowning and didn't know how to swim to the surface. Where was her life preserver? It had to be out there somewhere. Only she didn't have faith that she would find it in time.

Her eyes flickered, then closed while she contemplated her next move.

Honey indulged in a high volume of dating, but always on her terms. Men occasionally got her attention, but never more than that. She never allowed anyone to get close, and ended relationships long before they became complicated. Staring down, she rubbed her palms together as she stood. With a sigh she remembered several months ago, when one man had come painfully close to making her think twice about her frigid behavior. Suddenly struggling against emotions she couldn't control, Honey saw Jay's fine ass invading her senses as clearly as that warm summer night he'd appeared on her doorstep.

Jay stood about six-three, with a sexy-ass body. He had the most gorgeous cocoa brown eyes. When Jay looked at her he made her stomach flutter, and his touch made her panties wet. Although she tried to deny the attraction, she'd always known it was only a matter of time before something kicked off between them. They had spent too much time together. Even though they had mutually agreed to maintain a platonic relationship, ultimately it became almost impossible.

Jay had somehow become a major part of her life. She had gotten used to seeing him daily for lunch, or even for an evening game of Scrabble. She was drawn to his sense of humor and wisdom. He was caring and adventurous. Honey began to think of him as she fell asleep at night, and he was the first thing on her mind when she rose in the morning. She became dependent on him, and had gotten used to his always being there. But it all came to a halt when Jay decided to take their relationship a step further.

Her lips tingled as she remembered the day she found him standing outside her window. She'd invited him inside, and within seconds, Jay had scooped her into his arms.

"What are you doing?" Honey asked with wide-eyed surprise as she realized what was about to happen. She had mere seconds to stop him if she dared. But she didn't. She trembled a little but didn't dare move away.

Jay reached up and curled his fingers around her delicate neck, stroking her jaw with his thumb. "What I should have done a long time ago," he answered in a voice husky with desire. "You're driving me crazy."

Dipping his head low, he gently slid his tongue across her mouth, sending juices to puddle between her thighs. Her small frame molded perfectly against his. Her robe gaped open, and he felt her warm flesh through her satin gown. Placing his hands inside her robe, he allowed them to roam up her smooth thigh all the way to the middle of her back. Honey gasped against his mouth. Tilting her head back, he teased her skin across her jaw and along her collarbone.

Abandoning all resistance in her desperation, Honey reached for him, enjoying how wonderful it felt being touched by him as he took her mouth in a hungry kiss that paralyzed her. In her wildest dreams, she had imagined this happening between them, but she had never expected to act upon her feelings. Delight flooded through her as he coaxed her lips apart and sought refuge for his moist tongue. As she opened her mouth wider, he deepened the kiss. The warmth of his arms was so embracing. Honey had found herself relaxing against him, her body tingling from the contact. His lips were persuasive, weakening her senses and confusing her mind. . . .

Honey quickly shook off the intrusive memory and raised the coffee mug to her lips. Taking one last sip, she swallowed the large lump in her throat. So many months had passed since she'd last seen Jay. She had tried desperately to return to life as she'd known it, but still fought daily to curb a passion she'd never expected to experience. No other man had ever come close to making her feel the way Jay had made her feel. He had awakened desires within her soul she never knew existed, making her want things she was incapable of having.

Honey closed her eyes and tried again to calm the battle that continued to rage inside her. Since Jay's departure, she had resumed her frigid behavior. But this time things were different. With Jay no longer in her life, she found herself increasingly lonely. She tried to curb her loneliness by burying herself in work; thus far, she had been unsuccessful. Jay continued to fill her thoughts, and there was nothing she could do to erase them.

Rubbing a palm across her blue knit sweater, Honey reminded herself that she couldn't afford to indulge in useless memories. She knew no matter how much she missed Jay, there wasn't a damn thing she could do about it. She had panicked that night and asked him to get the hell out of her house, all because she had been so fuckin' afraid, afraid that if she gave in to her desires, she'd be taking the chance of his discovering her secret.

Honey blew out a quick breath. "I don't need this shit." Brushing her thoughts aside, she picked up the phone and dialed the bakery to order the cake for Sasha's baby shower.

Exiting the hospital's double doors, Jay headed across the parking lot through a maze of cars until he located his gray Lexus. After stowing his large overstuffed duffel bag in the trunk, he climbed into the car and defrosted the windows before driving to the nearest highway.

Jay's eyes were on the road, but his thoughts were a million miles away as he sped down the long stretch of interstate. Working the knotted muscles at the back of his neck, he leaned back and again tried to relax against the black leather seat. He found his efforts a fuckin' waste of time as his brain replayed the events of the last several weeks.

After Kendra's visit, Jay intended to take a few days to think things through and then speak with her as soon as he returned from Memphis. However, what had started out as a three-day trip had somehow turned into four long weeks.

As a private investigator, Jay had spent the last month working for a large insurance company trying to uncover a scam artist. By the time he figured out who the hell was responsible, a gun had already been pointed at his head. Had he not managed to remain calm and duck when he did, the bullet that had been fired in panic would now be lodged in his brain instead of a painting on a wall. A flesh wound on his right temple would be a constant reminder of how close he'd come to dying. Jay had spent the last three nights awakening in a cold sweat after watching his life flash before his eyes.

The temperature in the car had finally climbed to a comfortable level, and Jay reached down to adjust the heat. Leaning against the headrest, he began to chew the inside of his lower lip as thoughts raced through his mind. Not once in his fifteen-year career had he ever come so close to death. Now he found himself wondering if the shit was really worth it.

Jay had entered private investigation because he thoroughly enjoyed it. A former police officer, he'd grown tired of the constraints of the law and had started his own investigation and security firm. His expertise came to be in high demand as he solved cases that had baffled even the St. Louis Police Department. Jay had dedicated the last five years to his business. His life had been one big adventure after another. But was it worth it? The long hours, the aliases, the danger? Jay scowled. He just wasn't so sure anymore. He kept wondering, if he had died three days ago, what impact would he have made on the world? Would he have been missed? Would he have been remembered?

He kept coming up with the same answer. *Hell naw.*

Reaching for a pack of cigarettes from his breast pocket, Jay lit one and took a long drag. He had a lot to be thankful for. The Lord had spared his life and given him a chance to make shit right, and he planned to do just that. First on his agenda was Kendra.

He could no longer make excuses as to why he'd gone with her that night. Excuses like he'd had too much to drink, or that he felt rejected and needed someone to make him feel good about himself. The simple truth was he'd been horny and his dick hard. He also didn't have an excuse as to why he hadn't once bothered to pick up the damn phone to call her during the last four weeks. No matter what excuses he made, it didn't make a damn bit of difference. They simply didn't change the fact that he was trying to run away from his problems. *Again.*

Jay swore as he slammed his hand down on the steering wheel. A beauty pageant's worth of women had shared his bed over the years. He loved sex and considered himself a master of the art, but he'd always been careful. Never desiring marriage or children, he couldn't afford to be careless. Yet somehow he'd managed to have unprotected sex and was now faced with the consequences. Jay just couldn't understand it. What he *did* know was that it was time to quit running and do the right thing. As much as Kendra wanted him to marry her, he couldn't. Not as long as he loved someone else. The free-spirited playboy he once was had somehow vanished.

Women had come and gone in Jay's life because he preferred it that way. He grew bored easily, and most of the women he met were interested in commitment, something he definitely wasn't looking for. That is, until he met Honey. His sister-in-law's best friend, Honey often found herself in the same circles with him. She had practically knocked the fuckin' air out of his lungs with her beauty, and her sultry voice kept his dick brick-hard. They'd become instant friends; in a matter of weeks they had developed the habit of spending evenings together, watching old reruns on *Nick at Nite*, playing Scrabble, or just sharing and listening to each other's dreams. What started out as simple friendship had eventually developed into something stronger, and so powerful that Jay had found it difficult to continue thinking of Honey as just a friend. Friendship was suddenly no longer enough. Honey stirred his deepest, darkest passions. Soon she was all he could think about, and Jay found himself frantically racing to her every evening, longing to be close to the sweet fragrance of her lovely beige skin, near the radiance of her irresistible smile, and within inches of her luminous gray eyes. For the first time in his life, Jay didn't want to fuck. He wanted to make love.

Jay stared ahead at the clear sky and remembered

their time together, just as he'd done during the past several months. Honey had managed to get to his black ass in a way no other female had. The more time they spent in each other's company, the harder it became to resist. Somewhere along the way, Jay had realized that life as a ladies' man no longer interested him. Single life had suddenly become lonely, and for the first time he considered the possibility of spending the rest of his life with one woman.

Jay frowned as he remembered that final night. He had thought he read mutual desire in her eyes, and because of it, had taken a chance. As a result, he'd jeopardized everything they had worked so hard to gain.

He had appeared on her doorstep that evening, uncertain of what he was going to say but knowing he had no desire to be anywhere else. Still embedded in his mind was the clinging negligee she'd worn when she greeted him at the door, a chocolate nipple peeking out of the corner. Unable to resist any further, he'd pulled her into his arms, where her body had melted against his. They had shared an intimate encounter, on the verge of making love, before everything came to an abrupt halt.

Honey's eyes flew open as she scrambled upright on the couch and pushed him away. Jay reached out for her again but she quickly rose and walked away, covering herself with her robe.

Jay saw the fear etched into her face and reached out to comfort her, to reassure her there was something special going on between them, but she looked ready to dash across the room.

Finally, he broke the silence. "We need to talk." He stepped toward her but Honey backed away, as if not trusting herself to be touched by him again.

She shook her head and said, "Not right now. I need time to think."

Jay muffled a curse, then said, "I'm not leaving until we talk."

"Please, Jay, not today," she said, her words a plea.

He'd seen her pain, and against his better judgment, he'd ground his teeth and nodded. . . .

Her rejection had slashed him so deeply that he'd buried himself in his work, taking every assignment he could that led him far away from St. Louis.

Now as he looked back on that night, he realized that if he'd thought things through with a level head instead of focusing on his wounded pride, he would have noticed that Honey's expression wasn't one of disappointment. It wasn't until last night, while his life was flashing before his eyes, that Jay suddenly realized that her wide-open eyes had been clouded with pain. Something had frightened her. Something had been wrong. Could she be a virgin? Jay shook his head, unconvinced. *Hell naw.* Honey had to be experienced. She had an active social life and was a full-fledged flirt who always appeared to be hard-nosed when it came to the opposite sex.

And yet . . . he'd seen the vulnerable side. What if she *was* a virgin? It would answer so many fuckin' questions. As Jay thought about it further, it began to make sense. Yes, Honey had to be. Why else would she have panicked that night? He'd been too damn blind to see that then. Selfishly, he'd thought only of his own feelings. Now it was too late to repair one of the biggest mistakes of his life.

With a scowl, Jay remembered leaving her house that evening, and his decision to patronize a local bar to nurse his pride. He had felt rejected and hurt after receiving a massive blow to his ego, and believed that if he got drunk enough, it would erase the pain of his broken heart. As misfortune would have it, Kendra had walked back into his life, taking a seat at the bar beside him.

Then his mothafuckin' life changed.

Jay released an irritated sigh. What would Honey think if she found out that on the same night she'd asked him to leave he'd gone home with an ex-girlfriend . . . who was now carrying his child?

But was Kendra really carrying *his* child? He wouldn't put anything past that bitch. He'd been so drunk that night he wasn't really sure. What happened was one big blur. He scowled at his careless behavior and thought he felt some relief that Kendra was considering giving the baby up for adoption. What the hell would someone like him do with a baby, anyway? He was a private investigator; his days changed at the drop of a hat. It would be unfair for him to take on the responsibility of raising a child, because he knew absolutely nothing about being a father. So why did he feel like shit?

Because you were given a second chance.

Jay took his foot off the gas and put the Lexus on cruise control. He'd never known what it was like to have loving and nurturing parents. His own father had fallen victim to a drive-by shooting before he was even born. His grief-stricken mother had died only seconds after giving birth to him. The only parent Jay had ever known was a controlling, manipulative grandfather who had refused to acknowledge his illegitimate son conceived during a brief encounter with a local waitress. Jay wasn't like his older brother, Terraine, who had recently married and was expecting his first child.

Jay rolled down the glass and flicked his cigarette

out of the window into the chilly air. One thing he'd learned over the past several days was that he couldn't continue to run from shit. He'd run from so much shit all his life, and made too many damn mistakes along the way. It was time for him to come to terms with his decisions, put his pride aside, and fight for the things he wanted most.

How much was he willing to give up in the process? *Every fuckin' thing.*

This time he was going to make everything right.

"It's time," he whispered.

Even though he was still unsure of which direction his life was headed, Jay pressed down on the accelerator, no longer afraid of what the future might hold.

Two

"Oh, this is so cute!" Sasha cried, holding up a tiny pair of pink booties. "These are the smallest I've ever seen!" She showed the gift to her guests and listened to their awed reactions.

Both the large Persian rug and the polished hardwood floor under her feet were covered with gifts for the upcoming birth. When a recent ultrasound confirmed that her first child was a girl, friends and family had taken advantage of that vital piece of information to purchase plenty of pink and yellow gifts.

Honey passed Sasha another beautifully wrapped package. "This one's from the future grandmother," Honey announced, then glanced over at Roxaner Moore, who sat, beaming, at the far end of the couch. Roxaner was a petite woman with a girlish figure who managed to look superb in a washed-blue pantsuit. Her ebony hair, graying only at the temples, was cut into a short, tapered style that drew attention to a dark mocha face that was clear and free of wrinkles. Her gentle walnut eyes sparkled with pride. For years, Roxaner had waited patiently for the day to come when she could have the pleasure of a grandchild to spoil; now it was about to happen.

Sasha carefully opened the box, beautifully decorated in pastel purple paper, trying to prevent it from tearing. She believed anything worth saving could be used again. Even though she had married into wealth, she hadn't allowed it to spoil her.

Lifting the lid, Sasha gasped and stared down at its contents for several seconds. When she looked up at Roxaner, her hazel eyes brimmed with tears. She removed an antique carousel music box and held it up for everyone to see, then said softly to her mother, "I always wondered what happened to this."

Roxaner nodded knowingly. "I put it away, saving it for this day."

Sasha could hear the love in her mother's voice. The family heirloom had passed to all the women in their family for generations. It had once belonged to Sasha when she was a little girl. One day she had dropped it on the floor. It had broken, and because she'd never seen it again, she thought her mother had been unable to repair it. However, Roxaner had the miniature horse glued back in place, then stored the carousel away in a box on a shelf for years, waiting for this day to arrive. As a single tear rolled down her cheek, Sasha rocked her swollen body off the couch and rose to hug her.

Honey watched the play of emotion on her friend's face, sharing in her joy. Her future goddaughter was going to be born into a family surrounded by love. She envisioned a little girl with Sasha's caramel complexion and naturally curly hair, and Terraine's signature raisin-brown eyes. Honey's throat tightened as she was painfully reminded of her own personal loss. *Damn, girl! Don't even go there.* She swallowed quickly, then handed Sasha another box. "This one's from me."

Looking down at the wrapping paper decorated with *Sesame Street* characters, Sasha grinned. She raised the lid and eagerly removed a lovely white christening gown. "It's darling," she gasped before leaning over to hug her best friend.

Her own tears unshed, Honey gazed at her friend and said, "I can't wait to see her wear it! She's gonna look absolutely beautiful."

Several more gifts were opened. Sasha unwrapped a hand-sewn quilt, baby books, and several adorable outfits. Shortly thereafter, the group moved to the dining room, where a well-known caterer had delivered a sumptuous luncheon of teriyaki ribs, smothered potatoes, and a variety of salads.

Honey was cutting a long sheet cake decorated with pink candy booties when she felt a strange sensation. Sasha's husband, Terraine, had walked through the door, and Honey didn't have to turn around to know Jay was with him. She knew the brothers had gone ice fishing, and planned to return only after the guests had gone home.

Even with her back to the foyer, Honey was instantly aware of the exact moment Jay stepped into the room. A tingly sensation began to travel through her breasts making her nipples hard and aroused. Her breath caught in her throat as she turned slightly to her right. Jay was standing against the wall, laughing at something Roxaner had said. He still looked just as she had remembered him, the image etched in her brain for months: *sexy as a mothafucka.*

Honey looked away before Jay had a chance to notice her. She resumed cutting the cake, but realized her hand was shaking as she placed slices on the small decorative plates. She took several deep breaths, trying to calm her body. *Relax, girl.*

Echoes of laughter ricocheted around the room, but Honey couldn't hear anything above the hammering of her own damn heart. With great effort, she tried not to turn his way again, but Jay's silence and the feeling that he was looking her way made her feel too self-conscious. With her mind wandering, her eyes eventually looked up to see Jay still standing in the corner, making it no secret that he was indeed watching her.

Cheeks burning with embarrassment, Honey grabbed the empty punch bowl from the table and backed out of the room into the kitchen. Once she was alone she set the bowl on the counter and let out a deep, shaky breath, realizing she'd been holding it since she found Jay assessing her. She ran nervous fingers through her hair, displeased with her shameful reaction. She knew it would be difficult seeing him again, but she'd never imagined her reaction would be so powerful.

Honey moved away from the Formica countertop and shook her head, trying to remove any further thoughts. She scowled and mumbled, "Shit," as she reached into the refrigerator for punch ingredients. How the hell could one man have so much power over her? She didn't like it one bit. After being in control of her emotions for almost twenty-seven years, she was angered that one man was capable of turning her life upside down.

After mixing the tropical concoction, Honey poured herself a sample. Then, satisfied that she'd gotten the proportions right, she picked up the bowl, feeling more in control, and turned to leave. She almost collided with Jay, whose muscular frame filled the entire doorway. Even though punch sloshed onto the floor and all over her brown leather boots, Honey barely noticed. Even as she grabbed a dishcloth and hastily wiped up the spill, her eyes were drawn to his broad shoulders and those bulky arms folded comfortably across his massive chest.

"Hey, Honey," he said. Their eyes locked.

At the sound of her name falling from his lips, Honey's heart raced wildly, and her eyes moved appreciatively over his frame. His muscular, solidly constructed body was the color of bread toasted to perfection. He had the most remarkable brown eyes, accented by bushy coal-black eyebrows that connected slightly in the middle. Hanging from his left earlobe was a small gold loop that made him appear sexier than ever. Her eyes shifted to his full lips, and her memory relived the exquisite softness of their touch that had sent shock waves through her body. Sensing there was something different about him, she shifted her gaze and realized he was sporting a beard that had grown in smoothly across his square jaw, connecting with a thin mustache. It didn't appear unkempt, but added a little flava to his overall rugged image. She had to resist a strong urge to reach up and stroke it as soon as she placed the punch-soaked cloth on the counter.

As he stood there towering over her, Jay's smile broadened and two deep dimples appeared at his cheeks. His nearness sent a small shiver racing down her back, causing her to respond with a breathless "Hey."

Silence fell over them as Jay recalled the last time he'd seen her: at his brother's wedding. That afternoon, it had taken all he had not to get down on one knee and beg her for another chance. Instead, he'd acted as cool as he could possibly manage and kept his distance, giving her what he believed she wanted: to be left alone.

Jay dropped his arms and stepped inside the room to stand in front of her. "What's been up with you?" he asked, eyes glued to her face.

His broad, dimpled grin was contagious, and Honey managed to return the same friendly smile. "I . . . I've been well," she managed to say. The depth of her feelings at seeing him again made her voice raspy, and she cleared her throat. He was so close she could smell him. It was a dizzying combination of a spicy scent that was so much his own, but tainted with . . . stankin'-ass fish, compliments of his fishing trip that day.

She took a moment to regain her composure, stepping back from this giant who stood a foot taller than she, minimizing the electrifying potential of their bodies touching and attempting to steady her emotions. "I've been meaning to call you. I, uh, need to upgrade my security system." Her voice trembled, but she was surprised at how easily the lie fell from her lips. *Bitch, why did you say that? There ain't a damn thing wrong with your burglar alarm.* On the other hand, her words weren't completely untrue. If she got the loan to purchase the space next door, of course she would need to have the space rewired.

Jay's smile faltered. He, too, had felt the unforgettable heat generated when their bodies were mere inches from each other, and he wanted more of it. He felt so alive when she was near. Her matter-of-fact statement affected him more than he cared to admit. He felt a tinge of disappointment as he came to understand that she had intended to contact him strictly for business purposes.

Taking a step closer, Jay tilted his head and looked down at the tiny woman, happy to see that her gorgeous face still brightened an entire room. Shiny chestnut curls framed a heart-shaped face of delicate beauty. Long, dark lashes surrounded enormous gray eyes the color of a stormy sky, eyes that seemed to grow darker the longer he stared into them. He felt the strongest urge to trace her high, exotic cheekbones tenderly with his fingertips, to brush his fingers lightly across her charming little nose, and then caress the most beautiful creamy skin he'd ever come in contact with.

But that shit wasn't going to happen. Forcing himself back into business mode, he replied, "No problem. I'll have one of my technicians swing by your salon next week." He immediately changed his mind, but chose not to mention it. Not just yet. As the owner of Extreme Measures, a private investigation and security firm, Jay seldom worked the field unless his expertise was needed—he had employees trained for almost every type of case the agency accepted. But this time he didn't want to pass up an opportunity to spend time with her. In this particular case, he was more than willing to make an exception.

"All right," she answered awkwardly, telling herself she needed to be strong and resist him. Maybe she should say something to erase any thought that she regretted her decision to end their relationship. But his intense gaze caused her throat to tighten, preventing any additional discussion.

Granting him no more than an additional flickering glance, Honey swept past him and hurried into the dining room, trying not to let her nipples brush against his clothing. She placed the bowl at the center of the table and leaned against it, needing those few seconds to get her emotions back under control. Jay's presence had left her feeling vulnerable, and Honey was anxious to regain her better senses. Her brain seemed to stop functioning when Jay was near. Her heart was beating so fuckin' loud she could feel it pulsing in her ears. She had read the desire in his eyes, and because of it, her emotions had become a mixture of irritation and unwanted excitement.

For the rest of the afternoon, the women played silly baby games while the brothers sat out on the wrap-around deck drinking brews and cleaning fish. It was cold outside, but Jay didn't notice; he found himself repeatedly looking over his shoulder through the glass and into the living room at Honey, whose skin appeared to glow under the recessed lighting. She had paired a pink cashmere sweater with snug blue jeans that made her ass look sexier than ever. As he watched her mouth curl into a sensual smile, he felt a strong urge to go back inside and press her petite form against his, embracing her in a passionate kiss that would erase all insecurities and doubts from her mind. Once, when she turned toward the glass, their eyes tangled and love flooded the gaping wound in his heart as he remembered how painful it felt when she had shut him out of her life.

Jay's feelings for her hadn't changed. Honey still made his cheeks flush and his most intimate part hot and aroused. Gradually, as he observed her, he realized why he hadn't been successful in removing her from his heart. *That's what love does.* Jay's eyes widened with the realization. He loved Honey.

Terraine snapped two fingers before his brother's eyes, trying to release him from his trance. "Jay, man, when you gonna admit Honey's got your nose wide open?" Terraine teased.

Startled, Jay blinked several times, then frowned before reaching into the bucket for another fish.

The brother Terraine grew up with had always kept a string of women on hand, and flinched at the word *commitment*. But in the last several months, detailed accounts of one *phat* ass after another seemed to have ceased. Terraine was certain Honey had had something to do with Jay's unusual behavior. After observing Jay's far-off expression only seconds ago, Terraine was more certain than ever. He couldn't have picked a better woman for his brother.

After a while, Jay stopped skinning catfish and slowly raised his head. With a sigh of defeat he answered, "What good would it do? Honey ain't hearing it."

Terraine noticed that the look in his brother's eyes at the mention of Honey's name hinted otherwise, and was pleased by his observation. Maybe there was hope for his little brother after all. "There's more to that woman than meets the eye," he said.

"True, that." Jay shrugged. "But knowing Honey the way I do, she's got a string of brothas riding her coattail."

Terraine wagged his head. "Nobody special. I asked my wife this morning."

Jay's brow rose as he glanced over at his brother. Marriage had obviously turned Terraine's ass into a matchmaker.

"I think you need to take your time with her," Terraine said in a brotherly way.

"And have her bruise my pride again? Man, you got life fucked up!" Jay laughed dryly, then summarized the night Honey had kicked his ass out of her house.

Terraine frowned at his brother's sudden lack of confidence. "Since when do Andrews men back down from a challenge?"

"When their opponent is Honey Love." Jay shook his head, frowning at the memories. "That girl ain't no joke."

Terraine smirked. "And neither are you. Nothing good ever comes easy. You forget I went through hell trying to convince Sasha I wanted her in my life. I think if you're persistent, it'll pay off in the end." He pivoted his head toward the window. "I've noticed the way she be checking you out when you're not looking."

The corner of Jay's mouth curled into a quizzical grin. "Really?"

"Really." Terraine tossed another fish into the bucket of water. "So, was Honey what you wanted to holla at me about?"

Dread slid down Jay's back and settled like acid at the bottom of his stomach. He'd been putting off this discussion all day and debated putting it off a little further, but decided not to. He'd kept it to himself for more than a month. If he didn't share his dilemma soon, he was going to burst. "Naw, man," he said, then paused before adding, "I need to holla at you about Kendra."

Terraine's brow creased. "Natalia's friend? 'Fuckin' Fatal Attraction' Kendra?" He chuckled. "Is she still trying to get you to marry her crazy ass?"

Jay scowled at the memory of the two of them watching a football game at his condo while Kendra staked out his front door, demanding that he open the damn door. "Yep." He took a deep breath, then allowed the words to flow from his tongue: "Only now her ass is pregnant."

Terraine almost dropped the knife from his hand. "Pregnant? By whom?" A light of understanding finally dawned in his eyes. "You?"

When Jay didn't answer, Terraine let out a long whistle, flabbergasted. "Damn, Jay. How the hell you let that happen?" He noted the uncomfortable expression on Jay's face and frowned with concern. Damn, his little brother was slipping. In the past, Jay had been so careful. He wouldn't dream of sticking his dick anywhere without being strapped first. What had brought on this careless behavior? He dropped his arms to the table and leaned forward. "You want to tell me about it?"

Honey looked out onto the large wooden deck and watched the brothers sharing what seemed to be an intense conversation. She could tell by the deep lines across Jay's forehead that whatever they were discussing was important. Suddenly, she missed the long conversations they'd once shared.

She watched Jay for several more moments, taking in all angles of his body. He looked magnificent in a pair of faded blue jeans that made his backside look ever so *fine*, paired with a heavy navy blue hooded sweatshirt that covered his ears. Even though Terraine had carried a kerosene heater out onto the deck, she saw Jay rubbing his palms together in an attempt to keep warm.

On two occasions, she'd seen Jay taking furtive glances in her direction, and this had left her unglued. The kiss they had shared that night had forever changed things between them. Honey knew she would never be able to look at him again without remembering the caress of his hands and lips against her bare skin.

"He's gorgeous, isn't he?" a nearby voice inquired.

Roxaner's voice pulled her back to earth with a start. Roxaner had observed her steady gaze out onto the deck, and was now smiling brightly.

"I . . ." Honey looked at Roxaner's knowing smile while her heartbeat roared in her ears, and started to deny the attraction. But after one look at Roxaner's face, she didn't bother. Roxaner could always figure her out. Honey felt like a member of their family, and Roxaner was her surrogate mother. Honey had been around Sasha and her family since puberty. Because the Loves had had to struggle to make ends meet, Honey had loved the traditional middle-class lifestyle at the Moores' house. Roxaner, a college graduate in social work, had served as a positive role model in Honey's life and had steered her future in the right direction. Roxaner always kept a watchful eye on her, and the two communicated frequently.

Now, as always, Honey could not pull the wool over her eyes. On the one hand, she wanted to quickly deny her attraction, but on the other, she was tempted to pour out her heart to Roxaner. Seeing Jay again had brought desire spiraling from the depths of her soul. Was her attraction that obvious? Honey only shrugged, but the pink color in her cheeks positively revealed her feelings.

To Honey's shrug, Roxaner laid a gentle hand on her arm. "I might be old, but I know the signs of love when I see them." She moved in closer to whisper, "Good choice." She then winked and rose to carry a tray of chips and dip into the kitchen.

Honey felt a rush of heat to her face. She thought she could control her emotions, but found herself being magnetically drawn to Jay again. Tense now, Honey also rose and carried a bowl of peanuts into the kitchen. The shower was ending, and she had promised Sasha she'd stay behind to help clean up. With Jay only a few feet away, and with the possibility of him coming in from the cold at any moment, she wanted to get it done as quickly as possible.

While Sasha said good-bye to her guests, Honey loaded the dishwasher, then stood admiring the room. She loved Andrews Manor, with its high-ceilinged, massive rooms, especially the enormous kitchen with its state-of-the-art appliances. Grabbing a dish towel from the sink, she began mopping the countertop. Totally engrossed, she was unaware of Jay standing in the room until she heard his familiar voice behind her.

"You look good doing domestic duties."

Spinning around, Honey found herself again face-to-face with him, and her nervousness soared. Jay wore a crooked smile as he leaned against the island that sat in the middle of the room. She found it almost impossible not to stare back at the man who'd haunted her dreams for months, and realized how much she'd missed him. *Damn him for being so fuckin' fine.*

"Boo, I've missed you," he said, almost as if he'd read her thoughts.

"I've missed you, too." She couldn't have stopped the words falling from her lips even if she'd wanted to. Deep down, it was how she felt. But the surprise on Jay's face made her wish she could take them back.

Jay felt an inkling of hope at this candid revelation. He pushed away from the island and stepped forward. "Then why haven't you called me?"

Honey saw the curious expression on his boyishly handsome face, then looked at her hands, not wanting him to even suspect that she'd so much as given him a second thought. She quickly turned her back to him, crossed the kitchen, and began to wipe down the stove top before answering, "I thought it was best."

Jay came behind her, and his breath teased the hairs along the back of her neck. He lightly grasped her shoulders, causing her to gasp. Briefly closing her eyes, Honey tried to steady her heartbeat. Jay turned her toward him, taking her chin and forcing her to look at him. His eyes gleamed with curiosity, and she trembled at his touch.

"Best for whom? You or me?" he said, needing to fully understand why she had ended their friendship.

Honey's dark lashes fluttered and lowered, breaking eye contact. She didn't want him to see the fear in her eyes. How could she tell him she cared too much for him? That because she was aware of the extent of his feelings, she felt it unfair to mislead him into believing there was a chance of anything permanent developing between them?

Trying to regain self-control, Honey straightened her shoulders, met his gaze, and mumbled, "For both of us." Her heart was thundering beneath her breast.

Jay concluded she was lying and snorted, "I'm not buying that shit this time. I shouldn't have taken this long. I should have confronted you months ago, but I let my pride stand in the way." He moved closer and raised a hand to her cheek. In doing so, he felt her shudder. "Why do you insist on running away from your feelings?" When she didn't answer he continued,

"I'm not going anywhere this time." No longer thinking about his pride, he gazed down at her lovely face and said, "I want you, Honey. And I know you want me, too."

Her shuddering intensified as she stared numbly at the figure standing before her. Jay now surrounded her with his warmth and the scent of his skin, so close she felt suffocated. She continued to gape up at him, her mouth open and dry. Finally, she managed to swallow. But she couldn't stop her coochie from contracting or the juices from saturating her thong as she remembered the night they'd come close to making love on her living room couch. Why couldn't she just tell him how he affected her?

Because I'm scared, she answered silently. What would happen when he found out about her past? And the secret that weighed heavily on her heart?

Quickly getting her feelings under control, she frowned and pretended not to be affected by his response. Jay was the only man capable of making her feel things she didn't want to feel. How did he always manage to rattle the knob to the locked door that hid her heart?

"Whatever, Jay." She forced a frown and tilted her head back to look at him. "You're wrong, and you're wasting your time. It would never work between us. We're too much alike."

Jay was silent, but her eyes gave him reason to doubt her response. She was still running, but why? He smiled, then said, "All the more reason for us to be together. We can do this, boo."

Honey's eyes were now as gray as an overcast sky. Inside, her heart ached at the possibility of giving in to her feelings. She wanted to with all her heart. If only things were different! *Damn Walter's mothafuckin' ass!* With a great deal of effort she narrowed her eyes and said in a disapproving tone, "How many times do I have to tell you? I don't need a man in my life. Didn't we agree in the beginning we were only gonna be friends, nothing more?"

Mere inches from his face, the familiar fragrance of Honey's skin tantalized Jay. He wanted to take her into his arms and cover her lush mouth with his, reliving the kiss they once had shared. His dick was hard and he wanted to do something about it. Instead, he tightened his grasp and exhaled as waves of desire washed over him. He moved in closer, dropping his hands to capture both of hers, and spoke in a low, husky voice. "Things change. People change. What happened between us surpassed friendship. Boo, we've got somethin' special." He spoke the words slowly, as though still considering their meaning as he uttered them. The longing look he gave Honey told her he was thinking about the night she'd melted with desire beneath him.

Jay was so close his hot breath fanned her lips, sending heat down to her toes. Her cheeks burned with embarrassment. Were her emotions that easy to read?

Honey panicked. Jay was more determined than ever to find out the truth. Her excuse about wanting to remain friends was bullshit. Did he know this?

Stunned by his words, mesmerized by his smile, Honey couldn't move as she watched him step forward. Her nipples hardened and her lips parted as she yearned to relive their kiss. How she wished things could be different! But fate had dealt her a bad hand.

"Jay, it's over."

Jay wanted to shake her senseless, then pull her into his arms and kiss her breathless, but he had seen the pain behind those gray eyes. Although he wanted her to feel what he felt, he decided he would have to give her time. If he didn't want her to clam up again, he'd have to be more careful and not rush her.

Jay leaned toward her and tenderly kissed the slender bridge of her nose. "That's where you're wrong. It'll never be over." As he moved away, he shot her a lopsided grin that caused her knees to wobble. Jay then bade her good-bye with the parting words, "We'll talk soon."

Honey stood for the longest time, completely immobilized as a warm feeling flowed through her.

With moonlight pouring into her room, Honey stared out at the dark sky and sighed for the hundredth time since she'd arrived home. Feeling a sudden draft, she pulled the pink velour blanket over her shoulders and curled into a ball.

After what had happened, she was more confused than ever before. Her mind had managed to travel back into the past, and the unwanted feelings returned. Despite the intervening months, it had taken only one glimpse of Jay to realize she still desperately wanted him.

Honey shifted her head on the pillow and stared up at the ceiling. She'd hoped that the next time she saw Jay her feelings would be different. Instead, they had been the same, maybe even stronger. Seeing Jay today had forced her to admit that her attraction hadn't diminished, and neither had his. She'd seen his heart through his eyes and knew he still cared for her. It had all been too much.

She closed her eyes and pictured his handsome face.

She hadn't fully realized how much she'd truly missed him until today. Ending their relationship had created a sense of loss she never would have expected. *How lonely my life has become.* She took a deep breath as emotion choked her. The desire that had lain dormant in her heart for several months had resurfaced. Now it was alive and burning between them. How was it Jay was able to make her feel that way? Her head told her to stay away, but her heart was saying something else. Desire mingled with fear, and Honey realized her feelings were in turmoil. She swallowed hard, trying to stay calm as she savored their latest encounter.

Standing so close to Jay, she had ached to reach up and stroke his face. She wanted to relive the feel of his body against hers, the taste of his succulent lips, and the soft caress of his fingertips across her nipples. She shook her head and tried to escape the memories, but a shiver raced through her and made it unbearable to lie still. She moved to a sitting position and leaned against her headboard. Her bed felt so cold, alone. How wonderful it would be to have Jay's warm body lying next to her, holding her tight. Honey drew her knees up to her chest and dropped her head on them. Tears welled up in her eyes. It bothered her that she was so distracted by him. She hated that Jay had the power to destroy the tranquility of her life. She tried to be angry with him, but couldn't. She tried to dismiss the memory of how he had made her feel that afternoon, but she failed at that shit, too.

Jay's voice came again, echoing through the silence of her room: *"Why do you keep running?"*

Although Jay had suspected her fear, she couldn't answer. What would happen when he found out the truth?

She was so afraid he would. Then what would he think of her?

The look in Jay's eyes meant he was more determined than ever to find out why she ended their relationship. Panic squeezed at her chest. She couldn't let that happen! But Jay had a strange power over her that was difficult to control. Fighting to calm her mounting fear, Honey took a deep cleansing breath. No. She was doing the right thing. As much as it hurt, there was no fuckin' way things were going to change. As much as her body wanted otherwise, she had to continue to keep him at bay.

She and Jay could never be together.

Honey removed the pillow from behind her head and held it to her throbbing nipples, then groaned and closed her eyes. She wasn't sure how much more of this shit she could take.

Jay stepped out of the bathroom and quickly realized the cold shower had been unsuccessful at getting rid of a hard-on.

"This is getting fuckin' ridiculous," he groaned with frustration.

He hadn't had sex since that night with Kendra. Because of Honey, he'd lost the desire to be with anyone else. It had taken all his strength tonight not to pull Honey into his arms and devour her lips, sampling their sweetness once again. Torn between wanting her but afraid of frightening her off, he intended to spend a lot of time plotting ways to win her heart.

Jay strolled into his room and reached for his underwear drawer. Honey was more gorgeous than he'd remembered, and her large eyes had seemed to swallow him whole. Her petite frame gave her an image of fragile vulnerability, yet she was the same strong-willed, stubborn little fireball who initially attracted him. Tonight he'd watched her struggle as she tried to deny her feelings for him. But Jay knew better. Honey had forgotten that she had allowed him an opportunity to see inside her head. He knew her defensive wall acted as a shield against something that had happened to her in her past, something that prevented her from allowing anyone to get too close. In all the time they'd bared their souls, she never once shared that piece of information. Now Jay was determined to find out what it was. Once he obtained that information, he'd have the piece of her he desired most.

Her heart.

Sitting on the bed, Jay dropped his head in his hands. His life had grown too complicated, and it frustrated him. Even though he'd wanted to stay and make Honey confront her feelings, he'd made progress with her tonight. He wanted her with him now, here, sharing his bed instead of his having to spend another night alone. He wanted to bury his dick deep inside her and show her how good it could be between them. But he knew it wasn't time. Right now, something else took precedence over everything else.

Terraine had ragged him about his decision not to keep the baby. What else could he do? He damn sure wasn't marrying Kendra. Besides, she'd made it perfectly clear that she didn't want the baby if he refused to be her husband. Jay was convinced he was incapable of raising a child. Moreover, he didn't want his child raised by a nanny, as he had been.

Jay ran a frustrated hand through his hair. It wasn't

that he was trying to run away from his responsibilities. Shhiiit! The simple truth was that he'd make a lousy single parent. Although he felt terribly guilty, he knew a loving family would be better equipped to raise his child. He would never be able to raise a child alone, and he certainly could never do it with a selfish-ass woman like Kendra Johnson. He'd given it a lot of thought, and knew he'd made the right choice.

With that firmly in mind, Jay reached for the phone and dialed Kendra's number. But a familiar twinge of guilt assailed him before the second ring.

"Damn." Then with a sigh, he lowered the receiver.

Kendra looked down at her caller ID box and smirked. Jay's conscience was finally getting the better of him. *About damn time.* She had dropped by his condo more than a month ago, and hadn't heard one word from his sorry ass. Only the infrequent hang-up calls all week. Had it not been for Natalia, she would never have known Jay had gone out of town.

She snorted and brushed a long red fingernail across her cheek. She realized it had been a mistake to tell him about the baby. What had she expected to gain by going to see him that morning? A father for her child? A husband for herself? Kendra threw her head back on the pillow and gave a cynical laugh. *Hell naw.* She knew better. Jay was no more fit to be a father than she was to be a mother. He was a true playa. He'd proven that time and time again. He loved his freedom as much as he loved his career.

But anyone was capable of change. She had awakened that morning feeling the slight possibility that perhaps his unborn child might shock some sense into him. Instead, he'd left town on one of his stupid-ass rent-a-cop assignments the day after her visit. Was he that confused? Chickenshit, maybe? It was so unlike Jay to be afraid. His predictably strong exterior never revealed any of his internal feelings. Maybe it was a sign his ass was finally weakening.

Kendra reached for the remote control and clicked the television off. To Jay, she'd never been more than a booty call. She had accepted this because the brotha was no joke in bed. He had a colossal dick and knew how to use it. Also deep down she'd hoped he would eventually develop stronger feelings for her. He never had. Jay wasn't interested in commitments or attachments. At least, not with her. Her wet coochie was the only thing he had been interested in.

But all that shit was about to change.

Kendra's brow furrowed as she remembered the last night they'd spent together. Jay had ended their relationship several months prior, and no matter how much she tried, Kendra had been unsuccessful at getting him back into her bed. Then, as luck would have it, she'd found his fine ass sitting alone at the bar, drunk. She'd snatched his keys and told him he was in no shape to drive, and he was going home with her. Jay had been too intoxicated to disagree, giving her the perfect opportunity to put her plan into action. He may have been asleep but his big dick was wide awake. She buried all ten inches inside her wet coochie, then rode his ass all night. But the next morning he played her and pissed her the fuck off.

Before she could decide how to retaliate, Lawrence had come along, and she'd been swept instantly off her feet. At the time, it didn't matter that he had an itty-bitty dick. All that mattered was his fat pockets and status in the community. When Kendra realized she was pregnant, she was so afraid of losing him she'd quickly scheduled an abortion. Lawrence found her bent over the toilet, puking her guts out, and asked her if she was pregnant. When she confirmed his suspicion, he'd shouted with glee. He shared with her his inability to have children, then asked her to marry him, saying he would raise the child as his own. Relieved, Kendra immediately began to plan a wedding, spreading the word that she was carrying Lawrence's child. She had almost had it all: a new dental practice, a rich and successful husband, prestige, and a baby to make the package complete. Everything was perfect.

Then, just like that, it had all slipped away. Two weeks before their wedding day, Lawrence announced that his urologist had made a mistake. He'd been fucking his nurse and had impregnated her and no longer needed Kendra. Feeling used and abused, and too far into her pregnancy to terminate it, Kendra had quickly run back to Jay, hoping he would be pleased to find out he was going to be a daddy.

Even though Lawrence had been an excellent substitute, Jay really had everything she'd ever wanted in a husband. He was gorgeous, sexy, and rich and had a big fat dick. As she leaned back against a stack of pillows, she reminded herself that it wasn't about money. Jay was the perfect choice as a husband. Oh yeah . . . and the perfect father for her unborn child.

Now, with no other option, Kendra didn't even want to consider the possibility that Jay wasn't interested in resuming their relationship. Things had cooled between them several times before, but whenever she was ready to start again, Jay had always been compliant. She had always believed her tight coochie was difficult for him to resist. The sex was off the hook. Only Jay knew how to find her G-spot. Only he made sure she was satisfied before he would come. The mothafucka could eat pussy almost as good as she could suck a dick. He challenged her in bed and brought the freak out in her. Their time in bed was innovative and buck wild. Closing her eyes, she reached down and stroked her clit as she pretended it was Jay touching her.

They'd maintained an on-again, off-again relationship for years, allowing her ample time to sample other possibilities before returning for more of Jay's good loving. But the day following his drunken stupor had been different. Jay had cut her ass completely off. At first Kendra had taken it personally, but when she met Lawrence, she put Jay on the back burner herself.

It wasn't until recently that it dawned on her that Jay hadn't called or even tried to get in touch with her once during the entire seven-month span. Could things possibly have changed that much? Maybe it was time for her to pray. Kendra chuckled at that. She hadn't prayed in so long, God would probably ask, "Now what did you say your name was again?"

Kendra shifted on the bed and reached for a bag of potato chips, stuffing several into her mouth. She rubbed her hand across her swollen belly, anxious to have this tormenting, disfiguring pregnancy end.

She refused to be a single parent like her mother. Throughout her entire childhood, Martha Johnson made damn sure Kendra knew her ugly ass was the reason she couldn't keep a man. No good man wanted someone else's nappy-headed kid. As the years progressed, Kendra learned to think just as her mother had. She desired something she'd never had and was determined to get: love, marriage, and family.

Pressing her lips tightly together, she dragged one leg up alongside her inflated stomach. It had to be an all-or-nothing deal. Either Jay married her and they raised their child together or she'd get rid of the baby as soon as it was born.

With that in mind, Kendra leaned over and removed a business card from her nightstand. She stared down at the name of a very influential member of the St. Louis community. After gazing at it for several more seconds, her lips curled into a twisted smile.

"Oh, hell yeah!" she chimed.

Either way it went, she would triumph in the end.

Three

Honey put her pencil down on the desk and stretched her arms high above her head, allowing a yawn to escape her lips. Planning to be out most of the afternoon, she'd arrived at the salon early, hoping to weed through most of the work piled high on her desk. However, after two hours, she was long overdue for a break. She rose from the chair and stepped out into the lobby, eager to claim a cup of coffee.

While adding sugar to her mug, she heard the small bell hanging over the front door ring. She glanced over her shoulder and saw Mercedes strolling into the building.

"Hey, girl. What're you doing in so early?" Honey said, and stopped stirring her coffee long enough to gaze down at her watch. She raised an eyebrow in surprise. It was only nine o'clock. Mercedes typically didn't book her first appointment until after ten. Even then, she usually ran late.

Before answering Honey's question, Mercedes whizzed

over to her workstation at the far end of the room, pulled out the middle drawer, and placed her purse inside. "My car broke down," she mumbled. "So I had Dean drop me off on his way to the garage." She removed her coat, slipped a red smock over her head, and tied it around her waist. "Besides . . ." She stopped to give Honey an innocent expression before pointing to her head. "I thought maybe you could tighten my weave."

Honey gave Mercedes a sidelong glance, not missing the glint from her gold-toothed smile while she remained silent, waiting to hear more. Nothing was ever simple with the stylist whose life was *drama* with a capital D.

"Uh-huh," Honey murmured, then removed the wooden stirrer from her mug and tossed it into the nearby wastebasket. She raised her mug quickly to her lips and took a sip of the hot liquid. *Not bad.* The brew wasn't quite as good as Candy's, but it would have to do. The receptionist wasn't due in until late afternoon.

Honey moved toward her workstation, the heels of her brown leather pumps clicking against the vinyl tile, and set her mug on the counter. With the wave of her hand, she motioned for Mercedes to come and take a seat in the chair. Honey reached for an identical smock and slipped it on, covering her long chocolate wool skirt and creamy silk blouse. It was her power outfit. Scheduled to meet with the bank later in the day, she needed the confidence the combination provided her.

When Mercedes moved in closer, Honey sucked in her breath at the sight of the conspicuous dark bruise beneath her left eye that she had tried unsuccessfully to conceal with foundation. Honey quickly summed up that there wasn't a damn thing wrong with Mercedes's car. Dean had once again dotted her eye, then had taken her keys away in hope of keeping her from straying too far from home.

Realizing her boss had noticed, Mercedes lowered her lashes away from Honey's critical squint and climbed into the chair.

For a long moment, Honey stared down at Mercedes's reflection in the mirror, studying her. A pretty, mahogany-colored woman with a voluptuous body and large, doelike hazel eyes fanned by thick, dark lashes, Mercedes could do a lot better, Honey knew, than Dean's no-good ass. With a great deal of effort, she pressed her lips tight so she wouldn't comment and reached for a wide-toothed comb. Along the way, she had learned to mind her own damn business.

Mercedes had been with her since the first day she opened her doors, and played a major part in the salon's success. With her reputation as being a fabulous hairstylist, an overbooked schedule proved the girl made money. The only fault Mercedes had was her baby's daddy, Dean, who sucked her dry and continued to keep her down. For years, he'd been controlling her life by keeping her in line with an occasional black eye. Honey had tried several times to offer her assistance, but it never lasted for long. Mercedes was determined to hang on to Dean. Consistently listening to his weak-ass explanations, she always took him back. Because of their last disagreement over the way Dean dogged her dumb ass, and the rift that had developed between the two women, Honey decided it was best to stay the hell out of it, as would the rest of her staff when they arrived later in the day.

Pushing aside her ill thoughts, Honey parted Mercedes's hair and ran her fingertips along the ebony weave. "It doesn't look that bad," she said after a quick observation. "After I tighten your tracks, I'll wash it for you." She hoped her offer would bring some comfort to her stylist's fucked-up life.

"Thanks, Honey," Mercedes said, and released a long sigh as her shoulders relaxed. She'd obviously been holding her breath, anticipating a reaction from Honey regarding her battered face, and was relieved Honey had remained silent. She raised her head and looked at Honey's reflection in the mirror. "Mind if Lil' Dee and I stay with you tonight?"

Honey placed a comforting hand on Mercedes's shoulder as her eyes came to rest on the questioning face reflected in the mirror before her. "Girl, now you know you don't have to ask." Since the first time Mercedes and her five-year-old son sought shelter at her home, Honey had kept a spare key under a small rock at the edge of her garage. When the abuse became frequent, she hadn't seen any sense in removing it.

The warmth in Honey's voice echoed in a smile the two shared, until Mercedes lowered her eyes to her hands. Honey knew her employee had no intention of discussing the situation any further, so she just reached for a sewing needle and proceeded to fix her hair.

Honey had Mercedes under the dryer when Sasha came waddling through the door and said, "Hey, y'all." She waved before moving to the coatrack. "Can you believe it has the audacity to snow?"

Honey rose from her chair with a startled expression. "You're kidding?"

Sasha shook her head.

"I ain't surprised." Mercedes elevated her voice, trying to speak over the hum of the dryer.

Honey moved over to the large window. Using her

palm, she wiped away the frost from the glass. Sure enough, light flakes were falling to the ground. Even though it had been a mild winter, Missouri was known for its strange weather. Her thoughts filtered to the ground-hog that had seen his shadow, indicating six more weeks of bad weather. She wished she could ring his fuckin' neck. Honey was never one to believe in superstitions, but lately she was beginning to wonder. "Damn," she said. "I thought we were through with snow. I left my heavy coat at home."

Sasha shrugged out of a black cape, followed by a matching beret. "I thought the season was over myself, but you know as well as I do Februarys are always so unpredictable."

Honey turned away from the window, nodding in agreement, then walked to her station. She signaled for Sasha to follow.

Sasha plopped down into the chair. "I don't know how much longer I'm gonna be able to sit in this chair," she grumbled. "I'm getting bigger by the hour."

Honey leaned over and placed a palm on her pro-truding stomach. "How's my godbaby doing today?" she cooed.

"Gettin' on my damn nerves!" Sasha tried to sound annoyed but giggles of joy escaped her lips. "She's been break-dancing all morning. I woke Terraine this morning and told him he needed to tell his daughter to go back to sleep. Instead, he spent an hour talking to her." She stopped to drop a loving hand to her middle. "I tell you, she's already got her daddy wrapped around her little finger."

Honey snorted. "And you wouldn't have it any other way. The child's gonna be spoiled rotten."

Sasha grinned. "Yeah . . . I know."

Honey swung the chair around and removed the rubber band from Sasha's honey-colored hair, allowing it to flow freely around her shoulders. Running her fingers through it, Honey quickly summed up that Sasha needed a touch-up and told her so.

"Go 'head. I got nothing but time to kill. Terraine's takin' me to dinner later." She paused to look at Honey's reflection in the mirror. "He and Jay are painting the nursery today."

Sasha watched the way Honey's face lit up at the mention of her brother-in-law's name. Even though Honey never admitted it, Sasha had known for quite some time something was going on between the two of them.

But Honey brushed it off. "Hmm, that's nice," she said, trying to keep her voice steady even though her palms had begun to sweat.

Lips pursed, Sasha waited impatiently to hear more. When she realized she wasn't getting it, she sighed. "Honey, what's up with ya?"

"Whatcha talkin' about?" Honey stuck a comb into a tub of chemical relaxer and began applying it to Sasha's roots. She tried to appear engrossed in her work, but Sasha wasn't born yesterday.

"Jay's been asking a lot of questions about you."

Honey froze for only a heartbeat. "Questions?" Comb in hand, she twirled the chair around until Sasha was facing her. "What kind of questions?"

Sasha smirked. "Oh my! Aren't we suddenly interested?" Holding her stomach, she gave a jolly laugh. She didn't intend to say anything more, but seeing her friend's I'm-ready-to-strangle-your-ass expression, Sasha decided it was wise to continue. "He wanted to know if you were seeing anyone."

"And . . . what the hell did you tell him?"

Sasha looked down at her hands and mumbled, "I told him the truth." She paused to raise her eyes and met Honey's curious gaze again. "Naw, she ain't."

Honey's arms fell against her side. "No?" she repeated.

"It's the truth!" Sasha challenged.

"How the hell do you know?" Honey asked. Especially since she never bothered to mention she'd ended her relationship with Lavell.

Sasha gave a defiant smile. " 'Cause I know you."

"What-the-fuck-ever," Honey murmured.

Rolling her eyes, Honey tried to turn the chair back around, but Sasha latched on to her wrist. "Don't you want to hear the rest?" she asked, her tone one of faked innocence.

Honey's eyes sparkled. "There's more?"

Sasha nodded, releasing her grip. "I was eavesdropping on the two of them this morning, and I heard Jay talkin' to Terraine about you."

"What did he say?"

"Well, when I heard your name, I tried to lean in so I could hear better, and . . . well, shit, my stomach got in the way and pushed the door open."

Honey's lips curled downward. "You ain't no help."

"Help for what?" Sasha asked. Receiving no response, she folded her arms on top of her stomach. "Girl, you know you like him, so quit trippin' and tell me the truth."

Honey positioned herself behind the chair and resumed her work. "There ain't nothin' to tell. Jay and I are friends."

Blowing out an exasperated breath, Sasha sputtered, "But you two barely speak to each other any-more. I do have the right to know."

Honey smirked. "How the hell you figure that?"

" 'Cause I'm supposed to be your best friend."

Parting her hair, Honey snorted. "Girl, puhleeze."

"I want to know what the hell happened," Sasha said, her request a demand now.

"Quit trippin'. Nothing happened," Honey said, combing the relaxer through Sasha's hair. "Jay and I decided we were spending too much time together. So we backed off." She looked down at Sasha through the mirror. "Damn, Sasha. We're just *friends*." She said the word slow enough for even a five-year-old to under-stand. "Do I need to spell the shit out for you?" Using hand gestures, she gave her best shot at sign language.

Sasha huffed. "Friends, my ass! I've seen the way the two of you look at one another. Like y'all need to go rent a room or somethin'. Why can't you just admit that you like him?"

"Okay . . . I like him," Honey said.

"I knew your ass was lying!" Sasha gave a tri-umphant laugh.

"That's it, Sasha . . . nothing more."

Sasha clicked her tongue knowingly. "Uh-huh, whatever."

Honey had had enough. "Why don't we talk about somethin' else? Like . . ." Forced to think fast, Honey said, ". . . Like what're we gonna name my goddaughter."

Sasha rolled her eyes heavenward. Sooner or later, Honey had to open up to her, because the secrecy was driving her crazy. Even her own husband wouldn't tell her what the hell was going on, and she felt left out. She hated secrets.

She and Honey had known each other since high school, and she couldn't ask for a better friend. They had gone through a lot of shit together over the years. Honey always had her back. Sasha had tried to return the favor, but felt like Honey was hiding something. No matter how much she tried to get Honey to open up she never would, telling her only what she wanted her to know. Well, Sasha was sure there was a lot more going on between Honey and Jay. At one time she was certain that the two of them were fucking, and she was going to find out the truth if it killed her.

With that in mind, Sasha decided to leave the shit alone for now, and began rattling off the list of baby names she and Terraine had come up with.

Dory McDonald looked up from her computer to find her boss standing over her desk wearing a Cardinals baseball cap, a tattered T-shirt, and a faded pair of jeans spattered with paint. "I'm almost afraid to ask what you've been doing today."

Looking up from the pile of mail he was thumbing through, Jay smirked. "Terraine conned my ass into helping him paint my niece's nursery."

Dory's eyes were wide with delight. "Sasha's havin' a girl?"

"That's what her doctor says." Jay tucked the mail under his arm and headed toward his office door, located behind Dory's desk. "Let's hope they haven't made a mistake."

Dory twirled around in the swivel chair. "Why's that?"

"Sasha'll go off." Jay was shaking with amusement. He knew from experience that once his sister-in-law set her mind to something, it was next to impossible to change it.

Jay took a seat in his chair and set the mail on the corner of his desk to go through later, then reached for the stack of pink message slips sitting on top of his phone. Kendra had already called twice this morning. Damn! She'd been calling him for three days, and there was no point putting the shit off any longer. They needed to talk. Soon.

"Where's Chad?" he said. Chad Hamilton was the firm's most promising investigator. As a former St. Louis police officer, he was thorough, reminding Jay of himself.

"He's in his office," Dory said, closer than before.

Jay glanced up to find Dory leaning against his door frame.

"I think he's interviewing another missin' person's case," she added.

Jay frowned. "Shit. That's just what we need." Chad had been reassigned to handle all missing persons— one thing Jay preferred not to do. Most of them were due to broken homes or sexual abuse cases. Things that pulled at his heartstrings.

"I'm on my way out to lunch, you want anything?" Dory moved toward his desk, carrying a straw purse over her shoulder.

Looking up at her friendly, light brown eyes, Jay smiled. Dory had been twenty-one when he first met her. She'd just given birth to a son and was desperate for a job. Responding to an ad he'd run in the newspaper, she arrived at his office looking like a straight-up hoochie in a skintight, lime-green dress with white platform shoes. Dory had very limited skills, but was willing to learn. She had pleaded with Jay for a chance. Jay saw something in her that he hadn't found in any of his other candidates. Determination. He hired her on the spot, and not once had he regretted his decision. Two years later, she stood before him dressed appropriately in a gray turtleneck sweater dress, her jet-black hair pulled back neatly with a hair clip.

"Yeah, grab me two cheeseburgers and a large fry." Jay reached into his pocket, pulled out several bills, and handed them to her.

Unzipping a side compartment, she slipped the money in her purse. "You're gonna clog your arteries," she scolded. The health-conscious Dory was planning on picking up a salad for herself.

"Yeah, but at least I'll die happy," he joked.

After Dory departed, Jay laced his fingers behind his head. Rocking in his brown swivel chair, he allowed his eyes to travel across the parade of framed news clippings and awards that adorned the walls. Fifteen years of accumulation. He sighed as his mind filtered back to thoughts of self-worth. There was proof right in front of his face that his career meant something. The number of cases his firm had been successful at solving was a phenomenon in itself. Yet it still wasn't enough.

He needed something more.

Jay heard heavy footsteps moving across the floor outside his office. Looking up, he watched a rugged ebony man stroll through his door. He reared back in his chair and propped his feet on the end of his desk. "What's up?"

Chad pulled a chair away from a small conference table in the corner. Planting the chair in front of Jay's desk, he straddled it with his large legs and rested his arms against the back. "I just had an interestin' interview." He lowered a thin manila folder onto the desk.

"How so?"

"I met with this fine-ass widow who is certain her husband's still alive."

Jay's eyes sparkled with interest. "How's that possible?"

"Check this shit out. She was in Kansas City for a conference over the weekend and says she saw her husband coming out of a restaurant with another lady."

Jay's brow quirked. "Why didn't she just go over and ask him?"

"She tried, but the brotha pulled off in a Benz before she could stop him."

Jay reached for the file labeled *Jocelyn Price*, and without looking at Chad, asked, "Do you think she's a crackpot?"

"Naw," Chad said, and smiled. "She's a pediatrician." Rubbing a hand across his chin, he added, "With a nice body."

Jay opened the file. "You never could resist."

Chad flashed him a pearly-white smile. "One of the pleasures of being single."

Jay looked up to see the man's walnut eyes sparkling with mischief. Chad loved beautiful women in all shapes and sizes. Commitment was impossible. He believed there were too many options. Only a damn fool would settle for just one chip when he could have the entire bag. As active as Chad's personal life was, Jay was amazed at the time and dedication he was able to put into his cases.

Breezing through his notes, Jay read that J.W. Price had died a year before in an automobile accident, his body burned beyond recognition. "So, I guess you want to take on this case?"

Chad raised a hand and ran it across the ten jet-black

cornrows his younger sister had braided the night before. "I do. For more reasons than one."

"No doubt," Jay replied in a dry tone.

"Actually, man, I think you should take it."

"Why me?" He closed the file and placed it on the corner of his desk.

"Shit, man. I already have a heavy caseload. Tyler and Paul also." They were the operatives responsible for all the grunt work.

Jay dropped his feet to the floor and, turning in his chair, quickly logged on to his computer. Dory input all cases into a database, and each was flagged active until solved.

Jay whistled. There were over thirty active cases. "Fuck! When did all this happen?"

"Since your black ass left town."

"Naw. They weren't in here on Monday." The day after he returned from Memphis he had dropped by the office. There had only been twelve active cases then.

"That's 'cause I asked Dory not to enter them until you were officially back in the office. I knew if you saw them as soon as you got back, you wouldn't have taken a few days off."

Jay smirked. "You think you know me well."

"I do. It's like looking at a mirror image of myself."

Jay agreed . . . except that Jay had changed in one aspect. "Leave the file," he said. "I'll look at it tonight."

"I thought you'd say that." Chad rubbed his hand across his goatee. "Did I mention she's fine?"

"Yeah, you did." Jay frowned. "But unlike you, I don't mix business with pleasure."

"Since when?" Chad looked at him with surprise.

"Since I realized there are other pleasures in life."

Chad chuckled. "That bullet did more damage to

your ass than I imagined." But he had the perfect cure for his boss—fine-ass Dr. Jocelyn Price.

"So, how did it go?" Mercedes asked when her boss returned to the shop later that afternoon. The snow had stopped falling. Honey's cheeks were rosy from the cold wind, but an excited light was in her eyes.

"I got the loan," she announced.

"Yes!" Candy exclaimed.

"Hell yeah!" Mercedes and all her other staff—Aisha, Sonya, Terry, and Peaches—chimed in from their workstations.

"I can begin construction as soon as the permit is ready." Honey frowned, then mumbled, "That is . . . as soon as I can find my brotha's worthless ass."

Mercedes stopped applying styling gel to a customer's hair long enough to point toward the back of the building. "Speak of the devil, Rashad's in your office."

Honey's eyes widened with delight. She quickly removed her jacket and headed toward the rear. Entering her private office, she found him sitting behind her desk on the phone.

"Get off my phone," she mouthed while trying to keep a straight face. Her recent good fortune kept her from truly getting an attitude. However, after her last encounter with one of her brother's women—who took it upon herself to dial star-sixty-nine to find out what number Rashad was calling from, then bark, "Who da hell is dis?"—Honey had banned him from using her office telephone.

Rashad dropped his brand-new Jordans from the edge of her desk and put a fingertip to his full lips, signaling for her to be silent. Honey, in turn, propped a hand on her hip, then pressed her lips tight with false annoyance and tried to disguise her admiration.

Both of her brothers were fine, but Rashad had always been the looker. While Honey inherited petite features like her mother, Rashad took after their no-good-ass father, with a tough, stocky build and broad shoulders that filled his green and white jogging suit. His complexion was similar to his sister's, and also considered "high yellow." He had sandy brown hair that was startling against his fair skin, and eyes so gray they were often mistaken for contacts. With large fingers wrapped around the receiver, he ran his tongue across thick, sensual lips surrounded by a carefully trimmed goatee.

"Boo, I'll holla at you tonight," he whispered into the receiver, trying to keep his sister from overhearing.

Honey, finding his discomfort amusing, suppressed a chuckle and edged across the desk.

Giving her an annoyed look, Rashad swiveled the chair away from her outstretched ear and told the unseen caller, "All right, baby, later." Turning back around, he hung up the receiver, leaned back, and grumbled, "Damn! Can't a brotha have privacy?" Then his face melted into a buttery smile.

Honey clicked her teeth, resisting a grin. "Not in my office you can't. Out of my seat," she said, pointing her thumb at the door.

Rashad pushed out of the chair, surging to his full height of six feet, and perched his hip on the end of her desk.

"I haven't heard from your ass in almost two weeks." Honey rose on tiptoe and planted a kiss on his cheek, then stood back with arms folded beneath her breasts.

"Whatcha been up to?" When younger, she often felt like the big sister, especially when Rashad worried their mother about his whereabouts.

Rashad smiled and tilted his head, then said, "You know I'm always doing a lil' somethin' somethin'."

Honey pursed her lips before replying, "Uh-huh. That's what I'm afraid of." Suddenly, that little *somethin'* caught her attention. She leaned forward to take a closer look. "Is that another gold tooth?"

Rashad nodded with pride. There wasn't much he could get past his little sister. Widening his smile, he gave Honey a clear view of all three gold crowns dominating the front of his mouth.

Honey groaned at the gold open-faced heart that added to his collection and walked around her desk, shaking her head. St. Louis had the reputation of being the gold-tooth capital of the Midwest. With Rashad, Mercedes, half of their clients, and the cashiers at Church's Chicken, she could no longer argue the statistic. "You look straight-up ghetto," she said.

He waved a dismissive hand at his sister's disapproval. "Damn, sis. I thought you'd be happy to see a nigga." Pulling a stick of chewing gum from his pocket, Rashad quickly stuffed it into his mouth. When she chose to roll her eyes instead of commenting, he decided to change the subject. "How'd it go at the bank?"

Lowering into her chair, Honey nodded, amazed that he had remembered, but she found herself often surprised by her unpredictable brother. "It's on like popcorn. I got the loan."

Even though her face was unchanged, he heard the excitement in her voice. "All right, lil' sis!" Rashad gave her a high five, then slapped his palms together roughly as if they were on fire. "Shit, I knew my hands were burnin' for some reason. So when do we get down to business?"

"I'll get the check on Tuesday." Honey leaned forward in her chair and pointed a stern finger at him. "But let me tell you something, Rashad Dante Love . . ." She narrowed her eyes. "I'm not putting up with any of your shit."

Rashad sucked his teeth. "Girl, puhleeze."

"Don't 'girl, puhleeze' me!" She planted both hands on the desk and rose out of her chair. "If you're gonna do this job for me, you're gonna have to forget I'm your sister and think of me as one of your clients."

"Yeah, what-the-fuck-ever." His lips twisted. "I know how to handle my business."

"Good, then we shouldn't have any problems," she said. She knew the saying "never mix family with business," but she was proud of Rashad. Even though she was giving him shit, Honey knew he was the best man for the job. He was a skilled laborer who learned the job while working as an apprentice for an older gentleman who'd taken him under his wing many years ago. There wasn't much Rashad couldn't do. He was an all-around journeyman, and because of it, Honey knew she'd get top-quality work at half the price.

The only problem was making sure his ass came to work. Rashad had a tendency to get a little lazy, and from time to time, he seemed to drop off the face of the earth. "I'll have the plans for the addition drawn up on Friday," she said. "Then you can get me an estimate on the cost of materials."

"Not a problem." He smiled in the old, familiar way that used to make her relinquish the last cookie in the jar, but was all business when he said, "I'm lookin' forward to workin' with you." Extending his hand, they shook.

"Don't make me regret this." Honey rolled her eyes and returned to her seat. "Mom advised me not to even fuck with your sorry ass." She remembered all of the projects Rashad had started at their mother's house that he had yet to complete. Rashad's excuse was "Freebies are done when I have free time."

Rashad scowled at being scolded like a child. "Good ole' Mom, what would we do without her?" He'd moved around her desk and now stood across from her. Having enough of his sister's nagging, he shifted to something of mutual interest. "Whadda you want to do for her birthday?"

Honey shrugged. Helen Love's sixtieth birthday was in three weeks. "I don't know. Dinner maybe?" Last year, they each chipped in and bought her a new stove. This year Honey wanted to do something extra special.

Rashad lowered his eyes and sighed. "Maybe a day to relax. I wish she'd stop working for those mothafuckin' white folks."

Honey could detect the anger in her brother's voice. "You know that's a losing battle." They had fallen upon a touchy subject. For years, Helen Love had worked for a prominent white family as their housekeeper. No matter how much her three children complained, she refused to quit. She took pride in her job, and wasn't ashamed of what she did for a living. It was her kids who seemed to have a problem with it.

Honey gave him a thoughtful look. "I'd like to send her on a cruise."

"That's a possibility," Rashad mumbled before looking down at his vibrating pager. "Sorry, sis, got to go. I have a bathroom I'm supposed to be finishin' on the Southside. I'll holla atcha this weekend." He reached for his bomber jacket and headed for the door, where he turned around to say, "You know, you should let me hook you up with Darrius. He's been beggin' me for your number."

She remembered bucktoothed Darrius, who'd lived next door to them until junior high. "Don't even try it." She waved him away in disgust. "I'll see you this weekend."

"Yeah, okay." He chuckled. "Peace."

Honey absently stroked the leather binder in front of her and found herself deep in thought long after he left. Even though she'd ended her relationship with Lavell only last week, she already missed having a male companion. She raised her hand to her face, resting it under her chin, and sighed. A hundred years ago, she would've been considered an old maid at her age. *Then, maybe the shit wouldn't matter.*

Pushing away from her desk, Honey moved over to a small refrigerator that she kept in the corner of her office and removed a diet soda. She found her mind drifting to Jay again. He'd been the subject of her thoughts for the last forty-eight hours, and it was driving her crazy. She'd succeeded in keeping him out of her life for months. Now, after one afternoon, she couldn't stop wondering what he was doing. Now, after her discussion with Sasha, she knew he was also thinking about her.

She desperately needed something else to think about, so after contemplating a minute further, she moved around her desk, reached for her phone, and dialed her brother in his car.

"Yeah, sis?" he asked after the first ring.

Honey frowned, hating Caller ID. "What's Darrius look like?" she asked.

Rashad chuckled. "Girl, you know I don't be judging no dudes."

"Quit playing!"

"Have you ever known me to hang around with a bunch of bustas?"

Honey hesitated only a second before she found herself saying, "Go ahead and give him my number." Then she added, "He'd better not be a scrub." She hung up before Rashad could respond. Taking a deep cleansing breath, she inhaled the smell of fresh-baked bread coming from the Wonder Bread factory on the corner. *What the hell was I thinking?* She groaned.

She was still wondering if Darrius had ever gotten his teeth fixed when she was roused by a knock at her office door. Looking up, she saw Candy, her shoulder resting against the jamb.

"Can I get the hookup?" She smirked.

Honey sighed. Since the first time Candy met Rashad, she had expressed an interest in getting to know him better. "Girl, you can do that on your own. After next week, you'll see him every day for several weeks while he's workin' on the expansion."

Honey was kind of surprised Rashad hadn't tried to make a move on Candy himself by now. Then again, Candy probably wasn't his type. She was adorable and soft-spoken, and attending college in the evening, so she probably intimidated her brother's thuggish ass. Rashad was usually attracted to aggressive women with one or two babies by different daddies. The one exception was Diamond, a college student he'd dated for almost two years. Honey never knew what happened between them; Rashad refused to talk about it.

"Mmm-hmm-hmm. I can't wait," Candy said, bringing Honey back to the moment. Candy's chocolate eyes lit up like a Christmas tree and she turned to leave, then remembered why she had walked to Honey's office. "Oh yeah. I almost forgot. You asked me to remind you about a four o'clock appointment."

Honey looked down at her watch, then pressed her lips together in a gloomy expression. "Yes, I did. Thank you."

Kendra faced the presence that darkened her doorstep and frowned. "Look what the cat brought in," she muttered, voice cutting with sarcasm. Without bothering to invite Jay to follow, she turned away and returned to lounge across her floral jacquard couch.

Knowing her attitude was justified, Jay flashed Kendra an embarrassed smile, which she chose to ignore. He shut the front door to the plush apartment and reluctantly joined her in the living room. Then, looking down at her sour expression, he replied, "I guess I deserved that one."

"Good fuckin' guess," Kendra snapped before dropping her gaze to her manicured hands.

Jay removed his leather jacket and draped it across a burgundy swivel rocker before taking a seat beside her. He dropped a hand to Kendra's knee and squeezed it. "How you been?"

Jay's voice was so tender it took Kendra by surprise, taming her facile tongue. Tilting her head to the right, she considered his question for a moment, but when she saw his mellow expression her irritation brewed, and she raised her perfectly plucked eyebrows in a scowl.

What did the sorry mothafucka want to hear? That she hadn't seen her clit in months and it was driving her fuckin' crazy? That she spent over an hour looking at herself in a full-length mirror this morning, and found her swollen nose and massive stomach repulsive? Or that she'd gorged last night on a gallon of butter pecan ice cream and a bag of chocolate chip cookies? Shhiiit! Whoever said being pregnant was a wonderful experience fuckin' lied.

"Still pregnant," she answered, and was surprised when Jay's gaze traveled over her with admiration.

Kendra's hair was pulled up into a bun secured with several decorative bobby pins, with bangs that lay flat across her forehead. Dressed as she was in a navy blue corduroy jumper with a coordinating white blouse, he found her appearance quite adorable. *Too bad her beauty's only skin deep.* "Babe, you look good," Jay said, then patted his thighs, motioning her to prop her feet up across his lap.

Kendra, taken aback by his concern, complied with a smile. Leaning comfortably against the arm of the couch, Jay removed her leather moccasins and gently massaged her stocking feet. A sigh of relief escaped her lips. She'd had a long day at the office and as usual, by late afternoon her ankles had begun to swell. Her obstetrician insisted that she cut her days short and spend the rest of the afternoon with her feet elevated, but Kendra shit on that idea. With a new dental practice, it was important that she be available to her patients, especially if she wanted to compete with the numerous established offices in the area. She had learned a long time ago that customer service and flexibility were important to any business's success. Besides, she depended on the money. Lease payments were high, and she needed new equipment for her office.

While Jay kneaded the bottoms of her feet, she made herself comfortable and closed her eyes. This was what she missed most with Jay. The attention he used to shower her with. The pampering. Although a freak behind closed doors, Jay had always been a complete gentleman. She wanted that back in her life. Sure, maybe she had been a little pushy at times, but she'd learned long ago that men had no respect for weak-ass women. Women who knew what they wanted, and weren't afraid to do whatever the fuck it took to get it were the winners. Men didn't want women like that princess in the movie *Coming to America*. You now, the kind you can tell to bark like a damn dog. She had learned that shit the hard way.

Once upon a time, she had tried being nice. But being nice never got her no-fuckin'-where. Being a bitch was much more appealing. How else had she been able to keep Jay's chocolate ass in her life all these years? *Because he couldn't get enough of me.* Even pregnant, Kendra knew she still made his dick hard. She'd seen his appreciative gaze as he assessed what her current condition had done to her body, and was pleased to find that he still found her irresistible. *Maybe there's some truth to the saying that men find pregnant women desirable.*

Under lashes heavily coated with mascara, Kendra gave him a sidelong glance and saw his somber expression. She wondered what had brought Jay to her home this evening. She didn't want to get ahead of herself, but was certain he'd finally made a decision.

Jay observed her silence and sighed heavily, certain

that she was upset with him for his slowness. "I'm sorry it's taken me so long to come to my senses," he said, looking for a good place to start. "It was very inconsiderate of me."

Kendra opened her eyes and gave him a hopeful smile. She had dreamed of this moment; Jay had finally decided he wanted to be a family. She felt renewed hope that she wasn't going to be alone like her stupid-ass mother had been. She was going to be with her baby's daddy.

Jay turned to her and looked at her intensely for several seconds, then lowered his gaze to her sand-colored carpet, already regretting the outcome of their conversation. He'd read the hope in her eyes; Kendra wanted to marry and raise their child as a child should be raised: by two loving parents. However, he knew they could never do that, especially not as long as Kendra was incapable of loving anyone other than her own selfish ass . . . and not as long as he loved someone else. "Do you have any idea what you're carrying?" he asked, trying to prolong his decision a little while longer.

Kendra shook her head. "I had an ultrasound at the beginning, but it was too soon to tell." She sighed innocently. "All that matters is that he or she is healthy."

Silence stretched between them before Jay finally replied, "I tried calling you several times, but I figured that some things were better discussed in person."

"I agree," she said, urging him to continue. She wondered in which pocket he was hiding her phat-ass engagement ring. A cruise this time of the year would be ideal.

Carefully avoiding her eyes, Jay stared down at his

shoes. "I know what it feels like to be raised without parents, and I never want my child to ever go through that."

Kendra looked up at him, chestnut eyes wide and hopeful. "I agree," she said hastily. *Now hurry the fuck up!*

Jay bit his lip, trying to find the best way to phrase his thoughts. He shifted his gaze and watched the light dancing in her eyes . . . a light he knew would soon fade. Placing a palm on her leg again, he shifted on the couch to face her. "I believe your decision to put the baby up for adoption is a reasonable choice."

"What!" Kendra couldn't believe her ears. "But I want to keep the baby."

"You do?" he answered, confused. Her statement was a complete contradiction of what she'd told him several weeks prior.

"Of course I do," she answered. "But only if you do it with me."

With a groan, Jay found his eyes traveling to a pair of pleated drapes covering the window on the other side of the room. There wasn't anything left between them but their unborn child. Why couldn't she fuckin' see that? Instead, he'd seen the hope in her eyes. Guilt lumped in his throat, and he swallowed hard before allowing his gaze to travel back to her face. "I guess I misunderstood. I thought you wanted to give the baby up for adoption." Before she could respond, he raised a hand to silence her. "If you want to keep the baby, I'll be there for you. But you gotta understand, I ain't marrying you."

Kendra glared at him. *Be there for you?* What the hell did he plan to do? Come over and play house a couple of times a week? She stifled a bitter laugh, then, stinging with rejection and humiliation, she barked, "I guess I was good enough to fuck with but not enough to marry?"

"Kendra, this ain't a game. You tricked my black ass and you know it! I was too drunk to have any control over what happened that night. If I had, we wouldn't have had unprotected sex. As a matter of fact, I wouldn't have fucked you at all." Feeling his temperature rising, he tapped his hand lightly against her leg. Kendra always did bring out the worst in him. He calmed himself and began again. "It's over between us. It has been for months. I don't love you. Nor do I want to make the mistake of marrying you because I feel obligated to do so. If you're gonna keep this baby, then we need to try and be friends."

"I don't want to be friends. I want to be your damn wife!" she shouted. Then, realizing shouting would get her nowhere, she reached over and ran her fingers caressingly along his arm. "We can make it work," she cooed.

Jay stiffened at her touch and quickly removed her hand. "We've tried, Kendra, and it doesn't work between us." He sighed, realizing their discussion was going to be harder than he had imagined.

Her demeanor calmed and she fixed pained eyes on him. "But things are different now. I've changed."

Not wanting to hurt her, Jay thought about keeping the truth to himself, but decided it was best to be honest with her. "Would you really want to be with me knowin' that I love someone else?"

"What!" She dropped her feet to the floor with a thump and began wagging her head furiously. "Jay Andrews doesn't fall in love, remember?" She laughed a bitter laugh.

He patted her hand and said kindly, "Kendra, you're making this difficult."

"No, *you're* makin' this shit difficult!" she countered, jerking her hand away. Her voice was unsteady with disbelief. "Don't lie to me. I know better than to believe that you're in love." She dismissed his confession with a toss of her hand. "If you don't want to have anything to do with me or this baby, then fuck, just say so, because as I stated before, I'm not gonna raise a baby alone. Do you really want to put your own flesh and blood up for adoption?" She glared at him with contempt.

"No, I don't want that. But to be totally honest, I think we'd both be lousy parents. There are so many married couples out there ready to give a child all the love it needs." Jay stood and moved over to the window to find big flakes of snow falling in blankets across the lawn. There was no use talking. She was only going to listen to what the fuck she wanted to hear. Still, he had to try. He turned to face her. "I don't think I know how to do that. Be a parent, I mean." Kendra rolled her eyes while Jay paused to run a hand through his hair. "But if you want to keep the baby, I'll stand by your decision and support you in every way."

She leaned back against the cushion and said, "I don't think so. If I can't have you, then I don't want your ugly-ass baby either."

Jay tried to sound as reasonable as he could. "It's ultimately your decision, but please keep in mind I'll be there for you and my child. Money will never be a problem."

She flinched. His insinuation was like a slap in the face. "You think this is about money?" She laughed.

"Well, it's not! It's about me being forced to be a single parent like my mother."

"No one forced you to have this baby," he said, feeling his temper surfacing.

Kendra's eyes grew large as she spoke in a slow voice that chilled him. "You're right. No one did, and no one will force me to keep it either."

There was a prolonged silence before Jay asked, "So, what do we do now?"

"*We* don't do anything," she said with a tone of indifference. "I'll find a lawyer in the morning and arrange a private adoption." She cringed inside. The discussion hadn't gone as she planned. Jay still hadn't gotten used to the fact that she was carrying his child. *How long is this shit gonna take?*

Jay sighed heavily. "I guess it's settled then."

Chin raised, eyes glittering with anger, she said, "Yes, it is."

"Look . . . I didn't come over here to fight with you. Let's try again tomorrow." Jay reached for his jacket and looked down at her disappointed face. "I better get goin'. A storm was scheduled to move in from the north tonight and it looks like it's already here. I'll call you in the mornin'. Call me if you need anything before then."

Arms folded above her belly, Kendra responded with a temperamental sniff. Her frosty glare told him her attitude toward him now was nothing compared to what he'd have to face from this day forth. Finding no reason to stick around any longer, Jay turned and headed for the door.

Kendra was about to toss a pillow at his head when the baby took the opportunity to give her a swift kick in the ribs. Her eyes sparkled with an idea. "Oh!" she moaned.

Jay rushed back to her side, his eyes wide with concern. "Is somethin' wrong?"

Kendra shook her head vigorously, wearing an angelic look. "No. Nothing's wrong." She giggled. "Your child has a tendency to kick field goals against my ribs."

Kneeling down beside her, Jay focused on her stomach and asked, "Does it hurt?"

"No." She gave him a pathetic smile. "Why don't you feel for yourself?"

Jay laid a nervous palm on her stomach. As luck would have it, the baby moved again and Jay flinched. "Oh, shit! Was that the baby?"

Kendra nodded.

"Damn, he's got some kick."

She frowned. "Who said anything about it being a *he*?"

Jay was stunned. He hadn't thought about it much, and had used the word in a general way. But the little person kicking could be a future football player, or even a little ballerina.

As she watched the awe on his face, Kendra had to fight the urge to smile. When he'd first arrived, she saw the way he watched her move, staring down at her stomach. And only moments ago, she saw his eyes as he felt his child move inside her womb. All of those were signs of a father curious about his unborn child. There was no way Jay was going to be able to resist his child. *Especially if it's a boy.* She was certain of that. She just needed time to make him realize it. All she had to do was put a plan in order. All she needed was time. "Can I ask you a favor?"

He looked at her, startled from his daze by her mellow tone. "Yeah, girl, anything."

"Can you come with me to my doctor's appointment next week?" She dropped her head, then raised it. "I wouldn't ask, but all the other women . . . well, their husbands are usually there, and, well . . . I seemed to be the only one—"

Nodding, Jay placed a hand on her shoulder, silencing her. "No problem. I'll be there." He flashed a reassuring smile.

She batted her eyes and lowered her hand to cover his that was still lying flat on her abdomen. "Thanks. I really appreciate it." Then, wanting to test the waters further, she added, "Maybe I can make an appointment for us to see a lawyer the same afternoon."

Jay's froze at the word *lawyer,* then remembered his decision to give his child up for adoption. As he felt the baby shift inside her womb, guilt traveled to his heart. Was he really making the right decision? Shhiiit, he didn't know what the hell to do. He removed his shaky hand and rose to his feet. Wearing a far-off expression, he exited.

After he left, Kendra stretched leisurely across the couch, wearing a triumphant smile. She had finally made it to first base.

Honey left the clinic after stopping at the reception desk to schedule another appointment. Climbing into her car, she breathed in the cool air and hoped spring would soon arrive. When she looked at her reflection in the rearview mirror, she sighed at the sight of her red eyes. *You look like shit.* She couldn't go back to the salon like this. There would be too many questions.

She reached into her purse, removed her compact, and put a little powder on her face.

She'd had a breakthrough in her session today, and prayed for many more. Why had she been crying? Today was a new beginning for her. A time for healing. Something she should have done years ago.

She steered the car in the direction of the salon, but as tears began to fall again she made a sharp left turn, heading toward home.

Four

"You've got to be pulling my leg!" Natalia croaked with laughter in her voice. But even as she said it, she knew Jay wouldn't dream of joking about something so serious as Kendra being pregnant.

"What do you think, Nat?" Jay said, frowning at the beautiful mahogany woman he'd known all his life, the closest thing he'd ever had to a sister. After his meeting with Kendra the evening before, he was curious as to why Natalia had never mentioned that her best friend was carrying his child.

"Shit, I didn't know that was your baby." Her tone was apologetic now, as if she should have known. After all, Kendra always shared everything with her. Kendra had called her only moments after Dr. Hill's square-headed ass had proposed, and in the same breath had added, "Oh, by the way, I'm pregnant." Natalia had assumed the baby was Dr. Hill's, and Kendra hadn't bothered to correct her.

Brow drawn with worry, Jay regarded Natalia's innocent expression with skepticism, waiting for her left eye to twitch—an immediate telltale sign her ass was lying.

Natalia chuckled again at Jay's incredible revelation and pressed a slender hand to her chest. "I swear, Jay! I thought she was carrying his baby."

Jaw clamped tight, Jay held her gaze without so much as a blink before finally concluding that Natalia was in fact telling him the truth. Then he sighed and rubbed his hand across the nape of his neck, feeling even more frustrated.

Natalia leaned over and placed her hand on his arm. "You sure it's your baby?" she asked, her voice sympathetic. "I mean . . . it was Dr. Hill's baby, and . . . well . . ." She tossed a finger in the air. "For all we know, next week it could be Jed Clampett's baby." Falling back against the couch, she laughed.

Jay gave her an irritated look for finding humor in his present situation, and pressed his back against the brown leather chair. After giving the possibility a lot of thought, he'd decided the odds were stacked heavily against his ass. "If my dates are correct, the baby she's carryin' is mine. Which brings me to the subject of my visit." He edged forward and placed a large hand over hers. His voice low, he said, "Sis, I need a big favor."

When she met his gaze, she immediately realized what he was about to ask. Snatching her hand back, she shook her long auburn curls. "Oh, hell naw! I'm not getting mixed up in this shit."

"You're the one that introduced us," Jay reminded her.

"But I didn't tell you to drop your fuckin' pants." With narrowed eyes, she asked, "What happened to the safe-sex sermon you used to give me?"

Jay didn't need to be reminded that he'd been thinking with his dick. Terraine had already done that for him. "Well . . ." He paused, scratching his bearded chin. But he decided not to protest—he knew he'd allowed his good senses to be altered by alcohol. "Come on, Nat," he pleaded.

Natalia rolled her eyes heavenward. "No way. You got yourself in this mess," she managed through stiff lips.

Jay shot her a desperate look. "You owe me, Nat."

Seeing his pitiful expression, Natalia knew he was trying to lay on the guilt trip. Unfortunately, it was working. She groaned, hating to be in the middle of other people's problems. But she had to shoulder her part of the blame. It was she who'd planted the bug in Kendra's ear that Jay was single, wealthy, and ripe for the picking. Her intentions were good; she had wanted to see the two people she loved most together. Even so, what a mistake that had been! But because she loved him dearly, she couldn't possibly say no to his plea for help. He needed her. "All right. All right." She threw up her hands in resignation, ready to kick herself for letting him talk her into getting involved.

Dressed casually in black leggings and matching tunic, she curled her stocking feet underneath her, leaned slightly closer, and said, "I'll speak to her."

Deep down, she was disappointed Kendra hadn't trusted her enough to share the truth about her unborn child— the child who would become her godchild. The bitch was still sneaky as ever. The two had been friends for eight years, since meeting during their freshman year at UMKC. They'd shared the same dorm, and spent many nights passing the time talking about their lives instead of studying. Even though they were born on different sides of the tracks, Natalia had found their lives a lot alike. Homes with very little love. Parents with very limited time.

At her agreement to help, Jay dropped his shoulders with relief. "Thanks. I 'preciate it."

A teapot whistled, and Natalia escaped to the kitchen to prepare a cup of hot chocolate for the both of them.

Jay rose from the couch and moved across the gleaming hardwood floor into the dining room to take a closer look at a new African artifact sitting on top of a floor-to-ceiling shelving in the corner. An elephant carved out of ivory was the perfect addition to Natalia's already large collection. She frequently traveled, and purchased the pieces from the countries she had visited. Jay was proud of her talent in design. Natalia appreciated his admiration, even though what she yearned for most was to earn praise from her self-centered parents.

Senator Bonaparte and his wife had been so busy building his career that their only child went neglected. When Natalia was sent away to a boarding school, Jay's grandfather, also Natalia's godfather, intervened. When he took a personal interest in Natalia's life, she had become the daughter he never had. Growing up with the spoiled and attention-starved Natalia wasn't easy, especially for Terraine, whom Nat had a childhood fantasy of someday marrying. Jay, on the other hand, grew to love Natalia and protected her as if she were a real sister. She had always been a beautiful woman. At eighteen, she set out to become a model, landing numerous contracts with major cosmetic and clothing lines before becoming a spokesmodel for Diva Designs.

Brushing past a large oak table, he moved to a pair of white French doors and remembered the tulips last spring that made the large glass windows the central focus of the room. High ceilings added dimension to the area, blending with the cool cream color of the walls and the mosaic tiles covering the floor.

"Do you want marshmallows?" Natalia called from the kitchen.

"Yeah."

Jay moved back to the living room, where African-influenced prints were mixed with crisp black upholstery. A bay window with a bench seat was in the corner next to a large built-in bookcase where Natalia spent many hours curled up among the colorful pillows, reading.

Flopping back in the chair, Jay found his thoughts wandering to Honey. When they first met, she had just purchased a new house, and he'd had the privilege of helping her move in. She'd had so many plans for her home. Together they had built a bookcase in one of the spare bedrooms she intended to use as a den. He wondered if she had ever finished redecorating.

Resting his elbow on his knee, Jay dropped his chin to his hand. Seeing Honey again had given him hope. He had expected her to hide her feelings, but he'd seen the desire dancing in her eyes behind a fake smoke screen. Even though she'd made it clear that she didn't want to have anything else to do with him, Jay knew better. He had seen her nipples harden beneath her sweater. Now all he had to do was come up with a way to make her finally come to terms with her feelings. Dealing with Honey would be no easy task, but it would definitely be worth every minute.

Natalia returned carrying a tray with piping-hot mugs of cocoa and an assortment of store-bought cookies. Looking over at Jay, she met his wary expression. "What if Kendra *is* carrying your child? What're you gonna do about it?"

Jay was silent, lost in his own thoughts as he remembered feeling his child move inside Kendra's body. He had created a life. The experience still stirred him. "Be a man and take care of my child," he said at last.

Giving him a wistful smile, Natalia replied, "Good. You'll be a good dad." Setting the tray on her oak coffee table, she latched on to the handle of a large green ceramic mug and offered it to Jay.

Jay reached for the mug and frowned. "I tend to disagree." He took a sip, then continued. "Besides, Kendra and I agreed to put the baby up for adoption."

Holding her own mug, Natalia almost dropped the hot liquid onto her lap. "You can't do that!" she shrieked, then looked at him in alarm as she lowered herself onto the couch. "Why in the hell would you even consider giving up your child?"

Jay looked up from his mug and stared at her for several seconds before saying, "I'm not capable of nurturing a child properly. What do I know about love?"

"Yes, you can. I've never known a more loving individual. *I'm* the one who's a spoiled-ass brat."

Jay's eyes sparkled as he balanced the hot chocolate on top of his knee. "True, that."

Natalia pouted. "Don't get smart," she said. "What I was trying to say is that it never mattered to you how I behaved, because you love me unconditionally. That's what it's supposed to be about." She paused long enough to roll her eyes. "Shit! The only time my parents ever patted me on the back or said they were proud of me was when my skinny ass was strutting down a runway, or when one of their fake-ass friends saw my face on the cover of a magazine." Natalia took a deep breath, suddenly upset at allowing her thoughts to tread in that direction. "Anyway . . . you can always get a full-time nanny to help you out."

He shook his head. "No. That's the way we were raised."

Natalia sighed. Bringing her mug to her lips, she remembered the attention she never received as a child, and the way her parents had pushed her off on several different nannies who'd only done it for the money.

Even though she had loved her godfather, Richard Andrews, Natalia knew he seldom ever showed physical affection with his grandsons, believing it would make them punks. Like her, Jay had been raised without the nurturing a child needed.

"Then I'll help you," she said, her voice quiet.

Jay chuckled. "You don't know the first thing about raisin' a child."

She puckered her lips in protest. "Well . . . no. But at least I'm willing to try! That's my little niece or nephew we're talking about. I would love to have someone to spoil."

"You sound like Terraine," Jay grumbled.

"Well, at least he and I agree on something for a change." Natalia's words were dripping with sarcasm. She was thinking about the debate they'd had earlier. As the CEO of Diva Designs, Terraine insisted on recruiting a new marketing director. It was the beginning of the spring season. As fashion director for Diva Designs, she took marketing their gowns very seriously. In the interim, she'd been wearing both hats. In her opinion, it wasn't a good time for someone new to step in. She, along with a full marketing staff, had been doing quite well, and she wasn't ready for any outside interference at that point. Natalia shivered at the thought of someone coming in who knew nothing about the history of the corporation, initiating a lot of no-frills ideas.

Brushing aside her dilemma, Natalia noticed Jay was a million miles away. She lowered her mug to the tray with a bang, getting his attention. As Jay raised the mug to his lips, she saw his uncertainty and said, "You'll make an excellent father. Now, Kendra's motha-fuckin' ass . . . that's a different story." And a sigh escaped her.

"There's my baby boy." Honey leaned down, and her four-year-old nephew scrambled into her arms. Wrapping his tiny arms around her neck, she squeezed him tight against her chest. "I missed you, sweetheart."

"Marcus, let your auntie get out of the cold first," her sister-in-law, Tequila, scolded while wearing a warm grin. Tequila opened the door wide so Honey could enter Helen Love's quaint little house. She barely managed to plant a peck on his chubby cheek before Marcus dashed out of her arms to the family room at the end of the hall.

Stepping into the living room, Honey asked, "Where's my bigheaded brother?"

Tequila shut the door, then turned to face her. "Mama Love and Shaq are in the kitchen. Rashad hasn't made it yet."

Honey nodded while taking in Tequila's new look. A couple of weekends ago, the ebony woman had convinced Honey to cut her long dreadlocks. Now her jet-black hair was short and natural. The effect was perfect for her round face and chocolate eyes.

Honey adored her sister-in-law. Shaquil had met Tequila while managing a small bar on the city's Southside. She had worked as a barmaid, and it was her suggestion to begin selling food. Tequila's hot wings were heaven-sent. Shaquil eventually opened his own bar and grill and took Tequila along with him. It had taken five more years before he realized she was the woman of his dreams.

Honey removed her coat, laid it across the couch, and walked to the kitchen where the air was thick and smelled of something familiar cooking. "Mmmm, some-thin' sure smells good."

Following close behind, Tequila acknowledged the compliment. "That's my greens with smoked turkey," she said, unable to keep the pride from her voice.

The woman could *burn* in the kitchen. Just thinking about how wonderful it would taste made Honey run her tongue across her lips. The ham and cheese sand-wich she'd had for lunch was now history. "I can't wait."

Tequila had begun teaching cooking classes last year. Since then, she'd added several additional pounds to her thick hips that Shaquil commented made his wife look even more delectable.

Honey entered the kitchen to find her mother bast-ing a turkey on the stove and Shaquil standing at the sink buttering fresh-baked rolls. An aluminum pan of corn bread dressing was on the counter. One would have thought it was Thanksgiving. She zeroed in on a delicious-looking Dutch apple pie cooling on the table. Baked goods were Tequila's specialty; she prepared a crust so light and flaky it melted on your tongue.

"Hey, everybody," Honey greeted, then strolled over and wound her arms around her brother's neck, kissing him soundly on the cheek.

Six years her senior, Shaquil turned green eyes on her and smiled broadly. "Hey, sis." He was dressed in an orange sweatshirt that enhanced a cinnamon complexion she had always envied. Shaquil wasn't as tall as Rashad, but still towered over Honey's petite frame.

Moving to the stove, she planted a kiss on her mother's forehead.

"Hey, sweetheart." Tiny lines around her eyes crinkled with Helen's smile. She was a beautiful woman. Her fine wavy hair was brushed away from her face, showing a clear picture of her mixed heritage: creamy beige skin and gray-green eyes inherited from an Irish mother, and a wide nose and full lips that were the distinct qualities of her Haitian father.

Honey looked down at the juicy turkey. "That sho' looks wonderful, Mom. Can I have a sample?"

Helen playfully swatted her daughter's hand away, but not before Honey reached for a small, tender piece of white meat. Then she removed the oven mitt, reached for a large spoon, and began stirring a pot of pinto beans. "It will be time to eat soon enough. Grab a knife and put icin' on that cake."

Chewing, Honey reached for a butter knife with a smile. Moving to the far end of the counter, she spread homemade chocolate icing over her mother's fabulous marble cake, anticipating the sinfully sweet chocolate taste. Making certain Helen wasn't looking, she ran her index finger across the knife, then raised it to her mouth. *That shit is finger-lickin' good.* She couldn't match her mother's recipe, no matter how much she tried. Helen never wrote anything down. Her cooking lessons were "observe and learn." Even watching, Honey never could perfect the taste.

"What would you like for me to do, Mama Love?" Tequila asked.

"Get some fresh vegetables out of the refrigerator and make a tossed salad."

Honey watched Tequila move to the sink to rinse her hands, a smile tugging at the corners of her mouth. Everyone was used to her mother's direct personality, knowing it was just Mama's way.

Honey looked forward to Sunday dinners. It was a tradition; they prepared the meal together as a family. She watched as her mother reached into the stove to remove a pan of bubbling sweet potatoes, glad she was enjoying the new oven after they'd had to insist she let go of the old stove she'd had for over fifteen years. The almond self-cleaning oven was the perfect complement to the earth tones of the kitchen. Last year, Rashad had laid nutmeg ceramic tiles on the kitchen floor, and they were gleaming bright as ever. Helen could spend all week cleaning another family's home, but always found time on Saturdays to clean her own home. Although small, her house was just as immaculate as any mansion in West County.

They were setting the table when Rashad strolled in with Yolanda, his girlfriend. Honey noticed her latest ensemble. Cold weather never seemed to matter to Yolanda's hoochie ass. She was wearing a red leather miniskirt with matching jacket and knee-high black suede boots, highlighting ruby-red lips and eighteen inches of weave. But even with her outrageous getup, she was a sweet girl. Honey hadn't had a chance yet to find out how important Yolanda really was to her brother, but she had her suspicions. Yolanda knew Rashad saw other women, and she seemed okay about that. Although for one month straight she was the only one he had brought to their mother's for dinner.

"Hey, Honey," Yolanda called from several feet behind.

Honey flashed a warm smile. "What's up, girl?"

Catching her off guard, Rashad came up behind her and scooped her off the floor. "What's up, sis?"

Honey squirmed in his arms. "Put me down, Rashad," she demanded between giggles.

He slowly lowered her to her feet and planted a kiss on the back of her neck. After quickly looking around, he asked, "Where's Lavell?"

Honey glanced over her shoulder and mumbled, "Who?" before swiftly moving back to the kitchen.

Following her into the room, Rashad stopped long enough to plant a kiss on his mother's cheek before moving to the counter to stand next to Honey. He tilted his head, his smile taunting. "Lavell . . . the guy you brought to dinner last Sunday?"

Honey cleared her throat and murmured, "He couldn't come." Refusing to meet his eyes, she quickly moved to the refrigerator in search of salad dressing.

"He couldn't come, or you didn't invite him?" Rashad now stood beside the refrigerator door with his hands folded across his chest. Grinning, he shook his head . . . little sister was at it again.

Shaquil was removing silverware from a drawer. Listening to the exchange, he couldn't resist teasing and chimed in, "She probably broke the man's heart."

Honey closed the refrigerator and shifted her gaze from one to the other. They were baiting her. If her mother wasn't in the room, she would have cursed both of their mothafuckin' asses out. "No," she said, trying to keep her tone light.

"Then what?" Shaquil asked, nudging Rashad in the shoulder. Their eyes locked with a mutual grin.

How she hated being put on the spot. But this time, she wouldn't give them what they wanted. She placed several bottles on the counter and gave her brothers a sidelong glance.

Rashad stepped forward and playfully poked her in the side. "What gives this time?"

Honey responded with a look of annoyance.

Shaq wagged his hand, then chuckled, knowing she had no intention of explaining. "How many does that make this year, sis? Three? Four? And it's only February." He made tsking sounds with his tongue and gave her a sly wink. "At this rate, you're gonna beat last year's record."

His antagonizing voice flustered her, and she was on the verge of exploding. Hands on her hips, she slanted an irritated glance over at him and said, "Shut up, Shaq!" Out of the corner of her eyes, she saw that the others were watching and waiting for the answer she refused to provide. Why couldn't they just leave her the fuck alone? Was it that hard for them to understand that her priorities were different? That her career came first? A man and his dick was the last thing she needed.

Shaquil turned around and leaned against the counter with his ankles crossed. "Are you ever gonna settle down?" His question was serious, but his tone was teasing.

Honey's lips flattened. "Marriage isn't meant for everyone." She moved over to the sink and reached for a dish towel.

"Apparently," he dryly noted.

She twirled on her heels, her eyes shooting daggers. "Unlike you, I'm not afraid to sleep alone at night."

"Ha, ha!" Rashad chuckled, bending at the waist. "She got you, bro."

Yolanda tried unsuccessfully to stifle a grin, and even Helen snickered.

"Funny," Shaq said, pretending to be annoyed that his sister had brought up the fact that as a child he'd been afraid of the dark.

Tequila was dividing her attention between putting food in serving dishes and listening to her nosy husband. *Serves him right.* After lowering a pot into the sudsy dishwater, she walked up behind Shaquil and placed a comforting hand on the center of his back. "We don't have that problem anymore." She cupped her mouth as if she were telling a secret and pretended to whisper. "I bought him a night-light." Then she turned and kissed his parted lips before exiting into the dining room, leaving her husband wearing an embarrassed expression.

Yolanda whipped around in front of the cabinet and quickly brought a fingertip to her lips, causing Honey to chuckle. Rashad was cracking up so hard he fell against the refrigerator.

Helen was used to her children picking on each other. With a hand planted on a lean hip, she moved toward the refrigerator and found Rashad blocking her way. "Boy, move! I need to get the butter." Taking note of his mother's stern expression, he sobered quickly and moved out of her way. She opened the door and reached inside. "I don't know why the three of you pick on each other so much."

Shaquil looked flustered. "Why you cracking on a brotha?"

Honey saw the flash of Shaquil's grin before he tried

to conceal it. Thank the Lord for sisters-in-law. "Why're you in my business?" she countered.

As he rested his elbow on the counter, Shaquil's mouth lifted in a boyish grin. "All I meant was, you need to at least give us some warning. As soon as I get attached to one of your friends, you give the brotha the boot."

That did it. Honey flung the towel at his head.

"Hey!" Shaquil ducked, his eyes holding amusement. "Give a brotha a break!"

"You two leave your sister alone," Helen scolded, ending any further discussion. "Honey has plenty of time to settle down. She's still young." She removed the country-style apron from around her waist and moved to take a seat at the kitchen table.

Honey was grateful for her mother's intervention. She was used to her brothers nagging about her personal life. Usually she ignored them, but for some reason, today she had taken it personally. "Thanks, Mom." She flashed her a loving smile.

Rashad laughed and flicked his sister's nose. "My bad. You know I got nothin' but love for you."

Honey waved his hand away, then, carrying the salad dressings, moved through the archway heading to the dining room. Shaq followed, saying, "Sorry, sis." When she purposely ignored his apology, he came up behind her, tickling her under the arm.

Honey was extremely ticklish and flinched, trying to push her brother away. "Stop, Shaq!" she said, laughing and dancing away to avoid being goosed.

"No, not until you accept my apology."

She dropped the bottles onto the dining room table and dashed for the living room, her brother chasing her. Honey waved her arms, her efforts useless. She was laughing so hard her sides hurt.

"Say it, sis," he ordered as he tickled her under both arms.

"All right, all right!" Honey fell onto the couch and gave him a shove. This time, he stopped. She placed her palm against her chest and panted. "I accept your weak-ass apology."

Shaq leaned over and planted a wet one on her forehead. Looking down at her flushed face, he said, "I only want to see my little sista happy." He then turned and went back into the kitchen, stopping along the way to swat his wife across the behind for her tall tale.

After getting her breathing under control, Honey went to help. As she entered the dining room Rashad appeared, carrying a steaming bowl of beans. He placed it on a pot holder at the center of the table. "Everything's ready."

"Good. I'm starved," Honey said, then walked into the kitchen, picked up some serving dishes, and carried them out to the dining room. The table was beautifully decorated with her mother's favorite china and an old ecru tablecloth that her grandmother had crocheted when Honey was a little girl. She missed Grandma Dee.

The doorbell chimed as Honey placed a basket of rolls on the table, and she went to the living room to answer it. She opened the door and found a handsome old gentleman standing before her with straight black hair liberally streaked with gray, dressed in a white shirt and tie.

"May I help you?" Honey asked with a warm smile.

"I'm here to see Helen."

His eyes were friendly, and Honey's curiosity got the

better of her. She raised her brow, but before she could find out his name, Helen stepped into the room.

"George, you made it!" she exclaimed from behind Honey. She moved past Honey, took her guest by the hand, and pulled him into the room. "This here's my daughter, Honey. Honey, I would like you to meet my friend George."

Honey extended her hand, accepting his firm handshake.

"The pleasure is all mine," he said in a pleasant voice.

Honey watched her mother take George by the hand again and lead him into the dining room where the others had gathered. Honey entered just in time to see the surprised expressions on everyone's face, especially her brothers.

"Let's eat," Helen announced. Tequila yelled for Marcus to join them, then the family formed a circle around the table and held hands as Helen said grace.

As usual, dinner was fabulous. George was sitting to her mother's right with eyes gleaming with admiration. When had Mom sought male company? Honey wondered. She wasn't mad or anything, just surprised. *Damn, Mama's gettin' her freak on.* It had never dawned on her that after all these years her mother was probably lonely too. Since Curtis Love had walked out on his family when Honey was five, Mom seemed to have resented men. Never once had Honey seen her date anyone. Mom had sacrificed so much for them, and had once told her that her children were all she ever needed. Now that they were all grown with lives of their own, Honey knew that was no longer true.

Glancing at George out of the corner of her eye, she

wondered how long the relationship had been going on, and suddenly felt envious. Helen had lived a long, hard life, but maybe Honey was the only one that thought her life had been hard. Her mother had worked over thirty-five years as a maid while raising three children, doing the kind of work her children were ashamed of. But never once had Honey heard her mother complain. When her brothers were old enough they found part-time jobs, and against their mother's wishes they contributed to the household income. Honey had shared a room with her mother until junior high, when they were finally able to move to a larger apartment. By high school, Mom was finally able to purchase the home where she still resided. She was a proud woman and even now, when her children tried to give her money, she refused it, saying she didn't need it. Maybe she didn't, but they still used Christmas and her birthday as an excuse to shower her with the luxuries they believed she deserved.

Rashad and Shaquil took turns asking George his life history, while the women ate and listened. When the questions became too damn personal, Helen put an end to their interrogation and announced that George would be a regular at their Sunday meals.

Shaquil exchanged a long look with his brother before turning to Honey. "You know, sis, when you do find yourself another date, we're gonna have to buy Mom a new dining room table. It seems like the last chair has been taken." His statement earned him an elbow to the ribs from his wife.

"You're a real comedian," Honey replied dryly, and rolled her eyes with annoyance. Shaquil never could leave well enough the fuck alone. Then she turned to Marcus, who was sitting to her left, and draped an arm around his neck. "I don't need a date as long as I have this little sweetheart." She lowered her lips to kiss the top of his head.

Helen grunted. "I don't need another table. I've had this one for years. We can always pull up a chair from the kitchen."

Tequila brought her napkin to her lips briefly before asking, "Any hints for your birthday this year, Mama Love?"

Helen shook her head. "Nothing. Absolutely nothing." She allowed her eyes to travel around the table. "I have everything I could possibly ever want right here around this table. What else do I need?"

"A day of pampering," Honey mumbled.

Helen looked at George, who nodded. Then she turned to look at the others and said, "I do have an announcement to make."

Honey lowered her fork and looked over at her mother with curiosity.

"I'm going away for my birthday this year."

"What . . . where are you going?" Rashad asked

Helen reached over and grasped George's hand. "George is takin' me to Vegas."

"You? Vegas?" Honey was flabbergasted. Her mother never went anywhere.

Tequila smiled. "What a wonderful idea!" She ignored the frown her husband gave her.

Helen observed her children's stunned expressions. "I know what you are thinkin'. I never go anywhere. But things are gonna be different from now on."

"I can definitely see that," Honey mumbled and resumed eating. Everybody was getting some but her. She didn't even want to think about her mother in bed with George and his ole' shriveled-up dick.

"Well, I'll be damned," Shaquil murmured. "Our little girl is growin' up."

Helen pursed her lips. "Watch your mouth. Don't forget who still wears the pants in this house." She paused to reach for another roll. "It's about time I start enjoying my life."

"I agree," Rashad said.

Not saying much else, Honey wore a grin on her face during the rest of the meal.

After dessert, the family moved to the living room. Shaquil and Tequila were curled on the couch together, with Tequila's head pillowed against her husband's chest. Rashad and Yolanda were on the love seat; her legs were draped across his lap. Marcus was lying across the floor, head propped up with his elbows, engrossed in a rerun of the *Steve Harvey Show*. Helen and George insisted on stacking the dishwasher. Honey didn't argue, assuming the two wanted some time alone.

Honey carried a cup of hot chocolate into the living room. Slipping off her shoes, she curled up in her mother's favorite recliner and covered her feet with a small blue flannel blanket. Watching the couples together, Honey found her thoughts drifting to Jay. She remembered the Sunday evenings she'd hurried home from her mother's just so the two of them could watch the Sunday night lineup together. She had never invited him over to dinner because she knew if she had, she wouldn't ever have been able to get rid of his ass—her family would have taken an instant liking to him.

She shifted in the chair uneasily, not wanting to think about Jay anymore, and listened to the sounds of Shaquil snoring on the couch. Good food did that to you, she thought as she rubbed a palm across her belly.

She had eaten too much and would be paying for it in the morning.

A commercial came on, and Honey found her thoughts wandering again. She was still unable to dispense of the memory of seeing Jay's sexy ass the weekend before. Even though she knew they could never be anything more than friends, she found herself hoping to see him again. She remembered his sweet smile and easy laughter. How she missed sharing moments like this together. She so wanted to hear his voice, maybe even share the rest of the evening with him. How easy it would be to pick up the phone and call him. But she couldn't. She couldn't take the chance of him rejecting her when he found out she'd been hiding something from him. It was too damn risky.

Remembering her conversation with Sasha, she now knew Jay was up to something. Why else would he have been asking questions about her? The answer nagged at her heart. Visualizing his devilish smile, Honey anticipated disturbing quakes in her tranquility. The thought brought a frown to her face. Yep. Knowing Jay the way she did, she believed he had some shit up his sleeve.

Five

Honey pushed open the door and stepped into the dark room. Running her hand along the side of the right wall, she found the switch and flipped it up. The lights overhead flickered before pouring into the room. Following several blinks, she glanced around at the dirt, the abundance of repairs needed, and the old furnishings. Honey cussed and said aloud, "I've got my work cut out."

It was a dusty old room with faint reminders of gleaming white walls, now dingy and gray with cobwebs hanging from the ceiling. She planned to cover the walls with washed-out mauve paint and murals, courtesy of her cousin Ben, a spray paint artist. She intended to show the little wannabe gangsta how to put his talent to some other use than on the sides of several city buildings.

She pulled her sweater snug around her. Despite the heavy material, she felt a chill. The snow had finally stopped, and the weatherman had forecast sunshine, with a high near thirty degrees. The room was cold, but there was no point in turning on the heat; she didn't plan on being there long.

Stepping around an overturned chair, Honey moved toward the left side of the room and envisioned the changes to come. She had plans to knock out the wall separating the two suites, making the salon twice as spacious.

Moving behind the counter, she saw an old industrial stove and grill, covered with years of grease and grime. It was to be removed, and she would purchase a residential stove and refrigerator. Then she could finally remove the dormitory-sized refrigerator from her office that was taking up needed space. The rest of the kitchen was salvageable, but would require major scrubbing. Drywall would be hung to hide the kitchen from the work area.

Coming from behind the counter, she stepped across the dusty room and spotted something lying on the scuffed floor. She stooped down and picked it up, then dusted it off with the front of her skirt. Staring down at it, Honey smiled and released a cry of delight. It was a lunch menu preserved in a plastic sleeve.

She remembered when Freddy's Diner was opened for business many years ago. In high school, Freddy's was the shit. It was the place to hang out on Friday nights for chocolate malts and Freddy's thick-ass burgers. Somewhere in the back of her mind, she could still hear teenagers laughing, and could almost smell the scent of the greasy quarter-pound hamburgers they all had adored. The burger joint had been closed for almost six years.

Honey strolled over to the counter where three old stools were still screwed into the floor. Dusting off one red vinyl seat, she sat and took a twirl. "One chocolate

malt, please," she ordered, smiling at her own reenact-
ment.

"Make that two."

Honey whirled around sharply and found Jay standing several feet away. Her smile vanished as she stared
at him with her brow arched high in surprise. *Well, I'll
be damned.* It was becoming a habit of his, sneaking up
on her. Cheeks flushed, she felt embarrassed and pissed
the fuck off that he'd caught her goofing around.

Standing with his legs wide apart, he spoke again.
"Hello, Honey."

While remaining silent, she allowed her eyes to linger
over his appearance. He looked sexy as hell, dressed in
his usual eight-to-five attire. Crisp blue jeans outlined his
long muscular legs and fit as if they had been molded
to his body. Covering him was an unzipped quarter-
length leather jacket, and his large hands were tucked
in the front pockets. Honey watched the rise and fall of
his solid chest covered by a green sweatshirt.

His beard had grown since she'd last seen him, but
was still neatly trimmed, adding tantalizing dimensions
to his fine chocolate ass. Brown eyes dancing, he
looked deliciously edible. Just as she reached his thick
juicy lips, Honey tore her focus away and frowned. "I
wasn't expecting you. I thought you were sending one
of your employees."

Jay's mouth lifted in an irresistible smile. "I decided
to do this job myself."

"Oh." Shhiiit. She'd never even considered the possibility of him doing the work. Now Honey knew she
was in trouble. Her decision not to get involved with
him had been challenged at the baby shower, but now
that he planned to invade her space while installing her

security system, she'd have to stay on her toes. Otherwise, her efforts were going to be futile.

Jay had been watching her from the moment he entered the room. When he found her holding the menu in her hand, he had witnessed a tickled smile and eyes huge with delight. The sight had warmed his soul and made his dick stand to attention. Now he allowed his gaze to wander over her appearance, and took pleasure in looking at her. Honey had paired a white turtleneck with a red corduroy skirt and oversized sweater. White tights covered her shapely legs. Her hair was pulled away from her face, highlighting the attributes of a long delicate neck and giving him a full side view of her small, charming nose. Her skin was smooth, cheekbones high, lashes long and thick, eyes wide and bright, a complexion so natural that if she was wearing cosmetics it was impossible to tell. Her mouth looked delectable: red, pouting, and begging to be kissed.

Honey braced her weight against the countertop while her heart slid back into her chest. As soon as she found her breath she asked, "Did you ever visit Freddy's when it was open?"

Carefully maneuvering around an overturned table, he answered, "No. I never did. We weren't allowed on this side of town."

She nodded, remembering the stories of his strict upbringing. Jay had grown up in a big-ass house in the Central West End with servants and shit.

She watched Jay thoughtfully as he moved across the floor to a window in the corner, where he ran his hand across the sill, as though trying to determine a good location to install wiring for her security system. She had a bird's-eye view of his phat ass.

"Well, you missed out."

Jay turned and lifted his gaze to her, giving her a sexy, lopsided smile that sent her pulse racing. She spun around and stared down at the dirty countertop as she took several deep breaths. "Freddy's was the bomb. Anybody who was anybody hung out here. His burgers were big and juicy, and his malts were so fuckin' thick you had to use a spoon." She unconsciously traced figure eights in the dust with a slender finger. "Yeah, you missed out."

"Sure sounds like it." Jay pulled out a rickety old chair, resting his foot in the seat and his elbow on his knee. His eyes swept across the room. "I never had a place like this to hang out in. This looks like something we saw on *Happy Days.*"

"That it was," she mumbled, then looked over her shoulder in time to catch Jay staring at her. With his eyes centering on her face, she found it next to impossible to escape his penetrating stare.

"And you want to change it into a beauty parlor."

She nodded before her eyes wandered to his lips. They were full, moist, and curved slightly with amusement. Again, warmth rushed through her as she remembered what they had felt like brushed against hers. Her nipples tingled as she imagined his lips suckling her breasts like a newborn baby.

Honey slid off the stool and walked across the room to distance herself. She reached a booth once occupied by the in crowd. Staring down at the table was like déjà vu as she remembered standing in the same spot while enjoying good times with her friends. Combing fingers through her mass of shiny brown hair, she also remembered a time she'd rather forget.

It was right at this very booth that she had fallen in love with Walter. He was captain of their high school football team their senior year, and since she was a cheerleader, they both traveled in the same circle of friends. After victory games, the entire team traveled to Freddy's. Honey remembered sitting at that very spot with her chin resting in the palm of her hand while her eyes found their way across the room to where Walter was sitting. Sometimes they'd all share the same booth; other times Walter would sit close to the malt machine with his fellow teammates. She had thought him handsome with dark mocha skin, long nose, dimples, and coal-black eyes. He was so damn fine that she'd refused to listen to Sasha's assessment of him as a conceited dog.

It wasn't until months later that Honey painfully realized Walter was a self-centered bastard. He believed the world owed his tired ass something, and being in his presence was considered a privilege. Even Honey's being a member of the in crowd meant little to him. He ignored her. It wasn't until she became captain of the cheerleading squad that he finally found her worthy of his time. Honey had caught him staring at her on several occasions with looks of interest, causing a warm tingle down to the end of her toes. Then one afternoon, she found Walter standing in front of her locker. Her heart had raced so fast she thought she would faint. She believed herself to be the luckiest girl in the world when he asked her out.

How wrong she had been.

Returning from her reverie, she looked at Jay for

several seconds without blinking before turning away from the puzzled concern in his eyes.

Jay's brow wrinkled. He'd watched the disturbing play of emotions on her face, and could barely restrain himself from comforting her in his arms. Honey had shaken her head, as if to relieve herself of painful memories. He hadn't missed the sadness her eyes held. Now she looked like she wanted to kick somebody's ass. He wanted to push for answers, and wondered again for the hundredth time how much longer it would be before she decided to share her pain with him.

"Hey, Jay, come here." He heard the slight giggle in her voice. Whatever the hell had bothered her had quickly vanished. Jay walked over to the corner of the room and stood beside her. She pointed to the end of an old wooden booth, and he saw her name carved on the table.

Jay looked into her wide eyes. "Wow, you're famous." His irresistibly sexy smile reappeared as he reached out to squeeze her shoulder.

Feeling heat emanating from his hand, Honey backed away, afraid of the closeness she felt. She turned away and reached up to pull a wooden board from the window, allowing sunlight to pour into the gloomy room. "Why are you really here?" she asked.

Jay wasn't at all surprised by her blunt question. He would never expect anything less from her. But he paused a second too long, and she turned around in time to see the desire dancing in his eyes as he replied, "Why do you think?"

"Shit, if I knew, I wouldn't've asked," she answered shakily. "You tell me."

"Because I want to be here," he answered, taking a

step forward. "I want to be near you," he added, slowly, searching her face.

"But why?" she asked again, her voice a frantic waver.

He reached up to stroke her face, then dropped his hand again. "Why not?"

Only silence greeted him. Jay noticed her pained expression, and decided to restrain himself from sharing his feelings with her. It obviously made her uncomfortable.

Then a thought washed over him. Maybe Honey wasn't hiding anything. Maybe she wasn't afraid. Maybe the reason she wasn't interested in a relationship was that she truly wasn't interested in him.

Oh, hell naw, he told himself. No fuckin' way. His pride wouldn't let him accept such bullshit.

Honey shrugged her shoulders, almost as if to say, "What-the-fuck-ever," then turned away. She didn't trust herself to respond when near him. She felt like crying and didn't know why. *There'll be none of that shit,* she scolded herself inwardly. Taking a deep breath, she moved to remove another board from the window.

Jay broke the silence by asking, "When will construction begin?"

Relieved he had changed the subject, she whipped her head around. "My brother's company will begin next week." Putting some distance between them, she moved to the center of the room. "They'll knock down that wall over there." She pointed to the wall dividing the two suites. "And add six more booths and a smaller kitchen." She faced him, her mouth curled into a smile. "I plan to have a full-service salon. Everything from facials to manicures."

Jay nodded, clearly impressed. "Congratulations. It sounds like this is gonna be *the* happening place."

Hands clasped in front, Honey's smile broadened. "I hope so."

Strolling around the room, Jay stopped within inches of her. "So, you want this room wired and operating on the same system as next door?"

She could smell the spicy scent of his body. Dizzy with desire, Honey barely managed a nod.

Once again, he witnessed the same sweet smile he'd taken to his bed at night for almost eight months, and knew it was only a matter of time before she would share his bed. He could already imagine her lying on her back with her legs spread wide apart and him taking them on a long hard ride. Oh, hell yeah, it was going to happen. He would just have to be patient.

"You have some dust on your nose," he whispered. He lifted his hand and with the pad of his thumb, gently wiped the dirt from the tip of her nose. She glanced up at him, and Jay saw a reflection of his own desire. He stared into her eyes, trying to see deep within her, hoping to find some hint of what Honey was feeling.

"Honey, I—"

She held up a hand and broke in with a crisp tone. "If we're gonna work together, we need to get somethin' straight from the beginning." She gathered her emotions, getting them under control, then pushed them to the back. Fixing him with a glacial stare, she continued. "I'm not getting involved with yo' ass."

Jay's expression stilled, and his gaze held her stormy eyes for a long spell as he witnessed her visible struggle to keep herself together. "Aw'ight."

Honey's lips compressed into a thin line. Jay didn't appear to be offended; his tone was casual and his smile, although small, was friendly. She couldn't believe he was giving up so easy. Part of her wanted him to keep pursuing her, while the other half knew that was no good.

"I'm glad we got that straight," she said, her tone soft now.

"Friends?" Jay asked, extending a hand, and saw the lines of worry in her face ease.

Honey noted the mischief twinkling in his eyes, and knew being friends wasn't going to be easy. Jay was going to tempt the hell out of her every chance he got. But she was determined to fight him all the way.

"Friends." She clasped his hand and ignored the searing heat.

Jay released her grip and winked. "See you in a couple of days." Then he headed for the door.

Natalia arrived at the Galleria Mall just in time to find Kendra descending the escalator.

"Oh!" Kendra waved several bags in the air. "I was hopin' I hadn't missed you!" She embraced her friend in a bear hug.

When they pulled away, Natalia lowered a hand to Kendra's belly and patted it playfully. "Looka here. My little godchild is sprouting like a weed." Natalia chuckled. "You're as big as a damn house!"

Kendra cut her eyes and said, "Thanks for remindin' me." She wasn't in the mood for teasing, especially after spending half the morning trying to get ready. It was becoming fuckin' impossible to do even the simplest tasks.

"But no less beautiful," Natalia said, beaming at her friend. It was true, Kendra's full mocha face was adorably round and glowing. The burgundy jumper and turtleneck blouse she was wearing made her look every bit the part of the expectant mother. But from the look on Kendra's face, Natalia knew "cute" was the last thing she'd want to hear. She remembered reading that pregnant women became increasingly sensitive during their last trimester, and she had to agree Kendra was a perfect example.

Natalia looped their arms together. "I can't wait to hold that baby in my arms!"

Kendra clicked her teeth and turned her head to gaze up at her tall friend, and felt the usual pang of jealousy. Kendra had always been envious of Natalia's beauty and talent. When she'd first begun modeling during their freshman year, Natalia covered the expenses so Kendra could travel with her during the summer. It had been the most memorable experience of her life. At that point, she knew she wanted to have as much control of her life as Natalia had, not shackled down with a baby. Natalia had money, power, and beauty. Her model's figure, her greatest asset, had an amazing effect on men. She was also the first real friend Kendra had ever had. She felt proud Natalia had chosen her.

"How about you taking this baby off my hands and raisin' it yourself?" Kendra blurted.

Natalia looked down at her for several seconds before realizing Kendra was dead serious. "Girl, please! I don't even know how to change a damn diaper." She chuckled. "I'm definitely not ready for motherhood. I need to get married first. Then I'm depending on you to teach me a few things."

Kendra gave her a choked laugh. "And you think *I'm* ready? Nat, you know I don't know shit about babies. I don't have a family to help me. Unfortunately, babies don't come with instructions."

The pair grew silent as they strolled side by side, passing several specialty shops while Natalia wondered if it was time to mention her reason for asking Kendra to meet her this afternoon.

Natalia had a lot of admiration for her friend. Kendra's mother gave birth to her at fifteen, and had never pulled herself together. Kendra grew up living in and out of foster homes until she turned ten, when she returned to her mother and was verbally abused until she was old enough to get away. An honor student, she was granted a full scholarship to UMKC's school of dentistry. Unlike Kendra, Natalia had grown up with a college trust fund. Kendra had made something of her life through a lot of hard work and determination, and Natalia admired that.

"Oh, look!" Kendra shouted, pulling Natalia out of her reverie. She was pointing at a cashmere coat in the window of Lord & Taylor. "The coat's the bomb!" She rushed toward the door, dragging Natalia alongside her.

"You're pregnant! What good is that coat gonna do you?" Natalia teased, amazed at how fast Kendra could maneuver her body if she needed to.

Kendra dropped a hand to her thickened waist and muttered, "Hmmph! This is a temporary situation," before stomping off with a look of disgust.

Natalia found her reaction oddly disturbing. She'd always imagined that when Kendra decided to have children, she would cherish the moment and give her child all the love she had been deprived of in her life. Instead, she was acting the complete opposite.

They entered the department store, and Natalia

scanned a rack of wool slacks while Kendra went in search of the coat. Natalia quickly found a pair of royal-blue pleated slacks on sale and was pleased. She had a dinner party to attend next week, and was dying to wear a two-toned blue blazer she'd purchased while at a conference in New York.

Natalia smiled, thinking of the dinner. She was certain her boyfriend, Jacob Stone, was planning to propose. While at dinner together the night before, he'd casually asked her if a woman preferred a marquise or a round-cut diamond, then quickly added that he was planning on purchasing a pair of diamond earrings for his mother. However, when they dropped by a jewelry store on the way home, instead of looking at earrings he'd moved over to the ring display and asked Natalia what she liked. With that in mind, her heart lurched with happiness at the prospect of spending the rest of her life with him.

Not too long ago, she had believed herself to be in love with Terraine Andrews. Now she knew that had only been infatuation. She'd been jealous of Terraine loving someone other than her. She had been young, too. He was like a big brother to her, and she his pesky little sister going through puberty. When Terraine began dating and no longer paid attention to her, she became pissed off. One night she switched his allergy pills with sleeping pills, and once she was sure he was sleep, she slipped into his bed. Terraine awakened the next morning to find her lying naked next to him, and immediately assumed they'd had sex. Natalia did nothing to correct him.

A month later, she announced that she was pregnant. Richard Andrews immediately stepped in, as Natalia knew he would, and demanded his grandson marry her.

But shortly before the wedding was to take place, Natalia was offered a modeling contract and regretfully admitted she had lied. It had taken Terraine falling hard for fashion model Sasha Moore for Natalia to finally see the light. Now, with Jacob Stone in her life, she realized the difference between love and infatuation. Last night he had fucked the shit out of her and then they had lain in each other's arms, curled together in satin sheets. She had never felt more at peace.

She removed the size-five pants from the rack and disappeared into the dressing room, where she slid them over her narrow hips, then admired herself in the mirror. Jacob would be pleased. Slipping her jeans back on, she walked out to the sales desk where she found Kendra paying for the coat.

"Oh, Nat! I was able to snatch the last one," she said, eyes dancing with delight. Kendra fingered the material one more time before the sales rep placed the coat in a hanging bag. Then she moved out of line so Natalia could pay for her slacks, and they exited the store together.

Natalia looked down at all the bags Kendra was carrying and took several from her hands. "I've never seen you shop like this."

Kendra turned to her and grinned. "And it feels so damn good. I've got a lot on my mind these days."

"Anything you want to talk about?" Natalia asked with genuine concern.

Kendra's smile faded as she pressed her lips together tightly. "Yes, but let's do it over lunch."

They decided to indulge at California Pizza, a popular spot that usually had a line out of the door. Today, however, they were lucky to be seated right away. They ordered a chicken pizza and two Diet Cokes, and engaged in casual conversation before Kendra blurted out, "Oh, Nat, I've fucked up big time."

"How so?" A wave of guilt washed over Natalia as the nickname reminded her of how close the two really were. There was no reason for either of them to play games when they'd always been so honest about everything else. Natalia leaned forward and listened while Kendra told her about her breakup with Lawrence.

"That's terrible!" Natalia said. "I can't believe he was messing around with his nurse." Natalia was, in fact, flabbergasted. They had double-dated on several occasions, and she had believed Lawrence to be a kind, gentle man and a large contributor to the community.

"The ho!" Kendra fumed. Even though Natalia was her best friend, it was difficult sharing her humiliation. "I should have suspected somethin' by the way she was lookin' at him with those big bubble eye of hers, pantin' like a dog in heat."

Natalia covered her mouth and laughed. "You're mean."

"It's true! She even had the audacity to call me last week on behalf of Lawrence and ask me to return the gown he purchased for our wedding. If I wasn't pregnant, I would have beat that bitch's ass."

Natalia's brow rose as she remembered the beautiful satin gown Kendra had insisted on having. It had cost Dr. Hill close to five thousand dollars. "So, what happened?"

"I sat up that night and cut it into shreds, and then had it FedExed to his office the next mornin'."

"You didn't?" Natalia asked, even though by the look Kendra gave her she knew she had. "Girl, you're crazy."

"Hmmph! That was just a start." Her nostrils flared. "I plan on gettin' even." She reached for her glass and took a long drink before adding, "You just wait until he asks me for this ring back."

Natalia dropped her eyes to the three-carat solitaire Kendra was still wearing. "What are you planning on doin'?"

Kendra's eyes danced as she leaned across the table. "Cubic zirconia, baby." She screeched with laughter.

Natalia brow rose. "You wouldn't?"

"Girl, you know I will. Lawrence doesn't know who he's playing with. I already found one that looks just like this one at the pawnshop." She stirred the ice in her glass with her straw. "I was going to be *everything* for that man. Why else was I willin' to have a fuckin' baby?" She dropped her eyes to the table. "Then he decides he wants to dump me when it's too late to get rid of it."

Natalia's face clouded with uneasiness as she pushed back several unruly curls. She knew Kendra was a strong believer in an eye for an eye, but in all the years they'd known each other, she never would have guessed Kendra could be so vindictive. The rage blazing in her eyes made her shudder.

Their waitress returned with their food. After she departed, Natalia decided it was time to mention the baby. She cleared her throat and said, "What are the two of you gonna do about the baby?"

Kendra bit into a slice of pizza and finished chewing before she spoke. "Please don't think any less of me when I tell you this."

Natalia heard the plea in her friend's voice, and reached across to squeeze Kendra's hand. "Of course not. We're friends no matter what. What is it?"

Kendra didn't say anything for the longest time, and when she did, she spoke in a soft voice. "I'm carryin' Jay's baby." She stared intently at Natalia, analyzing her reaction. Instead of surprise, she noticed a look of relief. "You already knew, didn't you?"

Natalia looked at her pained expression and nodded. "Yes, but I wanted to hear it from you. But . . . are you sure it's Jay's baby?"

Kendra looked hurt for a moment, then realized the question was warranted. She'd fooled Natalia into telling everyone she was carrying Lawrence's child. "I'm sure," she said, then sighed and rested her head in her palm. "The worst part about it is Jay's tryin' to play games."

Natalia squeezed her hand again. "Jay intends to do right by you and the baby."

Kendra pulled her arm away and laughed bitterly. "The right thing to do would be to marry me."

Giving her a sympathetic smile, Natalia said, "I don't think that's going to happen. But I can reassure you, Jay will take care of his responsibilities."

Kendra thought about the restless nights she'd been having. The baby's rapid movement in her womb was constantly interrupting her sleep. "He'll have to marry me, or I'm givin' this baby up for adoption."

Natalia shook her head. "You don't mean that."

"Yes, I do."

"But why would you do that? Jay would provide financial support for both you and his child."

"This has nothin' to do with money. If that were the case, I'd have this child and take Jay Andrews's mothafuckin' ass to the cleaners." She shook her head. "I don't want to be a single parent. I want the husband *and* the child, not the child."

Natalia found herself unable to argue her point. She would probably react the same way if she suddenly found herself pregnant and alone. While she could run to her parents for help, Kendra couldn't. Once she'd left, she never looked back. Now she was pregnant and alone. Natalia never wanted to be in the same predicament. She would be terrified. That alone made Kendra braver than she. In fact, the only flaw she'd noticed in her friend was that, starved for love, she usually looked for it in all the wrong fuckin' places—which was why Natalia had introduced her to Jay in the first place. She'd hoped to see the two people she loved most find happiness with one another. How wrong she had been.

She looked up to see Kendra staring at her and said, "You would just give your child away to some stranger?"

"If I had to, yes, I would." Kendra shifted uneasily in the chair.

Natalia shook her head with disapproval. "I can't believe you'd even consider adoption, especially after the way you grew up."

Kendra's expression stilled. "I'm doin' it *because* of the way I grew up. I know nothin' about being a mother, because I never really had a mother. And when she was around, she spent most of her day trying to beat me upside my head for my existence and for ruinin' her life. I don't want to look at this child someday and think about what could have been if he or she were never born."

"Everything could work out in the end." Natalia gave her a comforting smile.

Kendra dropped her shoulders and blew out a long breath. "I'm not cut out to be a single parent, Nat. Even you know that. I don't need baggage. It would be too hard for me to find a husband who'd want a ready-made family. I was stupid enough to believe Lawrence did, and I'll be damned before I take that chance again." Her eyes became misty, and she lowered her head and dabbed them with her napkin. "Jay will have to marry me. That's the only option."

Natalia stared at her, watching the rise and fall of her chest. There had to be some other way. "It sounds as if your mind is made up."

"Yes, with Jay and this baby, it has to be all or nothin'." She blinked back fresh tears and took a deep breath. "Are you mad at me?"

"No, because I know you're too damn selfish to be anyone's mother."

Hurt darkened Kendra's eyes, and she blew air between her teeth. "Damn, girl! Why you have to be so hard?"

"It's true, but I love you just the same. I just hate that I'm now in the middle of this shit." Natalia bit into her pizza. "However, my godchild is not being put up for adoption. I'm gonna convince Jay he's ready to be a father."

Kendra's face shone. "Oh, hell yeah! I knew you would help me hook his chocolate ass."

"I didn't say that."

"Yes, you did. You know as well as I do that Jay isn't cut out to raise a child on his own. He needs me. This baby needs him."

Natalia shook her head. "I don't think it's gonna work."

"Yes, it will. I just need your help to pull it off." Her eyes glimmered with hope.

Natalia groaned inwardly. How did she get herself involved in this shit?

* * *

Honey was curled up on the couch with a large bowl of buttered popcorn. It was her favorite night of the week. She never scheduled a date on Monday, not wanting to take the chance of missing her favorite lineup on UPN. She either laughed or cried at the characters, knowing there were other people out there beside herself with drama in their lives. The characters dealt with something different each week. They were survivors, like her.

Today's appointment with her psychologist went quite well. She felt that she was really beginning to heal. Soon, she would be able to put her past where it belonged forever . . . in the past.

Glancing at the clock on top of her television, she noticed that she had still another five minutes before the first show began. She placed the bowl on the couch and returned to the kitchen for a big glass of chocolate milk. Nothing was better than chocolate milk and popcorn.

As she was pouring the syrup into a tall glass, the phone on the kitchen wall rang. Who could be calling her now? With a scowl, she reached for the phone as she retrieved a spoon from the drawer.

"Hello?" she asked while she stirred.

"May I please speak with Honey?" asked a raspy male voice.

Honey stopped stirring and tried to identify the voice, but failed. "Who is this?"

"Who's this?" the man countered.

Honey huffed and dropped a hand to her waist. "This is Honey, and I'm 'bout to hang up on your ass." The brotha called at the wrong damn time to be playing games.

He chuckled. "My bad. Would you like for me to call at another time?"

"That depends on who's calling."

"Dis Darrius."

"Oh yeah," she mumbled. Rashad hadn't wasted any time.

"Oh yeah," he mocked. "You sho don't sound too happy to hear from an old friend."

Honey snorted. "You were never my friend. All you ever did was pick on me, making my life hell."

"Then why did you tell Rashad to give me yo' number?" he challenged.

"Because I . . ." She paused. He did have a point.

Darrius laughed at her silence. "What's wrong? Cat got your tongue?" He lowered his voice to a mellow tone. "Why don't you give me a chance to make it up to you?"

Hmmm, baby's got style. Not used to such a bold introduction, she twirled the phone cord around her index finger without thinking. "Whatcha have in mind?"

"How 'bout I drop by your salon this week and we discuss dinner?"

Why the hell not? If she sat in the house alone another day thinking about Jay's mothafuckin' ass, she was going to go crazy. Besides, Darrius did sound good over the phone. "I guess so."

"Either you do or you don't."

She laughed outright at the blunt statement. *Talk about nerve.* "You're bossy, aren't you?"

"No. Just direct. It comes with havin' big balls." She could hear the smile in his voice.

"And I like it in you. That's cool." Looking toward the living room, she added, "But I got to go. My show just started, and I hate to miss the beginnin'."

Chuckling, Darrius said, "I'll see you soon."

Honey raced back to the living room and flopped down on the couch, wearing a wide grin. *Time must have done a brotha some good.* Darrius sounded quite interesting. He just might be what she needed to keep Jay off her mind. Maybe things really were beginning to look up for her again.

Six

Natalia sat behind her desk feeling a tremendous amount of frustration. She peered miserably around her lavish office as she pondered the problem at hand.

Last night she had planned to spend a quiet evening alone with Jacob. She'd prepared a fabulous lasagna dinner for two, including garlic bread and a tossed salad. She'd expected Jacob to come over straight after work, but when he hadn't arrived by eight o'clock she became worried and decided to page him. Jacob returned the call within minutes, but instead of apologizing for being late, he accused her of trying to keep track of his black ass. Natalia had laughed it off, explaining she was only concerned as to why the fuck he hadn't showed up yet for dinner. Jacob told her in a far-off voice that tonight wasn't a good night, and not to expect him for dinner. He finished by informing her that he'd be in touch, and then hung up.

In touch! His words had struck a nerve. Who the fuck did he think he was talking to? Gritting her teeth, Natalia searched for a meaning behind his words. She wasn't furious; instead, she was anxious to know what the hell was going on. Her eyes wandered restlessly to the phone, hoping Jacob would call with an explanation for his rude behavior.

Trying again to shake off the gloom, Natalia picked up a pencil and began making changes to a sketch in front of her. Diva Designs was hosting an AIDS benefit fashion show in April, and alterations were still being made to the season's new designs.

Diva Designs created exquisite evening wear made of the finest fabric in brilliant colors that complemented women of color. The two-piece sketch in front of her consisted of a flattering metallic gold duster and black slacks; however, Natalia wasn't quite pleased with the design. Diva Designs contracted with designers from all over the world, but this was one of her own creations. With a degree as a fashion designer, she had a flair for style. The olive wool pantsuit she was wearing was just a sample of her talent.

After several attempts, Natalia gave up. She couldn't concentrate. There was still a lot to do if she was going to be ready on time, but her thoughts were in turmoil. She dropped her pencil, sagged back against the leather chair, and asked herself again what could possibly be going on. The question stabbed at her heart. Since last night, she'd found herself feeling insecure about her relationship. It gnawed away at her confidence. Insecurity was one emotion she didn't particularly enjoy; she'd experienced it enough as a child.

Pushing back a wayward strand of hair, she reflected on the last nine months. She loved Jacob, and knew he also loved her. Not because he had told her so many times, but because he showed her in so many ways: romantic dinners, breakfast in bed, showering her with gifts, but most of all being there when she needed him the most.

She had given as good as she got. When his father, Sly Stone, passed away a month before, she'd been there to help him through it, giving him all the love and support she could provide. Which was why it was so fuckin' hard for her to understand why he was shutting her out. Something was obviously bothering him. Maybe her fears were premature; however, she wouldn't know for sure until he called.

Glancing down at her watch, Natalia discovered it was well past two o'clock. She'd missed lunch. Shhiiit. It didn't matter. Since last night, she had been unable to put anything down.

Before she could strike up the nerve to try reaching Jacob on his cell phone again, the door to her office swung open. It was Jay. Smiling, she relaxed in her seat, glad to see him. It gave her something else to think about, at least for the duration of his visit.

"What are you doing on this side of town?" she asked.

Jay strolled across the plush mauve carpet and sank into a Queen Anne chair opposite her desk. "You forgot who shares controlling interest in this corporation," he said with a smirk. Jay had inherited half of Diva Designs and thousands of dollars when his grandfather died. But because he knew little to nothing about fashion designing, and really didn't give a fuck one way or another, he chose to be a silent partner and allowed Terraine, who had once worked side by side with their grandfather, to run the corporation the way he saw fit. Three months ago, Terraine took the corporation public. Together, the two shared the controlling 52 percent.

Jay laced his fingertips behind his head, then stretched out his long legs, crossing them at his ankles. "I got your message late last night. So I thought I'd show my face around here and visit with you at the same time. Did you get a chance to speak with Kendra?"

"Yes, that's why I called." Natalia placed her red finger-nails on the edge of the desk and peered into Jay's warm brown eyes. "It's your child."

Feeling as if someone had punched him in the chest, Jay considered the revelation for a brief moment before asking, "How can you be so sure?"

Natalia blinked, surprised, then said, "I'm sure. I've been around Kendra enough years to know when her ass is lying." She gave him a knowing look.

Jay nodded and leaned forward, then ran over her words in his head as he contemplated what he was going to do now that he knew for certain the baby was his. His eyes shifted away from Natalia briefly, then back again. "Did she say anything about givin' the baby up for adoption?"

Natalia rose from her chair, lips pinched. "Yes, and just as I told her, I think the two of you are making a big mistake."

Jay shook his head. "I can't marry her, Nat."

"I'm not asking you to marry her," she said. "All I'm asking is that you raise the baby yourself."

He looked up, confused, and said, "I don't know," wishing he were as convinced of his ability to raise a child as Natalia.

She planted both hands on her trim waist. "Well then, you better figure it out, because that baby is gonna need a father. A mother, too, if you have any possibilities." Natalia noticed Jay flinch slightly, and was surprised at what she read on his face. Her gaze narrowed. "You mean to tell me there *is* someone in your unstable life?"

Jay shrugged, then said, "Yes and no." He paused then, but Natalia waited. Finally, he added, "Yes, I love someone. No, she won't have anything to do with my black ass."

"Damn!" Natalia wagged her hand as if she'd been burned, then giggled. "Someone has finally sunk her teeth in you. Well, it's about time." Moving merrily around her desk, she pulled up a chair so she could sit facing him. "Who is she?"

Jay chuckled at Natalia's response despite his anguish, and told her about Honey.

"She sounds lovely," she said, and her eyes sparkled with approval. "When do I get to meet her?"

"Nat, don't start," Jay groaned. "Honey isn't interested in being anything but a friend."

Natalia ignored his look of opposition. "Maybe you haven't tried hard enough. A good woman is worth fighting for." She crossed one leg over the other. "Remember, I waited for Terraine to come around for fifteen years."

A grin stole across his face. "Yeah, and look what good it did you."

Natalia frowned, and Jay opened his mouth to speak, but she jabbed him in the arm before spitting out a simple warning: "Don't even go there."

Honey had to pinch her arm just to make certain she wasn't dreaming. She had arrived at the salon around eight to find Rashad and a crew of five out front waiting in two trucks bearing the company's logo NOTHING BUT LOVE.

The rest of the morning breezed by in record time. Rashad instructed his crew, and by eleven o'clock most of the rubbish had been hauled away. Freddy's was beginning to look less like a diner, and Honey could almost visualize the changes to come.

While going over the layout of the area with her brother, she heard someone call his name. Rashad looked up first, then her eyes followed to find a fine brotha moving toward them. With eyes glued to the handsome stranger, Honey slid off the stool, brushing the dust from the back of her jeans. Her lips curled when she realized the stranger was Darrius. Gone was his frail, skinny body; in its place was a bomb-ass body. No longer slouching, the man moved with earned dignity.

"Hey, man, what's up?" Stepping forward, Rashad greeted him with a firm slap on the back.

"Just keepin' it real," Darrius responded before his eyes traveled over to Honey. He honored her with a charming grin, causing her to blush.

My, my, Honey thought as she took in his explosive good looks. A gorgeous brotha the color of roasted peanuts, Darrius was a tempting package. He was blessed with good hair that he once wore in a curly ponytail, but now was cut low. The gray two-piece suit added distinction to his features, and complemented his tall, solid frame. The years had definitely been good to him.

He greeted her with a warm brotherly hug. "You're still as fine as I remembered," he said, pleased at what he saw. Pulling away slightly, he kept his arms wrapped loosely around her small waist while his dark eyes feasted on her pretty face.

Honey smiled up into a pair of magnificent tawny eyes and said, "You didn't turn out bad yourself." The scent of his expensive cologne filled her nose. She waited, hoping to feel a warm tingle traveling through her veins or even a couple of drips in her panties. But her jaw sagged with disappointment. Nothing, not even a spark.

Damn!

Darrius finally released her and Honey took two steps back, smiling brightly up at him.

Rashad poked Darrius in the arm. "Didn't I tell you she was somethin' else?"

Still gazing down at her with admiration, Darrius licked his lips before speaking in a low tone. "And for once you didn't lie."

Honey rolled her eyes and grimaced, dying to knock a silly-ass grin off her brother's face. Standing next to her, Rashad began engaging in a conversation about her love for flannel as if she weren't there. She couldn't believe her ears. Matchmaking was bad enough. However, Rashad knew she didn't share her personal life with anyone. By the time she overheard him revealing she was a lousy cook, Honey decided to nip the conversation in the bud. *Enough is enough.* Agreeing to go out with one of Rashad's boys was becoming a grave mistake.

She propped her hands on her waist and said, "Rashad, don't you have work to do?"

The irritation in her voice got his attention. Realizing that he probably said more than he should have, Rashad smiled and said, "Yeah, I guess I do." He gazed at her for a second as if to say, "My bad," before turning to Darrius. "Man, I'll holla atcha later." They gave each other dap before he returned to his crew.

Honey clicked her tongue at her brother's retreating back and said, "You have to excuse him. Sometimes he doesn't know when to shut the hell up."

Darrius chuckled at her irritated look. "No problem." Hearing hammering behind him, he allowed his eyes to wander around the room. "Rashad says you're expanding your salon?" He faced her in time to watch her nod proudly in response. She was excited, and had every right to be. He was always happy to see a sista reach her dreams. Darrius's heart warmed with affection, and a smile crept to his lips. "Congratulations," he added. "You've come a long way from my boy's pain-in-the-ass little sister."

Honey slugged him playfully in the chest, and Darrius reacted as if she'd knocked the wind from his lungs before he laughed.

"Watch it, buddy," she warned. "The way I remember it, you had a mad crush on me."

"True, that." He allowed his eyes to travel the length of her again, taking a quick appraisal of her curves. "Damn, you look good! How have you been?"

"I've been good. And yourself?"

"I can't complain." He stuck out his chest. "Life has been good to me. I'm a stockbroker."

"Ooh! Wall Street," she said, impressed. She could just see him racing around the stock market trading floor.

He chuckled. "Yeah, about as close as I'll ever get."

She admired the way the corners of his eyes crinkled when he laughed. "Well, you definitely wear it well," she murmured.

They grinned stupidly at each other.

"So, when can I take you out to dinner?" he finally asked.

She made a face. "I'm not sure if I want to go out with someone who thinks I'm a pain in the ass."

Darrius dropped a hand to her shoulder and squeezed, then gave her a devilish grin. "You can pester me anytime."

Staring up at him awhile longer, Honey waited for some kind of reaction. She hoped for at least a shiver. However, once again she didn't feel even an inkling of a response. She sighed. It was fuckin' hopeless. "I don't care." She shrugged, then smiled. "I'm always game for a free meal."

He looked surprised, and said jokingly, "You mean I'm paying?"

With narrowed eyes, she said, "Don't even play."

Darrius laughed openly at her expression until her face softened. "How about tomorrow night?"

She grinned. "Tomorrow's good."

Straining his ears, Jay heard enough bits of the conversation to confirm that the two were indeed dating. Only seconds ago, he had entered through the salon and stood behind the makeshift door that separated the two suites. He hadn't intended to eavesdrop. Hearing Honey's voice, he assumed it was business, and had decided to wait. It only took a matter of seconds for him to realize he'd been wrong. That shit had nothing to do with business.

Watching them standing so close together was pissing him the fuck off. A slight frown marred his features as he looked the man up and down through the crack in the door. He didn't like the way his hand rested on

Honey's shoulder either. Observing them, Jay remembered how easy it used to be for him and her to carry on a friendly conversation, and even flirt with one another as she was doing with the stranger. That closeness was lost. Now there was only tension between them. A bolt of jealousy sliced into him.

Feeling the overwhelming need to storm into the room to stake his claim, Jay shifted to his right leg and resisted the urge. Time was running short, and if he planned to make Honey his, he'd have to act fast. It was time for her to realize there was more going on between them than could be denied.

Jay cleared his dry throat and the two turned toward him, wearing identical stunned expressions. Honey moved away from the man as if she were caught doing something she shouldn't have been doing.

With hands deep in his pockets, Jay moved forward. "I'm sorry, did I interrupt somethin'?" His apology didn't quite reach his eyes as they slid from the stranger to Honey's flushed face.

Even before Honey turned around, she was aware of his presence at the door; the hairs at the nape of her neck had suddenly stood up. She hated her traitorous body when Jay was near. He wasn't even touching her, but by simply looking at her, his gorgeous eyes kindled a flutter at the pit of her belly. Darrius's touch did nothing, but when Jay was near, every vein in her body came to life.

Shaking her head, Honey quickly recovered and threw him a less-than-welcoming look. "Yes . . . Yes, you *are* interrupting us," she said. "Will you excuse us a moment?"

"No problemo," Jay said, flashing a mouthful of perfectly white teeth. But instead of leaving them alone he

stood nearby, rocking back and forth on his heels, staring at them like he was ready to fuck somebody up.

Glancing briefly over at Jay, and realizing he had no intention of leaving, Honey turned her gaze to Darrius and raised her brow as if to say *I'm sorry*.

Darrius nodded knowingly. "Handle your business. I need to get back to work myself." He leaned in to kiss her on the cheek. "I'll give you a call tonight." After acknowledging Jay with a stiff nod, Darrius strolled to the front of the building. Jay's muscles tensed as he fought for control when what he wanted to do was grab the cocky son of a bitch around his neck and choke the shit out of him.

Not wanting to make Jay aware that his rude behavior had affected her, Honey stepped past him and walked toward her office. When she heard his footsteps, she paused halfway down the hall to glare at him over her shoulder. "Can I help you with something?"

"I thought I'd get started tomorrow."

"Check with my brother and make sure you won't be in his way." Without another word, she turned and walked into her office.

Following Honey, Jay breathed deeply, taking in the familiar female fragrance. Even dressed in faded blue jeans and a green sweater, she still managed to look damn good. As far as he could tell she wasn't wearing any makeup . . . but with flawless honey-beige skin, why would she? Her hair had been gathered loosely at the back of her head, then twisted and secured with a comb. She was seated at her desk now, head tilted down, and he warmed as he stared at the curls that had escaped and lay against her neck.

"So, you're datin' that cat?"

Her eyes immediately snapped to him. "Yes . . . not that it's any of your business."

His brown-eyed gaze held hers for several seconds while he moved to take a seat on the end of her desk. "He doesn't seem like your type."

Honey thought she saw a sign of jealousy, but his expression changed before she could be sure. Pushing a strand of hair behind her ear, she asked, "And what *is* my type?"

"Well, not the stuffed-suit type. He looks like he works at a bank."

Honey smirked, amused at his behavior but also relieved. He *was* jealous. "Your claws are showin', Jay."

"Hey." He raised his hands and shrugged. "I'm just tryin' to be a good friend."

"How? By being rude?" Arms folded beneath her breasts, she waited for an apology.

"Okay, please forgive me. But was I right?"

"About what?"

"About him being a banker?"

"No, you're wrong." She watched his jaw drop a fraction. "He's a stockbroker."

His triumphant smirk gone now, Jay scratched his bearded face and said, "That's even worse."

Her lips twisted to one side. "I'm not about to have this conversation with you."

"Why not?"

" 'Cause I'm not," she answered coolly, annoyed by his questions.

Jay was pissed, but he hid it well. Getting her to reveal her feelings about the stranger was like prying open a lion's mouth. She left him no other choice but to ruffle her feathers a little bit.

"Actually," he said, then hesitated briefly, "you should tell me all about him, just in case I need to rescue you again."

She gaped at him. "Excuse me?"

He folded his arms across his chest. "Don't tell me you forgot about the doctor."

Oh, how could she have forgotten? She grinned despite her best effort not to. "I could have handled him myself. I do know Tae Kwon Do."

His lips curved into a lopsided grin. "Is that what you were doing?" He paused to give a harsh laugh. "That shit looked more like Tae *Bo*."

She couldn't resist a chuckle. Last Fourth of July, she'd had a date with a resident physician who simply refused to take no for an answer. By the close of the evening, she'd planted a knee hard between his legs, causing him to buckle only momentarily before he lunged at her. Luckily, Jay had been lurking in the bushes. She pressed her lips together. Those had been the good old days. That is . . . before Jay ruined everything by kissing her.

Still daydreaming, she didn't see Jay round her desk. Before she had a chance to object, he dropped both hands to her shoulders and began massaging them.

"You're tense."

She nodded. She hadn't realized how tense she was until she felt his warm, gentle caress. Her mind flooded with memories of the two sitting in her living room with Jay commencing an evening massage.

Jay leaned in close and whispered, "You need to be with a real man, one who's got his woman's back. Not those wimps you've been dating." His hot breath against her ear caused goose bumps to rise on her arms.

Honey tried to fight the need to respond; however, his fingers commenced a slow assault of her senses while his male fragrance wrapped around her like a nylon rope. She felt weak. Helpless. Her eyelids fluttered closed and she moaned. It felt good to be touched by him again. For the moment, she forgot her vow to keep her guard up, to stay away from him, and allowed herself to enjoy the heat radiating from his hands.

"What you need is *me*," he whispered against her ear.

His cocky words snapped her back to reality. Swiveling around in her chair, she disengaged his hands. "What I need is for you to get the fuck out of my office."

Jay stepped back and looked at her with an intensity in his gaze that caused the same fluttering feeling inside her. Suddenly, she felt as if the room were closing in on her. She'd always found her office small, but now, with Jay invading her space, the room seemed almost claustrophobic.

Admonishing herself for the desire stirring at her core, she took a stabilizing breath and regained her senses. She didn't want Jay to misconstrue her reaction to his touch. As soon as she could trust her voice, she said, "I have work to do."

Jay grinned while shaking his head. Honey tried to act tough, but he knew there was a soft and vulnerable side to her. He'd already seen it. Leaning over, he cupped her chin in the palm of his hand. "When are you gonna quit resisting me and give a brotha a chance?"

The arrogant arch of his forehead as well as the knowing smile on his face told her he was thinking about that night they had almost shared. Although her coochie throbbed, she rolled her eyes. A burst of fire radiated from his palm; however, she pushed aside all emotion and moved away from his reach. "In your dreams. Now . . . would you please leave?"

She managed to sound as if she wasn't at all disturbed by his words, when in fact she felt like she was about to lose control. It was a shame she couldn't lie across her desk, spread her legs, and invite him in. Honey could tell he wasn't all that upset at her rejection, and it irritated her that she couldn't shake his confidence. If she was able to deny her feelings, why the fuck couldn't he do the same? "Is working together gonna be a problem?" she asked.

He plastered on an unruffled expression to hide his frustration and said, "No problem," but paused when he met her brief gaze. He watched her lips part with a sigh. The same lips that kept him awake night after night. "No problem at all." He then stepped out, closing the door behind him.

She closed her eyes after Jay left and allowed her head to fall against the back of the chair. She needed to stand strong, but there was nothing she could do about the warm, sensual current running through her veins. The man made her toes curl, but she had to find a way to keep up the pretense that she felt nothing for him except friendship. It wasn't going to be easy. Why couldn't any other male have the same effect on her? The more time she spent with Jay, the more she wanted. Why the hell couldn't she just tell him that she didn't need his help, that she'd found someone else to do the work? With a sigh, Honey reached over and logged on to her computer.

She was looking forward to her date with Darrius, even though they would never be anything more than friends.

But Jay didn't need to know that.

*   *   *

Jay was ready to put his fist through a fuckin' wall. The thought of someone else being with Honey, with his dick buried between her legs, bothered him. It was one thing to be led to believe that she wasn't interested in a relationship. It was another thing to know that the stupid-ass rule only applied to him.

Then there were the times when she made him feel as if he had imagined it all. Her lips. The warmth of her skin. The night they almost shared together. Even on days like today when he could feel her body relaxing beneath his fingertips. All those things reassured him it wasn't a dream. So why was she fighting the inevitable?

His cell phone vibrated at his hip, eliminating any further deliberation. Looking down, he saw that it was Kendra calling him from the clinic.

"I hope the hell you hadn't forgotten about my doctor's appointment."

Guilt washed over him. He *had* forgotten. "No, I haven't," he lied. "Want me to pick you up?"

"That would be wonderful," she replied with glee. "I have one more patient to see, then I'll be ready to go."

"I'll see you shortly." He snapped the phone shut and tossed it on the passenger's seat, then reached into his coat pocket for a cigarette. Luckily, his schedule was clear for the rest of the day.

Leave it to Kendra to help him keep his priorities in order.

"Wasn't that exciting?" Kendra exclaimed.

Jay nodded. Excitement was putting it mildly. If he hadn't been there, he would have never fuckin' believed it possible.

He had heard his baby's heartbeat.

"Four more weeks and this will all be over," Kendra sang. Leaning over in the seat, she clutched his biceps. *And not a moment too soon,* she silently added.

She had insisted that Jay accompany her to the examining room, knowing that hearing his child's heartbeat would have just the right effect. However, she'd forgotten that it also meant Jay would see her disgustingly distended stomach. She'd never forget the way his eyes practically fell out of his head when she raised her shirt. With a sidelong glance, Kendra noticed he was still wearing the same stupid expression. She groaned. How could she have been so dumb? The sight of her own protruding belly button was enough to make *her* sick. She could just imagine how it looked to him. He hadn't said a word since they left the office.

"I can't wait to hold *our* child in my arms!" she said, hoping her words were convincing enough to capture his attention.

Jay merely nodded and continued to stare straight ahead. Overcome by a rush of tenderness, he too had images of holding his child.

She glanced over at the dazed expression on his face again. "Well, say something," she demanded, hating to be ignored.

Her whiny voice broke the spell. Jay looked over at her. "I'm sorry, did you say somethin'?"

With an artful pout, she moved away from him and slumped down in the seat. What could he possibly be thinking about that was more important than her and this baby? "You're a trip."

Jay swallowed and reached over to lightly squeeze her arm. "Damn, Kendra. This is all new for me."

His soft smile reassured her that she was on to

something. She moved his hand to her belly. "I wonder if she's gonna look like . . . you or me?"

"I hope she'll look like you."

She was taken aback by his kind comment. "You do? That's so sweet of you!" She sighed with relief. *I knew he still found me beautiful.*

He returned his hand to the steering wheel. "I've always found you attractive," he admitted as if he'd read her mind. Seeing the dreamy look she gave him, he stared out in front of him again. He didn't want her to misinterpret his comment. "As long as the baby is healthy, I don't care what he . . . or she looks like."

"How the hell can you say that?" she shrieked, then her face fell and she added, "If this baby is ugly, I'ma have a fuckin' cow!" She hurried to explain. "I have patients coming in all the time cuddling their babies as if they're the most precious things in the world. But when I move in to take a closer look, I have to hide my surprise." She rolled her eyes. "Just yesterday, this lady brought in her new baby. He was pink, with a big-ass mothafuckin' head and little bitty eyes." Kendra squirmed in her seat for added emphasis.

Jay shook his head, not at all stunned by Kendra's response. He expected as much from her. "A mother's love is 'posed to be unconditional," he said. "Regardless of what the child looks like, you are to love it because it was created inside you."

"Whatever," she mumbled, looking unconvinced.

Jay pursed his lips.

She tried to come to her own defense. "I'm entitled to my own opinion."

"True, but it's that attitude that makes it hard for me to understand your ass."

"How can you say that?" She reached over to cradle

his arm as she wiggled closer to him again. "It was my attitude that drew you to me in the first damn place, and it's my attitude that kept your black ass coming back," she cooed.

"And it's that stankin'-ass attitude that's now keeping us from figuring out what's best for this baby."

"Why are you saying such hateful things?" Her lower lip quivered.

He glanced down at the fingers wrapped around his arm. "Why the hell are you still wearing that man's engagement ring?"

She smirked. Jay was jealous. "Do you know how it feels to be pregnant and unmarried?" she whined, trying to sound as pitiful as she could manage. "Well, it's embarrassing. And I refuse to have people staring and pointing their fingers."

"Kendra, this ain't the fifties," Jay said, keeping his voice even and light. "Single women have babies every day."

"You are so insensitive," she said, pouting. "You know I'm not like everyone else. I'm an old-fashioned type of girl."

"Since when?"

"I always have been."

He chuckled. "You are so full of crap. You don't even want this baby." His words were harsh, but his voice was kind.

"Yes, I do. I just want you, too." Her features transformed into a plea. "Things will work this time. I just know it."

Jay felt himself weakening as his conscience whispered to him. He fought it, taking a deep breath as he pulled into the clinic parking lot.

He turned to look at her long face. "Why don't we work on being friends?"

She snorted. "I'd rather you come over tonight and fuck me." She folded her arms over her belly.

Even though it had been a while since he'd had some, he declined. "Nah."

"Why not? It would work between us if you tried." Her voice was almost a wail.

I've tried. Lord knows I tried. Besides, he doubted his dick would even get hard. "Kendra, listen—"

She cut him off before he could finish. "Shhiiit! I almost forgot." After pulling herself out of the car, she crooked a finger and signaled for him to follow her into the building. A reluctant Jay got out of the car and followed. Once in the building, she grabbed his hand and led him to her office. Moving to a shelf in the corner, she retrieved a small box and handed it to him.

"What is it?" he asked.

Her eyes glittered. "Open it and see."

He lifted the lid and stared down at the tiniest pair of booties he'd ever seen. He removed one and placed it over his thumb. It was a perfect fit.

"Aren't they darlin'?" She pressed her round body against his. "One of my patients gave them to me," she lied. Actually, she'd bought them herself the night before, hoping to stir Jay's emotions even further.

"Take them with you," she insisted, and rested both hands on top of her stomach. "We created this life together. Whether it was love or not, this baby is ours."

Jay asked quietly, "Does this mean you decided to keep the baby?"

She moistened her lips. "Have you decided to marry me?"

His thoughts clouded with sympathy, but he knew better than to voice them. She would think she was wearing his ass down.

He shook his head, then took a hard breath and surprised himself by saying, "No. But I'm thinking about raisin' the baby myself."

She dropped her hands. "So one of your hoochies can raise my child?" She rolled her eyes. "You got life fucked up."

"What's the difference?"

Before Kendra could retort, she looked up to find Claire, her hygienist, entering her office without waiting for permission. "Oops!" Claire skidded to a halt. "I didn't mean to interrupt, but we're ready for you."

"Can't you see I'm busy?" Kendra snapped.

Jay noticed Claire didn't bat an eye. She was probably used to her boss flying off the handle. He gave her a sympathetic smile, then turned back to face Kendra and patted her hand as he said, "I'll holla atcha later." It was time to leave; the last thing he needed was for her to go the fuck off.

After he left, Claire shrugged an apology. "I'm sorry."

"Well, it's a little late for that," Kendra spat. Dropping into her chair, she scratched her stomach and sulked with displeasure. *This shit had better work.*

"I still can't believe it," Jay mumbled.

Terraine watched his brother pacing back and forth in front of the floor-to-ceiling window with his hands clasped behind him. Speaking about his unborn child, he had a noticeable glow of happiness about him. Terraine smirked, believing it a sign that Jay was finally coming around. "It *is* somethin' else. I remember the first time I heard my daughter's heartbeat. I was overwhelmed. Words couldn't begin to describe the experience."

Staring out at the snow falling, Jay merely nodded, still in awe. He hadn't even known something like that was even possible. But after Dr. Rosalyn Gaye finished examining Kendra, she squeezed some cold jelly—he couldn't remember the name—onto her abdomen and with a monitor she was able to pick up very loud sounds. It sounded like an underwater submarine—rapid swirling sounds that Dr. Gaye said were his child's heartbeats. Hearing that, he felt his heart swelling with pride.

Terraine leaned forward on the gleaming mahogany desk. "It sounds like this experience has really shaken you up. Are you havin' second thoughts?"

Jay turned and shrugged. "Yes. Maybe." He paused to blow out a breath of frustration. "One minute I'm sure, then the next minute my head is all fucked up again." He shook his head, overcome by a sense of responsibility. "I just don't know. I want to do this, but, man . . . I'm scared. What if I can't get it right?"

Terraine folded his hands. "Being a parent ain't somethin' to take lightly. So I can understand your frustration. My daughter isn't even here yet, but already she's changed the entire course of my life."

After turning the words over in his mind, Jay moved to a black wingback chair and leaned against it. "I guess it would be easier if it wasn't Kendra." What he didn't tell Terraine was that he resented the fact that Kendra was putting the future of their child in his hands with some stupid ultimatum. Why was she so dead set on marrying him?

"What if it was Honey?"

Jay blinked and glanced over at him. "What did you say?"

"What if Honey was pregnant?"

He gave a faint smile. "I wouldn't give this shit a second thought." His eyes lit up as he envisioned Honey's stomach swollen with his seed. "I lay awake the other night asking God, why Kendra of all people? There has to be some underlying reason I just haven't figured out yet." He leaned forward to briefly bury his face in his hands, then looked up again. "I've messed around for years, sticking my dick in anything with titties and a big ass. I had my pick of any woman I wanted. Even had them falling at my big-ass feet, and I didn't want any of them. Then here I am, ready to settle down and spend the rest of my life with one woman, and what the fuck happens? She doesn't want me. Instead, I get a woman pregnant I can't even stand to be around." He laughed in frustration. "What the hell does that mean?"

"I don't know, man," Terraine said, watching Jay gather his thoughts. "I think that's somethin' you're gonna have to figure out for yourself." Seeing the lines of stress around Jay's eyes, Terraine wished he could be of more help.

"I know, bro. I know," Jay said, his thoughts in a frenzy. Terraine was right; he had to make the decision himself. "That child deserves better than me."

"All that kid will want is to be loved . . . by his daddy."

Images of a foot the size of his thumb flashed before his eyes.

The door to Terraine's office swung open and Sasha waddled into the office, holding her car keys.

"Hey, Jay," she said merrily.

He moved to plant a kiss on her forehead and said, "Whatcha doin' driving?"

She frowned and hugged her swollen belly. "You're as bad as your brother. I'm pregnant, not handicapped." Moving behind the desk, she landed in Terraine's lap. He met her lips with a quick yet passionate kiss.

Watching the exchange, the love that clearly showed in their eyes, Jay felt a brutal stab of warmth and jealousy combined. *Shhiiit, why can't I have the same thing?* He moved toward the door.

"Uh, Jay?" he heard Sasha say.

He turned around. "Yeah?"

She couldn't keep the humor from her voice. "You talk to Honey lately?"

His blood surged at the mention of her name. "I saw her this morning."

Her brow rose. "Business or pleasure?"

Jay chuckled. His sister-in-law was about as nosy as Natalia. "Strictly business."

With an exasperated look, she asked, "What are you waiting for?" Terraine tried to get her to mind her own business, but Sasha shooed his hand away and told him she knew what the hell she was doing. Then she turned back to Jay. "Well?"

"It's all about timing," Jay said as he reached the door.

"Well, you need to hurry up," she mumbled as he exited the room.

Sasha mouthed something off to her husband, then everything was quiet. Jay was certain Terraine had found a way to silence her.

While he was waiting for the elevator, his cell phone went off.

"Jay speaking."

"Mr. Andrews, this is Jocelyn Price."

Oh yeah. "Thanks for returning my call. I spoke with my partner, and I'd like to hear more about your case. Can we meet?"

"Yes, definitely," she answered. "I'm free tomorrow evening. How about dinner, my treat?"

Jay smiled. "Dinner would be fabulous, as long as I get to pick the place."

"Fine," she agreed. "I'll call you tomorrow."

Seven

Honey was squeezing into a pair of panty hose when the phone rang. *It better be important.* On one leg, she hopped over to her nightstand and retrieved the cordless.

"Who are you going out with?" Sasha barked before she even had a chance to say hello.

"Damn," Honey muttered under her breath. While struggling to get her other leg into the hose without ripping them, she asked, "How'd you know I was going out?"

Sasha hesitated, then said, "Jay told me."

"Jay!" Honey said. "What's he doing running his fuckin' mouth?" Blowing out a breath, she lowered herself onto the edge of her red satin comforter before asking, "What did he say?"

"He wasn't gossiping or anything. Jay just happened to mention it to Terraine." She clucked her tongue. "So, who is he?"

Honey groaned. She didn't need this shit, not after a long day. Candy had cleared most of the afternoon so she could leave the salon by four, only to find that she had nothing to wear, which meant she had to race to Northwest Plaza. After spending an hour trying on dresses, she'd finally settled for a simple black turtleneck sweater dress she found on a clearance rack at JC Penney.

Rising, she peered at the clock and realized she had less than fifteen minutes before Darrius was to arrive. "It's no big deal," she said by way of dismissal. "Just one of Rashad's bucktooth friends from junior high." She padded to the adjoining bathroom decorated in rose and reached for the facial cleanser.

"Then why are you going out with him?" Sasha asked.

Honey spread the cream generously across her cheeks while wishing she hadn't bothered to answer the damn phone. "Not that it's any business of yours, but last time I checked I was still single and could do whatever the hell I wanted."

"Well, Jay is pissed."

Honey stopped scrubbing her face long enough to snarl, "I don't give a fuck!"

"Yes, you do."

"No, I don't," she snapped louder than she intended.

"Then why are you getting mad?" Humor had crept into Sasha's voice.

"I'm not getting mad." Staring at her reflected image, Honey saw evidence of frustration. "I'm just sick of everyone gettin' in my damn business."

"Girl, puhleeze! Your business is my business. Don't you know we're joined at the hip?"

"And I guess since you're married to one brother, you expect me to be dating the other?"

"What's wrong with that?"

"Bye, Sasha." Honey depressed the button, ending the call on her best friend's giggles.

Leaning against the sink, she took a moment to grin at the fact that Jay had been discussing her. She wondered what he was thinking. *Who gives a fuck?* she reminded herself. Brushing the thought aside, she splashed her face with cold water and reached for a face towel. She had a date to prepare for.

Moving to the full-length mirror behind the door, she glanced at her reflection and was pleased with what she saw. The dress was narrow, fitting her small breasts, narrow hips, and phat ass to perfection. *Not bad for a last-minute decision.* After one more quick look, she went in search of her black leather boots.

Tonight, Jay would be the furthest thing from her mind.

Max's Steakhouse was already crowded when they arrived. Luckily, they didn't have too long a wait. With his hand at the small of her back, Darrius escorted her to a cozy table for two at the left side of the room. The lights were dim, giving an intimate atmosphere. Soft dinner music was in the background, and the aroma of grilled meat filled the air.

Darrius pulled out a chair for her at a small table covered in white linen. A red rose was on display in the center. After the waitress took their drink orders, Darrius chatted away about the stock market. Honey had expected to be completely bored by the topic, but quickly found herself intrigued. He even agreed to help her put together a small portfolio when she was ready. During the conversation, she found her eyes lingering on his chest. She liked the way the peach rayon shirt fell from his wide shoulders. The color contrasted well with his skin. Darrius definitely had it goin' on. Intelligent eyes, full, juicy lips . . . it was a shame she wasn't attracted to his sexy ass.

When the waitress returned with their drinks, Honey took the opportunity to peer out the window. She loved Clayton in the evening. Bright lights everywhere, the prestigious community was like a city within itself. Everything was right at your fingertips: shopping, art, restaurants. It even had its own downtown.

"What're you thinking about?" Darrius asked.

She turned to him, a smile on her lips and in her eyes. "Nothing. I was just lookin' at how beautiful the city is at night."

Sitting opposite her, Darrius studied her face a moment, then said, "I disagree. The scenery in here is better." He gave her a devilish grin.

Honey pursed her lips playfully. "Don't even go there."

"My bad." He threw his head back and chuckled. "You haven't changed a bit. You still don't believe in givin' a brotha a chance." Pausing briefly, he sobered up before continuing, "All jokes aside, how's life been treating you?"

Honey fingered her water glass. "I haven't any complaints. Business has been good."

With his arms on the table, Darrius leaned closer. "What about your personal life?" he probed. "Anyone special?"

"Nope," she answered. "And I prefer to keep it that way."

"That's understandable," he agreed with a nod. "I'm recently divorced, with two little girls, Becky and Theresa. My pride-and-joys." Reaching into his back pocket, he pulled out their photos, holding them out for her to see. They were the spitting image of their father, except for the large brown eyes Honey was sure they had inherited from their mother.

"They're beautiful children."

"Yes," he agreed as he returned the wallet to his pocket, his voice proud. "They made it quite hard to leave . . . but my ex-wife didn't give me much of a choice." His voice drifted; the divorce obviously wasn't of his choosing. He cleared his throat. "But enough about me. When are you gonna slow down long enough to start a family?"

Honey lowered her lashes and shook her head. "I have plenty of time for that later." A lump rose to her throat. Reaching for her frosty strawberry margarita, she leaned in and took a cautious sip from the straw. She wasn't taking any chance of getting a brain freeze.

Darrius nodded. "Don't rush it, believe me." His expression turned thoughtful as he paused. "It *is* a lot of hard work. Marriage can be rewarding, but also a lot of pain."

Honey pinched her lips. Pain was something she was familiar with.

Darrius moved a hand to hers and gripped it gently. "I'm gonna be honest with you." He stopped to sigh, looking her directly in the eye. "I'm not ready for another serious relationship. I'm still tryin' to get over the last one." His smile faltered at the reminder. "I hope I haven't misled you in any way, but I'm only interested in conversation and company."

Honey heaved a silent sigh of relief. This one wasn't going to be a problem. "That's fine by me."

He smiled, pleased with himself. "Good, I'm glad we got that out of the way." Before removing his hand, he added with a wolf grin, "But if I change my mind, you'll be the first to know."

She was tempted to tell him not to even waste his time but thought better of it.

The waitress returned with a large sampler platter. When she departed with their dinner orders, Honey dropped a spicy wing in ranch dressing, then parted her lips and took a bite. "Ooh!" Eyes watering, she reached for her water and gulped until she could breathe again. "This shit is hot!"

Chuckling, Darrius appeared unaffected as he licked his fingertips. "The hotter the better."

Honey decided to stay the hell away from the wings and helped herself to the fried zucchini. While enjoying their appetizer, she and Darrius talked about the good old days and their old neighborhood.

"Do you remember Ms. Curtis?" Honey asked.

Twirling a straw around in his Long Island tea, Darrius answered, "Sure. The old woman with the 'fro."

She choked with laughter at the memory and nodded. Miss Curtis had been the principal of their junior high school. "Well, she married Ole' Man Smith."

"You're shitting me?" he said. A retired Vietnam veteran, Ole' Man Smith was once the neighborhood drunk.

Honey nodded. "Miss Curtis cleaned his funky ass up and made an honest man out of him. Mom says he's a deacon at her church now."

Darrius shook his head. "I can't believe it." He was still chuckling when something over her shoulder caught his attention. He cocked his head toward the entrance. "Isn't that your boy over there?"

Honey shifted in her seat so she could see behind her, and what she saw made her drop her food. Stepping into her line of vision was Jay. With a woman. Every muscle in Honey's body tensed. Taking a deep breath, she tried to pretend she couldn't care less, when in actuality she felt her heart turn over in her chest. She suddenly lost her appetite and pushed her plate away.

Jay was wearing a pair of tan pleated slacks and a rust-orange turtleneck that skimmed his chiseled chest. The outfit looked specially made for his tall physique. He had replaced a gold loop earring with a half-carat diamond stud, and gold chains were draped around his neck and wrist. He'd visited a barber recently; his wavy hair and beard were both neatly trimmed. Her heart thundered. Damn, Jay looked good.

And his chocolate ass knew it.

Moving as he was with a dignified grace, she could feel the power in his solid form. His arm draped around the woman's petite waist, he steered her in their direction, and Honey could only stare at him.

"Honey, what a pleasant surprise," Jay greeted her.

She glowered at the man in question, who flashed a blinding smile at her, and snorted under her breath, "Yeah, right."

Her gaze held his, and he knew she was voicing the silent irritation he knew all too well. Jay smirked in return, ignoring her obvious displeasure, and said, "Honey, let me introduce you to Dr. Jocelyn Price."

The woman greeted her with a warm smile and an extended hand. Honey didn't miss the emphasis on "doctor." Again, her eyes swung to the toasted almond–colored woman with freckles standing by his side. She was tall and willowy, and wore a slamming midnight-blue pantsuit. Draped over her arm was a winter-white wool coat. Her natural red hair was swept back in an elegant French braid, adding an air of sophistication. Eyes tawny, cheekbones high, she looked like something out of a glamour magazine. *The bitch ain't all that.*

Jay rocked back on his heels in silent laughter, finding the exchange amusing. His behavior infuriated Honey. Pasting on a fake grin, she managed a choked greeting. "Hello, Dr. Price."

"Please, call me Jocelyn," she said sweetly, her ringless hand outstretched. Her long lashes fluttered as she spoke.

Leaning forward to shake her hand, Honey caught a whiff of her rich fragrance. Honey lowered her hand and gently dropped it to Darrius's arm, and her eyes swung up to Jay. "The other day, I didn't get a chance to introduce you two. I'd like both of you to meet Darrius."

While Darrius and Jocelyn exchanged greetings, she watched closely for Jay's reaction. As she waited, she flashed a brilliant smile at her companion and leaned closer to him. As she had hoped, Jay's smile faded into a deadly expression, and jealousy flashed in his eyes before he could mask it with a smile. *Paybacks are a mothafucka,* she thought.

The men stared at each other before Jay initiated a courteous handshake.

"Would you care to join us?" Darrius offered politely.

As she swallowed her cry of protest, Honey's gaze slid from Jay to Darrius and back, and she was greeted by Jay's wide grin. *Don't even think about it,* she warned with her eyes.

Now that the tables were turned, Jay was enjoying himself. Even though he had no intention of sharing a table with them, he paused a little longer, making Honey suffer. While he watched her increasing discomfort, a knowing smile crept over his face before he finally answered, "Maybe next time."

"Well . . ." Honey hesitated as though unsure what to say next. Couldn't he tell she was uncomfortable?

But Jay didn't appear concerned. Silence enveloped them. The next minute felt like a fuckin' lifetime. The tension was thick. If she had a knife, she thought without a hint of amusement, she could have sliced the shit. It was uncomfortable seeing Jay in the company of another woman, and she wished he'd go take a seat at the table his waitress was preparing.

She finally got her wish.

Jay placed his hand at the small of Jocelyn's back and, after making their excuses, moved with her to a table at the center of the room.

Their food arrived, and Honey picked up her knife and eagerly carved into her steak. Focusing on her food kept her from looking across the room. Normally she looked forward to a juicy steak, but tonight the meat had somehow lost its flavor.

Darrius didn't seem to mind carrying the conversation while Honey, who was deep in thought, said very little. Though her attention was focused on her date, her thoughts and occasionally her eyes strayed to the man across the room.

After a while, Honey's lips tightened with annoyance. This was no coincidence. Jay had purposely showed up to spy on her ass. She knew she wasn't being full of herself. Jay was snooping. Only thing she didn't know was how he found out where Darrius had planned to take her tonight.

What was even worse was that he'd brought along a date of his own. A beautiful date. Not that she cared. *Who am I trying to fool?* It pained her to admit it, but it bothered her to see him with someone else. Especially an attractive female. Out the corner of her eye, she assessed her, one female to another. *I'm not hating.* She took a deep breath and tried to release her rising frustration with a forceful, ragged, exhalation.

It shouldn't matter, but it bothered her to know that Jay had moved the fuck on, and had no qualms about finding someone else. *I guess he got sick of my bullshit.* What infuriated her the most was that he was rubbing the shit in her face.

"Honey?" she heard someone say.

"Huh?" she managed before her gaze shifted to Darrius, her breath coming out in a sigh.

He leaned toward her, lowering his voice. "You haven't heard a word I said."

"Yes . . . Yes, I have." But even as she spoke, she found it hard to keep from looking past his shoulders.

Darrius tilted his head to the side, blocking her view. "Then what did I say?" he asked, drawing her gaze again.

"You . . . uh . . ." She lowered her head, then looked at him beneath her lowered lashes. "I . . . I guess I wasn't listening," she admitted.

Darrius didn't appear offended. In fact, he seemed amused. "Is somethin' wrong?"

"No, nothing at all," she said, still distracted. Things were getting out of hand. Ever since Jay's return, her life had been turned upside down.

Darrius bit back a smile. "I haven't had your attention since your boy arrived." He placed a palm over his heart. "I'm insulted."

Honey eyed him doubtfully, even though his gentle face appeared trustworthy. "He's not my boy. It's just a coincidence," she said, putting on a cool expression. "I was thinkin' about somethin'."

"Or some-*one*, maybe?" Darrius reached across the

table and clasped her hand. "Is there somethin' you're not tellin' me?" His eyes were warm with concern as he searched hers.

Lowering her gaze, she stared down at her plate. "Why would you say that?"

"Because you look as if you've lost your best friend," he added with a chuckle that vibrated through her body.

She lifted her chin. "Whatever," she mumbled. He didn't know how close he was to the truth. She *had* lost a very good friend.

"In fact, you look the same way Jay did when he saw you and me together yesterday." His gaze narrowed with curiosity, but she could tell he was teasing her. "Is there somethin' goin' on between the two of y'all? 'Cause I don't want to step on another man's toes." A knowing smile touched his lips, causing her cheeks to warm.

She really wasn't fooling anyone, and now she knew it. "No, there ain't shit going on," she said quietly. "I'm fine."

"You sure?" he asked with such a charming smile she couldn't resist smiling back.

"Really, I am." It was fuckin' ridiculous to be jealous. After all, she was the one who had put the brakes on their relationship. Jay had every right to be with someone else.

"Good." Releasing her hand, Darrius leaned back against the chair, still unconvinced, but he decided to leave it alone.

Their waitress arrived with their dessert, ending further discussion.

Digging into a large slice of New York cheesecake, she asked herself what right she had to be mad. From the corner of her eye she caught Jay staring, his gaze burning into hers, and her appetite disappeared. She sighed with relief when Darrius finally signaled for the check.

Despite his best intentions, Jay found himself watching Honey over the rim of his glass. Even from across the room, he couldn't keep his eyes off the soft features of her face—nose delightfully small, lips gently full. The dim light made her eyes appear larger and more luminous than ever. Her hair was shiny and fell into layers around her shoulders. Simply dressed, even covered up to her neck, she made his dick hard.

Jay pulled his eyes away and tried to focus on what Jocelyn was saying, but found himself comparing her features to Honey's. He watched her perfect, sensual lips parted with surprise. Lips covered in the deep, penetrating red that he was fond of. Lips he had kissed. Lips he imagined wrapped around his dick. Jealousy brewed in him as he watched Darrius reach across the table and squeeze her hand. He wondered how well they knew each other.

It had been a bad idea to bring Jocelyn here. It was fuckin' impossible to conduct business. While Jocelyn was just as beautiful as Chad had promised, she didn't have shit on Honey. There was no doubt about it— Honey was special to him.

Jay was delighted to think that she just might be jealous. Showing up with Jocelyn, he had only wanted to give her something to think about, and felt confident that he'd done enough for one night. As stubborn as Honey was, she would never admit jealousy. He'd have to keep hammering the nails until he finally broke through that damn shell.

Seeing Jocelyn smile at him, his mind sprang back to the present. She was chairman of a pediatric charitable organization, and for the past five minutes had been giving him her sales pitch, hoping his company would be a sponsor for an upcoming event.

He cleared his throat. "I'd love to be a sponsor. Maybe I can get a couple of my operatives to dress up like clowns and do face paintings or something." He smiled. "Just give my secretary a call."

"Wonderful," she said, with bold eyes beaming and a kind smile that surely put her patients at ease.

Soon he was watching Honey and Darrius rise to leave. He took a long sip of his drink to quell the sudden emptiness, and decided it was time to get down to business.

"Let's talk about your husband."

Jocelyn gave him a thoughtful look before she began. "I was a second-year medical student when I met James in ninety-two. He swept me off my feet. He was a wonderful man. It never mattered to me that he was ten years my senior. Age was nothing but a number. James spent his life trying to make sure everyone around him was happy . . . his patients as well as me. He was a strong believer in commitment, and put a lot of time into keeping the spark strong in our marriage."

"Sounds like you were a lucky woman," he said with sincerity.

She nodded. "I was." Pain shadowed her eyes.

"What happened that night?"

She crossed her legs and rested her elbow on the table. "The last time I saw him was at breakfast that morning. Mama Price was turning seventy on Saturday, and there was no way James was missing his mother's birthday." Her lips compressed. "After work, he hit the highway for Des Moines. He made it as far as Boonville, and I guess he must have fallen asleep, because that's where his car flipped over and exploded. He was burned beyond recognition."

Jay didn't miss the deep emotion in her voice. "I'm sorry for your loss, Dr. Price."

"So am I." Her lips curved into a sad smile. "Please, call me Jocelyn."

"Why didn't you accompany your husband on that trip?"

She took a few seconds to chew on her bottom lip. "There was no love lost between my mother-in-law and me. She never thought I was good enough for him. She blamed me for his death. That didn't come as a surprise. She even had me believing it for a while. I know I shouldn't have let him drive that night after a late night at the clinic. But she knew better than I did that once James had his mind made up, there wasn't a damn thing anybody could do about it."

"When was the last time the two of you spoke?" he asked, tapping a forefinger against his chin. "Your mother-in-law, I mean."

"Six months after the funeral, I called her. At first, she acted like she didn't even know me. Then she told me in so many words never to call her damn house again." She tensed, as if to fight off the rush of memories.

Then Jay asked the question he'd wanted to ask all night. "What makes you so sure that was your husband you saw that night?"

"I'm positive it was James." She paused and raised

her hands to cup her face. "I feel like I'm losing my mind. No one believes me, but I know my husband." Her voice lowered to a mournful whisper. "I lived and slept with that man for almost ten years."

Jay looked at her and, just as Chad had, he believed her. Something about her eyes proved her a sincere individual. "I'm sorry."

She blinked long lashes, fighting back tears. "I buried this. I put this behind me. I just started dating a colleague, trying to get on with my life. I . . ." She paused again to take a deep breath. "I desperately need to move on."

"I understand."

She reached into her pocket, pulled out a photo, and handed it to him. "James took this photograph right before he died."

Jay stared down at the wallet-sized version of James Price. He had salt-and-pepper, close-cropped hair. Fine lines were visible under velvet black eyes. And he was clean-shaven; the only facial hair he had were fine eyebrows. His lips were large, displaying a distinctive gap between his two front teeth. His most distinguishing mark was a cleft in his chin.

"Do you think you can help me?" Jocelyn gave Jay a desperate look that told him he was her last hope.

He handed the picture back. "I'm gonna do more than help you. I'm gonna find your husband."

As Darrius turned his black BMW onto her street, Honey groaned, "Can my day get any worse?"

"Is somethin' wrong?" he asked, peeking at her out of the corner of his eye.

"No, nothin's wrong." She sighed.

He grinned. "I believe you have a bad habit of lying."

"And I believe you ask too many damn questions." As they pulled into her driveway, she looked at the light on in one of the bedrooms upstairs. "I have company."

He gave her an arched look. "Another man?"

Honey turned to him and rolled her eyes. "I'm starting to remember why I never liked your ass."

Darrius pretended to wince. "Why, 'cause you can't handle the truth?"

Honey couldn't hide her smile. "You know what they say . . . the truth hurts." She reached for the door handle. "Thanks for dinner and being a friend."

"The pleasure was all mine. I'll give you a call so we can do this again."

"You do that," she said, and then he leaned across the seat and kissed her cheek.

Honey climbed out of the car and reached into her purse for her key, but before she could stick it in the door, it opened.

"How was dinner?"

Honey looked at the image in front of her. Mercedes's jaw was faintly black and blue. Honey forced a smile and said, "It was nice." She waved at Darrius, then stepped past her and moved toward the coat closet. "Lil' Dee sleeping?"

Mercedes nodded.

She would check in on him on her way up. Nothing pleased Honey more than to watch the darling little three-year-old sleeping peacefully. She could guarantee her home was a lot quieter than his had been tonight.

After hanging her coat in the small hall closet near

the front entrance, she moved across the plush desert brown carpet into the living room and set her purse on the coffee table.

"Did Jay catch up with you?"

Honey's head snapped around. "Jay?"

Mercedes flopped onto an overstuffed chair. "Yeah, he called the salon, said it was important that he get in touch with you. He wanted to know where you were goin' for dinner tonight." She paused to shrug. "So I told him."

Ain't that a bitch! Honey thought. *So that's how his sneaky ass knew. Wait until I see him again.*

Honey took a seat on the couch and removed her boots. Her corns were screaming for relief.

"I know the two of you are only friends, but I think he wants to get with you," Mercedes said.

Honey concealed her smile behind a frown. "What makes you say that?"

"It's just the way he looks at you. It's like he wants to fuck the shit outta you." Curling her legs beneath her, she sucked her gold tooth. "Girlfriend, you better hop on his fine ass."

Drawing her legs up before her, Honey hugged them with her arms and looked over at her friend. *Love hurts too much*, she thought. Mercedes's face was proof of that.

Eight

The construction crew was in and out of the salon on a regular basis. Between the noise and the traffic, everything was fuckin' chaos. In addition, business had suddenly picked up. Honey had a strong suspicion that word had traveled, and their clients wanted to catch a glimpse of the fine-ass crew working next door, especially when they shuffled through the salon periodically to use the vending machines. Honey was certain she'd seen some of the same damn clients twice in one week. Candy was especially intrigued by Rashad, and if he walked through the waiting area while she was on a call, she was bound to lose her train of thought. Even the stylists were found flirting in one corner or another.

Although Honey had to agree that several of the men did look good enough to eat, things were beginning to get a little out of hand. She expressed her concerns to Rashad, who found the entire situation funny; however, one stern look from his sister and he immediately understood it was no laughing matter.

To top it off, having Jay's ass around left her unglued.

Every time she looked, he was standing somewhere watching, his eyes devouring her. She could feel when he was near because the hairs on her neck stood up. While she tried to stay busy, she was constantly aware of his presence. She tried to spend as much time in her office as she could manage, away from his watchful eyes, avoided lingering glances, and didn't engage even in small talk. To stay in control of her beating heart, Honey had decided to maintain a businesslike relationship with him and only interact when it was necessary. After all, it would all be over soon. How long could it possibly take to install a damn security system?

By Friday, she was so busy that it was easy to ignore his presence. She was just putting a client under the dryer when Jay strolled through the work area carrying a white sack.

Mercedes met his twinkling eyes and couldn't resist asking, "Whatcha got in the bag?"

"Lunch." His eyes traveled to the right just in time to catch Honey casting a disapproving glance his way. He winked. "Come on, boss lady, let's eat." He motioned with his head for her to follow him. Refusing to take no for an answer, he moved toward her office.

Mercedes and two other stylists, Aisha and Sonya, exchanged a sly look full of amusement.

Feeling unnerved, Honey shook her head. "I don't have time," she called after him. "I have a customer waiting."

Mercedes intervened. "Go ahead and get your grub on. My one o'clock ain't even here yet. I can wash Deirdre's hair for you."

Honey gave her a dead stare that Mercedes dismissed with a wave of her hand. She knew what was good for Honey even if she didn't. She hadn't forgotten the joy on her friend's face at seeing Jay, and the disappointment when he no longer came around. Now that his sexy ass was back in town, she was going to do everything she could to make Honey realize Jay was the man for her.

At first Honey looked as if she would refuse. Then with a shrug, she followed Jay to her office and dropped into her chair. Ignoring him, she swiveled in front of the computer and pulled her keyboard drawer out. From out of the corner of her eye, she saw him standing in front of her desk waiting in silence.

Jay could tell she was stalling for some plausible excuse to kick him out of her office.

She was wasting her time.

She had withdrawn since that night at the steak house; he knew it had to have something to do with him following her. Shit, he didn't have time to care. He'd been trying all week to get her to have lunch with him, and she had refused each time. However, today he'd completed his work and no longer had an excuse to see her every day.

"I'm not hungry," she said, her voice cutting the silence.

Jay yanked the wool cap from his head and said, "That's too bad. I brought one of your favorites."

Honey shot him a sideways look. "What?"

He shrugged. "It doesn't matter, remember? You said you weren't hungry." He then deliberately stepped forward and waved the sack in front of her face.

Her eyes grew large. "Ah, damn! Egg fu yong."

Ignoring her outburst, Jay tucked the sack under his arm and headed for the door.

"Wait!" Honey sprang from her chair. "Where the hell you going with my lunch?"

He smiled before turning around and forcing a straight face. "I thought you weren't hungry."

She shrugged. "Can't a girl change her mind? Bring that bag back." Honey cleared a spot on her desk for them to eat while Jay reached for a chair and pulled it near. Sliding out of his bomber jacket, he draped it over the back, then removed two Styrofoam containers and placed one in front of her.

"Thanks," she managed to say as she flopped back down into her seat. Reaching for a plastic fork, she discovered that she was hungry after all. She'd been so busy scraping ice off her car this morning she hadn't had enough time to scramble herself a couple of eggs. She shoveled a forkful into her mouth, savoring every bite. "Mmm, this is good."

Jay's eyes had been glued to her since he heard the soft moan escape her lips. Those incredibly sensual-ass lips. He took several bites, taking the time to pull himself together before he spoke. "I'm done with your system."

"Already?" she asked, not realizing she sounded disappointed.

Jay nodded. Actually, he'd finished yesterday. Honey just didn't know enough about systems to have figured that shit out. "All I need now is for the phone lines to be installed and then I can connect the unit."

Honey momentarily stopped chewing when she realized that he wouldn't be hanging around any longer. A wave of sadness overcame her. She'd been looking forward to this day, but now that it had come, she wasn't so sure. "Thanks for all your help," she managed, looking up at him.

"No problem. You know there isn't anything I wouldn't do for you." His eyes met hers, and when she read the emotions dancing in them, she felt her heart-beat accelerate and her coochie clench. She had to do everything in her power not to groan. Her gaze shifted to a drop of sauce that clung to the corner of his mouth. As if he knew she was watching, his tongue darted out to capture it. Quickly, she dropped her eyes back to her food.

Jay was quiet while he finished his meal. Then curiosity got the better of him. He had to ask. "How was your date?"

She gazed at him but didn't reply right away, trying to suppress a smirk. She hated throwing her personal life in his face, but if that was what it took for his chocolate ass to believe she wasn't interested in him, so be it.

"Very nice. How was your date?"

"Interesting." No need to mention that Dr. Price was a client.

"I just bet," she mumbled. That night, she'd been unable to sleep a wink as she lay awake tossing and turning, thinking about Jay and Jocelyn Price. She'd been increasingly agitated lately, and only she knew why. She was jealous and hated to admit it. After all, she was the one who had decided she was only interested in being friends. But it did nothing to curb the thoughts she'd been having of him being with someone else.

In an attempt to shift her rising emotions, she spat, "I didn't appreciate you snooping on me."

"Who was snooping? I was having dinner."

His cocky grin only fueled her anger. "Mercedes told me all about your call."

He shrugged, appearing unbothered that he'd been caught in a lie. "So . . . when are you gonna see Darrius again?"

"Soon," she said simply. *Boy, he has a way of turning the tables.*

"How soon?" His question was more of a growl.

"That's really none of your damn business," she said, this time in a tone that left little room for further discussion. Or at least so she thought. However, before Jay could explore the depth of her relationship, he found Honey looking past his shoulder.

"Tequila . . . what's wrong?" she said.

Jay swung around in his seat to find a lovely lady standing behind him holding a little boy's hand.

Tequila stepped into the room. "My grandmotha was just rushed into the emergency room." She paused, as if trying to pull herself together. It was apparent she was panic-stricken. "I can't reach my b-babysitter, and Shaquil is in a s-seminar," she stuttered, nervous.

Honey rose from her seat, moved to Tequila's side, and placed a soothing hand on her shoulder. Tequila's mother had died when she was a child. Being that her father was a truck driver, she'd grown up with her grandmother. "Don't worry about a thing. Leave Marcus with me," Honey said, then looked down at his adorable face and winked.

Tequila sighed, her relief evident. "Thanks. I'll be back as soon as I can." She leaned down to kiss Marcus on top of his head, then whispered near his ear, "Baby, I'll see you later."

"No rush, take your time. Marcus is in good hands." Honey smoothed his curly hair with her hand. "In fact, I'll keep him tonight, and you can get him in the morning." She hugged her sister-in-law and then pushed her out the door.

When Honey dropped her hand to her nephew's shoulder, he sagged against her and latched on to her leg. "Marcus," she said, her voice a coo, "this is my friend *Jason.*"

Jay's eyes shifted to her smug expression. *Oh boy, she's back to her old tricks.* Honey knew he hated his given name. However, he pretended not to be swayed.

Jay moved from the chair and came over to them, where he stooped so his eyes were at the same level as the little boy's. "Hello, Marcus. It's a pleasure to meet you." Jay extended his hand. "Why don't you call me *Jay*? All of my friends do." He raised his eyes to meet Honey's frown, then back down again.

Marcus liked the idea of being considered one of Jay's friends, and his shyness vanished as he looked up at him with a big grin while he shook his hand.

Mercedes appeared at the door with her lips pursed. "Deirdre doesn't want nobody touching her weave but you." She rolled her eyes.

"All right," Honey said, and threw her hands in the air. "Come on, Marcus, let's see if we can get Candy to entertain you for a while."

Jay grasped her hand. "Marcus can hang out with me."

Honey glared at him. "Don't you have things to do?" The job was done. There wasn't any reason for him to stick around.

"I'm free for the rest of the day." Rising from his squatting position, he moved toward the door. "Marcus can help me load up my tools."

"Can I, Auntie?" Marcus's face beamed, and his dark round eyes pleaded for permission.

How could she resist? "All right." She sighed and then gave Jay a hard look to make sure he understood she was doing this for Marcus, not him.

Grinning like a kid with a new toy, Jay motioned for her nephew to follow. "Ready to have some fun?"

Marcus nodded and bounced up and down with anticipation.

Honey arrived at Chuck E. Cheese to find children of all sizes running everywhere. The hostesses were trying to keep up with the crowd as they came into the noisy restaurant.

After scanning the room, she found Jay and Marcus in the corner playing video games. Jay looked like a kid himself, laughing along with Marcus as he appeared to be beating Jay at a game. When Jay saw her, his face lit up. He whispered something to Marcus and then moved toward her. Honey felt a heat ripple beneath her skin as she watched him approach her with the grace of a lion, unconscious of the admiring glances he was receiving from the other females. Honey was tempted to stake claim to his fine ass and cuss them bitches out.

"I see you made it."

As the seductive sound of his voice vibrated through her, she stared up at his lean, dark-skinned face nervously, her hands clasped together. "Yeah, I finally made it."

"Our table is over here." Placing a hand on her waist, he guided her to a booth on the other side of the wall. Honey took a seat, which appeared to have been occupied earlier by Marcus. A cheese pizza lover, he had picked off the pepperoni and stacked the pieces on his plate.

"You've already eaten." It was more of a statement than a question as she reached for the last cold slice and took a bite.

Jay slid onto the bench across from her. "Marcus was pretty hungry. You want me to order another?"

She shook her head. "Maybe in a few minutes." She looked to her right to make sure Marcus was playing where she could see him.

"This is the first time I've ever been here," Jay said softly, bringing her attention back to him.

"I knew the second you offered to take Marcus to get somethin' to eat, he was gonna suggest this place." She couldn't help the smile that crept to her lips. "Thanks for your help today."

"No problem. I'm glad I could be of service." *I'd do anything to have you smile that way at me.* "I'm havin' a good time."

"You're good with him," she said. While working on her client's head, she'd watched Jay interact with Marcus, exhibiting a great deal of patience. She listened as he explained the different tools to the little boy, and even demonstrated their use.

"I'm gonna be busy working on another case for the next several days, so it feels good to have a chance to relax and spend a little time with you at the same time."

Honey ignored the jolt of her heart. Willing her hand not to tremble, she propped her elbow on the table and rested her chin in her open palm. "How's the detective business?"

"Good." Jay smiled. "Too good, as a matter of fact." For a moment, he considered telling her that Jocelyn was a client. But if he did, it would defeat his entire reason for popping up with her at the steak house. Now would be a really good time to tell her about the baby, too. But he decided against that too. So he said, "As soon as I get done with this new case, I'm gonna take a little time off and take care of some personal business."

"Why are you takin' on more work? Sasha said

you've been workin' yourself ragged for months. Don't you have operatives to do all that runnin' around for you?"

A light shone in his eyes, and his lips curled into a crooked smile. "You've been checking on a brotha."

"No. I have *not* been checkin' up on you," Honey snapped.

"Then what would you call it?"

"I wouldn't call it anything." She wagged a finger in front of his face. "See . . . that's why I can't be nice to your ass. You always take shit the wrong way."

He shrugged and said, "My bad."

A huff was her only response.

"Well . . ." Jay cleared his throat. "Just so you'll know, I'm leaving Valentine's Day open."

"So?"

"So, how about being my date?"

"For what?"

"For Valentine's Day."

"What about Dr. Price?" she blurted out.

Seeing her blank expression, Jay couldn't tell if he saw jealousy or not. "She already has a date."

She and Jay had never been out on a real date before, and now wasn't the time to start. It was too damn intimate. "Well . . . so do I."

"With who?" he pressed, even though he already knew what the answer would be.

"W-well . . . Darrius, of course." Her lie was smooth; she was certain if she asked him, he'd say yes. Shifting her attention away from his steady gaze, she watched Marcus play.

After a long silence, Jay asked, "Are you a virgin?"

She snapped back around with her mouth wide open. "What?" Astonished, she burst into laughter.

"It's okay," he said with a shrug. "It took me a while, but I finally figured it out. Now I know why you broke things off between us."

Just like a man. "Don't flatter yourself."

"So you're saying that you're not a virgin?"

"Yes, I'm saying that," she retorted.

"Are you attracted to me?"

Her upper lip stiffened. "You're attractive, but I'm not attracted to you."

"I don't believe you." He flashed a sly grin.

Honey had to chuckle. His line of questioning was ridiculous. "The reason you don't believe me is that you're used to women throwin' themselves at you." She waved him away with disgust. "And this girl ain't interested."

"I still don't believe you," he said. Why else would she keep up so much animosity?

He leaned forward, and the scent of him invaded her senses, so much so that she had to turn away, trying to suppress the desire churning inside.

"Well, believe it."

"Then prove it."

She rolled her eyes at that. "I don't have to prove shit to you."

"You're scared. Admit it."

She hated to be challenged. "I'm not afraid of anything."

"Then if you aren't afraid, be my date on Valentine's Day."

She frowned. "I don't have time for games. I thought we agreed to be friends."

"I've changed my mind."

Her body betrayed her again; his words caused a

stirring at the pit of her stomach, and she had to force herself to concentrate on what he was saying, and not on how good he looked. "Too bad," she forced between clenched teeth. "I'm not interested." She turned in her seat and looked over at Marcus again, glad for the diversion.

Jay was silent for a moment while he observed her stern profile. Honey was definitely a piece of work. He chuckled.

His laughter drew Honey's attention again, and she shifted in her seat. "What's so funny?"

"You're somethin' else. You know that?"

Crossing her arms on the table, she met the glitter in his eyes and couldn't hide her own amusement. "I am, aren't I?" She then laughed, a deep throaty laugh, finding herself relaxing for the first time in a long time.

The alluring sound warmed his heart. He hadn't heard her laugh like that in so long, and he missed it more than she could ever know.

Jay returned her smile and leaned forward in his seat, resting his arms on the table. "I miss this, us laughing, enjoying each other's company. I want that back with you."

"Then quit tryin' to make more of this than it really is." She caught herself, and her next words were gentler. "I'm sorry if it's hard for you to believe that I'm only interested in being friends. I don't have room in my life right now for anything else."

He didn't believe her, but decided not to argue. "No funny stuff," he pledged. "Friends again?"

Her face lit up with a beautiful smile. "Friends."

While returning her smile, he tried to force himself not to think about kissing her moist lips.

Marcus rushed over to them, out of breath. Honey held out her arms and scooped him up. "How's my baby?"

He frowned, obviously embarrassed, and squirmed out of her arms. He moved to Jay and patted him lightly on the arm. "Can you come and play with me?"

"Sure." Jay rose, smiling. "Let's get some more tokens first."

Marcus latched on to Jay's hand with worship in his eyes. Honey dropped her chin to her hand and watched the two of them together. Jay looked so right with Marcus. All the more reason they could never be more than friends. She would never deprive him of this happiness.

"I'm gonna order another pizza. You want somethin' to eat?" Jay's voice nudged into her thoughts.

"Pizza's fine."

"You still like sausage and mushroom?"

She nodded at his photographic memory, and caught herself smiling as she watched them stroll across to the cashier.

Jay moved to the token machine and stuck in a ten-dollar bill, giving Marcus a handful of tokens before he darted off ahead of him.

He couldn't believe his good fortune. After weeks of trying, he finally had Honey to himself. And this time he wasn't going to mess up. As much as he wanted to pull her into his arms and kiss her senseless, he knew he couldn't do that. Their friendship meant the world to him. The last time he jumped the gun, she quit speaking to him. He didn't want to take the chance of ruining their relationship forever. This time was going to be different. He was going to take his time and allow things to progress naturally . . . and on her terms . . . until he could slowly tempt her to the boiling point.

Reaching deep in his pocket for money to pay for the pizza, Jay realized he'd left his cell phone at the salon. Oh well. If there were any problems, Chad would handle them. Right now, nothing was as important as being with Honey.

He and Marcus returned to the table just as two piping-hot pizzas arrived.

"Perfect timing." Honey greeted them with a welcoming smile.

"You have a whiz kid," Jay said, ruffling Marcus's hair before he took his seat.

"Auntie, I beat Jay at every game," Marcus boasted. "Look!" He held up a long roll of tickets that were exchangeable for prizes.

"Wow!" Honey nodded as she slid off the bench so Marcus could sit down beside her.

"I don't know about you two, but I'm hungry again," Jay said as he grabbed a large slice of sausage pizza, then a slice of cheese pizza for Marcus.

"Why don't I get the drinks?" Honey offered. Rising, she headed toward the soda fountain.

"Pepsi for me," Jay called over his shoulder.

"Me too!" Marcus added.

Honey was tickled. Jay had an admirer. Marcus knew his hyper ass wasn't allowed to drink Pepsi. Caffeine was one thing he didn't need this late in the evening.

Jay and Marcus dominated the conversation during the meal. Marcus talked nonstop about preschool and video games. Jay told him how he used to be a Boy Scout. Honey found the discussion interesting, and added her experience as a Girl Scout, including some of her most disastrous camping trips.

After sipping her soda, she said, "I remember when we were at a campsite in Indiana. We thought a bear was right outside our tent. My troop was so scared we ended up knockin' the tent over tryin' to get away." Honey laughed as her mind was flooded with memories.

"Auntie, can we go camping sometime?" Marcus mumbled, his mouth full of pizza.

She licked sauce from her fingers before answering. "Maybe one weekend I'm not workin'."

Jay could see that she seemed relaxed and more approachable when her nephew was around. Maybe Marcus was the answer to getting close to her. "We'll see if I can't coax your auntie into lettin' me take the both of you real soon." Jay winked at Marcus, who beamed with joy; then they both directed electrifying grins at her.

Honey looked at both of them with raised eyebrows and knew that she'd better start shopping for sleeping bags.

The live puppeteer show started on the stage with Chuck E. as the star, but Marcus, who apparently had outgrown Chuck E. overnight, wasn't paying the stage any attention. All his attention was focused on his new buddy, Jay. Honey could tell that Jay found Marcus equally intriguing. She observed as Jay listened attentively to everything Marcus had to say without appearing annoyed with all his questions. Instead, Jay looked as if he was having the time of his life. He was a natural.

Of the three of them, the boys ate most of the pizza.

Honey didn't mind; for some reason, she didn't have much of an appetite.

Marcus began licking his fingers with exaggerated smacking sounds.

"Mind your manners," Honey scolded. Finding it amusing, Jay started laughing.

"Jay, can you come over and play video games with me and Auntie sometime?"

Jay looked over at Honey before answering. Unable to deny her nephew, she smiled even wider in approval.

"I'd like that very much," Jay said. His answer generated heat between Honey's legs, making her thong hot and wet.

Dinner was over much too soon, but it was getting late and nearing Marcus's bedtime. They put on their coats, and then Marcus dashed off to the counter to collect his prizes. Honey and Jay headed to the door with his arm draped comfortably around her shoulder, his male scent turning her ass on.

"You have a nice nephew."

"Thanks, I think so too," she said, beaming.

After his spending the afternoon with Marcus, thoughts of becoming a father were becoming overwhelming. "I never thought about having a family, but recently all that has changed." His words were soft, and his brown eyes gazed intensely at her.

Like a helium balloon, her entire mood fizzled.

Jay didn't seem to notice the change in her. "Give me your keys so I can go and warm up your car."

She reached into her purse and handed them to him. Jay pulled his hat down over his ears and exited the building. The cold February air hit him at the door. He reached into his pockets for a pair of thermal gloves. Unlocking the car, he climbed into the front seat and started the engine.

He had no control of his emotions when Honey was involved. He wanted to hold her, kiss her, and fuck the shit out of her. *Not yet, take it slow, let things happen naturally*, he chanted inwardly. He had to allow her a chance to make the first move.

He climbed out of the car, reached into the trunk, and pulled out the ice scraper.

Honey came out shortly after, bundled up in a camel-colored full-length coat with matching gloves and hat. Marcus ran up to Jay and showed him his prizes, which consisted of a plastic whistle and a fistful of candy.

"Thanks for a wonderful evening." Looking down at her nephew, she added, "Marcus, you need to thank Jay for a wonderful evening."

"Thanks, Jay," Marcus said quickly with a smile.

"No need to thank me, the pleasure was all mine," Jay said, smiling down at the little boy who looked swallowed up in a blue snowsuit. "I hope to get the opportunity to do this again."

Honey opened the car door so Marcus could climb in. "Thanks, Jay, I owe you."

"And I plan to hold you to that."

With a nod, she climbed into the car and was backing out of the space when Jay halted her.

"What is it?"

He scratched the back of his neck. "It sounds like you have a flat."

"A flat!" Honey threw open the door and hurried out of the car. Sure enough, her front tire was flat. She looked at Jay out of the corner of her eye but didn't say anything.

Jay was certain she thought he was responsible. Defending himself would only make him look guilty. He stooped down behind her tire and scooped up a palmful of broken glass. "Looks like you ran over a bottle."

"I don't have a spare," she mumbled.

"Why not?"

She winced. " 'Cause I'm already using my spare. I had a flat a month ago, and kept putting off havin' the tire repaired."

As if he didn't believe her, he popped the trunk and pulled out her tire. Sure enough, there was a large hole in it. "What the hell did you do . . . run over a barbwire fence?"

"Funny."

"I'll take you both home," he said.

She shook her head, already looking in her purse for her cell phone. "You don't have to."

"Yes, I do," he insisted. Not waiting for an answer, he opened the back door. "Come on, Marcus. You're both riding with me."

Marcus scrambled out of the seat. "Where's your car?"

"It's right over there."

Marcus's eyes traveled over to the gray Lexus. "Oh boy!"

Not wanting to argue in front of her nephew, Honey relented and shut off the car. She followed Jay over to his, wondering if he might have had something to do with her flat. Was it an excuse to spend more time with her? *Hot damn!* She couldn't resist the private smile that curled on her lips.

Marcus chatted away for about a mile, and then suddenly got quiet and drifted off to sleep. Honey forced herself not to look over at Jay's strong profile, and instead stared out the frosted window. Wanting to spend time with her private thoughts, she switched on the radio so neither of them would feel obligated to talk. Comfortable silence enveloped them, broken only by the sounds of Brian McKnight. There was a quiet intimacy in sitting in the car side by side, listening to a love ballad that put each of their emotions to words.

Jay pulled into the driveway of her house to find a couple standing outside. They appeared to be in the middle of a heated argument. Peering out his front window, he asked, "Isn't that Mercedes?"

Honey pursed her lips. "Yeah . . . and her baby's daddy."

He stopped in the driveway just as their voices elevated. By the time they climbed out of the car, Dean had swung the kicking, screaming Mercedes over his shoulder.

"Put me the fuck down!" she yelled at the top of her lungs.

"Not until you bring me my son," he demanded.

"Hell naw!"

Honey raced up the walkway with a hand doubled into a tight fist at her side. "You're not allowed on my property, Dean."

His eyes were dark with hatred as he turned in the direction of her voice. "Stay out of this, Honey. I'm tired of you meddling in my damn business."

"It's my business when you come to my house."

"You better back the fuck off!" he shouted.

"Put her down," Jay ordered in a low, hard voice.

Dean's mouth twisted as he looked at the man blocking his way. "Who the hell are you?"

"Your worst nightmare if you don't put Mercedes down." Standing about five inches taller, Jay stood before the rugged light-skinned brother with his legs planted wide apart and his arms crossed in front of him.

Dean lowered Mercedes to the ground, but continued to clutch her left arm tight.

Mercedes tried to adjust her terry cloth robe. The belt tied around her waist had loosened, revealing more than it concealed. Dean stepped forward, dragging her with him. Giving a humorless smile, he said, "Satisfied?"

"No, not until you leave," Jay said.

"I'm not going nowhere without my son," Dean challenged through gritted teeth.

"You're not takin' my son any—"

Dean cut off the rest of Mercedes's sentence with a vicious shove that sent her sprawling facedown in the wet snow. Honey quickly moved to help her up. Before Dean saw it coming, Jay's fist connected solidly with his jaw. Staggering, he nearly fell from the force of the blow.

"Don't you ever put your hands on her again," Jay warned.

With the back of his hand, Dean gingerly wiped the blood from his mouth. "I'll leave as soon as she brings me my damn son."

Jay step forward and Dean flinched. "You're either gonna leave now, or I'm gonna make you leave."

Dean's body tensed. "You can't keep me from my son."

"I can tonight."

"Come on, man." Dean shifted from one foot to the

other. "Do you know what it's like to be kept from your child?" He turned to glare at Mercedes. "That bitch won't even let me see him!"

"I don't want to get into yo' business," Jay said. "All I know is that this isn't the way, and it's too cold out here to be arguing."

"Leave, Dean, before I call the cops on yo' ass!" Mercedes shrieked.

"I think you'd better listen," Jay said.

Dean's eyes traveled from one to the other. "Y'all gonna regret ever messin' wit' me." He walked cautiously around Jay and climbed into his car, muttered exclamations flying from his lips.

Jay didn't pay heed to his threat. Any man that would hit a woman was nothing more than a bitch.

Always one to have the last word, Mercedes sprinted across the lawn, shouting obscenities as he sped away. "You sorry mothafucka!"

Jay walked over to Mercedes and dropped a comforting hand to her shoulder. Her lip cut and bleeding, her eye black, she looked fucked-up. "You okay?"

Gingerly pressing a hand to her mouth, she swallowed a sob and nodded.

"I'll get Marcus," Honey said.

"No, I'll get him," Jay suggested. "Why don't you take Mercedes into the house?" He tilted his head to the right. Honey looked over his shoulder and found several of her neighbors peeking from their doors and windows. Nodding, she moved toward the house with her arm draped around Mercedes's shoulders.

Jay returned to the car and scooped Marcus into his arms. Thankfully, the little boy had slept through it all. A child should never have to go through that kind of shit. That's why he knew he and Kendra could never raise their child together. It would be the same thing. A lot of arguments. Children could sense unhappiness. He would never do that to his child. Never.

He carried Marcus into the house and helped settle him into bed. After spending an hour trying to convince Mercedes's dumb ass to press charges, which she refused to do, he asked Honey to walk with him to his car.

She looked at him apologetically. "I'm sorry we had to end our evenin' on a sour note."

"Don't worry about it. I had a wonderful time tonight with the both of you. I hope we can do it again."

She looked down at her hands shyly. "I would like that very much."

"Does this mean we can go out on our first official date?"

"Are you asking me out?" she said softly.

He couldn't even stand next to her without wanting her. "Yeah, I'm askin' you out."

"Then I accept." Her face lit up with a beautiful smile.

He grinned, pleased at the progress he'd made. "I'll drop your car off in the morning."

Gazing up at his handsome face, she shook her head. "You don't have to. I can get one of my brothers to do it."

"I want to do it."

They stared at each other for a long moment before she said, "Thanks."

A cold wind was whipping around them, and the smell of snow was in the air. She didn't object when Jay slipped an arm around her shoulders.

"You don't have to thank me. I've always been there for you." Facing her, he ran a hand across her cheek, intensifying her shivers.

"I owe you one," she said as her teeth chattered.

He cocked a teasing smile. "Can you pay a brotha now?"

His voice was husky, causing something to lurch inside her. She knew what he wanted. She could read it in his eyes. Jay wanted to kiss her. He was waiting for a signal, a word, something, but she would have to initiate it. No pressure, just waiting for her to make the choice. At that moment, she wanted nothing more. Maybe it was because tonight he was her hero. "Yeah, I can," she answered in a shaky voice. She found herself leaning eagerly toward him until their faces were only inches apart.

The second their lips touched, she was lost. It awakened unforgotten memories of their first and only kiss. She had meant to make it brief, but suddenly she was doing more than permitting; she was participating. Her lips parted easily and he deepened the kiss, thrusting with his tongue in slow strokes. It was everything she remembered. Her arms found their way around his neck while his closed around her small waist, crushing her breasts against his hard chest. Confusion assailed her senses. What started out as a tender kiss deepened hungrily. Desire surged through her and she felt her nipples harden. Her hands slid down his neck, across his powerful shoulders, and then against his solid chest.

And then Jay ended the kiss.

They were quiet for a while, only the wind breaking the silence as he clutched her tight against him. He had dreamed of this day . . . a second chance at getting things right. Too much unnecessary time had passed. Time that needed to be made up.

Holding her away from him, his eyes lingered on her face a few seconds longer, then he left, leaving Honey feeling dazed and disoriented.

Kendra slammed the phone down onto the receiver and released a string of profanity. This was getting ridiculous. She'd been calling his cell phone for over an hour, and Jay still hadn't bothered to return her call. Who the hell did he think he was? Had he forgotten that she was carrying his child? Okay, so maybe she didn't really need anything, but how the hell would he know unless he bothered to call and find out? What if it was an emergency? She could have fallen, or gone into labor. She had every right to know where he was at all times. She needed to be able to reach him.

Pushing herself out of the chair, she moved into the kitchen and removed a carton of orange juice from the refrigerator. She poured a glass and drank it angrily; then, taking several deep breaths, she tried to calm the anger that was raging in her. She hated feeling fuckin' helpless. As long as she was pregnant, she couldn't have the upper hand. She took another deep breath and reminded herself there wasn't shit to get upset about. Everything was going to work in her favor.

She placed the glass in the dishwasher and returned to the living room, where she sank into her favorite chair. Tapping her index finger on the arm of the chair, she wondered where Jay was. She was horny as hell and could use a good long fuck. She had tricked his ass into her bed once and she could find a way to do it again.

After contemplating the possibilities, she remembered he had mentioned something about being in love. Could Jay be spending time with some other bitch? Naw. He wouldn't dare. But she didn't feel as confident as she did before. She pursed her lips. There was only one way to find out.

Natalia.

Nine

Despite the snow that had accumulated during the night, sunlight streamed into the room. With a groan, Honey rolled away from the window and tried to fall back to sleep. She couldn't. Her mind was racing with thoughts of Jay.

Sleep hadn't come easy. She'd had a fitful night, tossing and turning for hours with images of Jay dancing in her dreams. The attraction she had for him was scary. Every time she saw him, the pull was stronger. He made her feel things she'd never fuckin' experienced before.

Last night she had pulled out her vibrator and tried to break that bitch in half. She put in a brand-new set of batteries, then lay on her back and spread her legs. Slowly she eased it in and out of her coochie with one hand while she fondled her nipples with the other. With her eyes closed and Jay's sexy ass on the brain, it wasn't long before she had come. Just thinking about it, she was tempted to pull that bitch out again.

Honey took a deep breath and rolled onto her back. She wasn't herself around Jay, and felt herself weakening with every encounter. After all the hype of wanting to be just friends, she had blown that shit with just one kiss.

How had Jay known there was no way she could deny herself another kiss? The kiss had left her melting. He had aroused a deep longing inside her. Only this time, he made certain she couldn't blame him. She did the initiating. The scary part was that she didn't regret it. But she could never let it happen again.

"Auntie," Marcus whined, "I don't feel good." Wearing footed pajamas, he came into the room rubbing his eyes.

Swinging her legs onto the carpeted floor, Honey sat up. "Come here, sweetheart." He moved into her outstretched arms and she raised a palm to his forehead. "You're burnin' up," she said, worried. "Does anything hurt?"

He nodded. "My head hurts."

Honey rose. Curling her fingers around his tiny hand, she padded barefoot across the hall to the guest room. "Mercedes, Mercedes," she called softly, trying not to wake Lil' Dee. "Wake up!"

Mercedes opened her eyes and spoke in a groggy voice. "What?"

"Feel Marcus's forehead."

Mercedes shifted on the bed and raised a palm to his forehead. "He has a fever." Seeing the tears glistening on his thick lashes, she gave him a sympathetic smile. "How do you feel, big boy?"

"Not good." His chocolate eyes shed warm tears onto her arm.

Looking up at Honey she said, "He probably has that flu bug that's going around."

Honey nodded in agreement. "My poor baby," she cooed. "Are you sleepy?"

He nodded as he began to cry. "I want my mommy!" he wailed.

"I know," Honey said as she hugged him close to her chest. "I'm gonna call your mama, but first Auntie needs to make you feel better."

Mercedes scrambled out of bed. "I have some Children's Tylenol in my bag." She moved to the closet and pulled out a red duffel bag. "Here." She handed the bottle to Honey.

"Thanks." She quickly read the directions on the side of the bottle, then poured the liquid into the tiny measuring cup. "Open wide, sweetheart." Marcus, although fretful, cooperated. "Good boy." Handing the bottle back to Mercedes, she scooped his fevered body into her arms. "I'm putting you back to bed and callin' your mother."

"What are you thinking?" Chad asked.

Propping his feet on the end of his desk, Jay answered, "There might be some truth to what Jocelyn said about her husband."

"Oh my! We're on a first-name basis already." A teasing smile touched Chad's lips.

"Fuck you," Jay shot back.

Chad chuckled. He'd just returned from a weeklong investigation in Milwaukee, but had anticipated the two meeting while he was away. "Did you find her attractive?"

"Yeah," Jay answered without hesitation. "But I'll leave her to you."

Chad quirked a brow. "I thought maybe the two of you would have hit it off."

Jay was silent for a brief moment before answering. "My plate is full right now. I'm about to become a daddy."

Chad's eyes grew wide. "What did you say?"

Occasionally scratching his head, Jay told him. By the time he was done, Chad was doubled over with laughter. "I guess you don't have time for Jocelyn."

"Don't get me wrong, she's sexy as hell, but it's strictly business. However, she seems more your type."

"Not hardly," he scowled.

Jay was unconvinced. "She's beautiful, smart, and warm. What's there not to like?"

Chad shrugged. "I don't know."

"Maybe it's because she ain't interested in you."

"Funny." But in spite of his light answer, Chad wasn't sure what it was. He would never admit that in the short time he'd spent with her, Jocelyn had aroused something in him that he'd never experienced in the presence of another woman. Not only did he want to drag her ass into a corner and fuck the shit out of her, but he could see giving her his last name. He had thought by passing the case on to his partner, Jay would scoop her ass up for himself, freeing him of the need to do so. But that didn't happen. "So, getting back to your dinner, what makes you so sure she's tellin' the truth?"

Jay tapped a finger against his temple. "Instinct. I have a strong feeling about this. Dory's calling the hotel now, trying to find out if her husband was a guest."

"You think he staged his death?"

Jay shrugged. "It's possible. I'm gonna fly one of our operatives, probably Paul, to his hometown tomorrow, just to get us a little more background information."

Just then Dory stepped into the room, drawing their gazes. "Guess what I found out?"

Jay sank back against his seat. "What?"

"You know how good I am at getting information," she boasted.

"We know," they agreed in unison.

"Well, I just happened to talk to a sista who'd worked that afternoon. According to her, James Price wasn't registered in any of the rooms. However, all three conference rooms were booked that day."

"How'd you find that out?" Chad asked.

"Hmmph. It's a girl thang." Chest stuck out like a proud peacock, she strutted into the room and perched her hip on the end of Jay's desk.

"Women," Chad mumbled.

"Talk to the hand." She emphasized the meaning with an open palm pointed at his face. Chad and Dory constantly maintained a love-hate relationship. Turning to face Jay, she said, "Anyway, there was a desktop publishing workshop. The Missouri Kidney Program was holding a quarterly board meeting . . ." Counting off on her fingers, she continued, ". . . And last but not least, a symposium on oral hygiene."

Jay's brow rose. "You've got to be kidding?"

"Nope." A proud grin lifted the corners of her lips. "Did I do good?"

"You did damn good!" He reached across his desk to give her a high five.

Not following, Chad glanced from one to the other. "Can the two of you clue me in on what's goin' on?"

Dory pursed her lips. "I thought you interviewed this woman for an hour?"

"I did."

"He also took several pages of notes," Jay piped in. "I guess he was distracted by a great pair of legs."

Chad shrugged; no point in denying it. "It appears I wasn't the only one to notice," he said to Jay.

Dory rolled her eyes. She didn't approve of Chad's doggish ways, and never made her feelings a secret. "Well, if you had been paying attention to what she was sayin' instead of how good she looked, you would have remembered that Dr. James Price was a dentist."

By the time Honey carried Marcus up to his room, he was sound asleep. As he was already in his pajamas, she laid him beneath the cool cotton sheets and pulled the top sheet up under his chin to tuck him in. After turning on his night-light so he wouldn't be afraid, she found herself leaning against the door watching her nephew sleeping peacefully, without a worry in the world. After twenty-four hours, his fever had finally broken that morning.

Tequila stuck her head in the door. "Is he asleep?" she whispered.

Nodding, Honey stepped out of the room before responding. "He fell asleep after two episodes of *Scooby Doo*." Following Tequila down the stairs, she added, "He seems to be doin' better."

"A lot better," she agreed. "Yesterday, he could barely hold his head up." The two moved into the kitchen.

"Would you like a cup of coffee?" Tequila offered.

In no rush to return to the brisk cold, she answered, "A cup would be great." Honey pulled up a chair at the oak kitchen table.

Tequila reached for a canister on the counter. "I'm gonna take off tomorrow and stay home with him. I think another twenty-four hours, he'll be good as new." She moved to the table carrying two small plates. At the center of the table was a carrot cake. She sliced two pieces and placed them on the saucers.

"Mmm, thanks." Honey had never appreciated carrot cake until the first time she'd tasted Tequila's. Made with homemade cream cheese icing, the cake melted in your mouth.

While Tequila reached for two mugs from the shelf, Honey's eyes traveled around the small, cozy kitchen that was decorated in hunter green from the canisters all the way to the cushions on the seats.

"Mama Love called three times to check on Marcus," Tequila said.

"How's she enjoying Vegas?"

"I think she and George are havin' a blast. I'm so happy for her."

"So am I."

Tequila carefully placed a ceramic mug filled with the steaming brew in front of her, then took a seat to her right.

"Thanks, you're the perfect little housewife," Honey teased.

"Girl, puhleeze. You sound like yo' brother." Reaching for the sugar dish, she added two spoonsful to her coffee. Before bringing the mug to her lips she asked, "Who was that fine man in your office?"

In her frantic state, Honey had hoped Tequila hadn't

noticed. So much for wishful thinking. Honey concealed a smile as Jay came to the surface in her mind. "A friend."

Tequila didn't miss the hint of color now tinting Honey's pale cheeks. "Are you sure he's just a friend?"

Tequila was one of the best listeners Honey had ever met, and she often found herself opening up to her over a cup of coffee. But this was one time she couldn't. "I'm sure," she answered, and took another careful sip.

The back door opened and Shaquil stepped in, along with a short, bald-headed man wearing a quarter-length jacket that barely stretched over his big-ass stomach.

"Hey, sis," Shaquil said before turning to his wife. "How's Marcus?"

"Much better. He's sound asleep."

"I'm gonna run up and check on him." He dashed out of the room and up the stairs.

Honey felt the man's eyes on her. *How rude.* "Hello," she greeted him with a tight-lipped smile.

Tequila stepped forward to do the introduction. "Ray, this is my sister-in-law, Honey."

Ray's admiring gaze swept over her black tunic and stirrups that hung perfectly on her petite frame. "And she looks every bit as sweet as the name," he murmured before claiming her hand and turning it, palm up, to his lips. When he smiled, his beady eyes crinkled. "How ya doing?"

She didn't like the way this man was looking at her as if she were the flavor of the month. She gave him another weak smile. "Fine."

Shaquil reentered the room just as Ray released her hand. "Hey, man, you need to watch out for that one. She's a heartbreaker."

Here we go again. Fuming silently, she looked to Tequila for help. Tequila gave her one of those girl-you-know-how-your-brother-is kinds of looks.

"All I need is dinner in your company, and I'd be the happiest man in the world."

"Oh, brother," she mumbled. The last thing she needed was Ray's interest in her. She could just imagine his short stubby fingers reaching for her knee under the table.

"Hey, that might not be a bad idea, Ray," Shaquil said. "How about joining my family for dinner this Sunday? My sister could use a date."

Turning her head, Honey stared at him with wide eyes and mumbled, "No, you didn't?"

Tequila gave a sympathetic sigh. "I think he did."

Ray was all smiles. "I would love to be a guest at your table. That is, if you're gonna be there?" His eyes twinkled in devilment.

"No," Honey snorted, draining the last of her coffee. "I have a date."

Tequila lowered her lashes to hide the amusement in her eyes.

Shaquil gave Ray an I-told-you-so look.

"Too bad," he said, looking disappointed. "Maybe next time. Well, I need to get on home. I have an early day tomorrow at the morgue."

Oh, hell naw!

Shaquil thought that shit was funny and was still laughing long after Ray had left. Tequila excused herself to call and check on her grandmother, who was home and doing much better.

"You want somethin' to drink?" Shaquil asked.

"Yeah, a rum and Coke would be nice."

He signaled for her to follow him into the family room, where he kept a fully stocked bar.

Honey took a seat in an overstuffed chair. A fire was already roaring. Placing her elbows on the armrest, she leaned back, feeling the heat from the fire on her face. She then kicked off her shoes and rested her stocking feet on the wool throw rug below. The room was decorated in rich, dark woods. The dark hardwood floor was gleaming as if freshly waxed, with a large bear rug in the center of the room. There was a rust-colored couch and matching ottoman. Both windows were draped with gold curtains that Tequila had sewn. There wasn't a television in the room, but a stereo was softly playing classic jazz.

Drink in hand, Shaquil moved to where she was sitting and handed her the glass.

"Thanks." She brought the glass to her lips.

Instead of moving to his favorite leather recliner, he took a seat on the couch close to her. "What's wrong with you?"

"What do you mean what's wrong with me?"

"Why were you rude to my friend?"

She sipped her drink thoughtfully. "I wasn't rude." Her voice rose in annoyance. "I don't appreciate you tryin' to fix me up with your ugly-ass friends. You know that."

"If you could stick to one man, I wouldn't have to try and fix you up." He swung around. "Seriously, what's going on with you all these years? Why are you so against relationships?" He raised a hand to her knee. "Does it have anything to do with—"

"No!"

Shaquil raked his fingers through his hair with frustration. "Then what is it?"

"Just back off, Shaquil," she warned, her voice soft. Suddenly her expression was grim.

"Come on, sis, I'm serious."

Her exasperation barely controlled, Honey hissed, "I'm serious too. I'm not interested in dating anyone."

"Why?"

Honey sighed, hoping her brother would just leave the shit alone. She shook her head and looked him square in the eye. "Why are you always drillin' me about my personal life?"

"Because I'm concerned about you, sis." With his arms crossed, he stared at her. "You're never with anyone for any long period of time. What's up with that?"

"Can you just back the fuck off!" she shouted, tears suddenly stinging the back of her eyes.

"No, not this time."

Honey put her drink down and stood up to leave, but Shaquil was a step faster. His hand shot out to grasp her wrist, forcing her to stop.

"Move, Shaquil!" She tried to wiggle free but Shaquil held on to her, determined to find out what was really going on.

He turned her toward him and stared down at her. "Talk to me."

"Damn it, Shaquil, can you for once butt out!"

He loosened his hold and spoke quietly. "I wouldn't be a big brother if I didn't care. What's going on with you, sis?"

When she didn't answer right away, Shaquil knew she was fighting to keep her temper under control. He usually backed down, but this wasn't one of those times. Her behavior had been going on for quite some time, and he wanted the truth.

Honey was silent for several seconds as she remembered what her therapist had told her during their last session: *It's time to move on, which means letting go.* Squinting hard against tears, she raised her eyes to stare at him, pain shadowing her eyes. "I can't have kids."

His expression froze. "What?" he asked.

Eyes suddenly moistening, she whispered, "Nurse Donovan messed me up."

He looked puzzled for a moment, and then realization washed over him. "Shit, Honey." She felt his grasp tighten in shock. "I didn't know. I didn't fuckin' know," he mumbled. Shaquil looked down at his sister to see tears spilling from the corners of her eyes. It wasn't fair. The incident still hurt her deeply. He never mentioned it, hoping she would eventually forget the shit ever happened. He knew it wasn't the best way to handle a devastating experience, but she was his little sister. It stirred sad memories, which he tried to avoid. "Are you sure you can't have—"

With a raised palm, she silenced him. "I've seen three doctors, and they all confirmed it." Her lower lip trembled as she spoke. Then she lost it. She slumped against his warm chest, sobbing. Shaquil held her tight, allowing her to cry, remembering the devastating evening. They had carefully avoided any mention of the incident. Since that night, they'd made a mutual promise to keep the secret buried. Breathing a silent curse, Shaquil felt helpless, not able to do any more than hold her as their minds flowed with painful memories. He'd never forgotten the pain Walter brought into his sister's life. Silently, Shaquil repeated the same prayer he'd been saying for almost ten years, wishing he could take away the pain, wishing that he hadn't accepted that extra shift at work that night. If only he'd been there. If he had . . . things would be so different.

Honey raised her eyes to meet her brother's pained

expression, and instantly knew what he was thinking. It was the same look he'd given her the night she was raped.

Honey didn't even have to close her eyes; the memories of that night were as clear as the snow falling outside the window.

Walter had invited her to a movie on a Saturday night, and with slight hesitation, her mother agreed. At seventeen, Honey usually went out in groups or was chaperoned by one of her brothers, but Honey had begged and her mother, believing that maybe she was being too strict, agreed. When Walter helped her into his old Buick and held her hand during the movie, Honey thought him a perfect gentleman. After the movie, he suggested they take a drive before taking her home, and she had agreed. It wasn't until he pulled off into an unfamiliar wooded area that she began to panic. Walter immediately pulled her into his arms and she experienced her first French kiss. But before she could get used to the idea, the kiss became brutal.

Fighting off his advances was useless; instead, she angered Walter and in turn, he popped her in her mouth. Feeling her lips swell, Honey didn't resist when he slid her underwear down around her ankles. When he pulled her down on the front seat, Honey didn't fight and even stopped crying. She lay still as he tore into her, taking away her virginity. She became more numb with every painful thrust. Those few minutes had felt like an eternity while she closed her eyes and pretended she was at home nestled under her covers. After it was over, Walter drove her home as if nothing had happened.

Shaquil was waiting up for her when she returned, and at the sight of her disheveled hair and bruised lips, he'd demanded to know what the fuck had happened.

Honey had fallen into his arms with heart-wrenching sobs.

"How come you never told me?" he asked now, bringing her out of her reverie.

She shrugged. "I didn't want you to feel guilty."

He did feel guilty, even after all these years, because he should have been there. As soon as he'd found out, he wanted to bash Walter in his fuckin' face, but his sister pleaded with him not to and he'd reluctantly agreed. Then one evening, he ran into Walter hanging out in the record store with his friends, laughing and talking about some virgin he'd popped in the front seat of his car. Shaquil had snapped and waited for his punk ass to leave, then followed him to his car.

Honey watched Shaquil's jaw quiver, and she could feel his rising anger. She knew he was remembering, too. After skipping school for a week, she had returned to school to find that Walter had been badly beaten, and had received a double break in his throwing arm that guaranteed his football career was over. Honey never asked, but she had a sinking feeling Shaquil had been responsible. Even now, she couldn't bring herself to ask. All she wanted was for it to be over.

"All these years I thought you were . . ." Shaquil started, but allowed the words to fade.

Honey finished the sentence for him. "A ho. I know."

Several weeks after the rape, Honey had found herself pregnant, and made the painful decision to terminate the pregnancy. Instead of going to a hospital, as Shaquil urged, Honey had found a small clinic in East St. Louis run by a retired practitioner. Only last year had Honey found out that as a result of the severe damage to her cervix, she would never be able to bear children.

Ten years later the pain was gone, but the damage was still there. Because of it, Honey found it unfair to mislead any man—particularly Jay—into believing they had a future. She knew better than to believe in happily-ever-after, but it would be unfair of her to take away a man's pride at creating his own child.

"Does Mom know?"

"No!" she shouted, panic apparent on her face. "I'd appreciate it if you wouldn't say anything either."

"You know I won't."

She nodded. It was true. After all these years, he had kept her secret.

"But I think you need to talk to someone about this. You can't continue to keep this bottled up inside."

Honey playfully punched her brother's chest and moved to the couch. Shaquil took a seat beside her. She gave him a smile that didn't quite reach her eyes before answering. "I know. I've been seeing a shrink for six months. I had thought about it years ago, but thought burying it was the best way to pretend the shit never happened. Only it *did* happen, and no matter how much I tried, I couldn't cover it up. I thought breaking hearts would help me deal with the pain. Only I hated who the fuck I'd become. Then somethin' happened that finally caused me to face reality. . . ." Her voice faded as she tried to gather her composure.

Shaquil moved to his desk and returned with several tissues. She accepted them and blew her nose.

"What happened?"

Honey looked at her brother with misty eyes. "I fell in love."

With a look of understanding, Shaquil pulled her close.

How could I have been so damn stupid!
Honey tossed the book across the room. Finally, after months of denial, she had admitted that she was in love. And to all people, her brother. What was she thinking? How could she have allowed the words to finally form in her head? How could she have let the words slip from her tongue? She wasn't sure if she'd ever be able to look Jay in the eye again, afraid that he would see it in her expression. She'd been able to disguise the fact, even from herself. Now she could no longer deny the truth.

Heaven help her, she was in love with Jay.

The phone rang, startling her. She reached for it.

"How's Marcus?"

Speak of the devil.

When she had risen on Saturday, she found her car in the driveway with a brand-new tire. Later, she had called to thank him and told him Marcus was sick. Now she said, "He's better."

"Good."

"Mercedes says you left your cell phone at the shop."

"I picked it up yesterday."

"Oh."

They were quiet. Honey was unsure what to say, and Jay didn't want to push her.

"I really enjoyed the two of you Friday night," he said. "I hope we can do it again soon."

"Sure, Marcus would like that." *And so would you.* "I got to go. I . . . I left the bathwater running."

"Aw'ight. Talk to you soon."

After hanging up, Honey sagged back against the couch cushions and closed her eyes. Now what? Would it just be a matter of time before she gave in to her desires? As much as she tried, she couldn't forget the feel of his mouth against her lips, the masculine scent of his body pressed against her nipples, the way his hands felt against her bare flesh.

She shook her head. No, she couldn't let him find out. She couldn't take the chance. She would die if he looked at her with pity. Even worse, rejected her ass. It would be too much to handle. No, she would have to keep up the charade that she wasn't interested in being anything but his friend, no matter how much it hurt.

Jay hung up the phone. The call hadn't gone quite as he had planned. He had hoped Honey would invite him over, at least for a game of Scrabble.

He reached for a beer from the refrigerator, then removed his dinner from the microwave: fried chicken and mashed potatoes, courtesy of Banquet Dinners. He strolled into the living room and set his food on the coffee table. Easing down in his favorite chair, he reached for the remote control. Time for football. Just as the Rams scored their first touchdown, the phone rang.

"Jay, this is Jocelyn Price."

"Good evening."

"I spoke to Chad earlier, and he told me about the symposium in K.C." She stopped briefly, and Jay could tell that she was also eating. "I thought that was strange, but what I found when I went down to Vital Statistics today was even weirder. The receptionist is the mother of a little boy I saw in the emergency room a couple of weeks ago. She told me that American Family Insurance requested a copy of James's death certificate last week."

"Last week?" The man had been dead for almost a year. "Did he have any life insurance?"

"Yes, two policies. I was the beneficiary on one, his mother on the other. However, neither was with American Family."

"Maybe he had another policy you knew nothing about?"

"Maybe." She sounded unconvinced. "I've looked through all his things, and so far I've found nothing."

"If you don't mind, I'd like to have one of my operatives come by and look through Dr. Price's files tomorrow."

"That would be fine."

"Dory will call you tomorrow to schedule a good time. Meanwhile, see what you can get from the insurance company."

"All right. I'll let you know what I find out."

After he hung up, Jay reached for the remote and increased the volume. Before biting into a chicken leg he mumbled, "This case is getting more interesting by the moment."

Ten

Even though it was Valentine's Day, Honey didn't close the salon until after seven. Rita came in religiously every other Thursday at five o'clock for a wash and set, and Candy made sure she was always the last appointment of the day. The middle-aged woman was a talker; Honey knew the names of her children, her children's children, all her neighbors, and even the damn postman.

By the time she finally hustled Rita out the door, the other stylists were long gone, preparing for their own dates. Honey had brought her clothes along so she could change before Darrius arrived to pick her up for dinner. As she was turning out the lights, she heard a faint knock and moved to the front of the shop. She gasped when she found Jay standing outside the door.

Three days had passed. Other than a few brief phone conversations, she hadn't seen him. She had expected him to show up uninvited at the salon, or worse yet, her home. When he'd done neither, she had felt a mixture of relief and disappointment. Just this morning, she'd found herself wondering which of his female companions would have the pleasure of being in his company this evening. So what the hell was he doing here on Valentine's Day?

"Are you gonna invite me in?" he called through the door, pulling the collar of his heavy coat up around his ears.

Feeling her breath catch on her dry lips, Honey realized she'd been standing there gawking, probably like a lovesick puppy.

"Just give me a minute," she answered before reaching down to turn the lock. After several fumbled attempts, she opened it and stared at the handsome man in front of her.

Beneath a long tweed coat, she spied a black wool suit. His cologne filled the air. Oh, did he smell good! Jealousy raced through her chest. He was spending the evening with someone else. "You look nice," she forced herself to admit.

"And so do you. May I come in?"

She blinked hard. "Oh, yes, of course," she mumbled, almost tripping over her own feet as she moved aside.

Stepping into the room, he gave her a dazzling smile, then produced a small white box from behind his back and held it out to her.

Honey frowned down at it. "What's that for?"

"If you didn't know, today *is* Valentine's Day," he teased.

"I know what today is," she snapped, infuriated by what she was feeling. She forced her eyes away from his succulent lips. *Oh God, I want him to kiss me again.* "But why did you buy me a gift?"

Jay noticed something different in her eyes, but

wasn't quite sure what it was. Fear, and maybe something else. "I didn't," he mumbled, then shrugged. "My
date for the evening canceled, and I remembered you
like chocolate."

Honey looked at him, contemplating if what he said
was true before taking the box from his hands. "Sounds
like you're losing your touch," she said, feeling some of
her control return. She removed the lid to find a dozen
chocolate-covered strawberries. "Mmm," she moaned
before she bit into one. "This is delicious."

Jay stood to the side with his lips parted, watching
her. She licked her lips, and he had to resist the urge to
retrace the path.

Honey started to take a third bite, but stopped halfway
to her mouth to look at him. "You want some?"

His eyes twinkled. "I would love some." Before she
had a chance to reach into the box, he leaned forward.
Grasping her wrist, he raised her hand to his mouth and
swallowed the half-eaten strawberry.

Honey's fingers quivered, and a warm feeling traveled deliciously from her fingers down to between her
thighs. Jay took his time and drew each finger into his
mouth, licking the chocolate from her knuckle all the
way to her fingernail with his tongue, using slow, sensual moves. Her eyes traveled down to his lips, and she
swallowed. Honey found herself unable to move, and
the feeling of arousal consumed her as she envisioned
his tongue traveling to the private parts of her body.

Damn if he wasn't fucking her fingers! She jerked
her hand away, walked over to the reception desk, and
set the box on the counter.

"Thanks for the chocolate," she mumbled.

"No problem." He watched her out of the side of

his eye, hoping to see something to indicate what she was feeling. He hadn't intended to lick her fingers, but the melted chocolate had looked so inviting. "Do you have plans for tonight? Maybe another date I can rescue you from?" he said, smirking.

She waited until her quickened pulse quieted before answering. "I already told you I had plans." She moved across the room to her workstation and began putting her supplies away, trying to do everything in her power not to look at him.

"I was hopin' maybe you had changed your mind." His gaze traveled over her attire. He liked the way she looked in the brown leather skirt with high splits.

"What are you gonna do now that your date has canceled?" She couldn't help wondering who was stupid enough to call off a date with him.

"Sit in front of my television with a bowl of Edy's ice cream and a new video game." Jay crossed his arms. "I bought *Halo* yesterday for my X-Box."

She swung around, eyes wide. "X-Box! You have an X-Box?" He nodded. "I've been wantin' one of my own, but the price of those things is ridiculous." With a sigh, she moved to lock the cash drawer.

"Why don't you come over and help me break it in this evening?" he suggested, drawing nearer.

She shook her head. "I don't think so. I already made plans to have dinner with Darrius."

He studied her face. "You really don't want to go out with Mr. Stockbroker, do you?"

She shrugged, not trusting herself to speak.

"Come on, Honey. It's Valentine's Day. Why don't we spend the evening hangin' out like ole' times? I'm sure Darrius would understand."

Honey was tempted. She'd wanted to hold the joystick to that game for weeks. But the thought of being alone with Jay scared her.

"I even have cold Busch beer in my refrigerator."

She was almost swayed by his warm brown eyes, but dutifully declined. "Tempting, but not tonight. Maybe some other time."

Jay took a step forward. "You promised me a date."

Honey tried to move away, but damn if her body wasn't listening. For some unknown reason, her feet felt cemented to the floor. Desire was apparent in Jay's eyes as he moved in even closer.

He took another step, closing the distance between them, and backed her into a corner until she was trapped against the wall with his hands planted on either side of her. After gazing into her gray eyes, he let his eyes travel from her mane of brown hair down to the orange cashmere sweater hugging her itty-bitty breasts.

Honey drew in a swift breath mixed with fear and anticipation as she saw his gaze wander back to her mouth. He was so near and his lips so close she wanted him to kiss her. Even though she knew it would be a big mistake, she wanted it anyway. Rather than pulling away, she found herself swaying toward him.

Eyes roaming over her delicate face, Jay reached out and stroked her soft curls with the back of his hand. He could see the battle she fought within, but still leaned forward until she could feel his breath against her skin.

"Quit fightin' it, Honey. No one will ever be able to make you as happy as I can." He spoke in a low, husky rasp that caused her to shiver.

"Why do you keep doing this?" she gasped.

"You shouldn't be so damn fine," he said, his cinnamon breath hot against her throat.

Honey knew she should run, but couldn't. Even as his face moved closer, she couldn't. Even when his lips parted, she couldn't. For several seconds, she focused on his lips and she shuddered remembering how they felt. Her mouth went dry, making it impossible to speak. She felt caught beneath his brown gaze. Jay ran a thumb across her lips and she trembled, powerless to do anything but stand there frozen to the wall. His arm went around her waist, pulling her against his solid form.

Under dark lashes, Honey stared up at him with wide eyes, looking young and fragile. Her mass of curly hair was clipped away from her face, exposing a sensuous neck that was begging to be kissed. She dropped her eyes, and Jay rested his chin on her head. Taking a deep breath, he inhaled the scent of freshly washed hair and the herbal conditioner she liked so much. With her nipples pressed against his chest, he felt the throb of her heart. He allowed his lips to travel down the side of her face, then down the length of her neck, where he nibbled at the smooth honey flesh. Thinking of her with someone else made him furious with wanting to claim what was his. He'd sworn to take things slow. He'd made a pledge to allow her to initiate the relationship. But he was powerless against his desire.

With their faces only inches apart, he cupped her chin in his palm and drew it near. He dropped his head and claimed her mouth, her lips parted in shock. Then, cradling her waist, Jay pulled her closer to him.

"It could be so good between us," he whispered as he felt her heart flutter against his chest.

She took a deep breath, caught in a tidal wave of sensation as he showered her with kisses that made her shudder. She wanted his tongue in her mouth. There were no words for what she was feeling. She knew she should pull away, scream, even slap the shit out of him, but she could do none of that. Instead, dropping her head back, she leaned into him, allowing his tongue access, and he tasted, then explored as the fine hairs of his beard teased her. She tried to resist but found herself reaching out; she placed her hands on his shoulders and moaned.

"Let me love you," he whispered against her lips.

The kiss became so powerful Honey thought her knees would give way beneath her. Brushing her mouth back and forth in a coaxing movement, he plunged his tongue deep into her mouth, tasting lips softer than he remembered. Her hips pressed against the narrow heat of him and her thighs were nestled between his legs. He gyrated his hips against her, causing her to weaken.

The knock on the door ended it. Jay took his lips away. Still standing close, taunting her before backing away, he locked his eyes on hers. "We wouldn't want you to keep your date waiting." With that, he walked to the door and opened it, and found himself once again face-to-face with Darrius. The two looked at each other for a brief moment before Jay finally nodded, then brushed past him.

Leaving Darrius standing there, Honey escaped to her office, where she sagged against the office door. She raised trembling fingers to her throbbing lips. The passion-filled kiss had rocked her to the core, and had been every bit as explosive as the last time. Like before, Jay had left her nipples erect and her panties wet. If only he knew how damn close the phrase "I love you" had been ready to erupt from her smothered lips.

This had to end. She was weak around Jay, and if

she wanted to keep him from finding out her secret, she needed to stay away from him at all costs. Regardless of how much she loved him.

She just wished it were that easy.

As he steered in the direction of home, his cell phone vibrated.

"Jay, this is Kendra. I just hate to bother you on Valentine's Day, but I'm not feelin' too good."

He heard something unsettling in her voice. "What's wrong?"

"I—I'm not sure. I've been having lower abdominal pains all day. Ow! There it goes again."

"Hang tight, Kendra. I'll be right over."

Natalia arrived at Houlihan's to find Jacob already there, seated at a small table in the back, and her heart soared. She was dressed in the navy blue blazer and slacks she had planned to wear to his mother's birthday party before he declined her attendance.

"Sorry I'm late," she said as soon as he was in range. Moving to him, she planted a kiss on his cheek, loving the smell of her man, before taking the seat next to him. "I had a busy day at the office. You wouldn't believe all the last-minute problems I'm having with the designers. The spring season begins in four weeks, and I don't know if our new line is gonna be ready in time." She paused at seeing the distracted expression on his handsome mocha face, and smiled. "Listen to me, rattling on like a broken record. Happy Valentine's Day, baby. Ms. Kitty and I have a gift waiting for you at home. I hope Mandingo is up for the challenge."

Turning away from the suggestive look in her eyes, Jacob cleared his throat. "I have something for you."

Natalia bubbled over inside when she saw him remove a small black box from under the table. *Oh my goodness*, she thought, *this is it*. She took the gift and opened it.

Suddenly the joy left her face.

What the hell is this shit? She lowered her lashes to disguise her displeasure, then reached down to remove the two-carat diamond brooch. "It's beautiful." When she lifted her eyes, disappointment still flickered there. "Thank you." She opened the clasp and pinned it onto the lapel of her jacket.

"I have something to tell you," Jacob said, taking her hand in his. But then he paused.

"What is it?" she probed uneasily. She hadn't noticed the strained tone of his voice until now.

"I've been offered an opportunity to design a database for a large military installation."

"That's wonderful!" She knew he'd always dreamed of such an opportunity. "When do you start?"

His expression stilled as he looked at her. "I'll be moving to Germany at the end of the week."

Natalia felt her mouth go dry, and confused thoughts began to race through her mind. Was he really leaving? "What about us?" She tried to keep her voice steady, even though her heart was thundering.

Jacob dropped her hand. "I would like for us to remain friends."

She was stunned. "Friends. What the fuck do you mean, friends? I thought you loved me . . ." Her voice broke. ". . . that you wanted to marry me."

"Things have changed since my father passed," Jacob said, his voice heavy with emotion. "I spent my life trying to make him happy. Now it's time for me to live my own life. I'm not ready for marriage."

Natalia looked at him, angry, her mind working overtime. She stared across the table at him, wishing she had a bat so she could bust his head in two.

"I'm so sorry." Jacob lowered his eyes to the table when he spoke; his tone was apologetic. "I never meant to mislead you."

Natalia felt her heart break in two. How could she have been so damn stupid to believe that she had finally found love? How could he break her heart like this?

"You no-good mothafucka!" Her throat tight with rage, she rose from the table and scurried out of the restaurant.

Once home, she quickly undressed and crawled into bed, knocking the lacy negligee she had bought for Jacob onto the floor.

Ms. Kitty wouldn't be stroked tonight.

Honey looked down at the empty bowl of ice cream. She felt like a pig. Instead of eating a bowl, she'd eaten the entire carton. What a way to spend Valentine's Day.

Right after dinner, she had Darrius take her home. Even though she'd faked a headache, she had a strong suspicion Darrius knew the real deal.

Sighing, Honey let her head fall back against the couch and closed her eyes. Visions of Jay danced before her. She had tasted his lips throughout the depressing dinner, and even now as she sank back onto the couch. She could still smell the scent of his body, feel his breath against her earlobe, his dick pressed against her stomach. God, she was a damn fool. There was no harm in spending an evening with Jay. What was wrong with a harmless evening of video games?

She jumped off the couch and went in search of her cordless phone.

She let it ring five times before she hung up without bothering to try him on his cell phone. A pain squeezed at her heart as she thought of him with someone else. It was Valentine's Day; what did she expect him to do, sit and spend the evening alone? Jay had decided to spend the evening with another woman.

"I'm sorry, Jay. I didn't mean to ruin your night," Kendra said as they entered her apartment.

"No harm done," he said reassuringly. "Dr. Gaye said Braxton-Hick contractions are common in this stage of the pregnancy." He shrugged. "I didn't have any plans tonight anyway."

"I just assumed since you were all dressed up—"

"My date canceled," he said. Actually, he hadn't had a date. It had just been a ploy to make Honey jealous. An unsuccessful ploy after all.

"Oh." Kendra tried to hide a smile as he helped her slip out of her black cape.

While hanging it in the hall closet, he added, "Besides, I told you to feel free to call me. That's my kid growin' inside your body." He strolled into the living room with a proud grin lifting the corners of his lips.

Kendra moved to the couch and with Jay's assistance, lowered herself onto the soft cushions. "Thanks. I don't know how I manage anymore."

"No problem." He propped a pillow behind her head, then moved to elevate her feet onto the couch. "You don't have to apologize. Regardless of our differences, I said I'd be there for you, and I meant it."

"Thanks," she said, smiling. "You know, this is our second Valentine."

"It is?" Jay gave her a questioning look before he remembered. He had arrived home after a date with a schoolteacher to find Kendra lying across his bed, butt-ass naked and covered in rose petals.

He cleared his throat. "I'm gonna head on home."

"But you can't leave," she said. Seeing his puzzled expression, she quickly added, "I'm still not feelin' good. Can you please sit with me for a while?"

After a brief pause, he nodded. "Sure." He had made a pledge to help her through her pregnancy. He took a seat at the end of the couch, raised her feet to his lap, and reached for the remote.

"I think I found a lawyer that can handle the adoption," she said in slow, precise syllables.

He stopped channel-surfing and his eyes swung to her. "Let's hold off on that for a while."

"Why?" she asked. Lowering her chin, she regarded him through her lashes.

"Because I don't want to give my child up for adoption." There. He had said it.

She clapped her hands with glee. "That's wonderful! I—"

"Just give me a little time. Then we'll talk."

"All right." For the time being, she wouldn't push. Instead, she reached down for a small woven bag and pulled out a ball of yellow yarn and two needles.

Hearing a clicking sound, Jay turned to face her

again and was stunned by what he saw. "What're you doing?"

"What does it look like I'm doin'? I'm trying to knit a sweater for the baby. What do you think?" She held up something that looked like a dysfunctional sock.

Jay's head fell back in laughter.

Kendra pouted for the rest of the evening.

At the end of the ten o'clock news, Kendra switched off the television and, stretching her arms over her head, she released a restless sigh. She looked over at Jay, who was nestled comfortably against a pillow, snoring peacefully. From the end of the couch, Kendra watched the rise and fall of his chest. Damn, he was fine. Her coochie throbbed as she thought how good it would be to feel him inside her once again. It would take a little work on her part, but he loved it before and he would enjoy it again. Like they say, pregnant pussy is the best kind.

With little difficulty, she slid off the couch and got down on her knees in between his parted thighs. She then reached up, and gently unbuckled his pants. She watched Jay's face the entire time, making sure he didn't wake up. Lowering his zipper, she reached inside his boxer and found what she was looking for.

"Come to Mama," she whispered as she took hold of his big fat dick.

Kendra licked her lips as she gazed at its size and thickness. The brotha was truly blessed. Slowly, she stroked the head, then worked her way down the length and back up to the tip. His dick grew brick-hard and a low moan escaped from his lips.

Kendra tried to stifle her laughter as she moved in closer and filled her mouth with as much of his length as she could handle. She took him in and out, sucking his dick like a well-seasoned pork chop. It wasn't long before his hips began to gyrate against her mouth.

Jay couldn't believe how real his dream felt. He was in Honey's bed. Her legs were wrapped around his waist as he thrust in and out of her red-hot pussy. Oh, she was tight! The walls contracted and felt so fuckin' good wrapped around his dick. He was about to explode when he opened his eyes, wanting to see her face when he came. His eyelids fluttered open. He had to blink several times before he realized where the hell he was.

He looked down at his crotch to find Kendra's head bobbing up and down.

"What the hell are you doing?" He gasped although he did nothing to stop her.

"What does it look like I'm doin'?" she said with a bit of amusement before she took him deep in her mouth again. The she reached up and cupped his balls, massaging them delicately.

Jay knew he should put an end to her actions but he couldn't. He was too damn close to coming to stop now. He closed his eyes and lowered his head back against the couch.

"Yeah, baby. Just like that," he moaned.

Kendra didn't need any instructions. She knew exactly what he liked. She knew exactly how to perform her magic.

"Aaahh . . . oh, shhiiit! I'm gettin' ready to come!"

Kendra worked faster and harder and within seconds his cream spilled inside her mouth.

Jay waited until his breathing had returned to normal before he rose and went into the bathroom to clean himself up. He returned to find Kendra sitting on the couch pretending that shit never happened.

"What the hell you do that for?"

She sucked her teeth, then gave him a long penetrating stare. "I didn't hear you complaining."

"Girl, what-the-fuck-ever! You just don't know when to quit." Damn! She had played his ass again. And he had thoroughly enjoyed it.

Jay shook his head, reached for his jacket, and headed for the door.

"Come back anytime. I aim to please!" she shouted.

He could hear her laughter even after he shut the door.

"Damn!" he hissed as he slammed his car door. She had played him like a fuckin' harmonica. Kendra always had this unexplainable power over his dick that he never could understand. Nevertheless, he would have to learn to control his sexual urges around her. But damn, he hadn't had any pussy in months. Never in his life had he ever gone this long without getting some. He hoped to remedy that problem real soon. Only it wouldn't be with Kendra's triflin' ass. He wanted Honey.

As he pulled away from the apartment building, he lit a cigarette. Turning onto West Florissant Road, he wished he could go home to find Honey waiting in his bed.

He had meant to end it there . . . just a simple kiss to remind her of what they once had. Or rather, what could be if she allowed the chemistry between them to evolve. Something to put in her mind so that while she was with Darrius, her mind would be on him.

As he turned down Chambers Road, he was tempted to drive by Honey's house to see if Darrius's car was parked in her driveway. It was almost midnight; if he was there, it wouldn't be a good sign. But even though he still couldn't get the two of them out of his mind, Jay resisted the impulse.

When it rained, it fuckin' poured, and right now it was hailing on top of his black ass.

Eleven

A noisy commotion caught Honey's attention the moment she climbed out of the car. Tightening the wool scarf around her face, she reached for her purse and dashed across the snow-covered sidewalk. Entering the salon, she found the reception area overflowing with females.

"What the fuck?"

Honey pushed her way through the crowd of women waving dollar bills in the air. The music was so loud she thought she was at a rap concert. As soon as she reached the center of the room, she realized what all the commotion was. One of Rashad's employees, whom they called B-Daddy, was flexing and wiggling to the sound of LL Cool J's "Head Sprung."

A pissed-off Honey moved over to the stereo and hit the power button with her finger.

"What the . . . ?" Rashad's voice drained at the expression on his sister's face.

"What the hell's going on?" Standing only inches

away from her brother, Honey folded her arms across her chest as she tried to control her rage.

Rashad shrugged sheepishly. "Just havin' a lil' fun."

"Fun? *Fun*?" she said. "This ain't a fuckin' strip club! This is a place of business." Realizing she was making a scene, she lowered her voice to a heavy whisper. "Your mothafuckin' ass is supposed to be workin'." She peered around the work area with a fist planted on her hip. "All of you should be workin'."

Candy bolted to her chair, dropping her money on the floor along the way. All five stylists quickly scattered to their stations while the customers who'd been observing scrambled to take a seat.

B-Daddy reached for his shirt, mumbled, "Sorry, Honey," and rushed through the makeshift door.

Giving her brother one long stare, Honey stomped off to her office with all eyes on her. Rashad came behind her, trying to explain.

"Sis, we were on our break. B-Daddy just won first prize in one of those bodybuilding contests and one of the ladies wanted to see what the brotha was workin' with." He flashed her a twenty-four-karat smile. "It's all good."

"No, it ain't." Honey shook her head, hoping she didn't look as confused as she felt, then lowered her head in her hands.

She was falling apart. She'd spent half the evening wondering whom Jay was with, and the rest of the night fucking her vibrator. Part of her was ready. She wanted his lips. His dick. His love. *Lord have mercy.* Even now, desire shuddered through her, so intense that it stripped away all pretenses. Besides her rape, she had no sexual experience whatsoever, yet she wanted to be sexing it with Jay. Because they wouldn't be having sex, they would be making love.

She needed time to think, to sort this shit out. Everything was happening too fast. She was so scared of loving him. She was scared of him finding out she had been raped. Somehow, she had to deal with the fact that Jay wasn't going away. She kept telling herself she couldn't get involved with him. But she already was. One touch from him and everything had come tumbling down. Jay owned her heart. He had somehow managed to unravel every ounce of her resistance.

She had to get her turbulent emotions under control. The simple truth was she was in love and . . . yes, damn it, she was definitely losing it.

The other part of her was scared, so very scared of him finding out the truth and rejecting her. Her body was ready for intimacy but her mind wasn't. Once he found out, Jay would realize he was wasting his time. She couldn't bear for him to look at her with pity, and then deal with the rejection that would follow.

God, she was having a bad day. Last night, Mercedes had moved her stupid ass back home. This morning her fuckin' toilet backed up. The heat in her car had stopped working. Then she came in to work to find a man with a body that could put Tyrese's black ass to shame standing half naked in her salon. Trivial things never bothered her before. Now everything bothered her, trivial or not. She was in trouble.

And it was all Jay's fault.

Honey flinched in her seat.

"What's up, sis?" Rashad asked, his brow creased with concern.

Yep, she was losing it. She couldn't even stay angry. She had to be falling apart.

"Rashad, I ain't in the mood." She raised her head and looked at him. "Whatcha need to be doing is tryin' to make up for that shit."

Honey had spoken so calmly she had Rashad worried. "No problem. Whatcha need?"

"I need heat." *Jay can warm you to the core of your existence.* "Damn! I—I mean, I need the heat in my car fixed."

"No problem. I'll take care of it. You sure you're aw'ight?"

I am in love and about to pull my fuckin' hair out trying to deal with my emotions, but other than that, I'm just peachy. She nodded. "Yeah, I'm cool."

"Good." He breathed a sigh of relief, then turned to walk to the door.

She cleared her throat and called out to him, "Oh, and don't think your ass is off the hook. We'll talk later." *When I have my head screwed on right.*

"I had no doubt." He smirked before exiting the room.

Jay arrived in Chicago around noon, hailed a cab at the airport, and gave the driver directions to Pulsar's Medical Research. The corporation had devised a retractable syringe, which would cut down on the number of nursing personnel sticking themselves with infected needles. Until the product was completely tested, though, they didn't want any word of its existence to leak out. A security system was needed to ensure the secrecy of the product. Pulsar was a nationwide corporation. If Extreme Measures could outbid their competition, it would open up a lot of doors for the company. Luckily, the owner was a friend of the family.

As the cab pulled off the Eisenhower Expressway, Jay reached for his cell phone to check his messages. After listening to them, he only returned one call.

"Jay, I'm so glad you called me back," Jocelyn said after they exchanged greetings.

"I'm sorry I couldn't get to you sooner. I'm going to be out of town until Thursday. What did you find out?"

She sighed into the receiver. "Well, according to the insurance company, the policy was left to James's brother, Jhamil. But that's impossible."

"Why is that?"

"Because Jhamil is dead."

"Hey, everybody," Sasha called as she moved through the salon waving to all of the stylists.

Mercedes was saturating a woman's hair with a strawberry rinse, but glanced over her shoulder. "Hey, Mama."

Holding hot curlers in her hand, Aisha spied Sasha's stomach. "How much longer you got?"

Pausing to rub her red sweater, Sasha answered cheerfully, "Three weeks and counting." Then she looked over at the empty workstation and asked, "Where's Honey?"

Sonya swiveled around, flipping booty-length auburn extensions across her shoulders. "Girl, she's in her office. She fuckin' flipped out."

Sasha stopped in her tracks, eyes wide with wonder. "What happened?"

Moving over to the shampoo bowl at the back of the shop, Mercedes answered in a low voice, "She caught us goofing around and hit the roof."

"We deserved it," Aisha added as she reached for a can of hair spray. "Although Rashad is to blame."

Swinging around in her seat, Candy rushed to his defense. "Don't even go there."

Aisha held up an open palm and barked, "Whatever!" at the receptionist. Everyone was well aware of Candy's infatuation. They also knew she didn't have a chance in hell of getting Rashad's attention.

Turning back to Sasha, Aisha said, "Honey usually goes off, then she'll laugh along with the rest of us. But this time was different." She paused to glance down at her wristwatch. "It's been three hours and she still hasn't come out."

Sasha pondered the possibilities a moment, then headed across the floor. "I guess I better go talk to her." When she entered the office, she found Honey's head down on the desk. "Knock, knock."

"Go away," Honey commanded.

"Girl, what's wrong?"

Honey groaned. *Not Sasha.* "I'm just tired."

Sasha moved to take a seat in a chair across from her desk. "Rashad's friend keep you out too late?"

She snorted. "No. I just couldn't sleep."

"How was your date?"

"Fine."

"That's all? Just fine?" Sasha said, disappointed.

"I told you we were just friends."

"Your staff is worried."

"Let their asses worry! I'm sure they told you what they were doing."

"They told me."

Honey raised her head to find four heads peeking around the corner of her door. She couldn't resist a grin. "Get back to work," she ordered, and the heads disappeared. Then, reaching into her drawer, she removed a hairbrush.

Sasha leaned against her desk. "So what's really going on?"

Looking down into a handheld mirror, Honey said, "Why does everyone think something's going on? Maybe I've got PMS or something."

"And maybe you're hiding something from me," Sasha retorted, but decided not to pursue the big mystery until later. "I'm on my way to visit my mother. But I wanted to stop and invite you over this evening."

Honey looked at her for the first time since she'd entered her office. "Why? Is somethin' wrong?"

Sasha rose slowly from the chair. "Does there have to be something wrong for me to invite my best friend over?"

"No," Honey answered, but her voice held skepticism.

"Good." Sasha smiled. "Then I'll see you this evening."

Honey stopped brushing her hair and said, "Is Jay going to be there?"

Sasha looked down at her, and immediately sensed her apprehension. "Why?"

"Because if he is, I ain't comin'."

Honey shifted her eyes, but not before Sasha saw the pain she was trying to hide. Instead of what she wanted to say, she said only, "No, he won't be there. Jay left town this morning."

"Good," Honey said with a sigh. "I'll see you this evening."

* * *

The sun was melting the thin layer of snow when Honey pulled into the circular driveway at Andrews Manor. She rang the doorbell, then waited patiently for Sasha to waddle to the door, admiring the large wrap-around deck surrounded by shrubs. The twenty-room mansion dated back before the 1904 World Fair. Before Sasha had moved in and applied her creative skills, the grand house had reminded her of a mausoleum.

"Hey, girl." Honey smiled at her best friend, hoping the look was convincing.

"What took you so long?" Sasha scolded. She moved aside so Honey could pass. "I pulled the lasagna out of the oven an hour ago."

"Mmmm, you didn't tell me you were cooking," Honey said as she stepped into the huge marble foyer and hung her coat on the rack.

"What can I say?" she said, shrugging. "I was bored. Waiting on this baby, I have a lot of nervous energy. I think I've cleaned out all the closets. Our housekeeper had a fit."

Honey laughed.

"Anyway . . ." Sasha signaled with her hand. "Follow me."

Together they traveled up a winding staircase trimmed in rich oak to the suite at the end of the hall.

"Come on, girl," Sasha called as she waddled rapidly down the hall. Honey tried to keep up.

"I'm comin'. I'm comin'," Honey said, noting that Sasha was more excited than Honey had ever seen her before.

As soon as they reached the last door, Sasha turned to her and smiled. "Ready?"

Honey nodded.

Sasha opened the door and moved aside so her friend could step in first.

Honey walked in, and her heart swelled in her chest. It was the nursery for the baby.

The room was painted a pastel pink with balloons stenciled on all the walls. Balloons made from satin hung from the ceilings, and plush rose carpeting covered the floor. Moving across the room, Honey rubbed her hand along the white antique crib, noting the colorful balloon mobile at one end and windup music box at the other. Inside the crib was a comforter and sheet set that matched the décor, as well as several stuffed animals. The rest of the furnishings consisted of a wooden rocking chair, a changing table, and a tall white dresser.

"What do you think?" Sasha asked.

Eyes misty and voice full of emotion, Honey said, "It's beautiful."

"You think so? Mom and I spent hours getting this room together. She made all of the accessories. Terraine and Jay did all the labor. Can you believe it?"

Honey nodded, a sob lodged in her throat.

"I think Jay was more excited about getting this room together than we were. Maybe he's ready to have a family of his own." She brushed against Honey playfully and winked. "Hint, hint."

"That's nice." Honey moved away, reached for a yellow blanket draped over the rocker, and rubbed the softness against her cheek.

"What's going on with you and Jay?"

Honey looked down, lips twitching. She couldn't speak, afraid if she did the dam would give way.

Sasha's eyes flickered over her face. She hadn't missed the dark circles under her eyes. "I know how you feel about him."

"No, you don't," Honey said softly. "You couldn't begin to know."

"So why don't you tell me?"

The only thing to do was change the damn subject. "What's in here?" Honey asked, and moved to the closet and opened it.

Sasha removed one of several outfits hanging in the closet. "Isn't this adorable?" She was referring to a frilly peach dress with a matching bonnet.

Honey took it in her hands. The material was so soft, and the dress tiny. *A little life.* She couldn't wait to hold her godchild in her arms. A tear spilled over, and she quickly moved away to hang it back in the closet. "Are you ready?"

Sasha sighed, her eyes glowing. "As ready as I will ever be. I'm so nervous. I don't know the first thing about babies."

Honey moved to embrace her. "You're going to be a wonderful mother." When they pulled apart, Sasha's eyes were cloudy.

"I hope so. Thank God I have my mother."

Clenching her eyes closed, Honey tried to keep back the flood of tears burning in their depths.

"You're going to be a wonderful mother someday yourself," Sasha said.

Honey shook her head, and the tears started flowing.

Sasha's face creased with concern. "What's the matter?"

Honey began to cry outright now. Sasha took her by the hand and moved down the hall to the master bedroom, took a seat on the massive poster bed, and patted the spot next to her. "Sit," she commanded. Leaning over, she reached for a box of tissues from the nightstand and handed it to Honey. "Are you gonna tell me what's been botherin' you?"

Honey mopped her eyes again and swallowed hard before answering. "I can't have children."

Sasha's concern turned to a look of dazed disbelief. "What do—" She stopped, paused, then gasped, "Why?"

Honey's eyes locked with Sasha's. "Remember Walter?" she said, her voice breaking.

Sasha thought for several seconds, then her mind registered. "The football player?"

Honey nodded. "Our senior year . . . that mothafucka raped me," she said quietly, tears flooding her eyes.

"Oh no!" Sasha shook her head, horrified, and muttered something under her breath. She reached over and embraced Honey while her friend poured out years of bottled-up pain. "Oh my God," she cried, her own eyes flooding with tears. "All these years, I . . . I thought you were promiscuous, and you let me believe that. I'm so sorry!"

"I know you didn't mean it," Honey replied in a voice drawn and sad. Sasha held on to her until her cries subsided to soft sobs. Then Honey eased herself away, reached for another tissue, and blew her nose.

"Why'd you keep this bottled up inside?" Sasha said, hurt that Honey hadn't trusted her. "I'm your best friend. I would have understood."

"I tried to shut it out . . . pretend the shit never happened," Honey admitted.

Sasha hesitated, tears splashing down her face. "Does Jay know?"

Her eyes grew large with fear. "No, he doesn't, and I'd appreciate it if you didn't tell him." She wouldn't be able to stand it if she saw a look of pity in his eyes.

Sasha, still holding Honey's hand, nodded. The movement shook loose fresh tears. "I can assume that's the reason why you won't let him get close to you."

Honey nodded.

"You know, he loves you."

Lowering her eyes, Honey took a deep breath, hoping to stem the fresh flow streaming down her face. "How do you know that?" she asked, even though deep down she'd known all along how he felt about her.

"We've all known how much he loves you," Sasha said, smiling to show Honey comfort even though her heart filled with pain. "It's written all over his face. I also know you love *him*."

Honey sighed, refraining from making eye contact.

"Quit fighting it, Honey. You deserve to be happy." Sasha lifted her chin, forcing Honey's eyes to meet hers. The pain she witnessed made her stomach cringe. "I remember when I was in your shoes, letting Robby control my life. I didn't think I was worthy of anyone's love after that relationship. But you refused to let me wallow in self-pity. Now I look back and see that I almost lost the best thing to ever happen to me, loving Terraine." She touched Honey's hand. "You can't quit living. Don't you see? If you deny yourself happiness, then Walter has won. Don't let that bastard ruin the rest of your life."

The words hit home. How many times had her therapist told her the same thing? She wiped her eyes and slowly nodded. She wanted Jay with a hunger that surpassed mere attraction.

She was in love. But love and trust worked hand in hand. She would have to open up her heart to him. Was she willing to take that chance?

"Allow yourself to love," Sasha assured her, as if

she could read her mind. "Give Jay a chance and you'll see . . . he'll understand."

"Breathe, Kendra!" Natalia yelled as she coached Kendra through another contraction. She continued to count as the contraction peaked, and Kendra released a long breath as if she were blowing out candles on a birthday cake.

Seeing the serious expression on her best friend's face, she ended her breath in a fit of laughter. "Girl, you look like a damn fool," Kendra cackled.

Natalia stopped counting and pursed her lips. "Don't say anything when you *do* go into labor and you don't have the foggiest idea what you're supposed to do."

They were attending a Lamaze class. Twelve other couples were spread out on the padded training room floor.

"I feel stupid," Kendra said with a pout.

"Too bad," Natalia mumbled under her breath. "Now pay attention." Natalia turned her focus back to the clinical instructor at the front of the room, who was demonstrating how to bear down and push.

Kendra snorted, and Natalia gave her a look that said to shut the hell up. She was obviously getting into the spirit of the course. Kendra rolled her eyes at Natalia's disapproval. She had better things to do with her time than to spend it with a bunch of giddy-looking people.

Her eyes traveled around the room. Besides Natalia, there were two other female coaches. One was a mother accompanying her teenage daughter, so they didn't count. The other lady seemed to be quite pleased that her coach was a woman. *They're probably dykes*. All the other pregnant moms were accompanied by men. Couples were holding hands, husbands were rubbing their wives' stomachs, and here she was with her best friend.

"Come on, Kendra." Natalia waved a hand in front of her face.

"Come on what?"

Natalia sighed. "Weren't you listening? We need to practice pushing."

"Pushing?" She frowned, then said, "This is stupid."

"No, it's not! You need to be prepared."

"Who's gonna remember any of this shit when they're hit by excruciating pain?" she whispered, perplexed.

Natalia's eyes narrowed to slits. "That's why I'm here. Now breathe!"

"Fine." Huffing, Kendra lay back on the mat with her knees bent. On Natalia's cue, she lifted her shoulders off the mat, held her breath, and pushed.

"Good job!" Natalia said, and meant it.

"Oh, shut the hell up," Kendra mumbled, falling back to the floor in disgust. "I feel like Humpty Fuckin' Dumpty!"

Natalia cracked up laughing while Kendra rolled onto her side and sulked like a spoiled-ass brat. She had looked forward to the Lamaze classes when Lawrence had planned to attend them with her. Without him, or Jay for that matter, it just didn't make any sense.

Class was dismissed shortly afterward. Carrying two pillows, Natalia strolled through the building with Kendra. "You have to admit that was fun."

"For who . . . you or me?" she answered stiffly, not liking the fun Natalia was having at her expense.

Natalia curled an arm around her shoulders. "Aw, come on, Kendra, lighten up a little." A tender smile crossed her lips. "I'll be glad when you have that baby, 'cause you've been trippin'."

"I can't help it. I'm gonna be doing this all by myself, and I just have to get used to that." They were passing the information desk on the hospital's main floor. Kendra stopped and took a seat on a wooden bench. "It's okay, though. Jay and I talked, and I know it's over between us." She kept her lids low, knowing Natalia was watching her carefully. "He even told me he was in love with someone else."

Natalia slid in next to her. "He told you that?"

Kendra shrugged nonchalantly. "Yes, he did." She kept her dark lashes down over her eyes. "I'm okay with it."

"Wow!" Natalia cried, amazed. She was going to have a long talk with Jay when he returned. Then her brow bunched in confusion. "Are you feeling okay? I thought you wanted me to help you to get him back?"

Kendra carefully raised her eyes. "Do you think I still have a chance?"

Natalia squirmed in her seat. "I don't know," she said, feeling uncomfortable discussing Jay's personal life.

"Tell me, Nat. I can take it. Do you really believe he's in love?"

Remembering the way his face lit up when he talked about Honey, she didn't hesitate with her response. "Yes."

Kendra looked so pitiful. Natalia's eyes rested on her with deep affection and sympathy. She knew Kendra's pain; her own feelings since the breakup with Jacob were still too raw to discuss with anyone.

"Kendra, I love you both and only want to see everyone happy, but I can't lie to you. Jay loves Honey," she said, sorry to have to tell her, yet knowing it was necessary.

The sneaky bastard. Kendra tried to disguise her envy. "Honey . . . that's a pretty name. Is she good for him?"

Natalia didn't answer for a long minute, and Kendra thought maybe she could see through her ploy for information.

Finally, Natalia shrugged, palms up. "I haven't met her yet, but I'm hoping to drop by her salon and find out for myself."

"Salon?" Kendra echoed. *He's dating a hairdresser. Talk about uneducated.* "Which one?"

"Don't even go there," Natalia warned, realizing she'd said too much. Since her breakup, she'd found herself making a lot of careless mistakes.

Kendra batted her eyes innocently and said, "I was just askin'." It wasn't like she couldn't call every salon in town until she found where the hoochie worked. "I wonder how she feels about me being pregnant and all."

Natalia pondered the situation a moment. "I don't know if she knows."

"Hmmm, that's too bad." Feeling a sudden burst of energy, Kendra rose again. *I think it's time she fuckin' found out.*

Twelve

Honey could barely climb out of the bed on Saturday. Pain throbbed at her temples, while her body felt as if it had been run over by a truck. Moving on wobbly legs, she staggered to the bathroom where she swallowed three ibuprofens. Bringing the bottle and a full glass of water with her, she made it back under the covers, feeling disgusted that something so natural as walking had exhausted her. With a full schedule at the shop, she hated to cancel. But by nine she didn't feel any better, and called into the salon.

"Love Your Hair, Candy speaking."

She took a deep, shaky breath and said, "Candy, this is Honey."

"Girlfriend, you sound terrible!" Candy exclaimed in a high-pitched voice sprinkled with concern.

"I feel terrible. I think I caught the flu from Marcus." She paused to take a breath, then began again. "Can you reschedule my appointments for today and apologize for me?"

"No problem, boss. You know I got your back."

Even in pain, Honey couldn't resist a smile, knowing that the job would be done as professionally as if she'd handled it herself. "Oh, and, Candy?"

"Yeah?"

"Offer them all the standard ten dollars off on their return visit."

"I know, boss."

Honey was preparing to say good-bye when she heard Mercedes's voice come across the line. "What's wrong with you?"

"Sick. Tired." Honey gave a lifeless chuckle that ended with a groan. "Ready to sleep for the next week."

"Poor baby! Don't you worry, I've got everything under control. We might even be able to work in a couple of your appointments."

Honey sighed with relief. "I'd 'preciate it."

"Want me to bring you somethin' to eat later?" Mercedes offered. After all, it was the least she could do. Honey had always gone beyond the call of duty for her.

"That would be nice. Use the key, 'cause I might be asleep."

"I always do. Now get some rest."

Honey dropped the phone and rolled onto her back. Shivering, she pulled the blanket over her head and immediately fell asleep.

When Jay entered the salon later that afternoon, it was buzzing with activity. All six workstations were occupied, and the waiting area was just as full. *Soul Train* was showing on the tube up front, while MAJIC 105 was blaring from the speaker mounted in the work area.

Jay removed his gloves and shoved them in the pockets of his leather jacket, then moved past the front desk, saying, "Good morning, Candy."

"Hello, Jay," she said, returning his warm smile.

As he moved through the lobby, admiring gazes followed him across the work area.

"Hey, Jay," Mercedes called. He acknowledged her and the others with either a smile or a wave.

Strolling across the tiled floor, he tilted his head toward the back of the room. "Honey in her office?"

Sonya shook her head. "She ain't here."

Jay turned, his brow raised. "How come?"

"She's under the weather," Aisha answered.

While spraying a cloud of oil sheen, Mercedes nodded in confirmation. "She thinks she has the flu." Glancing down at her watch, she added, "I'm 'posed to take her somethin' to eat as soon as I can get away."

A light went off in Jay's head. *Opportunity.* "You look busy. Why don't I take her somethin' to eat?"

Mercedes bobbed her head. "Sure, go right ahead." *Who am I to stand in the way of true love?* Besides, her boss could use some dick in her life.

Jay found the spare key and let himself in. Standing in her living room, he was flooded with memories. The room was beige with a large wraparound cream Italian leather couch that Honey had complemented with burgundy pillows, drapes, and a matching area rug.

They had spent several evenings curled up on that couch together watching television, or sitting around her cherry-wood coffee table playing Scrabble. Honey was a sports fan; several sports video games were sitting beside the big-screen television. Jay's eyes traveled up to the second floor, where he knew Honey was lying in her room across a large iron-rod canopy bed.

He moved slowly up the stairs, trying to make as little noise as possible. Stopping at the first door to his left, he noticed she'd made an office of one of the spare rooms. Shelves lined one of the walls. A computer desk and file cabinets were to the left. A navy blue sleeper sofa was to the right, covered with a handmade afghan.

Curiosity got the better of him and he returned to the hallway. His gaze strayed toward the door in front of him. He moved the few feet, pushed the door open.

She hadn't changed a thing.

The room had once been a nursery for the previous owners. Everything was the same. The sky-blue room still had half-moons adorning the wall. She had added a twin bed where Marcus likely slept when he stayed over. There was a small white bookshelf in the corner filled with children's books and toys. A lump formed in his throat. Feeling like he was snooping, Jay returned to the hall, remembering his own child soon to be born.

Trying to be as quiet as possible, he slowly opened the door and entered her room. He found Honey lying on her stomach wrapped in a cocoon of blankets, sleeping soundly, her hair spread around the pillow. She appeared at peace. His gaze wandered to her face, where beads of sweat were apparent across her forehead. She looked so beautiful and innocent. Every time he saw her, the pull was tighter. He contemplated leaning over and kissing her forehead; he even considered joining her under the covers, but fought the urge and went back downstairs to wait for her to wake up.

*　*　*

With great effort, Honey dragged her eyelids open. Pain still throbbed behind them. Following a long stretch, she rolled over in the bed to see that her clock read three P.M. She couldn't believe she'd slept almost an entire day, yet still felt so damn tired she could have slept the rest of the week. Running the tip of her tongue around her mouth, she found her lips to be dry, chapped. She sat up and reached out a shaky hand for the glass of water and took a large gulp followed by three more ibuprofens. After returning the glass, she slid back onto the pillow and closed her eyes. She was hungry but too exhausted to walk down the flight of stairs to find something to eat. Hopefully, Mercedes would arrive soon. Honey sighed and pulled the covers over her shoulders again. It was then she felt someone watching her.

She opened one eye and rolled her head toward the door to find Jay standing in the doorway. He was here. At her home. *In my room.*

She bolted upright, and a wave of dizziness hit her. A small moan escaped her lips when she lowered her head back to the pillow. Pressing a fingertip to her temples, she asked, "How did you get in?" Her heart pounded in her chest.

Jay pushed away from the door and entered, carrying a tray of food. "I used your spare key. Mercedes was swamped, so I volunteered to bring you somethin' to eat."

Honey rolled to her left, suddenly self-conscious about her appearance. *Why the hell did he have to pick today of all days to come over?* She was certain her hair was fucked-up, and her face pale and haggard looking. Not to mention the bad taste in her mouth. She made a vain attempt to smooth down her hair, then opened her heavy eyelids again.

Jay walked around her bed and set the tray on top of the dresser. "I brought you some chicken soup and a grilled cheese sandwich." He leaned across her for another pillow. Ignoring the spark of electricity as he brushed against her, he gently stuffed it behind her head, then reached for the bowl of soup and took a seat beside her. He glanced into her sleepy eyes with a look of concern. "Here, eat," he ordered, holding the spoon in front of her mouth.

Honey hesitated, but the aroma caused her stomach to growl, and she opened her mouth and took a sip. "Mmmm, that's good." She opened her mouth again, eager for more. Jay brought the spoon to her lips several more times, and she dutifully obliged him.

Jay smirked, pleased that for once she wasn't giving a brotha a hard time. "I picked this up at a little shop on the way over." He fed her a few more spoons of soup. When Honey refused the sandwich he said, "Here, have some tea."

He handed her a thermos full of lemon tea. Just the way he knew she liked it.

She eagerly accepted the thermos and brought it to her parched lips.

While she drank, Jay studied her face. Even with the sleepy look in her lovely eyes, she was still a heartstopper. Her hair was in disarray, with several wisps draped across her forehead damp with perspiration.

Honey didn't miss his examination, and tried to keep her hand steady. Having him beside her, in her bed of all places, was jangling her insides.

"How are you feelin'?" he asked in a low voice.

She took another sip, then raised her eyes to meet

his concerned gaze. "Tired." Fatigue was settling in again, and she handed him the thermos. "And hot."

Jay reached over and touched a palm to her cheek, then forehead. "You're burnin' up." Sitting beside her, he stroked the damp curls away from her face as he noted the ibuprofen bottle and empty glass by her bed.

Honey swallowed. She never dreamed his hand would feel so gentle. Even in her sick state, her coochie vibrated with want, her heart pounded with need.

"Back under the covers now," he ordered, mistaking her reaction for a chill.

Honey didn't argue. She felt the heat from Jay's hand seeping into her skin before she lowered her head back onto the pillow.

Jay helped her settle beneath the cool sheet, then walked into the bathroom. Returning with a cold cloth, he placed it across her forehead.

Looking up at him, she smiled softly and muttered, "Thanks."

"Get some rest." He pulled the covers around her shoulders. "I'll be downstairs if you need me." He dropped his lips to her cheek, then strode out of the room, pulling the bedroom door closed behind him.

Sighing with exhaustion, Honey continued to smile. Already feverish as she was, his lips had only added fuel to the fire.

While Jay washed up the few dishes in the sink, he gazed out the window into the backyard at a playground set. Images of his own son swinging out there danced before his eyes. If he ever did win Honey's love, what was she going to say about the baby? Would she be willing to raise the child with him?

Shit, nigga, you ain't even hit it yet and already you thinking about marriage and raisin' babies together.

Annoyed at his thoughts, he went into the living room to catch the news. He sat down on the couch and propped his feet up on the end of the coffee table, making himself at home, then reached for the remote control. After switching to several channels, he found nothing of interest.

He could barely contain himself about being here again. It had been so long. Too long. Being with Honey was what he had wanted and needed all those months. He reached for a pillow at the end of the couch and placed it behind his head. It smelled of her. A fruity, intoxicating scent. The same scent that always made his dick stand to attention. He found himself looking up at the top of the stairs, wanting so badly to go back up, pull off his clothes, and lie beside her. Shit, he had just what the doctor ordered. Sex cured all things. But he knew Honey would kick his black ass if he did. He rubbed his palm several times across his bulging crotch while he contemplated his next move.

Mercedes removed the plastic cape from around the client's neck, then swiveled her around in front of the mirror. "All done."

"Thank you," the woman said, pleased at the transformation. "Thank you so much." She handed Mercedes a check and sashayed out the door as another woman entered.

Mercedes straightened up her work area and signaled for her next client to take a seat in the chair. While looking up, she noticed an attractive woman standing at the reception desk. Candy was on break, so she went to help the woman.

"May I help you?"

"Yes. I was responding to the sign for a nail technician." The woman pointed to the door where a HELP WANTED sign was posted.

"Are you licensed?"

"I wouldn't be here if I wasn't," she said, and smiled sweetly. Resting her arms on the counter palms down, she wiggled her fingers. "I even do my own nails."

Mercedes examined a pair of professional-looking hands and said, "Them are nice. Well, you need to speak wit' Honey, but she's out."

"That's fine, I can wait." She moved to take a seat.

"Then you'll be waitin' a long time, 'cause she's sick and won't be in today."

The woman stopped, and her grim expression indicated annoyance.

"If you'd like to go ahead and fill out an application, I can— "

"No. I'll come back." Then the woman turned and walked away.

It wasn't until she moved through the doorway that Mercedes noticed the woman was pregnant.

Her eyelids fluttered and opened, and Honey awakened to find the room dark. She rolled over to look at the clock and saw that it was well past seven. Had she really slept that long?

Swinging slender legs out of the bed, she rose. The movement caused her head to spin a little, and she stopped to lean against the door before trying again. After an initial wave of dizziness passed, Honey found she was able to stand unassisted. She retreated to the bathroom, needing to quickly empty her bladder, but stopped when she took a deep, rattling breath followed by a series of painful coughs. She was definitely sick.

Looking in the mirror, she found dried-up drool on the side of her mouth and eye boogers in the corners of both eyes. *Bitch, you gonna scare his fine ass away.* She stayed in the bathroom long enough to wash her face and brush her teeth. She attempted to run a comb through her hair and tied it back with a blue hair tie, then padded back to her room and took a seat on the end of her bed to catch her breath. The short walk had worn her ass out, stripping her of what little strength she had. She was tempted to climb back under the covers where it was warm, but then she remembered Jay was somewhere in her house. As quickly as she could manage, she slipped on her house shoes and reached for her flannel robe draped across a chair in the corner. Music led her to the family room, where a fire was roaring in the fireplace. The sounds of Luther Vandross came from her stereo at the same moment an aroma reached her nose, and she moved to find out what smelled so delicious.

She entered the kitchen just as Jay was removing a bowl from the microwave. Honey planted her hands on her waist and couldn't resist a smile.

"You look good doin' domestic duties."

Jay frowned when he saw her. As soon as he'd heard the toilet flush, he rose to warm her food with plans to carry her to the family room so she could lie in front of the fireplace. "What are you doin' up?" he scolded.

"I got hungry." She moved in closer and found that the delicious smell was beef vegetable soup. Her mouth watered.

"Take your sick behind on in there and have a seat in front of the fire. I'll be in shortly with your food."

Honey obeyed his command and curled up on her couch, staring at the cozy fire until Jay appeared. He came in carrying a TV tray, and placed it in front of her.

"Thanks." She gave him an appreciative smile.

Jay placed a hand on her forehead, and his brow furrowed. "You're still too warm." He reached for a throw cover on the end of the couch. Suddenly he became aware of her minty breath. Nothing tasted better than kissing a fresh mouth. He cleared his throat, trying to dissipate the desire brewing inside, and tucked the blanket around her feet. "Keep this on."

Honey smiled up at him and nodded in compliance. Her heart warmed having him here with her. So many nights she'd lain awake, with her vibrator between her legs, remembering moments like this. Jay's kindness and consideration mesmerized her. He was a wonderful man. She didn't need anyone to tell her that.

"While you were sleeping, your mother called."

"My mother?" Jay saw the confusion in her eyes. "I didn't hear the phone ring."

"That's 'cause I unplugged it," he said matter-of-factly.

She scowled at him. "You had no business doing that."

"Yes, I did. You needed your rest."

She stirred her soup for several seconds before asking, "What did my mother want?"

"To see how you were doin'. I reassured her that you were in good hands."

I just bet you did, she said silently.

"Does it bother you that I'm here?" Jay asked, thinking maybe he was stepping over his boundaries.

Honey raised her head to meet his eyes and shook her head. "No. I'm glad you're here." She smiled. "Thanks, Jay."

"What are friends for?" He returned to the kitchen, leaving her to eat her food in silence.

Friends. That's what they were. At least that was what she wanted to believe. But until she could let go of the past, she couldn't expect someone else to. She sighed and asked herself again, *Why me?* The more time she spent with Jay, the harder it was for her to keep her emotions in check. Her nipples were hard and her coochie moist, but she couldn't do shit about it.

Jay returned carrying a beer, and took a seat on the rug in front of the fire. "This is one thing I hate about my condo. No fireplace." He brought the can to his lips, but paused. "I've been thinking about buying a house of my own."

Surprise touched her pale face. "You, Mr. Playa-Playa, ready to take on the responsibility of your own home?"

Jay stared into the roaring flames. "Yeah," he answered. He knew part of it was his unborn child. The child would need room to grow.

She took a sip of the soup, then said, "Mmm, this is good. Where'd you get this?"

"I picked it up at the St. Louis Bread Factory."

She nodded. "They're one of my favorites."

Fixing her with a dazzling smile, he answered, "I know."

It grew quiet in the room, the only sound the crackling of the fire while they listened to another of Luther's ballads. She loved to hear the brother hum. Honey swallowed the last bite and leaned back on the couch with a sigh. "I'm stuffed."

Jay tapped the spot next to him on the floor. "Come sit by the fire. Bring your blanket with you."

Honey's heart began to race. If she got too close, she just might jump his bones. "I don't think so. I'm just fine lying up here."

They stared at each other for a long time before he said, "I insist." Jay set his beer down and pushed himself up from the floor. When he reached the couch, he scooped Honey up into his arms and set her down in front of the fire. He returned for the blanket and draped it around her shoulders.

The feel of his arms sent a thrill through her spine. Honey found herself speechless, unable to argue with him.

"Now, doesn't that feel better?"

Hell yeah, it felt better, but she didn't answer. When he carried her, her breasts had pressed against his body, and his male essence left her nipples tingling and her head spinning from the contact. Afraid to break the spell, she sat close to the flames with her knees drawn up before her.

Jay stared at the fire. He had to resist the impulse to kiss her. That was what had gotten him into trouble the last time. But it was no easy task. His emotions were screaming, out of control. Honey turned him on like no other woman had been able to. Her breath had been warm against his skin, and he had felt her breasts beneath her robe. It took all his willpower not to reach inside and fondle her nipples until they were as erect as his dick.

They both gazed into the depths of the crackling flames for a long while without talking before Jay spoke again.

"I'm thinkin' about stepping down from the investigative side of my business for a while and concentrating solely on security."

She turned to him, surprised. "Why? I thought you loved goin' undercover."

Staring into the fire, he answered, "I do. It wasn't until a bullet whizzed by my fuckin' head that I decided to take a closer look at my life. Now I find myself askin', what do I have to show for all the years I poured into the field? And my answer always comes up, not a damn thing."

"Now, you know that ain't true!"

He pressed his lips together thoughtfully. It was the perfect opportunity to tell her about Kendra and the baby, yet he still wasn't ready to talk about that shit. So instead, he turned to her and said, "Yeah, it is. I've been livin' life one day at a time for years, never thinkin' about tomorrow, only living for the moment. But all that's about to change. There are so many things I haven't done yet. And as long as I continue to live on the edge, I may never have a chance to do them."

Honey nodded in understanding. "I feel like that at times. There are a lot of things that I still want to do, like mountain climbin', hang glidin', maybe even jump out of a plane wearing a parachute."

Gazing at her beautiful face in the firelight, he gave her a sheepish grin. "That's not the shit I had in mind, but those are interesting ideas."

"Then tell me what you *are* referring to," she said, and smirked.

"Family."

His words knocked the wind out of her lungs. With a frown, she turned and stared into the fire again.

Jay didn't miss the sudden change in her demeanor. Family and marriage bothered her. But why? He sighed. What did he have to do to get her ass to trust him?

Pulling away from his puzzling thoughts, he noticed that several strands of her hair had worked loose from her ponytail, perspiration beaded her forehead again, and color heated her cheeks. Jay rose, taking Honey's hands, then swung her weightlessly into his arms again. "Maybe sittin' in front of the fire wasn't such a good idea. You look flushed."

Honey clung to his shoulder and stared up into his handsome face as he lowered her onto the couch.

"While you were asleep, I rented a DVD for us to watch."

Coochie clenching, she swallowed for control. "Which one?"

"*Tombstone*."

She smiled; he'd remembered it was her favorite western.

"Yeah, I remembered," he said, and when the passion flared in the depths of Jay's eyes, Honey trembled and cast her eyes away. She didn't dare look up again, afraid that he might see she had an itch that needed to be scratched. And she wasn't thinking about her back.

He helped her settle back on the couch and turned off the stereo. After putting the DVD on, he took a seat next to her and instructed her to lean against him. She pressed her back against his chest and stretched her legs across the couch. Jay took a deep breath, trying to keep his dick from moving. Drawing her closer to him, he wrapped his arms around her.

"How do you feel?" he asked in a gentle voice.

How the fuck you think I feel? "Fine."

While he mopped her forehead, Honey found herself relaxing against his shoulder, feeling his warmth and strength. It was almost like old times.

For the rest of the evening they were quiet as they both pretended to be engrossed in the movie when in fact they were thinking about each other.

She'd fallen asleep long before he had. Jay couldn't bear to wake her, or part from her embrace. Sometime during the movie, Honey had drifted, and was now lying curled against him, her head resting against his chest and an arm draped around him as if it were the most natural thing in the world. She was sweating through the fever; her body heat curled around him like an electric blanket.

A sigh escaped his lips as he listened to her steady breath and felt the gentle rise and fall of her chest. Jay closed his eyes, trying to fight back the image of her itty-bitty breasts and her chocolate nipples. One fit perfectly in the palm of his hand. He remembered they had been on this very couch. He was rubbing, licking, and sucking, only minutes away from fucking when Honey froze up and stopped him. Damn, his dick grew hard just thinking about it. If she would just give him a chance, she damn sho wouldn't be disappointed.

Dropping an arm to her shoulder, Jay eased her head, which had fallen slightly, back onto his chest.

He wanted to make her his woman, his wife. He wanted to protect her. To make her feel safe. To reassure her that he'd never do anything to harm her like he was certain some other mothafucka had done.

But how?

Thirteen

Honey woke the next morning to find herself on the couch with a pillow beneath her head and a blanket covering her. The aroma of fresh coffee led her to the kitchen, where she found Jay standing at the stove.

When he heard her house shoes slide across the linoleum, Jay glanced over his shoulder. "Good mornin', sleepyhead. Breakfast will be ready in a minute."

Lips curved into a sleepy smile, Honey lowered herself into a chair and felt a rush of delight. Jay didn't know the first thing about cooking, yet she was flattered he was making an effort for her.

Cupping her face with her hands, she leaned against the table and watched him with admiration. He had taken a shower; his hair was damp, and he was bare from the waist up. The muscles in his back flexed when he moved to the refrigerator on bare feet, looking right at home.

"You need some help?" she offered.

"No. I have everything under control," he answered

with a quick smile, then resumed chopping onions and peppers on a cutting board.

Honey grinned as a warm feeling flowed through her body and down between her thighs. Last night she had awakened briefly to find herself tucked snugly in his arms. Though startled, she couldn't will herself to move. For the rest of the night, she'd lain there, tingling with excitement. When she had arisen this morning alone, she felt a sense of loss.

"For you, madam." Jay padded to her, and with a spatula, lowered a beautifully browned ham and cheese omelet onto a plate.

Honey sucked in her breath as her eyes drifted down the length of his chest. Staring at his bare, taut skin, she licked her lips. Her awed gaze followed the trail of silky hair that spread over his sculptured pecs, then narrowed and plunged down a muscular abdomen, only to disappear below his belt. *Damn, that motha-fucka looks good*.

Dropping her eyes to the plate, she pretended not to be affected. "It looks great."

Jay took a seat opposite her and reached for his own plate.

Honey raised the fork to her mouth and was delighted by the savory taste. "Mmm, this is good. When did you learn to cook? The Jay I remember couldn't even boil water." He had always been too busy to worry about something as time-consuming as cooking.

He chuckled. "I took cooking lessons while doing surveillance on a thief who owned a restaurant."

Shaking her head, she mumbled, "Forget I asked."

They ate in silence for several minutes until Honey found Jay watching her. "What?"

The corner of his mouth twitched. "How you feelin' this morning?"

She couldn't resist a grin. "Much better." She reached for the pitcher of orange juice and poured some into her glass. "I believe my fever has broken."

He laid his hand across her forehead. Her skin felt cooler to the touch. "Good. You look better, but no point in rushing it."

"Rushin' what? The salon is closed until Tuesday. I have two days to lie around and maybe read a couple of magazines I've never gotten around to finishing."

"How about after you get back in bed, we play a game of Scrabble before I leave?"

"Sure." She managed to keep her disappointment from showing; however, it churned through her mind. She didn't want him to leave.

Jay gave her a sidelong glance. He didn't want to leave either, but he also didn't want to wear out his welcome. He wanted a repeat of last night. But the ball was now in her court. If Honey wanted him to stay, she would have to ask him herself. However, if she did she had better be prepared for a little extra TLC.

After breakfast, Honey excused herself and went upstairs to take a shower. Jay volunteered to clean up the kitchen. He had just loaded the dishwasher when the doorbell rang. He went to answer it and was greeted by Rashad.

Rashad looked at Jay for several seconds, not the least bit surprised to find him there. While the two had interacted at the salon, Rashad had had a strong suspicion something was going on between Jay and his sister. What he couldn't understand was, if she was fucking this cat why did she have him hook her up with his boy?

"Hey, what's up?"

Jay moved aside. "We just finished breakfast."

Rashad stepped into the room and looked toward the top of the staircase.

"She's in the shower," Jay answered, reading his thoughts.

At that moment, Honey came downstairs in a blue sweat suit. "Rashad, what are you doing here?" she asked, surprised to see her brother.

"Mom wanted to check on you." He gave her a long look. His sister couldn't be too sick if she had this pretty-ass nigga over. "She's in the car talkin' to Tequila on the phone."

Honey ran a hand through her damp hair and smiled. "Y'all didn't have to come over. I'm fine."

Jay stepped in and draped an arm around her waist. "No, she's not fine. Your sister still has a low-grade fever and refuses to get back in bed."

Rashad nodded. "She's always been stubborn."

"I know."

"I see." Rashad chuckled inwardly. Maybe this cat was just what his sister needed.

Jay's cell phone rang, and he excused himself and moved into the kitchen.

"Chad, what's up?"

"Breakthrough, man. We found a Dr. J.W. Price practicing right outside of Leavenworth, Kansas."

"Are you sure it's Jhamil?"

"Positive. I called and checked myself. It's also the same address the insurance company is scheduled to mail the check to."

Jay was silent.

"Who you want to send?"

If their suspicions were correct, things could turn

ugly when they confronted the dead man's brother. Jay knew that, as the head of the agency, he had to let the physical risk fall on him. With a silent curse, Jay answered, "Have Dory book me on a flight leaving tomorrow."

Jay returned to the living room to find Rashad missing; however, a lovely silver-haired woman was sitting on the couch. Aside from the tiny lines around her eyes, her face was virtually wrinkle-free.

Honey did the introductions. "Mom, this is my friend Jay."

Jay moved toward her. "We spoke on the phone. It's so nice to meet you."

"You too." Helen rose, extended her arms, and hugged him tight. Jay returned the embrace. When they pulled apart, she grasped his hand. "Thanks for taking care of my baby." Her eyes moved leisurely across his face.

"Your baby is hardheaded."

Helen squeezed his hand with affection while assessing the tall man before her. His voice hadn't lied. He was as handsome and kind as he had sounded over the phone. She gave an amused chuckle. "Yes, she always was." Still holding his hand, she returned to her seat on the couch. Jay sat beside her.

"So tell me, how'd you meet my daughter?"

Honey jumped in. "Terraine is Jay's brother."

Helen's eyes grew large. "Oh, your brother is a wonderful young man. Sasha's like a daughter to me. Are you anything like your brother?"

Honey's throat became dry. She knew where this conversation was going.

Jay looked down at the petite smiling woman. "I'd like to think we're a lot alike."

"Good," she said, her eyes mirroring approval, and they shared a knowing smile. What Honey didn't know was that they had shared a conversation the night before. Jay had instantly felt comfortable talking to Helen, as if she were his own mother.

Rashad came through the door carrying a large basket, tracking snow on the carpet. From the look on his sister's face, he realized his mistake. "My bad." He went back to wipe his feet on the mat.

Helen rose and took the basket from him. "I decided to cancel Sunday dinner since Shaquil's in Kansas City this weekend and you're sick. So I brought over some leftovers I froze."

"You didn't have to do that, Mom."

"Yes, I did. You have this handsome man over here taking care of you. We can't let him starve."

This is exactly why I have never invited him to dinner. She had known her family would take an instant liking to him.

The four sat in the living room and talked until it was close to lunchtime. Then Helen went into the kitchen to warm up the food. Honey didn't have much of an appetite, but she sat at the table while the others ate. She found herself watching Jay as he interacted with her family. Her coochie hot and moist, she had to squeeze her legs tightly together.

Jay looked at her in time to see her grace him with a dreamy, trusting smile. The glazed look in her eyes caused his mouth to drop open. *Is she thinkin' what I think she's fuckin' thinkin'?*

Helen watched them, her eyes shimmering with happiness. Jay had eyes for no one but her daughter. He was sitting close to her with his hand possessively resting over hers; she had also seen the look in Honey's eyes, and knew Jay was indeed the one. "Rashad, I think it's time for us to go." She rose and looked to her left. "Jay, I hope to see you at dinner next Sunday."

Jay also rose. "I'll be there." Taking her hands in his, he leaned over to kiss her smooth cheek. As he looked over his shoulder, his gaze collided with Honey's, and he saw that soft, familiar look in her eyes again. As soon as the two left, it was on and poppin'!

Together they stood at the window and watched them pull away. Jay clasped her hand moving her back to the couch. "I hope you don't feel pressured to invite me."

She shook her head, a smile on her lips. "I'd love to have you join us for dinner."

"Good. Now back to bed." He swept her up into his arms and carried her up to her room, their mouths only inches apart.

He didn't have to wait long for her to make the first move. Honey's hand came up and curled around the back of his neck, tugging him closer. Lowering her onto the bed, he leaned down beside her with her hot breath stroking his chin. She tilted her head back against the pillow and raised her lips to meet his in a fierce kiss. He used his tongue to open her mouth farther. Oh, it felt so good kissing her! He moved to kiss her neck and a moan escaped her lips. However, when his long fingers slid underneath her sweatshirt, she pushed against him and ended the kiss.

"Wait a damn minute!" she whispered, her breath coming out in short gasps. With her eyes closed, she had seen Walter lying on top of her with a devilish grin on his face. The image had scared the shit out of her. "N-not yet."

"Aw'ight," Jay whispered, his voice hoarse. Taking a

moment to catch his breath, he nodded, then held her close to him. "I would never force you to do anything you don't want to do."

And she knew he meant it.

After a long silence, she removed her arms from his neck and gazed up at him. She saw desire mirroring her own in his eyes. Jay was different. He would understand. Something told her he would be gentle and patient and anything else she needed to help overcome her fear of sexual intercourse. Fuckin' a vibrator she could deal with, fuckin' a man she wasn't sure if she was ready to explore.

She sat up in the bed beside him. "You want to know why I froze up that night and asked you to leave?" she finally managed to say.

"Only if you're ready to tell me."

"I'm not a virgin." Honey paused, then said, "I was raped."

"What?" Disbelief filled his face. He witnessed her pained expression. "How . . . When . . ." He broke off, unsure what to say, and pulled her close to him, resting her head on his chest.

Despite her best intentions, her eyes grew shiny with tears, and she reached up to wipe them away. "It happened during high school. I was on a date with this fool I really thought liked me. . . ."

As she poured out her story to him, Jay listened without interruption except for an occasional exasperated sigh. Someone had violated his boo. If he could have found Walter, he would have capped a bullet in his ass. He felt some consolation that Shaquil had beat his ass. God! All this time he'd been thinking about his own ego, how she kept rejecting a nigga and how hard his dick was, while all along she was hurting and needed someone to listen. To understand. He had been a selfish bastard. Her wounds were far deeper than he had fuckin' imagined.

When she finished, Jay pushed slightly away and gazed into her eyes. "Honey, baby, I'm so sorry."

She heard the sympathy in his voice. What she didn't want was his pity . . . which was why she'd decided not to tell him she was unable to have children. That might be more than either of them could bear.

Taking her hand, he said gently, "I'm glad you finally told me."

"Thanks for listenin'." She flashed him a smile designed to eliminate any pity he might feel.

"I'll never pressure you. When you're ready, you let me know." He had been without pussy this long, what difference would a little bit longer make? Drawing her close again, he planted small kisses on the top of her head.

Tears of happiness were in the corner of her eyes, but she didn't wipe them away. His words soothed the fear that lay just behind her heart. She was glad he understood and didn't judge her. But she should have known all along that Jay would be patient with her. "I want to," she told him. "I—I'm just so damn scared."

"I'll wait as long as it takes. When you're ready for me to make love to you, you let me know. I promise when I do, I'll take it slow. I want you to feel comfortable." He held her for the longest time after that. Finally, he said, "I hate to bring this up now, but I need to leave town for a couple of days, but when I return I want us to spend some real time together."

"I'd like that." His being away would give her a chance to figure out the 180-degree change in their relationship.

Jay stayed long enough to play a round of Scrabble.

When he left, she climbed back into bed. Honey found herself smiling lazily as she lay there thinking about what Jay had said. He was going to be patient. She silently prayed as her eyelids drooped closed. The next time he attempted to make love to her, she wanted to be ready mentally as well as physically.

After hanging up the phone, Kendra rolled onto her side and pulled herself into a sitting position on the bed. Her big-ass stomach itched. Raising her gown, she reached for a bottle of cocoa butter and rubbed the lotion generously across her abdomen. Shit, if she had known pregnancy could cause stretch marks, she never would have allowed herself to get pregnant. Her doctor assured her the generous use of lanolin or cocoa butter would help, but that was no guarantee.

Jay had called to inform her he would be out of town for at least a week. He reassured her that if she needed anything she could call his office and they'd get in touch with him immediately. Kendra was fuckin' insulted that he hadn't even bothered to come by. But she already knew where he had been. She had driven by that bitch's house last night and found his car still there this morning.

It was apparent Jay had changed his mind about her and the baby. He had kicked her black ass to the curb. Asking her to hold off on seeing a lawyer was his way of trying to con her into keeping the baby. *You got life fucked-up!* She was through playing games with his mothafuckin' ass.

Now it was time to get even.

Fourteen

"It's not my fault," Honey chanted as she exited her therapist's office.

Today she had opened up and discussed her relationship. When her therapist asked her if she was ready for intimacy, without hesitation she had answered yes. She was no longer going to be a victim. The rape wasn't her fault. She finally realized that it was time to let go of the past and move forward with her life. She deserved happiness. She was going to be a survivor.

Pulling away from the clinic, she stared out at the clear sky. The gorgeous day marked the beginning of March, and it was coming in as a lamb. Honey took a deep breath. Jay was willing to take things as slow as she needed. She giggled, feeling silly. *It might not be as long as he thinks.*

She was ready to be loved. It was time to put her vibrator away.

Relief rushed though Honey, its force making her light-headed. She had lived with the memories and the fact that she would never have children for so long that she feared she'd never be able to love. But Jay changed all that shit. When the time was right, he would understand. He had to.

He had been gone three days. They spoke on the phone each night. Last night when Jay asked her how she had been able to satisfy her sexual urges, she'd admitted she used a vibrator. Jay then instructed her to take it out of her nightstand.

"Now put the phone on speaker."

She did as she was told, then slipped off her gown and panties and slid under the covers.

"Rub your pussy for me, boo."

Lying on her back, she spread her legs wide as she stroked her clit with one hand and pinched her nipple with the other.

"You like that?"

"Ohhh, hell yeahhh!" she moaned.

"Now stick your finger inside your pussy and taste it."

She stuck her fingers inside her wet welcoming walls, then brought her hand to her lips.

"What's it taste like, boo?"

"Wet pussy."

"Aahh, yesss! That's some good shit!"

"Uh-huh," she moaned as she reached down again and probed deeper inside.

"Now take my dick and put it inside your wet pussy."

She reached for her vibrator and inserted it in her wet hole.

"Ohhh, yeahhh, now I'm strokin' you with my big dick. Movin' in and out of your pussy again and again just the way you like it."

"Oh, yesss!" As he chanted in her ear, she followed

his lead, pretending he was there inside her. She slowly slid the instrument in and out of her coochie again and again. Her body arched with shock and pleasure. As Jay continued to talk shit she plunged deeper, riding that vibrator as if it were a dick.

"Oh yeah, baby. You got some good-ass pussy. Damn, that shit is good. How you likin' this dick?"

"I'm lovin' it. Oh yeah."

"You got me stroking my meat just imagining being in that phat pussy. Keep workin' it, baby. Don't stop! I want us to come together."

"Aw'ight." She moved it faster and harder, feeling the rhythmic contractions of her inner muscles gripping the vibrator. Moans of pleasure escaped her lips when spasms coursed through her body.

"I'm getting ready to come, baby. Damn, that pussy is good. Come with me, baby."

"Oooh . . . weeee . . . I'm comin' too, baby!" It wasn't long before she erupted in a flow of spasms.

"Aaahhh . . . yesss!" he hissed.

They both lay there for the longest, breathing heavily over the speaker.

"Boo?"

"Yeah?" she whispered, still out of breath.

"That's what it's gonna be like with us, baby. It's gonna be good. It's gonna be so damn good."

"Uh-huh." It wasn't long after that that she drifted off to sleep with the vibrator still firmly in place.

When she arrived at the salon, she found it quiet for a Wednesday morning. The lobby was empty, and only three workstations were occupied.

Candy was returning to her desk carrying a cup of

coffee. "Hey, boss lady," she greeted. "A lady came by to talk to you about the nail tech position."

While hanging up her coat, Honey glanced over at her receptionist settling back in her chair. "Oh, good." She wanted to have her new staff on board and trained before the grand opening of the new addition. "Did she fill out an application?"

Shaking her braids, Candy answered, "Shit, I tried, but she said she'd wait until she had a chance to talk to you first."

Mercedes came out of the restroom. Catching tidbits of the conversation, she arched a sweeping eyebrow and asked, "Was she pregnant?"

Candy swung around in her chair. "Yeah, as a matter of fact she was."

Resting a hand on her hip, she nodded knowingly at Honey. "She's come by several times. I've tried to get sista girl to fill out an app, but she refused." She paused, her eyes narrowing. "She seemed pissed off you're never here."

Honey shrugged and turned in the direction of her office. "Well, if she'd fill out an application, I could call her and schedule an interview."

It was one minute after two when Jay entered his condo. Tossing his keys on the counter, he removed his jacket and draped it across the couch.

It had been a long week. He had arrived in Kansas City to find something that was only in the fuckin' movies. Dr. J.W. Price had risen from the dead. Only he died, was reborn, then died again.

According to the police, Jhamil Wayne and James William Price had been identical in every aspect, from their features to their dreams of someday becoming a dentist like their deceased father. Only James had what it took, while Jhamil didn't; James was an excellent student, but Jhamil's college grades were far too poor to gain entrance into dental school. While on a boat trip together, James drowned. The drowning was accidental, but Jhamil saw it as his lucky break; he assumed his brother's identity and attended dental school. In spite of his poor college grades, he was able to learn the hands-on dental techniques well enough to get by. Passing the academic courses was easier; by manipulating a fellow student who had fallen in love with him, he was able to pass the academic requirements, if just barely.

After graduation, he built a practice as Dr. James W. Price. When substantial gambling debts began to weigh him down he took out an insurance policy, leaving the money to Jhamil Price—his real name. By switching dental records with a patient named Timothy Madden, who was also a friend, he put his plan into action.

He invited Timothy to meet him in Columbia, Missouri, for a tailgating party at Mizzou, and then the two traveled to Boonville to a casino boat. James made sure he got Timothy drunk enough to pass out cold. Then he put his car in gear, and with a push, it went over the cliff. Dental records identified the body as Dr. James Price. He moved to Leavenworth and rebuilt his practice as Dr. J.W. Price, then waited a year to file a claim on the insurance policy.

Jay found not only J.W. but another wife, a newborn son, and a mother suffering from Alzheimer's, who didn't care which son he was as long as someone was alive. J.W. Price tried to deny ever knowing Jocelyn, but after the insurance company sent one of their investigators down and the police became involved, Jhamil, a.k.a. J.W. and James, took his own life, again.

Jocelyn had flown down with Chad to identify the body. Within a few hours, Jay saw the beautiful woman change. She had been betrayed. He finally realized what women meant when they said men make them the way they are.

Moving to his room, Jay removed his clothes, then fell facedown onto the bed. Sleep, that's what he needed. Once he woke up, he was going to spend the entire weekend showing Honey how much she truly meant to him.

He knew exactly what he wanted. He wanted her to love him. He wanted her to marry him and bear him several gray-eyed children. He wanted to spend the rest of his life making her happy.

It was time for Honey to realize she wanted the same, 'cause phone sex was no longer enough.

My husband is dead . . . again.

Jocelyn Price stared out the window as the plane prepared to land at St. Louis's Lambert Airport. *I'm not gonna cry again*, she told herself. She'd cried enough the first time she buried the bastard. Or, the man she'd always thought was James Price.

As the St. Louis Arch came into view, she remembered the first time James had taken her there. It had been on their first date. It was also the place he had proposed several years later.

Had she really been that fuckin' naïve? She had thought their marriage was ideal. James was a dentist while she was a pediatrician. Her friends all envied her relationship, and she thought she was the luckiest woman in the world. The only thing missing was children, but James had insisted that they wait until their practices were under way, and she had agreed.

Then a car crash brought her blissful world to a screeching halt. Or so she thought.

For several months, she lay awake at night, wishing they'd had a child so she would still have a part of him.

Jocelyn had tried to hold it together, and buried the man and a big chunk of her life. It had taken a year before she was able to pull her shit together. Her laughter had just recently returned and the tears lessened until finally she had felt ready to date again.

Then she attended a seminar in Kansas City, and it all came crashing back when she saw that sorry mothafucka crossing the street.

At first she'd thought she was losing her damn mind, but she knew her husband's strut, the way he tilted his head slightly to the left, his long neck, the way he always embedded his right hand in the pocket of his pants when he walked, the style of his tailor-made suits. Everybody had thought she was crazy, but in her heart, she knew she was right.

I wish I had been wrong.

But a deep emotional attachment for the man she believed had been her soul mate forbade her letting go. All she could think about was that maybe she had buried somebody else, and her husband was still alive . . . Maybe he had amnesia.

So she had hired a private investigator.

"Are you okay?"

She flinched at the sound of Chad's voice, then, without glancing at the man sitting in the seat beside her, she nodded and looked out the window again.

Jocelyn had lied. She would never be all right, ever again. She had given her all to one man, giving him her heart and soul. In turn, the man had made her look like a damn fool. He had crushed her heart and killed her spirit. He had taken something from her that would take years, if ever, for her to get back. Trust.

Chad watched Jocelyn out of the corner of his eye as she tried to come to terms with the last twenty-four hours. He couldn't begin to imagine what she was going through as she tried to accept the fact that the man she thought she knew, she'd never really known at all—and the man she thought she had buried last year had only died yesterday.

Chad had flown down with Jocelyn so that she could identify the body, and had watched the beautiful woman crumble right before his eyes. He wouldn't wish that kind of bullshit on anyone.

When the plane taxied in and pulled up to the terminal, Chad unfastened his seat belt and glanced over at Jocelyn again. "We're here."

She looked over at him with a dazed look, then blinked until her eyes cleared. She forced a smile and said, "Yes . . . yes, I guess we are." Unfastening her seat belt, she reached for the small overnight bag underneath the seat in front of her.

As he waited for the passengers in front of them to begin exiting the plane, Chad folded his hands in his lap. "Would you like to go somewhere and talk? I know a great restaurant in North County."

Jocelyn rolled her eyes. "No. I have a million things to do."

"Maybe another time?"

"Maybe not," she retorted, then paused, realizing that she was being rude. "I'm sorry. I really appreciate everything you and Jay have done for me, but right now, the best thing for me is to be alone."

He nodded in understanding. When their turn came to rise and depart the plane, they entered the terminal and went their separate ways.

Chad moved out to the parking garage, his ego bruised, but not beaten. He would give Jocelyn the time she needed to heal, then he'd come knocking at her door.

No one had ever turned him down before. That in itself made Dr. Price a challenge he couldn't pass up.

That afternoon Honey hung out with Marcus, giving his parents a chance to spend some time alone. She and her nephew had a wonderful time. They went downtown and visited the City Museum, an old warehouse that had been converted to house a collection of unusual artifacts. It also had a train and a man-made cave for the kids to explore. Honey found herself climbing through the tunnels alongside him. Afterward they went to McDonald's and pigged out on cheeseburgers, fries, and hot fudge sundaes. They returned to her house around dinnertime after stopping to rent some of Marcus's favorite movies. She checked her answering machine and saw that Jay had called several times. Her heart throbbed at the realization he was back. While boiling water for hot chocolate, she returned the call. He answered on the first ring.

"Hey, boo. I was beginning to think you were avoiding me," he teased.

She smiled at hearing the laughter in his voice. "No, I spent the day hangin' out with Marcus. He's spendin' the night."

"Mind if I come over and join you two?"

"I'd love the company." Just the thought of being in the same room with his fine ass made her nipples stand straight up. "I'm sure Marcus would be happy to see you."

"And what about you?"

She giggled, feeling like a breathless girl of eighteen. "Me too."

"I have a stop to make, but I'll be over right after."

Not seeing him for several days had elicited an emotional attachment she'd never thought she would experience. She knew the intimacy they'd had several times over the phone had a lot to do with it. "I can't wait."

Her words were magic to his ears. "Neither can I."

Kendra smiled weakly at the couple sitting across the table. The woman squeezed her husband's hand while gazing at Kendra with growing appreciation. "You are a dream come true," she said.

Kendra nodded, eyes wide with false innocence. "I'm just glad that I can help you both. My baby's daddy abandoned me as soon as he found out I was pregnant." She paused. Under lowered lashes, she found the husband sizing her up with dark, observant eyes. She sagged back against the bench, her hand resting on her abdomen. "There's no way I can raise a child alone."

The lady's eyes immediately filled with sympathy. "How terrible," she said, then closed her hand over Kendra's and squeezed it gently. "We've been trying for years to have a baby, and had given up hope." She turned to her husband, who leaned down to kiss her on the cheek.

Kendra wanted to throw up. They were the homeliest couple she had ever met. No wonder their ugly asses couldn't have children. The woman's infertility was a blessing in disguise!

Pulling her hand free, Kendra laced her fingertips on top of the table. "Let's get down to business."

"Yes, of course." The woman reached into a Coach purse and removed an envelope. "We're prepared to pay you the agreed-upon balance on delivery."

Kendra took the envelope from her and opened it, finding both a sizeable deposit and a contract inside. She quickly glanced over the fine print.

The woman's lips twitched nervously. "Our lawyer prepared all of the forms, but if there's a problem with the contract, we—"

"No," Kendra said with an impatient wave of the hand, sick of hearing the woman's whiny voice. "Everything looks just fine."

The woman beamed at her husband. To finally be parents, fifty thousand dollars was chump change.

Honey retrieved a bag of popcorn from the microwave and entered the living room, where Marcus was lying on the floor engrossed in a new *Rugrats* movie. She took a seat on the floor beside him and placed the bag of popcorn between them.

The movie had just ended and they were preparing to watch another when a knock came at the door.

Honey anxiously looked through the peephole, then threw open the door. Marcus ran up to Jay and embraced him around the waist. "I'm glad to see you again, Uncle Jay."

Jay's and Honey's eyes met and they both raised a brow, surprised by Marcus's choice of words, but neither bothered to correct him.

Honey looked down at the box in his hand. "What you got there?"

"A tent and three sleeping bags." His eyes twinkled with mischief. "I thought maybe we could camp in your living room."

"Oh boy!" Marcus shouted, and began jumping up and down.

As Jay reached down for the bundles, Honey watched the muscles flex in his powerful legs. She felt a warm shiver travel straight through her as she remembered making love on the phone last night. As she took in his appearance—his cap turned backward on his head and sweatshirt spread tauntingly across his massive chest—she ached from both need and longing. Even in a pair of worn jeans, he was sexy. She licked her lips as she envisioned him lowering his pants, followed by his boxers, and standing in front of her giving her a bird's-eye view of his colossal dick. She had never seen it but she had felt it through his pants and knew for certain her boo was blessed.

While Marcus and Jay set up the tent, Honey went in search of hot dogs and marshmallows, shaking with anticipation of the evening.

While she was piercing the hot dogs, Jay came behind her and wrapped his hands around her waist.

"You're an expert," he said. "Where did you find the sticks?"

"They're for makin' kabobs."

"Good idea." He dropped his head forward and inhaled deeply of her scent, then swung her in the circle of his arms until she faced him. "I've missed you."

"So have I." Staring up at him, she saw desire that mirrored her own.

He quickly devoured her lips with a kiss, quick but not lacking in intensity. Then he raised his leg and rubbed his knee against her coochie until she was dripping wet. When Honey moaned, he reluctantly pulled away. "We'll finish this later," he promised before exiting the room.

After ghost stories in front of the fireplace, Marcus finally dozed off, and Honey escaped into the kitchen to make two cups of hot chocolate. Reaching into the cabinet, she removed two mugs and grabbed the last of the marshmallows, then turned on the teakettle. True to his word, Jay followed her into the room, and she felt his presence behind her as his hands clasped around her waist. She felt the sensation of his lips against the back of her neck and swallowed, trying to stand perfectly still, but his touch left her unbalanced and trembling. His tongue traveled across to her earlobe, then moved around to the side of her mouth.

He swung her around and she allowed her body to fall limply against his chest. When he lowered his head, she felt the warmth of his mouth against her. She wrapped her arms instinctively around his waist and arched against him, her nipples pushing against the cloth that separated them, feeling the heat of his flesh through his shirt. Her mouth opened beneath his, and Jay swept his tongue inside. Their tongues met and Honey moaned softly. The intensity rushed up from her toes, bringing heat and overwhelming sensation. Jay slipped his hand under her blouse and found her heart hammering violently against her chest.

He pulled back. "You're shaking," he whispered against her right earlobe, sending Honey's heart into a tailspin. "I'm sorry. I didn't mean to frighten you. I just can't seem to help myself when I'm around you."

She shook her head and said, teeth chattering, "You didn't frighten me. It's the way my body responds to you that frightens me." No . . . she wasn't afraid of him; her body was begging him to make love to her.

A delightful shiver of want ran through her. Her skin was tingling. She wanted him, and was amazed at how much. Jay had her like putty in his hands, and she loved it.

Jay had given her the one thing she'd wanted all week. A kiss. One that left her gasping, panting, and shuddering. Oh, she wasn't afraid, not anymore. Jay had brought untried senses to life.

"We've got plenty of time," he said, his voice teasing. "The last thing I need when we finally make love is a four-year-old watching us. Come, let's sit in front of the fire."

She sat cross-legged in front of the fireplace and patted the spot next to her. Jay lowered himself and sat close enough for their legs to touch. They were quiet for several moments, enjoying the intimate feeling circulating around the room.

"I love you, boo," he said, breaking the silence. When he saw her surprised look, he asked, "Didn't you know?"

"How was I supposed to know if you never told me? I'm not a mind-fuckin'-reader." She faked a frown, but was in fact bubbling over with joy. Jay loved her. Honey gazed at him, saw the love pouring from his cocoa eyes, and knew he meant it.

"I fell in love with you the first time I saw you," he said. "I've missed you like crazy these past several months, but I was too stubborn and stupid to admit it."

Jay pulled her close, and she relaxed against his shoulder as he kissed the top of her head and nuzzled against her. "I want to share my life with you. When you're ready, I want to marry you and start a family."

Why the hell did he have to say that? When she turned her head to face him, her smile disappeared as she realized she hadn't told him the rest of her secret. The part that mattered the most.

Seeing the change in her expression, Jay realized that he'd said too much. *Shit, Andrews, you're scaring the woman.* Pulling her close, he resolved not to bring it up again.

Long after Jay was sound asleep in his sleeping bag, Honey lay wide-awake, staring at the paper moon and stars Jay and Marcus had taped to the ceiling. She tried to smile, but tears spilled from her eyes. Her confidence of only a short time before had evaporated. *This shit is fuckin' unbelievable.* She'd finally fallen in love with a man that loved her back, yet she couldn't give him what someone else had taken away.

Fifteen

Driving home from her mother's house, Honey looked over at Jay and smiled. Dinner had been everything she thought it would be.

Jay had met the rest of her family and, as she'd expected, won them all over. For the first time ever she was at a loss for words. By the end of the meal, the two were curled up on the couch together with her head resting on his shoulder, and she'd ignored her family's grins and her brother's smart-ass wisecracks. Perhaps she should have been embarrassed, but she wasn't.

They pulled into her driveway, then Jay walked her to the door. He looked down into her eyes glistening in the moonlight and felt desire spiral through his body. When he leaned over and kissed her he savored the taste; even though he pulled away, he wanted more.

Honey reached into her pocket for her key and fumbled with the lock. Jay was standing so close. "Would you like to come in?"

As much as he wanted to, he knew he couldn't. "I

don't think that would be a good idea. As hard as my dick is, I might not be able to control my actions."

She nodded, understanding. A sexual need like she had never experienced before had been brewing inside her all evening, and she didn't doubt the same was true for Jay.

"I'll call you tomorrow," he promised, then curled an arm around her waist and lowered his head to kiss her again.

Honey entered the house and pulled off her coat. Tossing both it and her purse on the couch, she climbed the stairs to her room. She sat on her bed and removed her shoes, then sighed. Shit, she didn't want to be alone tonight. But was she ready for Jay to make love to her?

Shaking off the question, she went into the bathroom to remove her clothes and slipped into red flannel pajamas and matching robe. After sliding into her house shoes, she moved past the window to turn on the lamp on her nightstand. What she saw outside made her stop in her tracks.

It was just like it had been the last time. Jay was standing in her driveway, puffing on a cigarette, gazing up at the second floor as though hoping she didn't notice while also hoping she would invite him in.

As Honey peeked from behind the curtain, a warm sensation ran through her body. *He is so fine and all mine*, she thought. His skin glistened under the streetlight and looked as creamy and smooth as if she'd melted chocolate in a saucer on the stove.

She watched him turn his head toward the window, and knew he'd suddenly realized she was watching. In the dim streetlight, his loving brown eyes seemed to be saying, "You have to make the next move." His dimpled grin radiated a sensual light that could brighten an entire room, and sent her heart beating rapidly against her chest. He confused her, made her believe love was indeed possible for her. He would understand. He wouldn't care that she would never be able to bear his child. She said a silent prayer, and after several seconds knew that it was time.

What was she going to do?

Never in her life had she imagined meeting one man who would make her want to throw all her fears away. But she had, and he was standing right outside her window, waiting and hoping she finally would. Of course, being the gentleman he was, Jay wasn't going to push her. He had promised. Instead, he would allow her to see the truth by gaining her trust and showing her he truly cared.

Finally, she'd met a man who made her want to learn what true love really meant. After the rape, and scared of being hurt, she'd closed off her heart. But with Jay, it was different. If she put her cards on the table, would he really love her? If she gave him the key to her heart, would he truly want her? For the first time, she had hope that the answer to those questions was "Yes." She'd been so afraid of taking a chance she had prevented herself from seeing what had always been right in front of her face.

Suddenly she wanted to know. *To hell with fear!* She no longer wanted to deny herself. Yes, it was easier not to know than to find out, but she no longer wanted to be a coward. Tonight, she decided to put her fears behind her and live for the present. Tonight. Right now.

She was ready to find out what true love really was.

* * *

When Honey had peeked through the window, Jay was sure she would invite him in. But he'd been wrong. *Damn.* He was going to have another sleepless night with a hard dick. Jay dropped his cigarette butt on the ground and walked around his car to get in. Just as he opened the car door, her porch light came on. Next thing he knew, Honey was standing in the doorway.

"Whatcha doing out here?" she asked.

Jay kicked his pride aside and said, "Thinking."

"Thinkin' about what?" she dared to ask.

The answer was obvious, but still he said, "About you, boo." His eyes raked in her appearance as she opened the screen door, hair pulled back and wearing her favorite pajamas. No other woman looked so damn good in flannel. He was magnetically drawn to her. Unconsciously, he shut his car door and moved toward her.

Honey saw him closing in on her and began to shiver with anticipation. There was no panicky feeling. It felt right. Finally, Honey allowed her heart to lead the way.

And damn if she wasn't going to follow.

"Why don't you come in before we both freeze to death?" she whispered.

Jay nodded and continued toward the porch where she was waiting. There was a chilly breeze, but neither of them seemed to care.

Honey stepped aside so he could pass into the living room, then closed the door. Her teeth chattered as she moved to where Jay was standing in front of the couch. She rubbed her hands up and down her arms, pretending to be cold, but instead she was shaking with an exhilarating combination of excitement and anticipation.

"Let me start a fire," Jay suggested, then shrugged

out of his coat and laid it across the chair. He moved toward the fireplace, but Honey stopped him with her hand.

She allowed her robe to fall to the floor. "I'm ready."

Jay felt an excitement bubble up inside, but he didn't want to assume too much. There was only so much a brotha could take. "Baby, tell me what you're ready for."

Honey swallowed and said, "For you to make love to me," hoping he wouldn't notice the tremor in her voice.

Jay, stunned, didn't dare move. If he did, nothing would stop him from making her his. "Are you sure?"

She had barely nodded when Jay closed the distance between them and pulled her into his arms. "You're so damn sexy," he whispered. Her heart was beating just as hard as his. "I want you so damn bad," he whispered. "I lie awake at night aching to have you lying beneath me, with your legs spread wide and my dick buried deep inside you."

As she pulled away, her most private area throbbed and her eyes became misty as she looked up at him and saw a reflection of his heart. Jay leaned in closer and dropped his mouth to the base of her neck, and she shuddered with desire. His lips traveled to several small places along her neck as he seared a path. "I promise not to hurt you."

She draped her arms around his neck and stood on tiptoe, arching her body against his. "The only thing I'm afraid of is the way you make me feel. I've been runnin' away from my feelings since I met you."

Staring down at her, he said, "I've tried to leave you alone, but I don't want to pretend anymore." His voice was husky with emotion.

"Yes." With that one word, Honey surrendered to the emotions she'd kept buried deep inside for years.

He lowered his head and took her mouth. The feel of her pressing against him was his undoing. She clung to him, making soft little sounds deep in her throat as he plunged his tongue and explored the warmth inside. Then he stopped.

"Look at me," he commanded.

She opened her eyes to meet the desire brewing in his.

"At any point you change your mind, I'll stop," he whispered.

She nodded. "I know you will."

He swept her up in his arms and made his way to the master bedroom, planting small wet kisses across her face and neck. Pulling back the covers, he eased her onto the bed and followed her down. He poised himself on his elbows, hovering over her, his gaze feasting on the sight of her lying beside him, sharing the intimacy of her bed. "I'm gonna take this slow."

He lowered his head, covering her lips with a passionate kiss while his hands began an exploration of her body. His hand moved downward, slowly caressing either side of her body to her thigh. The fabric of their clothing separated them, yet did nothing to slow the energy generating between them. Her breath came in shallow, uneven gasps.

"Are you okay?"

She nodded, touched by his concern.

"Try to relax." He pulled her close to him. "Baby, take as long as you need. I'm not going anywhere." While he held her tight, he expressed words of love and encouragement until her breathing became almost normal again.

She pressed her parted lips to his, and as their tongues did a soulful dance Honey sighed, surrendering to her desire and freeing something inside her. The days of running from Jay were finally over. She loved him. Love was her strength.

The sound of her breathing had quieted and was now coming evenly. Jay reminded himself that he needed to treat her like a virgin. No matter how fuckin' horny he was, he had to take it slow. He had to make it good for her too.

He made doubly certain she was relaxed before his fingers traveled under her top and he gently outlined her small perky breasts with his fingertips. He kneaded first one nipple, then the other, drawing them into hardened peaks.

"How does that feel?"

"Good," she whispered, and moaned with pleasure. His touch filled her with warmth.

He looked down at her, eyes closed, lips parted.

While nuzzling her hair he continued to circle her nipple slowly with one hand, while the other traveled down into her pajama bottom, skimming her hips and thighs. He quickly realized she wasn't wearing panties. His fingers brushed through the curls, seeking her clit.

Her stomach fluttered, her toes curled, and the walls of her coochie clenched and unclenched in preparation. The gentle massage sent currents racing through her veins. She could no longer lie still, and began squirming beneath his hand.

He ended the kiss, then lifted himself up and off the bed. With quick precision, he freed himself of his shirt and flung it to the floor.

Honey sucked in a deep breath, her nerves singing, her body yearning, as she looked at his naked hairy chest as if it were the first time. Broad, and muscular, his shoulders looked massive and his arms huge. He was without a doubt the finest man she'd ever seen.

As if he sensed her longing, he took a seat on the bed beside her. Then he guided her hand to his chest and encouraged her to explore. When he pressed her hand against his chest, she was amazed at the powerful beat of his heart. "That's what you do to me," he said in a low sensual voice. She caressed his chest, then ran her hand over his broad shoulder, loving the feel of his strength beneath her fingertips. Sliding her palm across his skin, she felt heat leap into her fingers and spread up her arm.

Feeling the electricity of her touch, Jay had to grit his teeth to keep from losing it as desire spiraled up in him. He reached down and raised her into a sitting position. Honey allowed him to lift her pajama top over her head and toss it on the floor.

As he gazed down at her with appreciation, her breathing quickened, lifting and lowering her breasts, her nipples tightening under his scrutiny.

"Sweet heaven," he moaned as he stared down at her perfect little breasts. He lowered his mouth, and filled it with the right one, then the left. He laved her nipples until they were marble hard.

She felt herself unraveling. Warmth spread through her, rapidly raising her temperature, and moisture pooled between her thighs. She had never known anything so incredibly sensual, so delicious.

His fingers touched and teased her nipples, giving her indescribable pleasure. His lips and tongue licked and sucked until she was mindless with sexual feelings unlike anything she'd felt before. Jay kissed her belly, then lifted her hips enough to reach under her and tug the elastic waistband of her pajamas down and over her legs. Just as skillfully, he removed the rest of his clothes. He couldn't believe his eyes. She was sexy as hell. Little breasts. Tiny waist. Flat stomach and a phat ass. What more could any man ask for?

He returned to her, and they both lay naked beside each other. While he planted a trail of kisses down from her neck to her breasts, and then to her abdomen, his fingers sought and found her core. He stroked her clit intimately, eliciting a cry of astonished pleasure from her before he inserted two fingers inside her pussy as if testing her readiness. Her tightness declared that she hadn't been touched in years.

"You are so hot and wet, Honey," he whispered before he lowered his head. With his tongue, he painted a damp trail up one inner thigh and down the other before he buried his face in the brown thatch between her legs. He then began thrusting and stroking his tongue from her clit down to her core.

"Ohhh, baby!" she moaned as she spread her legs wide apart, giving him complete access. "Don't stop! *Ahhh, yesss.*"

Honey shivered uncontrollably; she desperately needed more than his mere touch. A wave of ecstasy throbbed through her, and she was lost. "Please," she whimpered with sweet agony.

"Not yet, boo."

While he sucked her clit, he inserted two fingers in and out of her pussy. She rocked her hips against his fingers, fucking them as she would a dick.

"You like that, boo?" he asked in between sucks.

"Oooh! That's feels sooo good. Just like that, baby . . . just like that."

He continued to stroke her; her entire body tingled, and Honey felt she was ready to come.

"Puhleeeeze, Jay! I want you inside me."

Her cry was permission for what he was dying to do. Jay positioned himself carefully between her thighs and pulled her hips up to him. Honey stared down at his large dick and felt a moment of panic. Could she possibly accommodate something that size? But her fears were quickly put to rest when Jay began gently stroking the head against her clit. She closed her eyes and the image of Walter was nowhere in sight. All she saw was the man she loved.

She moaned and the tension slowly left her body. Jay decided she was finally ready. Finding her entrance, he pushed slightly while he watched her face. He pushed again, making sure there were no signs of pain or fear. He was at the brink of exploding, but if she had any doubts, he would stop. With the third push her eyelids flew open, and his eyes searched hers.

"Are you sure?" he asked with concern.

"More sure than I've ever been." She squirmed beneath him, pushing her hips forward, trying to meet him. Her eyes drifted closed as she moaned against his lips. With her encouragement, he pushed into her hot, moist pussy.

A cry tore from her lips that he smothered with a kiss. He lay still, trying to give her a chance to recover from the shock. However, she grabbed hold of his buttocks and continued the stroke on her own. Jay was met by a tidal wave of pleasure. He released a moan. Never had he felt so connected to a woman.

Honey felt full, expanded to the limit, and nothing had ever felt so right.

Jay withdrew from her but, moaning, she clung to him. He plunged again, deeply, completely, and she cried out from the sheer joy of having him inside her body.

Their rhythm began, slowly, gently, and together they found harmony with one another. They soared higher, the pace accelerating until the beat of their union grew faster and faster.

"Damn, this pussy is good!" he chanted over and over.

Her body jerked with release. Her juices flowed continuously. Jay intensified his actions, pushing her further and deeper into pure, explosive ecstasy. He was fuckin' her so good that Honey cried out his name repeatedly as they thrashed about on the bed, their bodies joined.

"Oooooooh!" she cried as she came harder than she ever did with her vibrator.

A vigorous tide of passion raged through both of them, bringing them to an earth-shattering climax.

Later, Jay pulled her into his arms, and Honey snuggled against him, praying the night would never end. He lifted the covers over them and draped his arm across her warm, damp body.

Honey couldn't believe she had finally given in to her feelings. She had finally made love to Jay.

Bitch, you still haven't told him the truth.

What was she going to do? she asked the nagging voice inside her head. Jay was bound to find out sooner or later . . . unless, of course, she was ready to end their relationship again. He loved her and she loved him. But nothing had changed. It was unfair to mislead him into believing they had a future. *This shit ain't fair.* It would be unfair of her to take away a man's joy at hav-

ing a child. She could never do that to him. Honey sniffled, anticipating the grief of losing him again.

Jay stiffened at the sound. "What's wrong, boo?"

"Nothing," she whispered before turning around
and leaning her back against his chest. The joy she'd
felt only minutes ago had suddenly faded, and she didn't
dare look into the future.

Now what the fuck is wrong? Jay asked himself as
he felt her body tense. Maybe she was regretting that
she allowed him to make love to her. He'd tried to make
it good for the both of them, and her actions told him
she had enjoyed every minute of it. *So then what the
hell was the problem?* He wrapped his arms tight
around her and planted light kisses on the side of her
neck, then whispered reassuringly near her ear, "I love
you, boo."

Honey awoke well after midnight and found her
head still resting on his broad chest. She eased out of
the covers and rushed into the bathroom to wash her
face and brush her teeth. Looking on the back of the
door for her robe, she cursed when she remembered
she'd left it in the living room. Wrapped in only a
towel, she decided to go downstairs before Jay rose.
But he was waiting for her outside the door, standing
before her with his dick sticking straight out.

"What're you doing?" he asked, leaning against the
doorjamb.

"Getting dressed."

He moved in closer, put his hands at her waist, and
gazed into her eyes. "Why?"

Honey hesitated for a moment. "I thought I'd go
down and watch a movie."

"Stop running from us, Honey."

She felt his dick rub against her thigh. "I—I'm not runnin'."

"Yes, you are, boo," he whispered against her hair. "I need you here with me." Jay brought his lips to hers, then broke away. "Whatever's bothering you, we can work out together. Nothin' is gonna change the way I feel about you. Absolutely nothin'. Now that I've tasted you, sucked you, fucked you, I ain't going no-damn-where." He captured her lips in another kiss, then dropped the towel to the floor, swung her into his arms, and carried her back to bed. "Are you sore?" he asked, staring down into her eyes as she lay beneath him.

"No."

"Good, 'cause I'm not done with you yet." Spreading her legs, he slipped into her pussy so easily it was as if he had never left.

Sixteen

Natalia quickly added the figures for next month's extravaganza. The expenses were increasing by the minute. Traditionally, Diva Designs' fashion shows were held at the historic Fox Theater; however, an incompetent marketing assistant booked the event on the wrong day, and Alicia Keys was scheduled to perform at the Fox on the same night. Now they were left with little choice: change the date or find another location. Luckily, Natalia had received a bid from the Black Repertoire Theater, located in the same vicinity. They were eager to bring the annual attraction to their location, and were willing to make all the accommodations needed.

All that was left was to find a master of ceremonies. Natalia tapped a pencil lightly on her desk, thinking. Normally they used one of the local radio personalities, but this time she wanted to do something a little different. Maybe even a stand-up comedian to entertain the audience during intermission. There was a lot of local talent in the area, but she wanted someone who wasn't only born in St. Louis but could also draw a large crowd. Someone like Cedric the Entertainer. She'd already assigned a competent team to work exclusively on the event, and trusted them to find the right person.

Natalia stretched her long legs underneath her desk, then moved her neck from side to side, releasing the tension. She'd been at it for hours now. Glancing down at her watch, she remembered she was scheduled to interview a candidate that afternoon for the marketing position. She dropped the pencil she'd been holding and laced her fingers. She was still pissed off that Terraine was determined to get the position filled before the spring season began, and although she'd stressed to him that now wasn't a good time, he refused to listen to shit she had to say. He was the boss, and what Terraine's pussy-whipped ass wanted, Terraine got. Natalia could try talking to Sasha, who seemed to have her husband wrapped around her damn finger. However, after the two of them bumped heads last year, she'd be damned before she kissed that prissy bitch's ass. Instead, she would have to deal with the shit.

She had to admit, if there were a marketing director in place, she wouldn't have to work quite as hard. Even though the two departments worked hand in hand, if she could relinquish marketing, she could concentrate solely on fashion.

In the meantime, the dual role was helping keep her mind off Jacob's punk ass. Leaning back in her seat, she found herself wondering what he was doing. He'd sent her a postcard, but nowhere in the note did he indicate he missed her, or provide a phone number. She gritted her teeth with renewed anger. *That bastard is gonna regret fuckin' with my emotions.*

That thought strengthened her, and she shuffled

through her in-box looking for the candidate's resume. She wanted to take a few minutes to review it for problem areas. The person had better be qualified, or Terraine was going to hear from her. Maybe she could take the problem before their stockholders. Wouldn't he be pissed? She frowned. No, maybe that wouldn't be a good idea. If pushed, Terraine could be vindictive. He would look for any excuse to remove her from the position her godfather had left her in control of in his will. And more than likely give her job to his wife. Nah, she wasn't having that.

Her eyes darted around her desk in frustration. After several more seconds with no success in locating the file, she buzzed her secretary.

Tiffany quickly entered the office, her dark brown eyes shining. She was young, and the daughter of a good friend of Terraine's. Initially, Natalia resented that she was forced to hire her, but as they continued to work together she realized Tiffany was quite qualified, and an asset to the office.

"You need something?"

"Yes," Natalia said. "I have a candidate coming in this afternoon, and I can't seem to find his resume."

"I'm sorry," Tiffany said. "I forgot all about the interview. I'll call Geri right away and ask for one."

"Thanks," Natalia said, and gave her a forgiving smile.

After she left, Natalia's stomach began to growl. Now was a good time to escape for lunch.

Sterling Mann stopped at the security cage and gave his name before pulling his rental car into the lot and parking on the third level. He took a few minutes to relax before climbing out of the car, then strolled to the elevator.

He hadn't had much time to enjoy being back in St. Louis again. His plane from San Antonio had been delayed, leaving him just enough time to check into his room at the Ritz Carlton and quickly change for his two o'clock interview. As he moved through the double doors, he was stopped at a security desk where he had to show his ID again. He wasn't surprised; Terraine had warned him that security had been tightened in their building since someone attempted to sabotage the corporation last year.

Exiting the elevator on the fifth floor, he entered the plush hallway and allowed his eyes to travel around the office space. He grinned, impressed by what he saw. Diva Designs had changed quite a bit since he'd worked as a college intern for Richard Andrews. It was then he had had his first encounter with his goddaughter, Natalia Bonaparte.

He winced at the memory. "Bitch" was the best way to describe her. Born into money, she probably never lifted a finger in her life. Richard had also given Natalia a job as an intern in the marketing department. She'd considered herself superior over everyone else, reveling in her position as the boss's goddaughter. Sterling had his concepts, she had hers, and the two never seemed to see eye to eye. They clashed on ideas with Natalia sulking, kicking, and screaming to her godfather. Richard had tried to be a mediator between the two, but nothing seemed to work. So Sterling worked as quickly as fuckin' possible to complete the project, and was relieved to take the next plane home.

Sterling sighed. He was back, and couldn't wait to see Natalia's face again. Their meeting would be a challenge, but he wanted this job and was willing to do anything to get it. Working for Diva Designs would finally put him on the map, and even closer to starting his own design label. The only thing standing in his way of making it was Natalia.

Even with that test in front of him, Sterling smirked with confidence. He'd have to see about that.

As Honey stared at the sunny sky outside her office window, she felt her lips curl into a dreamy smile.

She was in love. Now that she could admit it, love bubbled in her laugh and shone in her eyes. There was no rain in her forecast, only sunshine and warm weather. Being in love felt so damn good.

After their weekend, they'd spent almost every evening together. Last night Jay took her dancing, then to his condo, where they made love until sunrise. Honey had been certain she'd be exhausted this morning, but instead she felt more alive than she had in years.

Jay was an excellent teacher and she tried to give as much as she took. When she held the reins, she rode him as if he were one of those mechanical bulls. And when she took his dick in her mouth, she sucked it like a fuckin' Blow-Pop.

Exhaling a long sigh of contentment, she moved to her desk and looked at the huge arrangement of long-stemmed roses that were delivered this morning. Her belly fluttered with delight. She felt whole, complete. Jay had fucked dozens of women in his life, but even with his experience, he never made her feel inadequate. Instead, he made her feel like their lovemaking was just as fulfilling for him as it was for her. Jay was a wonderfully compassionate man and a gentle lover. To think that she'd almost ended things between them because of her fear!

Her lips turned slightly downward; he still didn't know she couldn't have children.

Honey ignored the ringing phone, not wanting to lose her train of thought, and took a seat in her chair. She was scheduled to leave tomorrow evening for Minneapolis, where she was attending a two-day convention.

Bolstered by her newfound love, she had finally summoned enough courage this morning. She would tell him tonight. That way, he'd have time to think it over while she was away. The mixture of uncertainty and anxiety was driving her stir-crazy. But as soon as she bared her soul, she would finally be able to put the past to rest.

What would he say? The question stabbed at her heart. But she was tired of not knowing. She had to finally know. Despite her apprehension and no matter how he reacted, she needed closure.

"Honey, someone's out front to see you," Candy said as she peeked inside the office.

Honey smoothed out her blue button-down blouse and khaki slacks and strolled out into the lobby. Standing at the front counter was a very pregnant woman. Honey felt a pang of envy as she admired her. Her skin glowed, and her hair, pulled back into a bun, was shiny and healthy.

Honey greeted her with a friendly smile. "May I help you?"

The lady turned malicious eyes on her and assessed her from head to toe. "Are you Honey?"

Puzzled by her expression, Honey raised a brow before nodding. "Yes, I am."

Kendra was fuming. She had hoped the petite beauty

she watched sauntering gracefully from the back of the salon wasn't Honey. But as soon as she saw her long brown curls and large gray eyes, she knew it couldn't be anyone else. Her lips curled in a sneer as she stood face-to-face with the woman who was fuckin' her baby's daddy.

"I would appreciate it if you'd leave my man the fuck alone!" she spat.

"Excuse me?" Honey gasped with surprise. Who the hell was this woman?

"You heard me, bitch!" Kendra said, loud enough to draw the ears of all the patrons in the waiting area. "I'm tired of you runnin' after my man."

Honey blew out a ragged breath, trying to keep her composure. Sista girl was obviously trippin'. But in her pregnant state, she was drawing sympathy from her audience—Honey's staff and clients. "I have no idea what you're talking about," she said. "But if you'd like to go into my office, we can discuss this in private."

"Don't play dumb with me," Kendra hissed. Glancing around, she made sure there were plenty of listeners, then rubbed her hand across her stomach for added emphasis. "My name is Kendra Johnson, and I want you to stay the fuck away from my fiancé!" Kendra chuckled inwardly when she saw Honey's gaze fall to the diamond sparkling on her finger. Thank goodness she'd been smart enough not to send Lawrence's engagement ring back to his bitch ass! It had definitely come in handy.

Honey was growing irritated. "Like I said before," she said, working to keep her tone even, "I have no idea who your fiancé is. And unless you want to discuss this like two adults, I advise you to get the hell out of my salon."

No, that bitch didn't try to make me look like a fool. Kendra's expression suddenly saddened as she pretended to be choking over tears. "Stay away from Jay! I love him," she begged between sniffles. "My baby needs her daddy." She then turned to walk away. Once she reached the door, she swung around and grinned wickedly before retreating from the building.

Hearing his name fall from the woman's lips, Honey gripped the counter for support; her legs felt like they would give out. One quick glance told her that several customers were whispering among themselves. She turned and headed toward the back, with Mercedes close on her tail.

"Girl, you need me to get you anything?"

Honey shook her head, still in shock. "No. I just need to be alone."

Mercedes squeezed her shoulder, then went back out to try and clear the air. "Damn!" she mumbled under her breath. "And I thought I had drama in my own life!"

Terraine completed his interview with Sterling and was very impressed with his credentials. He was definitely a top pick. Even though he was sure he'd found their man, he would wait until he received the opinions of his managers before making a definite decision.

He dropped Sterling's file in his out-box. When Geri returned from escorting him down to Natalia's office, he would have her schedule an appointment for him with personnel.

Terraine rose, smiling with satisfaction. He knew Natalia was against hiring someone, but she really didn't have much say in the matter. He was the CEO, after all.

Natalia was very territorial, and even though she would never admit it, he knew she was overworked. She would thank him later.

He moved to stare out of the floor-to-ceiling window at the overcast sky. His grandfather was probably turning over in his grave. Richard Andrews would never have agreed to Natalia taking on such a load. He never could understand the relationship between the two. Terraine had even learned to love her over the years despite all her flaws, and even forgiven her after she had tried to destroy his relationship with Sasha. Terraine grimaced at the memory of that.

Yet despite their differences over the years, he had to admit Natalia was good at what she did. The fashion world was in her blood. Nonetheless, he needed to hire someone dominant enough not to be easily intimidated by her. Terraine knew Natalia had a tendency to act like a spoiled-ass brat, but he could handle her. Years of knowing her and the bullshit she pulled made that possible. Chuckling, he returned to his desk. He had a strong suspicion Sterling would know how to deal with her, too.

Natalia whizzed back to her office and was sitting behind her desk trying to return several phone calls when her secretary buzzed. The candidate had arrived.

"Where's the file?" she asked with exasperation.

"It's sitting on the middle of your desk."

"All right," Natalia grumbled. "Give me a minute." She'd been so wrapped up in a conversation with one of their designers that she'd forgotten about the interview. Crossing her legs, she reached for the folder. Her eyes went straight to the work history before they rose to the top of the page. Staring down at the name, she felt her heart sink. *Oh, hell naw!* Sterling Mann! She hissed the name as if it were an obscenity, then slammed the file shut. Why hadn't Terraine warned her? But he wouldn't have known that the two had a history. Although she had little reason back then, she still couldn't stand his ass. She had thrown her weight around because she knew she could, and had behaved childishly. But she would never admit it—not to him, not to anyone.

"When it rains, it fucking pours!" she hissed under her breath as she reached in her drawer for a Tic-Tac.

Twirling in her chair, she decided to get the interview over and done with, then send him back on a plane to wherever he came from.

Her stomach clenched despite her resolve to numb her emotions. Glancing quickly in the mirror, she raked her fingers through her hair. Then, after straightening the lapel on her salmon-colored suit, she buzzed for Tiffany to send him in.

Before she had a chance to relax in her seat, the door swung open and there he stood. Conscious of a sudden dryness of the mouth, she fixed her brown eyes on the tall, athletic physique she had hoped never to see again.

Natalia instantly noted that Sterling still prided himself on his good looks. He was something no woman could ignore. Dressed in an expensive suit tailor-made to fit comfortably over his broad shoulders and massive legs, he glided through her office with an air of self-confidence. Once again, he commanded attention. A ray of sunlight from the window glimmered across his clean-shaven head and revealed the smooth-caramel face he held elevated with pride. He was still sexy as shit. How could she have forgotten the round face that was the home of a pair of compelling pecan-colored eyes and full, supple lips?

Sterling's eyes traveled to several cover shots of Natalia taken while she was modeling that now adorned the walls in her office. "I see you're still as vain as ever." His deep voice sliced through the silence.

Realizing she'd been holding her breath, Natalia released it slowly, then rose from her chair. Arms folded in front of her, she strolled from behind her desk. "Sterling, what do you want?"

Tilting his head, he met the vixen's ginger gaze head-on. He was tempted to tell her exactly what he wanted from her fine ass, but decided there was plenty of time for that later. Wearing an elegant suit that revealed the contours of her voluptuous figure, Natalia still moved with arrogance and the seductive grace of a queen. Her auburn hair was shorter than he remembered; instead of reaching the center of her back, curls tumbled around her shoulders, framing a stunning mahogany face.

"Didn't your boss tell you?" he responded in a mocking tone. "I'm interviewing for the marketing position."

At his taunting remark, she compressed her coral-painted lips and tried to think of a snappy retort, but couldn't find one. She couldn't think clearly with her heart beating against her ribs. Sterling made her nervous. She had never before been nervous around a man.

She looked at him with narrowed eyes filled with dislike. "You're gonna make this difficult, aren't you?"

Her reaction to him was amusing to say the least. Moving closer, he smirked. "Of course."

She laced her fingers together. "Then let's get something straight from the beginning. I don't like you."

"That's good, 'cause I don't like you either," he countered. He moved closer, then paused long enough to give her a dark, dangerous look before the sliver of humor returned to his eyes. "See, the problem with you is that you've never taken the time to get to really know me. You've based your decision solely on my irresistible charm."

She was appalled. "I think it has more to do with the fact that you fucked half of our models that summer."

He gave her an incredulous look. "I was only eighteen! I was experimenting with my sexuality." He shrugged. "I allowed my little head to think for the big head."

Trying to ignore the strong bones of his chiseled face, Natalia snorted. "You haven't changed a bit."

"Neither have you." He moved in closer. "Still the ice princess." His hot, sweet breath fanned her nose. "I want this job, Natalia. My bags are packed and I'm ready to start on Monday." He shot her a twisted smile before adding, "And I'll do whatever it takes to get it. Even bring up the fact that I wasn't the only one sneaking off behind the stage that summer."

Her eyes grew wide with alarm. Was he bluffing, or had he really seen her with their production assistant?

Leaning closer, he whispered near her ear, "I never knew they could put tattoos there."

The fact that he'd seen the small red strawberry tattoo on her inner thigh caused Ms. Kitty to gasp.

"Talk about the pot callin' the kettle black!" He barked with laughter.

He *had* seen her. She was silent as humiliation flushed her face. That summer she had had a fling with a man ten years her senior. If her godfather had found out, he would have kicked her ass. "Shit, I was a kid then."

"And so was I. Now that we've gotten that out of the way, are you gonna interview me or not?" Sterling stared down at her with laughter burning in his eyes as he waited.

Natalia clenched her teeth together in an ill attempt to stifle the rage that burned within her. She wanted to drop his ass out her window. She cleared her throat and said, "This won't take long, so we might as well get it out of the way." Rounding the conference table, she gestured for him to take the seat across from her.

"That's more like it." He strolled to the end of the table and extended his hand. "Sterling Mann, pleased to meet you, ma'am."

With a flash of horror, she stared down at the hand as if there was a big juicy booger on his index finger.

"Are you gonna just leave a brotha hangin'?"

His eyes gleamed with the love of combat, as if he was waiting to see how she would react to his peace offering. Shaking his hand would be like accepting defeat. Natalia stared at him, torn between rage and an inexplicable desire to touch his tantalizing mustache to see if it felt as soft as it looked. His supple lips were curled upward, causing dimples to appear in his cheeks. She swallowed. His aura of arrogance fascinated her. Heat stole into her face as she tried to put out the fire his presence caused to burn inside her. Ms. Kitty liked what she saw, which was rare because she was a tough bitch to please.

Natalia shook her head, trying to rid herself of the thoughts as well as Ms. Kitty's pleas. Ignoring his hand, she lowered herself into her seat. "I have more important things to attend to. So let's get this interview under way." She dropped her eyes to the table and admitted it—seeing Sterling again left her panties wet and a sour taste in her mouth.

Somehow Honey had managed to stay calm while she spoke with Jay over the phone. After changing into sweatpants and an oversized T-shirt, she had just slipped on her house shoes when the doorbell chimed.

"Hey, boo," Jay said.

Oh, he was gorgeous. He was standing outside the door wearing a brilliant smile and dressed in her favorite pair of jeans that molded his firm ass. Honey stepped aside and said, "Come on in."

He moved forward, trying to kiss her, but she pulled away. Jay frowned. "Is somethin' wrong?"

Honey walked to the kitchen and didn't respond until she heard him follow. "How come you didn't tell me about Kendra?"

His heart skipped a beat. Shit, he had fucked up big time. "I can explain."

Clutching a dishrag, she turned to face him, her jaw tightening. "Don't waste your breath. She already told me."

"She told you?" He should have known that bitch was likely to do anything.

Honey nodded, eyes narrowed with irritation. "She waddled into my salon, accusing me of stealing her fiancé."

"She's not my fiancée."

With as much defiance as she could muster, she said, "Then what is she . . . your baby's mama?" *Please tell me she's not carrying your child.* She waited for him to object. He didn't. And her world crumbled. "I saw the ring." She paused to swallow. When she spoke again, her voice had dropped an octave. "I saw her stomach."

While gazing deeply in her eyes, Jay placed a gentle hand on her arm. "If you give me a few minutes, I'll explain it all to you." He wanted so desperately to hold her and kiss the pain away.

"What is there to explain?" Honey said, her anger flaring. "She looks ready to pop any day, which means she's due any day now." She paused, waiting again for some kind of denial. When Jay remained silent, Honey opened her mouth wide with disbelief. "So you were with her the same mothafuckin' time you were trying to fuck me on my living room couch?"

Nodding, he raked a nervous hand across his head. Damn, he had fucked up. "It happened the night you threw me out."

Looking at him, she shook her head in dismay. "Because I wouldn't give your black ass none, you . . . you left me to find someone up for the job." Her heart was breaking in two. She had never expected him to remain celibate, but she hadn't expected this either.

"It was nothing like that," Jay said, rushing his words as his hand slid down her arm and latched on to her wrist. "I was hurt . . . wasn't thinking straight. I made a mistake."

She jerked her arm away. "You should have trusted my ass enough to tell me the truth!" Chest heaving, she glared up at him with tearstained eyes. "How could you do this to us? How could you do this shit to me?"

"I'm so sorry. I fucked up by not telling you about the baby." There was nothing more he could say. Now it was too late to undo the damage.

For a moment, time stood still as she watched him,

her gray eyes stormy with anguish and streaming tears. He reached for her but she swatted his hand away. If she allowed him to touch her, there was no way she could remain strong. Jay had played her ass like a violin. She'd thought he was different. She couldn't believe she had allowed herself to believe that he truly loved her.

Jay sighed heavily. "I didn't want you to find out this way. I was waitin' for the right moment."

"And when would that have been? After the baby was born? When he started school?" she cried. Not waiting for an answer, she continued, "Get the fuck out."

He moved forward and grasped her shoulder. "All right, I'll call you to—"

"No!" She jerked away, folded her arms across her chest, and turned to look out of the back window. She didn't want him to see the fresh tears spilling from her eyes. "Just get the hell out," she croaked. "Go home to your family. Go somewhere, anywhere, I don't give a flyin' fuck, just don't ever call me again."

After he left, all she could see were the clouds overhead. It was raining on her world again.

"How could you?"

Kendra gave a nonchalant shrug. "I thought she should know I'm carrying your child."

Jay was so sick of her playing games with his life. The only thing stopping him from choking the shit out of her was the fact that she was pregnant.

"You had no right!" he said as he dropped into the recliner across from her.

"You're wrong," Kendra huffed. "I have a right to know who's gonna be around my child."

"What does it matter, Kendra? You don't want the baby. You made that perfectly clear. I also made it clear that you and I are through. Why do you keep making this situation so damn difficult?"

Kendra leaned against the couch and scowled. Why couldn't he fuckin' cooperate? She was getting sick and tired of his shit. Nothing she was doing seemed to work. *First, he takes a seat across from me as if he can't stand being in the same room with me, and then he wants to get in my ass over his Tinkerbell-lookin' girlfriend. Well, I ain't having it.*

"I'm tired of trying to prove how much I love you," she said.

"You don't love me, Kendra, you never have. You only love the concept of being in love. It's not the same thing."

"You're one to talk . . . I thought you didn't believe in marriage and babies!"

"I didn't . . . but I've changed. I love Honey. I also love that child you're carrying. But I don't love you, Kendra, and it's time you realized that. I plan to raise our child, which means Honey will also be a part of that baby's life." Even though Honey was angry with him, Jay damn sho wasn't giving up.

"What?" Kendra blinked as if she'd been struck in the face. "You want some strange woman to raise our child?"

"Kendra, you were planning to give the baby away to complete strangers," he hissed in frustration. "I'm gonna raise our child. I now believe I'll be a great father." He sighed. "I should never have considered giving the baby up in the first place. I was scared."

Kendra folded her arms and openly sulked. "What about me?"

Jay groaned. The woman's head was made of bricks. "As I have said before, if you want to raise our baby, I'll stand by you and support you in every way. If not, I want full custody. Either way, we will not be together."

Throwing up her hands, she sighed. "Fine. You can have the stupid baby."

He shook his head. Damn, he couldn't stand her ass. She acted as if the baby were an old toy no one wanted to play with anymore. "Even though I'll be raising our child, I'll never keep him or her from you. Can we try to work on being friends?"

She rolled her eyes at the ceiling. "I don't think so."

Jay groaned. As much as he would like to never have to deal with her ass again, he knew Kendra would always be a part of his life, regardless of how difficult the situation would be. The big problem was that Kendra could be so fuckin' selfish, there was no telling what she might do or say.

He rose. "Is there anything I can do for you?"

With her lips still poked out, Kendra answered bluntly, "Yeah. Get the fuck out."

Jay cursed for the hundredth time. How could he have been so stupid?

He reached for a beer, fell back against the cushions of his couch, and picked up the remote control. He should have known her sneaky ass would find a way to tell Honey about the baby. Her vengeance should have come as no surprise. He'd heard her rant and rave on several occasions about getting even with one person or another. Once, Kendra had even gone so far as to start a rumor that one of the other dentists in the area was gay just so he would lose business. He couldn't understand why Kendra had a driving need to make other people's lives just as miserable as her own. She was out of control.

Yes . . . if he'd been thinking and had used his head, he would have realized that as soon as he told Kendra he loved someone else, she was going to cause trouble. Tilting his head back, he took a long swig of the beer.

It wasn't hard to figure out how Kendra found out who Honey was. He was certain Kendra had somehow wriggled it out of Natalia. His nostrils flared. She'd always been good at getting Nat to feel sorry for her ass. But he couldn't blame Natalia. It was no one's fault but his own. Terraine had warned him of the consequences, but he'd chosen to ignore that, wanting to do things his way. What a fool he had been! If he had told Honey the truth in the beginning, none of this would have happened. Now he had to find a way to make things right.

Jay took another angry swallow. He hadn't meant to hurt her. He had just thought . . . well, he wasn't sure what he thought anymore. At the time, keeping the truth from her was important, but now the reason seemed ridiculous.

While tapping the can across his knee, he tried to make sense of it all. He'd made a terrible mistake, and he was wrong . . . yet he refused to let the incident come between them. After months of melting her resistance, nothing was going to keep him from the woman he loved.

His eyebrows drew together as he pondered several possibilities. Honey wasn't taking any of his calls. He briefly considered popping up at the salon, but discarded the idea. There was too much of an audience there. After Kendra's performance, he was certain his showing up wasn't a smart idea. He considered going to her house and banging on her door until she let him in. But he couldn't guarantee that she wouldn't call the police.

The phone in the kitchen rang. Certain it wasn't Honey he ignored it, and after three rings the answering machine came on.

"Jay, it's Tee. Sasha's in labor."

Seventeen

Honey arrived at the hospital to find Roxaner pacing in the waiting area. With a smile, Honey headed to her and dropped a kiss on her check.

"I'm so glad you're here," Roxaner said, looking relieved. "This waiting is getting the better of me."

"Thanks for rememberin' to call me," Honey said as she moved to take a seat. "How long has Sasha been in labor?"

"It's been about eight hours. She called me early this evening when the contractions first began. When they were twenty minutes apart, Terraine brought her to the hospital." Although she was wringing her hands nervously, Roxaner's eyes shone with excitement. "Her obstetrician just went back in, so we should be hearing something real soon."

Honey laced her fingers in her lap and beamed up at her. "Then relax, Grandma. You'll need all your energy."

Nodding, Roxaner decided to walk down the hall

and try to calm her nerves. On her way out, Jay entered the room.

"Hey."

Honey looked up from a baby magazine she was thumbing through, and had to work hard to keep her voice calm as she said, "Hello." Being around him wasn't going to be easy. His greeting was a husky whisper that vibrated through her veins. Just the sight of him made her heart flutter wildly in her chest. However, as soon as she remembered his baby—and his baby's mother—the erratic rhythm stopped.

Part of her wanted to scratch his eyes out. The other part wanted Jay to assure her that everything was going to be the way it had been. But she knew there was no way they could turn back. If that were possible, she would have traveled back almost ten years. For her and Jay, things would never be the same. Not now. Not ever.

Face flushed with humiliation and anger, she dropped her eyes, but raised her head at the sound of a baby crying in the background.

Jay moved to take a seat next to her. "Sounds like somebody just had a baby."

His pants leg rubbed against her. She didn't dare look his way.

"Are you ready to be a godmother?"

Nodding, she couldn't resist the faint smile. "Are you ready to be an uncle?" she asked. She finally turned to look at him and found dark circles under his eyes.

"Actually, I am. I never guessed I'd be looking forward to holdin' a baby in my arms, but I can't wait."

Honey turned away. "Neither can I."

Jay didn't miss the flash of pain in her eyes. "Honey . . . baby, we need to talk."

With an exasperated sigh, she tossed the magazine back on the table. "Jay, we don't have shit to talk about."

"How can you say that? I love you, boo."

"If you loved me, you would have told me."

"I know, I know. I made a big fuckin' mistake." Feeling the overwhelming need to touch her, he grasped her arm. "But we can work this out."

Trying to ignore the hopeful glint in his eyes, she tried to pull away. "No, we can't."

"Yes, we can." He held on firmly. "How many times do I have to tell you your heart belongs to me?"

"And how many times do I have to tell you it's *over*?" she hissed. "You have a responsibility to your unborn child and to . . . to Kendra. I think you need to concentrate on them and leave me the hell alone!"

"Tell me you don't want me anymore . . . that you haven't thought about me once since I left your house . . . and I'll leave you alone." His voice was hoarse and tired.

"I don't want you anymore."

"You know your ass is lying." Her eyes told him so, and he sighed with rising frustration. "I'm not gonna beg."

"Then don't," she snapped.

He shook his head. "You've been looking for any excuse to keep us apart. Now you want to throw our relationship away."

She snatched her arm away and said, "*You* did that when you got someone else pregnant!" She couldn't help the bitterness of her words. She wanted him to hurt like she hurt.

The tension was still there when Roxaner returned carrying three sodas, but she missed their strained expressions as she handed one to each of them and asked, "Have we heard anything yet?"

Jay shook his head. "No, we haven't heard anything."

Honey leaned back against the chair and took a deep breath, grateful for the interruption, but also surprised by Jay's confidence that they still had a future together. However, she'd never been a weak woman, so there was no point in starting now. And what could he possibly say that would make a difference?

But Jay wasn't letting her get off so easy. He leaned toward her and whispered in her ear, "We're gonna talk later."

Just then Terraine entered the room, wearing a wide grin. "Well, like we already knew, it's a girl!"

Jay rose and slapped his brother on the back. Roxaner exclaimed and clasped her hands together as the tears came streaming down her face.

Honey also moved to embrace him. "Congratulations. I can't wait to see her."

"She's beautiful, just like her mother," he said, beaming. "They're weighing her now. I came out to bring her grandmother in to see her. See you guys in a few." Taking Roxaner by the hand, he escorted her down the hall, leaving Jay and Honey alone again.

Jay gave a whoop, then said, "My brother the daddy. Who would ever have guessed?"

Honey gave him a mumbled excuse and disappeared to the restroom at the end of the hall. Once inside she reached for a paper towel, wet it, and pressed it against her forehead. Her hands were shaking. This couldn't possibly be happening to her.

That man could make her so damn mad at times. How dare he try to turn the tables on her? She wasn't the one having a baby. She loved him, and he had gotten another woman pregnant.

And it bothers you.

Yes, she was so jealous she could scream . . . because she would never be able to give him a child.

Leaning against the sink, she took a deep breath. It was probably for the best their relationship was over, because otherwise she'd have had to tell him she couldn't have children. Their breakup saved her from the embarrassment.

So why didn't she feel any better?

Because you love his lying no-good ass.

She was supposed to be angry with Jay, but seeing him, she wasn't quite as angry as she wanted to be. Her body reacted to his presence, her heart hammered at the sound of his voice, being around him made it almost impossible to stay in control.

Deep down, she knew there had to be a logical explanation. Jay would never play both sides of the fence. But instead of listening to him, she was using his mistake as an excuse to end their relationship while she still could.

Yes, it was probably for the best. Jay had made his feelings clear with words, and she'd seen the desire in his eyes to have a child of his own. And he was . . . only it was going to be with another woman. How could she deny him such a blessing? Despite his deceptions, she still loved him. But there was no future for them. There was no way she could deny him what he wanted most—a family of his own.

Holding a hand over her heart, she attempted to release the emotional pain. The tears came streaming down her face. She removed the towel from her fore-head and used it to pat her eyelids while she gave her-self a stern command to pull herself together.

She reached for another paper towel to blow her nose, then looked at her red-rimmed eyes. She reached inside her purse and removed her compact. Once she was satisfied with her appearance, she returned to the waiting room.

She found Jay, Roxaner, and Terraine standing out-side the nursery window wearing smiles of joy. Blink-ing back a fresh set of tears, she joined them and pressed her face against the glass. When she looked down at the crib in front of the window labeled BABY GIRL ANDREWS, her heart swelled, and she gasped. She was beautiful.

She watched the nurse put a diaper on the baby and then slide a small pink hospital gown over her tiny body. Her hand was curled into a fist that she pro-ceeded to suckle. The little darling turned her head to-ward the window as if she knew she was being watched. She had caramel skin like her mother, with a head full of curly dark brown hair, and stared up at them with a pair of brown eyes identical to her father's. *And Uncle Jay's.* Honey sucked in her breath.

"I think we have another model on our hands," Roxaner said.

Honey nodded in spite of her pain. "You better get the shotgun ready. She's gonna be a heartbreaker."

"Don't let me catch any nappy-headed boys hang-ing around," Terraine replied.

Jay crept up behind Honey and locked his arms around her waist. Closing her eyes, she tried to stay in control as the strength of his body heated her own. He was trying to penetrate her resistance. If she didn't stand strong, he would succeed.

Dropping a kiss to the side of her neck, Jay whispered, "Our daughter will be just as beautiful."

Her spine stiffened as she turned to glare at him. "I wish you would stop it. You're already havin' a baby and it's not by me!" she whispered harshly as she wriggled free.

"Is everything okay?" Roxaner said, sensing something was wrong.

"Yes, I'm fine," Honey said, then moved over near Roxaner and curled an arm around her waist.

Jay was hurt by her rejection, but determined. Somehow, he would find a way to get her to understand he hadn't meant to deceive her.

Terraine came over and stood next to him. Still staring at the nursery window, he asked, "So, lil' bro, what do you think? You still want to give all this up?"

Jay peered at Honey out of the corner of his eye before answering, "Not in a million years."

Honey slowly opened the door and found Sasha lying in the bed, propped up by several pillows. She smiled down at her tired face. "Hi, Mommy."

Sasha gave her a brilliant smile. "Have you seen her yet?"

Honey nodded. "Yes, and she's beautiful." Honey moved to her and dropped a kiss on her forehead. "Have you decided on a name?"

"Ciarra."

"That's so pretty." A tear streamed down her cheek, and she quickly wiped it away.

Sasha reached over and squeezed her hand. "How are you doing?" Honey had called Sasha after Kendra left the salon and told her everything.

Honey bobbed her head. "I'm turning into a big cry-baby. I can't understand how he could do this to me." The tears began to flow harder.

"I believe in my heart that Jay didn't mean to deceive you. Listen to what he has to say. I know the two of you can work it out."

Honey shook her head. "I don't think so. It's probably for the best. You should have seen his face when he saw Ciarra."

Patting Honey's hand, Sasha said, "Girl, everything is gonna work out, I promise. You have to trust me on this."

Honey sniffled. "Oh . . . I really hope so."

"Are you gonna give him a chance to explain?"

She paused. "Maybe when I get back from the convention. Right now I need some time to think."

Sasha smiled with relief. "Good."

Honey rose from the bed. "I'm sure Terraine is dying to get back in here, so I'm gonna go. I just wanted to see you before I left and to tell you my god-daughter is beautiful."

"Thanks, girl. I'll see you when you get back."

Honey waved and exited the room, rejoining the others outside the nursery window. She found the nurse wrapping Ciarra in a blanket.

"It's feeding time," the nurse announced as she came out of the nursery door. "Follow me, Dad."

There was no mistaking the love in his eyes when, grinning from ear-to-ear, Terraine waved his hand and signaled for Roxaner to join him. "Come on, Grandma."

Once he was alone with Honey, Jay took her hands

into his and stared down at her. "We have a lot to talk about."

Eyes downcast, Honey nodded. "Can we save this conversation for when I return from Minneapolis? I really need to get home and pack, and I'm a little exhausted."

Glancing down at his watch, he saw that it was well past three in the morning. "Okay, I can live with that. But I want you to know that I didn't mean to hurt you."

What-the-fuck-ever. Honey raised her eyes and nodded.

"I love you."

Lowering her lashes, she nodded again. "We'll talk when I get back."

Before he could try to kiss her, she turned and walked away.

Eighteen

As she exited her office, Natalia's steps slowed when she found Sterling leaning against Tiffany's desk, whispering something in her ear that caused her to blush.

Ain't this a bitch? Sterling was already up to his old tricks.

After their interview, Natalia had stormed down to Terraine's office to voice her objections. For one thing, she considered two other candidates better suited for the position. But Terraine wouldn't budge in his decision to hire Sterling. When he received the seal of approval from the other four directors, it was a lost battle.

His second day on the job, and already Sterling had managed to charm over half the hoochies in the building. She, however, would never be one of his conquests.

Natalia cleared her throat as she approached them. "Excuse me, but my secretary has work to do."

Sterling straightened from his leaning position and said, "My bad," raising his hands to shoulder height. "I'm here to see you anyway."

"Me? What could we possibly have to talk about?" She turned and walked to the elevator, leaving him to stare at her backside.

With long strides, Sterling moved beside her. "Hey, hold up."

"What do you want?" she asked without stopping.

"I'm putting together a projected marketing plan for the coming year, and I thought maybe we could collaborate on ideas."

Natalia set her chin in a stubborn line. She didn't have time to waste; she had a million things to do before she flew to Los Angeles in the morning to meet with a potential buyer. Even if she wasn't leaving, there was no way she was helping Sterling keep his job. If she refused, in a matter of weeks he'd fall flat on his face. She bit her lip to stifle a grin. "Sorry, I'm too busy." Giving him a sidelong glance, she boarded the elevator.

Sterling also hopped on. "Why you got to be like that?"

"Why you got to be so damn ghetto?" she said, glowering at him. The doors closed, and as the elevator descended, she found herself once again alone with him. "This is a professional corporation. We don't need any *hood* ideas around here."

She had thought her words would have some kind of impact, but they didn't. His expression never changed. In fact, he laughed. "So I guess my MBA from Morgan State doesn't count for anything."

The challenge in his voice infuriated her. "Oh yeah! The full athletic scholarship." She slapped her forehead lightly with her palm. "How could I forget? Let's see now . . . you were the first-round draft pick for the Baltimore Ravens, and after two seasons, you sustained a knee injury, ending your career. At that point, you decided to go back to college and finish."

His face broke into a wide grin. "You've been checkin' up on a brotha."

"Not hardly. I just like football," she said and crossed her arms, looking away from his lean, muscular body as she did. Sterling apparently still worked out.

"Whatever you say." He laughed again. "What you fail to realize is that I *am* qualified for this position."

"I wouldn't know," she said with a shrug. "I barely glanced at your resume." Oh, he was getting on her nerves!

"Then let me break it down for you." Reaching out, he slapped his hand against the red button, stopping the elevator.

Natalia gasped, then turned away shaking her head.

"Straight out of college, I worked as a marketing analyst for Sears for three years before spending five years at Pepsi-Cola as their promotions manager. As marketing director for Jacqueline Giamanco . . . who, if I'm not mistaken, is now one of Diva Designs' most valued designers . . . I spent the last two years making sure her designs were in hot demand for every buyer on either coast. So . . . I think I'm more than qualified to market this corporation's upscale designs."

Natalia stayed mute, so he continued. "In my spare time, I've done volunteer work for Big Brothers Big Sisters and several other not-for-profit organizations to increase awareness in the community. I've already spoken to two such agencies, and plan to continue my efforts here in the Midwest."

That annoyed her. She didn't want to know that behind the playa there was a compassionate man concerned with the needs of the area. Anxious to escape his company, she leaned forward and started the elevator, then turned to face him. "I'm impressed—"

Her breath caught in her throat. His gorgeous eyes were staring down at her while a smile touched his beautifully supple mouth. For the first time, she noticed the tiny amethyst stone in his left earlobe, and this gave her a sense of relief. Sterling was a Pisces. She'd never gotten along with a Pisces man. *Then why is Ms. Kitty waking up?*

She took a step back from his scent, which was assailing her senses, and he closed the distance between them, trapping her in the corner with his powerful body. Standing so close, she could feel his heat.

"You don't have to pretend with me anymore." His voice was low and smooth.

"What? What are you—" Panic rose in her throat.

Sterling put a finger to her lips to shush her, and she became wildly dizzy and realized she wasn't breathing. At the touch of his warm skin, she was feeling something that she had never felt before, not even with Jacob.

He pierced her with his intense stare, and his voice was silken. "You want me, Natalia. You always have. That's why it used to bother you so much to see me with those other women."

He lowered his finger and ran it down along her collar, sending tingles down the length of her spine. She opened her mouth to deny his statement, but the protest lodged in her throat.

"You might as well get used to having me around," he whispered, his breath hot on her face. She found herself at a loss for words, and nibbled nervously at her inner cheek.

His hands traveled up again. Cupping her chin in his

palm, he brought her face closer to his. With his other arm curled around her back, he pulled their bodies close.

Then Ms. Kitty started to meow.

She gasped. With the heat of his flesh through his navy blue suit, her nipples hardened upon contact. Then his mouth caught hers, and the impact was like nothing she'd ever dreamed. When his tongue stroked her lips, she felt a hot tendril of pleasure unfold low in her belly. Suddenly, she wanted his tongue in her mouth. Desire shuddered through her when his hand slid down to cup her buttock. She responded with a moan, wanting more. But just as she reveled in his arms, he broke the kiss and backed away, and Natalia's eyes fluttered open in time to watch Sterling step off the elevator.

Hands embedded in his pockets, he turned to her again, wearing a wide grin. "It's a good thing I'm back. It seems that we have some unfinished business to attend to."

The following day, Jay landed the contract with Pulsar Medical Research.

Thank goodness something positive was happening in his life. Honey had left yesterday, and he hadn't heard from her once. Rocking in his office chair, he tried to think of a way to make things right between them. He had fucked up, and was prepared to admit it every day for the next year if he had to. But as stubborn as Honey could be, it wouldn't matter.

He'd tried to reach Natalia, but found out from her secretary that she had left town this morning. Maybe he could find a way to get her to help him. If not, he could always resort to Honey's mother. Since their introduction, the two had developed a mutual liking.

He heard a loud commotion outside his office only seconds before his door flew open. Dean barged in, followed by Dory. Dean's face was a mask of rage.

"I'm sorry, Jay. I tried to stop him," Dory said.

Jay waved off her words with his hand. "It's okay." After she left, he turned his gaze to Dean and noticed his clenched jaw. "Come on in and have a seat," he offered.

"I'd rather stand," Dean managed through stiff lips.

Clasping his hands behind his head, Jay asked, "What can I help you with?"

"Stay da hell away from my girl!" Dean barked.

"Mercedes?" Jay shrugged. "I haven't seen her. As far as I knew, she was back at home with you."

Dean moved to the end of his desk, lips thinned. "She left me again. This time she has a restrainin' order keepin' me from seein' my son."

Jay turned slightly in his chair and eased into a smile. "So, she finally came to her senses. That girl deserves a medal."

"Shut da fuck up," Dean demanded. "No one can keep me from my son. Not even you."

"I don't have anything to do with this," Jay replied honestly. "But you did bring this shit on yourself."

The answer infuriated Dean further. "How da fuck would you know? You don't know shit about me or my girl, so just stay da fuck away or else ___"

"Or else what?" Jay said, then waited.

Dean bunched his fists and moved forward. "Or else somethin' might happen dat will keep you away from your own kid."

"I don't have any kids."

"Yeah, you do." Dean smirked. "I know all about Kendra."

Jay's brow shot up in surprise. "How's that?"

Dean rocked back on his heels, apparently amused by Jay's reaction. "I was there when she came to the salon and acted a damn fool with that bitch you've been humpin'."

"I'd advise you to watch your mouth," Jay said, barely controlling his voice.

"Whatever, man." Dean chuckled. "It looks like we each got somethin' the other wants. Stay away from Lil' Dee, and I promise not to bring any harm to yo' expectant family. I would hate for dat child to be without his daddy."

Jay rose and walked around his desk. "You got a lot of balls coming into my office threatening me." He took another step so they were eye to eye. "If I was you, I'd get the hell out of here before I'm forced to hit you in your mothafuckin' mouth again."

Dean lunged at Jay, hitting him square in the stomach. The unexpected attack knocked the wind from Jay's lungs as they hit the desk. A lamp smashed to the floor, followed by stacks of papers. While Jay recovered, Dean was at an advantage and landed a punch on Jay's cheek. Thinking he had the upper hand, Dean smirked, then swung again. Only this time, Jay was prepared. He caught Dean's hand in midair and twisted it behind his back until he heard a pop. Then, with his foot, he pushed Dean headfirst into the wall.

Dean gave a high-pitched scream. "*Aahhh* . . . you broke my arm!"

"You better be glad I didn't crack your sorry ass in two."

The noise brought Chad through the door, followed by Dory.

"Is there a problem in here?" Chad asked, looking down at Dean crumpled in the corner.

Jay reached up and rubbed his knuckles across his cheek, breathing heavily. "Nah, there's no problem. I think we understand each other quite well. Dean, wouldn't you agree?"

Cradling his arm, Dean mumbled, "Yeah . . . Yeah, man, it's all good."

Dory planted both hands on her hips and huffed. "Well, if you're through throwin' your weight around, you need to get to the hospital right away."

"Damn, Dory. I don't think these minor bruises constitute a need to go the emergency room," Jay said, a trace of laughter in his voice.

"No, silly. A nurse from Christian Hospital called. Kendra's in labor."

Jay dashed out the door, cursing silently when he remembered that Natalia was out of town. With Kendra's birth coach away, he was left to deal with Kendra alone.

Damn! It was raining on his world again.

Nineteen

When Jay arrived, Kendra's legs were jackknifed up alongside her swollen stomach, her hair was hanging wildly around her face, and her eyes were wild with fear. The birthing bed had been disassembled, and her feet were propped up against the edge of the shortened bed, with Dr. Gaye positioned between her legs.

"About time your black ass showed up!" Kendra cried out between moans.

A nurse gave him a sympathetic smile before another contraction seized Kendra. Putting aside their differences, Jay moved to her and grabbed hold of her hand. She screamed and squeezed his hand so hard he thought she had broken a couple of his fingers.

"Kendra," Dr. Gaye said, "when your next contraction begins, I want you to bear down and push."

Her panting became rapid, and with the aid of the nurse, she leaned forward. Gritting her teeth, she followed the instructions and pushed between sobs. "I can't do this shit!" she screamed.

"Yes, you can, Kendra," Jay said while mopping her forehead. "You can do it."

The doctor smiled. "I see the baby's head."

A bubble rose in Jay's throat, and he released Kendra's hand and walked around to stand beside the doctor to get a closer look. *Shhiiit!* Was that a pussy he was looking at all stretched out and shit? Hell, he knew they stretched, but damn, not like that. He wouldn't have believed it if he hadn't seen it with his own eyes. Then he noticed the baby and his mouth flew open. When he saw the crown of wet, matted hair a warm feeling flowed through him, and he no longer heard Kendra's screams or the nurse coaching her along. The only thing he saw was his child's head suddenly appear. The doctor stopped to suction the baby's mouth and nose—a nose that was broad and so much like his own. Jay chuckled with excitement and placed a soothing hand on Kendra's knee.

"Come on, girl, you can do it," he encouraged her, anxious to see his child.

Kendra took a deep breath and gave an ear-piercing scream as she bore down hard. Within seconds, a small body appeared.

The doctor held the baby up for everyone to see, then gave Jay a satisfied smile. "Congratulations, you have a handsome baby boy."

A boy!

His son coughed, then squalled, and Jay couldn't stop grinning. He watched with the grin plastered on his face, tears of joy streaming down his cheeks. He didn't even try to stop them from falling.

His son was placed on Kendra's stomach while the umbilical cord was clamped and then cut.

"You did good, Kendra," Jay said softly before bending over to plant a kiss on her cheek.

Kendra stared down at her son and gave a weak smile that quickly faded. "He's all wet and slimy." Then she leaned back on her pillow and closed her eyes while the doctor repaired a minor tear. "Can you please take him away? I'm exhausted." She brought the back of her hand to her forehead for added theatrical effect. The nurse carried the baby to a warmer and wheeled him out of the room.

Jay moved like a zombie out into the hallway, following the warmer to the nursery, where a nurse met him at the door. She smiled and said, "Sorry, Dad, authorized personnel only. But you can watch over there." She pointed to the long picture window.

Jay was still grinning as he watched the nursing staff weigh and measure his son, footprint him, and put him in the tiniest diaper he'd ever seen. The nurse then put him in what looked like a small hospital gown and wrapped him tightly in a blanket. He tapped on the window, and she looked over and nodded knowingly. After she placed a small blue cap on the baby's tiny head, she carried him in the crook of her arm to the window so Jay could get a closer look. His son gazed up at him as if he knew who his daddy was.

How could he have ever thought about giving this child away? Jay's chest tightened just thinking about it. The pain of never knowing his son would have sliced through him worse than any bullet wound and haunted him for the rest of his life. How could he have ever considered such a thing?

This was his son, to love and to protect.

Thirty minutes later, Jay returned to Kendra's room to find her sound asleep. He took a seat in the rocker, and the nurse arrived with the baby. She lowered him into Jay's outstretched arms and exited the room.

Staring down at him, Jay was overcome with emotion. Never again would he believe his life worthless. This child gave him purpose. Made his life worthwhile. He'd never imagined he could become so quickly attached to another life. A life he had created. Already he felt a strong stirring of love and protection toward him. He would be there to watch him grow, to hear his first word. He would be there when he took his first step. He was going to be a father to his child. His son.

Cuddling him close, Jay reached down and gently stroked his silky black hair. His hand then slid down a soft arm to touch a tiny hand that curled around his thumb. Lifting him, Jay held him to his cheek and took a deep breath. His lips brushed across the baby's head while he whispered loving words.

"I'll always love you," he cooed, smelling the scent of his son.

He lowered him into his crib, laying him on his stomach with his little behind in the air, eyes closed, and tiny fist curled. He wasn't sure how long he stood there watching him before the nurse came to return him to the nursery.

It was almost impossible to leave him behind.

Jay headed straight to Babies-R-Us. Within minutes, he had several carts filled beyond capacity with clothes, diapers, and toys, including a football and a bat. There was a crib and rocker up front, waiting for him at the checkout. He was standing in line when he suddenly remembered he hadn't called the office or his brother.

* * *

Terraine was propped up on one elbow watching his daughter suckling at Sasha's nipple when the phone rang. He reached it on the second ring.

"I have a son!" Jay shouted through the phone.

"What? Congratulations! Why didn't you call us?"

"I forgot." Laughter floated over the line.

"What did he say?" Sasha eagerly asked.

Moving the phone away from his mouth, Terraine said, "Jay has a son."

"Congratulations, Jay!" she shouted, loud enough for him to hear; then she looked down at Ciarra. "You hear that, sweetie? You have a cousin."

Terraine chuckled heartily before hanging up the phone and saying, "He just bought out the store." Then he reached down and stroked his daughter's face before saying a silent prayer: "Thank God, he has finally come to his senses."

Sasha gazed up at him with a worried look. "Now all he has to do is work things out with Honey."

Jay returned to the hospital and held his son until he was sound asleep, then went back to his condo and spent the rest of the night putting the crib together. After finally getting some rest of his own, Jay returned to the hospital at ten the next morning.

Strolling into Kendra's room, he found her sitting upright in the bed, brushing her hair.

"Where's my son?" he asked with anticipation.

Without looking up from the bedside table mirror, Kendra gave a bored shrug. "A nurse took him to get some blood work done."

Jay took in her uninterested expression for several

seconds before he moved to the end of the bed and took a seat.

"I meant what I said, Kendra. I want to raise my son."

She frowned. "No problem. The last thing in the world I want is to be tied down with a child. Even though I have to admit, he is kind of cute."

"Kind of cute?" Jay said with a smirk. "He's handsome, just like his dad."

Kendra stopped brushing her hair long enough to witness the smug look on his face and snorted. "I wouldn't say all that."

After a prolonged silence, Jay rose again and crossed his arms across his chest. "I decided to name him Jason Junior. J.J. for short."

Ignoring his comment, Kendra put the brush down and glanced sharply at him. "I'm being discharged tomorrow morning, so make sure you're here to pick . . ." She wrinkled her small nose with displeasure. ". . . J.J. up by eleven."

"I can take you home," Jay offered.

"No need. I've already made arrangements."

"Then I guess I'll contact you when my lawyer has the paperwork ready."

"Fine, you do that." She looked down into the mirror again, signaling the end of their conversation.

Jay exited the room anxious to see the little tike, and eager to get away from the selfish bitch as quickly as possible. He was thankful that she had no desire to be a part of their son's life. J.J. would be better off without someone like her as a mother.

He rapped lightly on the nursery door, and an elderly nurse opened it.

"Came to take your precious baby to the room?"

He beamed. "Yes, ma'am. Baby Boy Andrews."

"Just a minute." She disappeared and walked between the glass bassinets. After checking all the names she returned, frowning. "We don't have a Baby Andrews."

Jay snapped his fingers. "He's probably registered under his mother's name, Johnson."

"Oh, one moment." She walked over again and slowly checked each crib, then reached for a log sheet before returning. "He's in his mother's room. We've been trying all night to get her to bond with that darlin' little boy," she said with an apologetic smile.

Jay scratched his head and gave her a sheepish grin. "Yeah, his mom isn't very affectionate." Then suddenly his expression stilled. "But I just left her room, and he wasn't there."

The nursed followed him down the hall to Kendra's room, and they found her on the telephone.

"Kendra, hang up," Jay said.

She covered the mouthpiece with her hand and snapped, "What do you want?"

The nurse moved around to the side of her bed. "Ms. Johnson, who came to retrieve your baby?"

She shrugged. "A nurse. Why?"

The nurse mumbled something under her breath and exited the room.

Kendra whispered into the mouthpiece, then hung up. "Jay, what's going on?"

He shook his head, surprised by her fear-stricken face. "I'm not sure yet." He walked out and found the nurse conferring with the other staff. Within minutes, everyone was scrambling around the wing while another nurse in the nursery checked each baby's bracelet one by one for a possible mix-up.

Jay caught a blond nurse by her arm as she came down the hall. "What the hell's going on? Where's my son?"

She wore a grave expression. "We don't know what happened to him." She pulled her arm free. "Please, we have to act fast." She dashed into the nursery and grabbed the phone. Jay took long strides down the hall to where a heavyset nurse was sealing off the exit doors.

Kendra raced out of her room wearing a blue satin robe she had brought from home. "What's going on? Where's my son?"

"He's missing," Jay said, his heart pounding. "J.J. is missing."

Jay caught Kendra just before she hit the floor.

Honey closed her eyes as the plane prepared for take-off. Attending the convention had been good for her. She was coming home with lots of new ideas for the salon. She'd spent a ridiculous amount on new equipment, but it was well worth it.

But her mind wasn't on the salon, or on the grand opening she was having next week. Her thoughts were on Jay. She stared out the window, thoughts floating in her head. She had done a lot of soul-searching, and realized Jay wasn't the only one at fault.

How could she blame him for keeping a secret, when she had done the same? It was ironic. She couldn't have children, and he had one on the way. It was so fuckin' unreal. Her heart filled with an ache. She was pissed at him. But even though he'd gotten another woman pregnant, it did nothing to change the fact that she still loved him, and he loved her, and she still wanted him regardless. When she got home, she planned to call him and give him a chance to explain.

The hospital was swarming with police. Every wing was checked and every nurse questioned, but there was still no sign of J.J.'s whereabouts.

After Jay contacted his brother, Terraine was there within minutes.

"Any word yet?" he asked as he joined Jay at the end of the hall.

Jay shook his head. Terror shuddered through him, drowning out all the frantic voices as he shuffled numbly down the hall. He spotted a female police officer coming out of the nursery, heading toward the exit.

"Hey! Aren't you gonna question the rest of the staff?" he shouted.

"Sir, we've already done that." She gave him a sympathetic smile.

Terraine reached for Jay and pulled him in the other direction. "Come on, Jay, let the officers do their job."

"I know, I know. I just can't fuckin' believe this shit is happening." Jay ground his teeth in helpless anger. It had already been two hours since J.J. was last seen.

"I can't believe it either," Terraine said. "If anything happened to Ciarra, I'm not sure what I would do."

"I think God is punishin' me."

"What're you talking about?" Terraine's eyes were large in disbelief.

Eyes filled with regret, Jay said, "For not wanting J.J."

"What?"

"No, I'm serious." Jay shook his head, then said, "I need to get some air. Go back to your family. Kiss Ciarra for me." Terraine heard the deep sadness in his brother's voice.

Jay traveled down to the lobby to smoke a cigarette, dodging TV cameras and newspaper reporters. The chill air met him at the door, temporarily numbing his pain.

There were clouds overhead again.

Honey walked into her house and, leaving her suitcase in the hallway, moved to the answering machine to check her messages, removing her coat on the way. There was a message from both her mother and Darrius, but nothing from Jay.

She reached for the remote control and clicked on the television, then strolled into the kitchen for an ice-cold soda.

"This just in . . . the newborn son of Jason Andrews, great-grandson of millionaire fashion designer Richard Andrews, was abducted today from the maternity ward at Christian Hospital."

Honey slowly walked back into the living room, and her eyes froze to the television.

"About seven this morning, a woman dressed in a nurse's uniform walked into the mother's room and told her she was taking the baby to have some tests. The little boy hasn't been seen since."

Honey watched, rooted to the floor, as Kendra appeared on the screen. "Whoever you are, please bring my baby back!" she said, then burst into heart-wrenching sobs.

Jay moved in front of the camera and pulled her into a comforting embrace. His pained eyes blazed onto the television screen. "All I want is my son back. No questions asked."

With a trembling hand, Honey managed to click the television off. Her knees turned to water as she lowered herself onto the couch, feeling as if someone had reached into her chest and crushed her heart.

It was well past midnight when the police finally convinced Jay to go home. The nurses were forced to give Kendra a tranquilizer to calm her down. When he left, she was sound asleep. Jay found it a relief to know that deep down she did care about their son. *She was probably just as confused as I had been.* It was a shame it had taken a tragedy to bring her to terms with her feelings.

Clicking on the television, he found the media still reporting on the kidnapping and clicked the television off again. They didn't know any more than he did. He walked back to the room he had all ready for his son, and seeing it choked him up. Who took his son? His heart wrenched with pain as he thought, *Are they feeding him? Is he okay?* He had to pray that whoever had taken him did it because they wanted a child of their own, and would make sure that all his needs were provided for.

The phone rang. Hoping it was news, Jay raced into his room to pick it up and practically shouted hello.

"J-Jay?"

"Honey?"

"I'm so sorry about your son," she said.

Taking a seat on the bed, he briefly closed his eyes. It was soothing to hear her voice. "Thank you. I really needed to hear that."

"Have they any leads yet?"

He lowered his head into his hands and answered in a troubled voice, "No, not a one."

Honey heard the pain in his voice, and wished she could be there for him. But did he need her? He and Kendra had each other. The thought of the two of them consoling each other caused her stomach to churn. "They'll find him. I can feel it."

"I hope so." There was so much more he wanted to say. "Honey, I want to . . ." His voice broke. He was an emotional mess, and now wasn't the time. "Honey, I've got to go."

She tried to hide her disappointment. "Good luck finding your son," was all she could muster.

Twenty

Natalia slumped back against the couch, shaking her head in disbelief. "Who could do somethin' like this?"

It had already been twenty-four hours. There were still no leads. Jay's eyes blazed with anger as he paced around the living room. "I'm not sure. But when I find out, they'll have hell to pay." And that was a promise.

Natalia's brow furrowed with worry. She had returned to St. Louis only hours ago. After catching word of the abduction at the airport, she headed straight to Kendra's apartment. "I didn't even get to see him," she whispered.

Remembering his son squirming innocently in his arms, he sighed, then lowered himself into a chair. "J.J.'s adorable. Big brown eyes and . . . wavy hair like mine."

Natalia didn't miss the catch in his voice. Jay was trying to appear strong, but she knew he was torn up inside. "What are the police doing?"

He leaned forward and rested his elbows on his knees. "They're building a case, but so far they've got nothing. I can't just sit back and wait for somethin' to happen." Jay stared down at the floor. The not knowing was killing him. To ensure that he didn't miss any news, all his calls were being forwarded to Kendra's phone. She'd been discharged from the hospital only hours ago.

Natalia leaned over and patted his hand. "We mustn't panic. They're gonna find him."

He turned to her with solemn eyes. "I hope so." The lack of leads was eating at his confidence, but he wasn't about to give up hope.

Kendra moved into the room. She was dressed in black pajamas, her eyes bloodshot and her hair in disarray. "Nat, when did you get back?"

"An hour ago." She rose and embraced Kendra, then kissed her cheek. "It's so sad."

"It's terrible!" Kendra shrieked, fear burning in her eyes. "How could someone do something like this?"

Natalia blinked in surprise. Jay had already warned her that Kendra was upset, but she had to see it to believe it. "They're gonna find him," she told her distraught friend. "It's just a matter of time."

"I wish I had that kind of faith," Kendra said as she took a seat on the couch next to Jay. "The Lord is punishing me for being a bad mother." She threw herself into Jay's arms and began to cry again. "I'm so scared. Can you hold me please?"

His arm curled around her waist, then his gaze settled on Natalia as he mouthed, "See what I'm talking about?"

As quickly as her tears started they stopped. Kendra moved her head from his chest and leaned back against his shoulder. "When are they gonna send the ransom note so we can get this shit over with?"

"I—I don't know." Jay was afraid to voice his darkest fears that maybe whoever had J.J. planned to keep him. Best to let Kendra believe that this was a ransom kidnapping.

Natalia wished there was something she could do to comfort the two. If anyone could find the baby, Jay would. He was an excellent PI, and finding J.J. was just a matter of time. Searching his troubled eyes, she tried to read into his thoughts. "Jay, do you think this could be directed personally at you? Maybe someone's trying to get back at you?"

"I've considered that." Jay had been racking his brain since yesterday trying to think of people who would be out to get him. The list was extensive; he'd made a lot of enemies over the years. He had assigned Chad and Alan to start narrowing down the possibilities.

"Look at my hair," Kendra moaned as she tunneled her fingers through the lifeless mass. "I look awful!"

Now, that's the Kendra I know, Natalia thought. Who else but Kendra would be thinking about her appearance when her child was missing? "Would you like me to make you an appointment?" she offered, certain she could get her hairdresser to see Kendra right away.

Lip quivering, Kendra nodded. "That would be nice. I have to do something to take my mind off of this."

Jay was no longer listening.

Dean.

Not only had Dean threatened him with harm to his child, but he had been in his office when Jay received the news that Kendra was in labor.

Jay took several breaths to calm the rage stirring again. Removing his arm from around Kendra, he moved to call his office, thinking, *J.J., Daddy's coming for you.*

He was going to hold his son again.

* * *

Now that the renovation was in the final stage, preparations were being made for the salon's grand opening.

Honey tried burying herself in her work, concentrating on the décor for the new space. She even overbooked her schedule so she had little free time to think. But nothing worked. Her thoughts kept returning to Jay and that bitch named Kendra Johnson. She couldn't even turn on the television without taking a chance of hearing some reporter talking about "the Andrews baby boy."

Every night when she turned on the salon's security system, her thoughts turned to him. Then she went home to spend a restless night of tossing and turning while he invaded her mind. He was hurting, but she was too. She needed to feel his arms around her, his lips on her lips.

She held back tears that she stubbornly refused to shed.

Yesterday she tried calling his house to give him some moral support, only to find that he wasn't at home. He was with Kendra. *Of course.* She tried not to be jealous because she knew they needed each other right now, but she couldn't help herself. She wanted him to need her.

As she rubbed the palm of a hand across her flat stomach, her heart churned. She was jealous of Kendra and Jay's son.

Dean was nowhere to be found.

Unable to sit still, Jay returned to work the next morning, anxious to dig into the investigation. The police had warned him to back off, but there was no way he could sit still and do nothing. Sitting behind his desk, he went over his notes.

According to the nursery, J.J. was taken to Kendra's room an hour before he was discovered missing. Kendra claimed that Nurse Jewel showed her how to properly hold the baby and feed him his bottle, then she had left Kendra to burp him. The idea of Kendra willingly burping a baby was far-fetched, but he decided to give her the benefit of the doubt. Kendra then reported putting him back in his crib, where he had fallen asleep. She was in the bathroom when she heard a nurse arrive, saying she had to take J.J. for some blood work. When Kendra re-entered the room, they were gone.

Jay lowered his head to his hands. By the time he had arrived twenty minutes later, J.J. had already disappeared. His chest cringed at the possibilities. The police had interviewed the entire staff, monitored all the exits, and confiscated the security tapes. But no one had seen or heard anything. The first twenty-four hours were the most critical. The longer it took to find J.J., the more likely they never would. It had now been forty-eight hours.

Jay rose from his chair and moved toward the window, shaking away the ridiculous thought. He would find his son. No matter how long it took.

As soon as Honey got home that evening, she decided to call Jay. She had promised him that when she returned, they would talk. Even though he had brushed her off the other night, she needed to let him know that she was there for him.

She dialed his number, and the phone picked up after the first ring.

"Hello?"

Honey hesitated at the sound of the female voice. "Sorry, I have the wrong number." She hung up and dialed the number again. However, the same voice came over the line.

"Is this Honey?" the woman asked.

She frowned. "Yes . . . who is this?"

"The same lady who told you to stay the fuck away from her man."

Kendra. What the hell was she doing at Jay's condo? "I'm sorry about your son," she said, trying to be nice.

"If you were really sorry, you would leave us to grieve alone."

Who does she think she's talking to? "Look, I know there's nothing going on between you and Jay."

"Hmmph! If that's what you want to think."

"That's what I *know*. Jay and I love one another. Now put him on the phone," she ordered. Baby's mama or not, Kendra was trippin'.

"Jay isn't available to talk to you. We're trying to . . . console one another."

"Excuse me?" Honey sputtered.

"You heard me, bitch," Kendra said. "Jay and I have discovered we still love each other, and are trying to work through our differences so J.J. can come home to a family. It's over, so I would appreciate it if you would leave us alone." She snorted. "The only woman who's gonna be ridin' his dick is *me*."

Honey's ear was then met by the dial tone.

*   *   *

His son had been missing almost seventy-two hours. With the help of a friend in hospital security, Jay was granted access to the maternity ward the following afternoon. He intended to try to reconstruct the events of that night.

Using a stopwatch, he monitored the amount of time it took from Kendra's room to the nursery. Without any stops, the short trip took forty-two seconds. He then walked down the hall again and observed all of the doors along both walls. There was an exit door near the nurses' station and a supply closet.

As he moved down the hall, a door swung open. He quickly jumped out of the way.

"Oh, I'm sorry." A tall woman stood behind a cart piled high with fruit juice.

"No problem." Smiling down at her, Jay found something oddly familiar about her gentle amber eyes. But he couldn't quite understand why.

She noticed the pad of paper in his hand. "Y'all still investigatin' the missin' baby?"

Jay nodded. "Were you working that night?"

She looked around her to make sure no one was watching. The staff had been instructed not to discuss the case with anyone. "Not on this floor. That day I was workin' up in the OR." She extended a slender hand that had rings on every finger and a diamond tennis bracelet dangling from the wrist. "Ledora Hayes."

"Pleased to meet you. I'm Jay."

She signaled for him to follow her into the supply room, where she put juices in the refrigerator while she talked. "I'm an on-call nurse. Normally I'm assigned to this unit, but there were quite a few C-sections that morning. They were pretty short-staffed, so I was sent up to the OR." She looked up at him, eyes narrowed. "I did, however, get the pleasure of meeting that hateful bitch the afternoon before. She had buzzed the nurses' station wanting a cup of tea, and even had the nerve to ask for lemon and honey. When I went down to her room, she was still pretty upset from the couple who had visited her earlier."

"What couple?"

Ledora ran a hand across her honey-blond weave as she tried to remember. "A fancy-looking couple dressed in furs and diamonds came in carrying a car seat. They asked me which child was the Johnson baby, and I pointed to him through the window. They were so excited."

What car seat? He didn't remember seeing any car seat. "Then what happened?"

"Well, later I was passing out supplies, and I heard loud voices coming from her room. I poked my head in, and the lady in the fur was crying. The gentleman . . . I guess he was the lady's husband . . . had his arm around her and mumbled something about money. Then they left."

Jay continued to stare down at her, eyelids blinking. "Thank you, you've been a big help."

"No problem. Just don't tell anybody I spoke to you."

He nodded, then watched her push the cart down the hall and around the corner.

Wondering who the couple might be, Jay strolled to the end of the ward and pushed the button for the elevator, suddenly anxious to talk to the only person who would know the answer.

Twenty-one

Jay arrived at Kendra's just as she pulled into the driveway in her Range Rover. She got out and moved up the sidewalk, carrying several bags with designer labels.

"Looks like you're feelin' better," he mumbled with intentional sarcasm.

"No. Not really," she said, pouting. "But what else is there to do besides wait?"

Jay took several bags from her and followed her up to her apartment. Kendra walked into the living room, removed her coat, and fell back against the couch.

"If I just sit around this place another day thinking about where my baby is, I am gonna fall apart." Her eyes became misty, and she moved to the bathroom to find a tissue.

After shrugging out of his jacket, Jay took a seat in the nearest chair. "I know exactly how you feel."

Kendra returned carrying a box of tissues and set it on the coffee table. She sat back on the couch and removed her shoes. "I went and saw a lawyer today."

"For what?"

She looked shocked by his question. "To sue Christian Hospital, of course. Our son was in their care, so they're responsible. Mr. Holmes says we have a strong case. The hospital will likely settle out of court."

"Kendra, I'm not interested in suing, I just want my son back."

"It doesn't look like that's gonna happen." She winced at her own words. "I spoke with the police, and they still have no leads. What about you? Any possibilities?"

He shook his head. He'd found out from the police that Dean had been arrested the morning of the abduction for violation of the restraining order. "No, no leads at all. However, I *would* like to know who the couple was that visited you in the hospital."

Kendra wrinkled her petite nose with confusion. "What couple?"

"The couple that brought along a car seat."

Kendra rose and moved toward the kitchen. "I have no idea what you're talking about."

He lunged after her, caught her by the arm, and spun her around before she made it into the kitchen. "Don't play with me, Kendra," he said, glaring down at her. "I know all about the conversation you had with them. The *heated* conversation."

Kendra nibbled on her bottom lip, then said, "Oh, *that* couple." She wiggled free of his grip and took a seat at the kitchen table.

Jay moved in and stood before her with arms crossed, waiting.

"That was my mother," she said after a moment.

"Your mother? I thought you hadn't spoken to her in years."

Kendra rested her chin in the palm of her hand. "I lied.

I contact my mother all the time. Christmas, birthdays, you name it. Only she never makes any efforts of her own." Rolling her eyes, she continued. "The only reason she came to visit me was that she found out that J.J. was the great-grandson of the legendary Richard Andrews."

"How did she know that?"

"I told her."

Jay raked a hand through his hair and moved away. "What did she want?"

Kendra raised her shoulders matter-of-factly. "Money, of course. She assumed that since I was having your baby you were taking care of me." She laughed bitterly. "She couldn't believe that I could take care of myself. Unlike her, I learned to be independent. She brought her newest beau with her, and the two of them walked into my room dressed like they were on their way to the annual BET Awards," she spat bitterly. "She asked me for a loan so her car wouldn't be repossessed, and I refused."

Jay returned to the living room and took his seat as he weighed the possibilities. He was so quiet that, after a while, Kendra came into the room and gave him a quizzical look.

"What's runnin' through your mind?"

He looked her squarely in the eye with his next question. "Do you think your mother could have taken J.J.?"

Kendra gasped, and it took her several seconds to speak. "I . . . I doubt it. She doesn't even like kids." But as she said one thing, her face was saying another.

"Money makes us all do crazy things."

She shook her head. "I don't know what to say."

"Think about it. You said yourself the only reason

she came to see J.J. was that she found out he was an Andrews. What more reason do you need?"

"I don't know," she mumbled.

"I'm gonna call Officer Holman. It's more than they have so far." Ten minutes later he returned to find Kendra still sitting in the same spot, her head hung low.

"Are you okay?"

She looked up at him with red-rimmed eyes. "I can't believe my mother would do something like this." She sniffled into a tissue. "She never wanted me, yet for money, she was willing to take my son." She threw herself into his arms.

After they tried unsuccessfully to reach her mother, Jay convinced Kendra to take a nap and didn't object when she asked him to hold her. When she was sound asleep, he called Chad and had him run her mother's name through the computer. If Martha Johnson had his son, she would have a helluva lot of explaining to do.

Honey didn't want to believe what Kendra had insinuated, but she hadn't heard from Jay since she returned. What else was there to think other than Jay and his baby's mama had gotten back together?

He had obviously accepted her decision to end their relationship, and while she was gone, he and Kendra had reconciled. What the hell did she expect? Jay had too much pride to keep running after her. Just like he'd told her, he wasn't going to beg. He had finally decided to move on and had left her high-yellow ass in the dust.

Her stomach churned at the thought. It was too late. Her boo was gone. She had sent him into the arms of another woman, and it was no one's fault but her own.

Honey tried not to be jealous. He was doing the right thing, and she didn't want to be responsible for taking him away from his child. She knew how it felt to grow up without a father, and the bitterness she'd harbored ever since.

Her life was fine and uncomplicated before he stepped into it. Damn him for curing her sexual fears, awaking her desires, and making her feel like the most beautiful woman in the world! Had he made Kendra feel that way also?

With renewed determination, she tried to put him from her mind and bury herself in her work, brushing aside the impulse to cry.

Her phone rang and she quickly reached for it, glad for the distraction.

"Honey, this is Sasha. When are you coming over to see your goddaughter?"

"I'm sorry. I've been so busy trying to get ready for the grand opening."

Sasha wasn't buying it. "You've also been ignoring my calls. Ciarra will be walking by the time you come by."

Honey couldn't resist a grin. "I'll be by this week."

Sasha heard the pain in her voice and said, "Terraine will be out tonight, and I could really use some company."

Honey only hesitated a moment. "All right. I'll drop by this evening."

"Oh, good! I'm dying to show you Ciarra's pictures."

"See you then."

* * *

"Nothing, man. I drove to East St. Louis myself, and there was no one there."

Jay slumped down in the chair. The search wasn't going anywhere. After he was unable to reach Kendra's mother by phone, he'd sent Chad to drive by her house with instructions to call him immediately if she was home. He would have gone himself, but he didn't trust leaving Kendra alone. As soon as he had turned his back, he found her trying to down a bottle of sleeping pills.

"I'll have Tony do surveillance on her apartment tonight. It's a dump. Not even fit for a dog to live in."

"Tell him the minute he sees anything to call me."

"I'll do that."

After visiting with her goddaughter for almost two hours, Honey could no longer resist asking, "Have they found out anything yet about little J.J.?"

Sasha met her friend's gray eyes. She had wondered how long it was going to take before Honey asked about Jay. Shaking her head, she replied, "No, and Jay is so torn up about it. He's practically put his business on hold while he tries to find out where his baby is. It's so sad."

Honey didn't comment, just rocked Ciarra in her arms.

"I've never known him to shatter emotionally. Jay's always been so calm and in control. If they don't find out something soon, he's gonna fall apart. He really loves that little boy." Sasha looked to make sure Honey was paying attention. She was. "And he loves you too."

"I miss him," Honey confessed. "But he should've told me."

"He didn't know himself until the last minute."

Her head snapped up. "What do you mean, he didn't know?"

Sasha quickly filled her in on how Kendra showed up on his doorstep, and on her ultimatum. "He spent the last several weeks trying to decide if he wanted to keep the baby or find him a loving home. It wasn't until right before he was born that Jay finally made the decision to be a father to his child." Sasha gave Honey a disgusted look. "That wench doesn't want any part of that baby. I'm not buying any of those Oscar performances she's been displaying on television. Terraine and I dropped by her apartment yesterday to give our support, and she kept throwin' herself in Jay's arms the entire time we were there. Jay is just trying to do what is right."

Sasha waited for Honey's reply, but when she saw her friend's distant look, she knew it would be a while.

Have I been too quick to judge? Honey wondered. If so, then maybe it wasn't too late to salvage their relationship.

But was she ready to take the risk of Jay rejecting her? She took a deep breath and nodded. Deep down, she believed her love for Jay . . . and his feelings for her were real enough to help them get through anything. Sasha was right. She was being stupid. She had everything she could possibly want in a man, and she was willing to give it all up because she was afraid that Jay's love wasn't going to be strong enough, that he wasn't going to love her anymore when he found out she couldn't give him a child of his own.

But he now had a child. Yes, he did. Jay had a little bundle of joy, something she could never give him . . . but someone they could hopefully share.

"I've been so stupid," she whispered.

Sasha smiled and said, "It's okay, girl. Just get it right, and go get your man before that bitch sinks her claws in him. He really needs you right now."

Staring down at Ciarra, Honey said, "Let me rock my godbaby to sleep, then I'm out of here." She prayed there was still time to make things right.

The waiting was getting to both of them. *Please let my son be okay.* Jay prayed to God and hoped that whoever was taking care of him heard, too.

While Kendra took a bath, Jay looked through her refrigerator for something to eat.

"Jay?" he heard her call from the bathroom.

He moved to the bathroom door. "Yes?"

"I forgot to bring a towel in."

He pursed his lips and moved to the linen closet for a bath towel, then knocked on the door. "Here you go."

"Just bring it in. It's not like you haven't seen me naked before."

He hesitated a moment, then opened the door. The room was steaming and smelled of her favorite Victoria's Secret bubble bath. Kendra was lying back in the tub with a washcloth covering her breasts. Her hair was wrapped in a towel. He moved to the sink, laid the towel down, and turned to leave.

"Jay, do you mind washing my back?"

She had been crying all day. It was almost impossible to say no. Like she said, it wasn't like he'd never seen her butt-ass naked before. Nevertheless, when he turned back around, he tried not to look directly at her.

Kendra removed the washcloth draped over her chest and held it out to him, exposing a pair of beautiful breasts. Jay's dick pulsed. They were larger than he remembered but just as succulent looking. He pulled a brass vanity chair near the tub and took the cloth from her hands. She leaned forward, and as he lathered her back she moaned, "That feels so good. I can't remember the last time I had my back washed."

Jay felt his body tense as blood started pumping to his loins. It had suddenly gotten hot in there. Clearing his throat, he circled the area one more time, then rinsed, relieved he was done.

"Thank you," she said as she leaned back against her bath pillow. She found his eyes on her chest and smiled inwardly. Reaching forward, she grabbed his hand and placed it on her left breast. "Please, Jay, I know your heart belongs to someone else, but right now I need you." Kendra's eyes brimmed with tears. "Can we make each other feel good just for the moment?"

Damn, he was a sucker for tears, not to mention her big-ass breasts. She was hurting and so was he. All they had right now was each other. What would it hurt for the two of them to console each other? Reaching for a towel, he carried her effortlessly to the room and laid her on he bed. He then lay beside her.

"Dr. Gaye said no sex for at least a month, but she didn't say anything about touching, finding ways to make each other feel good," she whispered in between kisses. She reached down and unzipped his pants, then took his dick in her hand and began to stroke him as Jay took a nipple in his mouth.

"That's it, baby. Make me forget everything that has happened," she said, breathless, as he took her other breast in his hand and began tweaking the nipple gently between his fingers.

Her eyes drifted shut as he sucked and licked. There

was no way she could concentrate on jacking him off with Jay touching her that way.

With her nipple still in between his lips, his right hand slowly traveled down her body until he found her clit. He stroked it with his index finger. Kendra rocked her hips against his hand. When Jay rubbed faster, she bucked on the bed.

It wasn't long before she moaned, "Oh, yeeesss . . . I . . . I'm getting ready to come! *Aaahhh!*" When she was done, she placed her head on his chest until her breathing returned to normal. "Thank you."

"You feel better now?" he asked.

She lifted her head and stared down at him. "Not until I make you feel good too."

He shook his head. "You don't have to."

"Yes, I do. Now roll your ass over."

Jay hesitated but he was too fuckin' horny to resist temptation. With her hand wrapped around his dick she didn't leave him much choice. *What difference does it make?* It wasn't like he was messing around. He was single and so was she.

Kendra straddled him, then took his length in her mouth. Jay moaned with pleasure as she slid her lips up and down his shaft.

"That's it, Kendra. Don't stop!" he grunted with each stroke.

She licked and sucked and when he began to tremble, she knew he was about to come. She moved her mouth away and stroked him until his cream spilled in her hand, then she rubbed it across her chest. Afterward they lay side by side until their breathing settled.

"You'll always be mine," Kendra murmured against his chest.

Then reality hit him. What the hell did he just do? He had allowed his emotions to take control again.

Jay rose from the bed and stared down at her smiling face. "I'm gonna go order dinner." He closed his pants and bolted from the room. He paused outside the door, amazed at himself. What the hell happened in there? He couldn't possibly still be interested in Kendra. He knew that. It was the pain that they were sharing, nothing more. He loved Honey. Boning Kendra because he was lonely and scared was a mistake. Fucking her because Honey had pushed him out of her life was even worse. *Isn't this what happened the last time?* Yep, this was exactly how Kendra had tricked his ass in the first place. Kendra was a seductive woman who knew exactly what she was doing. And she had played his ass again.

But he quickly brushed his most recent mistake aside. He and Kendra would have a long talk later. Now there was dinner to think about, 'cause a brotha was hungry.

Moving into the second bedroom that Kendra had converted to an office, he strolled across the plush, powder-blue carpet to a large mahogany desk and reached into the bottom desk drawer for a phone book. As he glanced down, something caught his attention.

Fifty thousand dollars.

His senses pricked as he reached down and picked up the document. It was a contract. Scanning through it, he felt sick inside.

Jerome and Deborah Adams.

Adoption.

His hand trembled, and was suddenly so weak that he dropped it to his side. What a fool he had been! Kendra had given his son up for fifty thousand dollars.

Furious, he stormed down the hall to her room. Kendra was sitting on the bed with a towel draped around her body, smoothing lotion on her legs. She looked up and smiled when he entered the room, but when she saw the stormy look in his eyes her smile faded and was replaced by confusion.

"How could you?" he said, his voice almost a whisper.

"What?" she asked. When she saw the papers in his hand, her jaw dropped.

"What kind of woman are you?" he said between clenched teeth.

Kendra rose, snatched the document out of his hand, and crumpled it. "You had no right to go into my office!" she shrieked.

"You had no right giving my son away!" he thundered.

"I didn't." She paused when she saw the lethal look in his eyes, and backed away.

Jay covered the distance between them and grabbed her by the arm. "Where the hell is he?"

"I don't know! I changed my mind. I swear!" She stared up at him with wide-eyed innocence.

"Then where the hell is he?"

"I don't know."

With a grimace of disgust, he shoved her away. Kendra fell against the bed sobbing while he paced the room like a caged animal.

"Please believe me," she begged. "I told them they couldn't have him."

"When?" he barked.

"When they came to the hospital."

His eyes grew wide. "The couple with the car seat?"

She nodded. "When you told me you wanted to raise

him, I called it off. They showed up that day threatenin'
to sue if I didn't give him to them."

"How much have they already given you?"

She hesitated. "Twenty thousand."

"Whatcha do with the money?"

"I went shopping."

His clenched hand turned into a fist, and she flinched.

"You are one sick bitch, you know that?" Jay shook
his head with disbelief. "How could you sell your own
son? I would have given you any amount of money!"

"I didn't want your money. I—I wanted you to suffer."

"You need to call them so we can give them their
money and get J.J. back."

"They can't sue me. He's a mayoral candidate. The
scandal would ruin him. Anyway, I wasn't selling him.
I was making sure he was going to a good home. Only
someone that's capable of properly caring for a baby
would be willing to spend that kind of money."

He grabbed her arm again and shook it, his eyes
smoldering. "I don't care about that. *Do they have my
son?*"

She couldn't bear the disgust in his eyes. "I don't
know. I swear."

He released her arm, shoving her away in the process.
"I don't think I have ever hated a person before today."

Unable to stop herself, she scrambled to her feet and
clung to his chest. "Please, Jay! I didn't know they
were gonna take him. I told them they couldn't have
him."

Jay pried her fingers from him. "Don't talk to me.
Don't ever bring your triflin' ass near me again." He
moved to pick up the crumpled contract off the floor
and walked out of the room.

"Jay!" she screamed after him. "Please come back!" When she heard the door slam, she flung herself onto the bed, kicking and screaming.

She had made so much progress; now it was all lost.

Twenty-two

Jay went directly to the address on the document. On his way there, he called one of his buddies on the force and asked him to send over an officer; otherwise he couldn't be responsible for his actions.

Pulling into the driveway of a large brick house, he got out of the car and knocked heavily on the door. The house was quiet. He was peeking through the windows when a patrol car pulled up and Eric Jackson, a former partner and friend, emerged from it.

Eric moved up the driveway mumbling under his breath, "You can't do that."

"Like hell I can't," Jay said. "My son's in there."

"Do you have proof?"

Jay flung the document into Eric's hands. "This proof enough?" Then he moved around to the side of the house and peered through the window. He saw a baby swing in the living room. "There's baby furniture in there."

"Jay, you can't do this." Eric reached for his arm but Jay shoved him away.

"Try to stop me." He moved to the back door and banged on it.

"I'm gonna have to arrest you if you don't stop," Eric said. "There are other ways to handle this."

Jay turned to him, his eyes fiery. "Y'all have been sittin' on your asses for days, and my son is still not at home! This is the closest lead we have, and I'm not leavin' until I get him back."

Eric shook his head. In all the years he'd known him, Jay was one stubborn dude. If he tried to stop him, Jay would resist, and he would be forced to arrest him.

"There's nobody home."

They both turned to find a white-haired man standing on his back porch.

Jay moved to the fence separating the two houses and asked, "Is this the Adams residence?"

"Yes, but they're out of the country."

Jay's brow furrowed. "Where did they go?"

"They were excited about adopting a baby boy, and left yesterday to visit family in Mexico."

Jay lay across his bed. There wasn't a damn thing he could do now but wait. The Adamses had left town with his son. Jerome Adams, a politician, had a debate scheduled in town for Monday, and hopefully would return on Sunday, three days away. Without proof that the Adamses had J.J., there was nothing the police could do but wait.

How could he have allowed Kendra to do this to him? One minute he was sucking her nipples, then the next minute he was trying to break her fuckin' neck. She was the most conniving woman he'd ever known. He should have sensed that something was up. There was no way she would just give up that easy. Kendra had played him like a fuckin' yo-yo.

His life was falling apart. One minute he was on top of the world, and the next it all had come collapsing down. The two people he loved most in the world were gone.

Honey, I need you.

He needed to find a way to bridge the rift between them. He needed her support, her love. He had made so many mistakes and couldn't blame her if she never forgave him. But he wasn't giving up. He loved her too much to let go.

When J.J. was back in his arms, the Andrews men were going to bring her home.

Honey knocked at the door. Just as she got ready to knock again, Jay opened it.

She stared up at the man she had fallen in love with and barely recognized him; his eyes were hollow with dark circles below them, and his beard looked tattered. But she still found her heart pounding fiercely in her chest. Even as haggard as he was now, he was so handsome. The way he looked down at her, his tired brown eyes sparkling with love, made her feel like she could tell him anything, together they could conquer. No matter how bad it was he wouldn't love her any less.

"Come here," he commanded, arms extended.

"Jay, I'm so sorry." She rushed into his arms.

"No, I'm the one who's sorry." He held her tight and kissed her hair, needing her strength, thankful she had finally come back to him. "I missed you so much," he whispered.

She wrapped her arms around his neck and leaned into his embrace, thrilling at his warm breath against her face. His kiss deepened, and she parted her lips to welcome his tongue.

As his mouth devoured hers the lost days slipped away, and all he could think about was that she was going to be his—his friend, lover, future wife, and mother to lil' J.J.

Honey pulled back slightly and looked up at him, eyes begging for understanding. "Jay, I was so wrong, I should have given you a chance to explain."

He shook his head. "You had every right to be mad. I should have told you about Kendra a long time ago."

She looked at him closely. After a deep breath, she replied, "I haven't been completely truthful with you, either." Slipping her arm through his, she led him over to the couch and took a seat next to him. "When I told you about my rape, I didn't tell you that I got pregnant." She saw his expression still, but pressed on. "I had an abortion, and because of it, I'm unable to bear children."

"Why didn't you tell me?"

"Because I was afraid that I would lose you. You talked so much about havin' a family, and I didn't want to take that away from you."

"Don't you know that without you, I don't have a family?" His gaze now was tender, understanding. "I have never loved anyone the way I love you, and nothing is gonna change that."

She stared up at him, unable to believe her ears. "You mean it?"

"Let me show you." He swung her into his arms. "Dear God, I need you," he whispered. He took her chin between his fingers and tilted her mouth upward, rubbing her lips against his. His tongue demanding and hungry, he kissed her repeatedly.

Jay moved to her ear next, taking the lobe between his teeth. Honey groaned, arching her body closer to his, her breathing stalled. His mouth was all over her now, smothering her face with kisses. She felt tightness in her chest, and desire surged through her.

As soon as they reached his bedroom, they quickly removed their clothes and climbed between the sheets. She closed her eyes while Jay traced the fullness of her small breasts. Catching a nipple between his thumb and finger, he tweaked it until a sigh escaped her lips.

"I missed these."

"They missed you, too," she murmured. His lips replaced his hand as he laved one and then the other. Honey arched up off the mattress gasping for air, unable to think.

While he continued to tease her nipples, his hand traveled down, searching between her delicate folds to find her moist and ready. He stroked her with the tip of his finger.

Her thighs became weak, and her coochie throbbed with immediate need. She rose to meet him, wanting all ten inches buried deep inside her, wanting his touch, his closeness.

"I need you, now!" she gasped.

Parting her thighs with his hand, Jay rolled on top of her, and Honey raised her hips to receive him as Jay eased into her. The heat inside her flared, and her hips met his thrusts as he moved in and out. Gasping, she drifted into a sweetness she'd never known before him.

Jay tried to slow his movements to prolong the pleasure, but he had gone too long without feeling her pulsate around him. The thrusts became faster and more powerful until they were both met by a wave of ecstasy.

Minutes later they lay together, sweaty and exhausted, with his hand curled around her waist. Jay kissed the top of her head and whispered, "I'm never letting you go."

Twenty-three

"Knock, knock."

Things had been so fuckin' crazy in the office with Jay in and out so much that when Chad looked up, he expected to see Jay standing at the half-open door. His expression stilled when he looked up to see another familiar face. "Jocelyn, so good to see you."

That was an understatement. Her red hair curled softly around her face, and the sienna paint on her succulent lips accentuated the redhead's radiance, as did the two-piece bronze knit outfit covered by a white lab coat. *Damn, the sista was blazin'!*

Chad rose from his chair, walked around the desk, and perched on the edge. "What brings you to our neck of the woods?"

Her generous lips curled upward as she sashayed into his office. "I wanted to drop this by in person." Reaching into the pocket of her coat, she removed a card. "Please give this to Jay for me. Tell him my prayers are with him."

While accepting the envelope, he took a whiff of her

expensive cologne. "I'll do that," he replied, then licked his juicy lips.

Jocelyn didn't miss the lust gleaming in his eyes. It was the same look he'd been giving her since the first time they met. *Give it a rest.* "Have they any leads yet?"

Shaking his head, Chad answered, "Nothin' concrete."

Her dainty nose wrinkled with worry. "That's too bad." She moved to take a seat in a chair in front of his desk. As she crossed her slender legs, her split skirt parted, giving him a bird's-eye view of her thighs. "I want to—"

"Did you get the flowers I sent you?"

She forced a smile. "Yes, they were very nice. My secretary should have sent you a thank-you."

She was referring to the impersonal card, courtesy of Hallmark, that had arrived a few days later. "No, I didn't receive it," he lied.

Jocelyn suspected he was lying, which was why she didn't like him. Chad Hamilton reminded her too much of her husband . . . manipulative. She was too distraught to remember before, but Chad had dated a colleague of hers a couple of years back. So she knew all about him. Chad was a womanizer, a love-'em-and-leave-'em kind of man. Although he was eye-candy fine, she despised him.

"This is very unprofessional," she said, "but I wanted to talk with you privately about something."

Aha! I knew she was feelin' my black ass. "Sure, dinner will be great."

"What?" She laughed at the absurdity. Chad was a mack daddy wannabe.

"You think it's unprofessional for us to date," he said, misreading her. "Well . . . it's not a problem."

"Chad, this is serious. I'm not trying to come on to you."

Recovering, he said lightly, "I know. I was just playin'." He then chuckled at his own joke. What was it about her that disturbed him so much? Shaking it off, he cleared his throat. "What did you want to talk about?"

"Like I said before, this is unprofessional . . . but a new patient came in today, an adorable little boy and his mother. What bothered me was that she said he was four weeks old, but there's no way he could have been any more than four or five days old."

With a slow nod, Chad understood what she was implying and shifted on the desk. "Did you ask her about it?"

"Yes, and she swore he was born four weeks premature."

"How can you be sure she's not tellin' the truth?"

Jocelyn pursed her lips. "I'm a pediatrician. We know the difference." In one fluid motion, she rose and strolled to his file cabinet, where she found a picture of him embracing a beautiful light-skinned woman. She found herself wondering if the woman was his girlfriend. Turning to face him, she said, "I had a parent once who wanted me to lie and say her daughter was premature because she was already four weeks pregnant by another man when her husband returned home from basic training."

Chad laughed richly. "The lies women tell."

"We learn from the best," Jocelyn retorted, wiping the smirk from his face. Secretly pleased, she shrugged and said with mock indifference, "Maybe this woman was trying to do the same thing. I don't know. I might never know. It was an initial visit, and the way I questioned the child's age, I doubt she'll ever come back."

Chad's eyes had never left her. "You might have something there."

"Then again, it may be just a coincidence. That's why I'd like you to check it out first to save us all from unnecessary embarrassment." She reached into her purse, removed a card with the mother's name scribbled on it, and handed it to Chad. "The baby seemed fine, and the mother seemed very affectionate toward him. However, if nothing develops soon with Jay's baby, I'll have to take my suspicions to the police." Placing a fingertip against her lips, she murmured, "For now, remember . . . you didn't hear this from me."

"Mum's the word," Chad promised.

"Good. See you around." She exited the room.

"You better believe it," he whispered at her retreating back.

Twenty-four

Jay stared out the window at the runway. He'd been at the airport waiting for almost an hour, and the tension was getting the best of him. It didn't help that some of the city police officers had insisted on being there, too.

Honey latched on to his arm. "Sweetheart, it's gonna be okay."

"Thanks for being here with me," he said, staring down into her loving eyes.

"I have to be with the man I love."

Jay looked down at her tenderly. It was the first time she'd expressed her feeling in that way, but even though she had never told him, he had known all along how she felt.

The past three days had been special. They came together as lovers, and talked through the nights as friends. When his son was safely in his arms again, he planned to ask her to marry him.

The plane finally landed, and as soon as the double doors opened, Jay sprinted to the gate.

"Jay, you need to stand back," Officer Holman called to him.

After half the passengers had departed the plane, a distinguished-looking couple came through the door. The woman was carrying a baby in her arms.

Ignoring the officer, Jay rushed to the woman and barked, "Give me back my son!"

"What?" The woman's thick lips parted with surprise as she clutched the baby protectively against her chest.

Her husband moved between them. "Get the hell away from my wife!"

"That's my son," Jay said angrily, standing in their way.

Officer Holman and the other two officers caught up with Jay, and Holman said, "Excuse me. Jerome Adams, we'd like to ask you a few quick questions."

"What about?" Jerome said. Reaching for his wife's arm, he tried to maneuver around them. "We're in a hurry."

Honey moved to Jay's side as he shouted, "You either talk to us or I'm gonna call the media and tell them how you paid a woman fifty thousand dollars for her unborn child!"

Jerome stopped in his tracks, and the color drained from his high-yellow face. "What do you want?"

"What do you think I want? I want my son back!" Jay could no longer control his temper. One of the officers seized his arm as he lunged forward.

Jerome shook his head, confused, but then recognition swept over his face. "If you mean Kendra Johnson's child, we don't have him. She changed her mind."

What? Could she have possibly been telling the truth? Jay pointed to the baby. "Then who's that in your arms?"

Mrs. Adams stepped forward and said, "This is our new son, Sanchez. We're bringing him back from Mexico. See for yourself." She lowered the bundle in her arm and removed the blanket, revealing his face.

Jay gasped. The dark-haired boy with the almond-shaped eyes wasn't J.J.

Sitting in his office, Jay again pored over the nursing schedule from the morning of the abduction. According to the report, J.J. had to have been taken during shift change. At that time, there had been eight nurses assigned: five to the floor, and three to the nursery.

"No wonder one hand didn't know what the other was doing, they were too damn busy trying to get off for the day," he grumbled, then leaned back in the chair while he thought. The nurses all checked out, so Jay pretty much had to eliminate them as suspects. There had been fifteen patients on the floor and ten babies. Two patients had been discharged before shift change, and then two more shortly afterward. The police had already questioned the four patients, and their babies matched their footprints taken at birth. Same as the remaining eleven patients and their babies.

"Think, Jay," he muttered. "What the fuck are we missing?" He leaned forward and looked at the schedule again. It appeared that most of the nurses worked eight-hour shifts, while some worked ten. There were even nurses who worked strictly on the weekends.

"I thought I was the only workaholic."

Jay looked up at Chad standing in his door and shrugged. "I've got to find him."

"I know." Chad entered the room and held out his hand. "Maybe I can be of some help. Let me see what you got." Chad looked down at the schedule, and his brow rose. "That's her!" He pointed to the name scribbled at the bottom. "That's the woman Jocelyn came to see me about. Ledora Hayes."

Jay's head snapped back in alarm. "What about her?"

"Jocelyn came by yesterday. I didn't mention it because we were so certain the Adamses had your son. But some lady came into Jocelyn's clinic, trying to pass off a newborn boy as a four-week-old baby. Her name was Ledora Hayes. The only thing I was able to find out was that her baby was born at a small hospital in Kansas."

Bits and pieces of Jay's memory fit together and, springing to his feet, he practically knocked Chad to the floor. "Get Jocelyn on the phone and get a home address, then call me in the car."

He finally remembered where he had seen those eyes before.

Twenty-five

The preparations had been made to unveil the new addition. Decorations adorned the room, and two long tables had been borrowed from a nearby church and covered with long red tablecloths.

Honey stood back and took everything in. Streamers were hanging from the ceilings, as well as large red balloons. She'd ordered twelve bouquets of fresh-cut flowers, and had positioned them around the area herself. "You think this is too much?" she said.

Candy looked up. "Hell no. It looks great." She walked over and removed two punch bowls from their boxes. "What time are the caterers comin'?"

"Around five." Their last hair appointments were scheduled for two so that all of the stylists would be available to attend. All of their customers had been invited, and everyone was looking forward to seeing the addition. Her new staff was scheduled to begin on Tuesday.

Honey left to take care of some last-minute items, and returned to the salon just in time for the caterers.

The smell of barbecue, meatballs, and egg rolls met her at the door. There were also several different types of salads, meat and cheese trays, and fresh fruit.

She was in the new ladies' room changing her clothes when she realized she hadn't heard from Jay yet. He'd promised he would call after he left his office, and would see her tonight at the grand opening. Honey felt almost guilty having a celebration when her man had nothing to celebrate. He was determined to find his son, and her heart went out to him. She loved him so much that she prayed nightly that he would find him soon.

At the back of her mind, she wondered what types of changes little J.J. would bring to their relationship. How would she fit into that picture? She sighed. Was she prepared to deal with it? Being with Jay meant dealing with Kendra and a whole lotta baby's mama drama. Did she really want to do that? Only time would tell . . . and only if J.J. was found.

Following the directions he'd mapped out, Jay made the drive to Dellwood and pulled onto Ledora's street. He drove slowly past her house to make sure she was home and then parked down at the corner. Jay got out of the car and, after ensuring that no one was looking, walked around to the side of the house and listened. He could hear cooing sounds at one of the half-open windows, and when he heard water splash, realized it was bath time. Jay felt a pang at the thought that he'd never had the chance to bathe J.J.

Ledora's voice became faint, and Jay knew that she'd taken the baby to another part of the house, probably to get him dressed. He walked back to his car and waited a few minutes before he called Officer Holman. Then he walked up to her door and knocked. After several seconds, he heard someone move to the door and stop, probably looking through the peephole, before opening the door.

Wearing a look of surprise, Ledora smiled. "Well, hello . . . what are you doing here?"

"I had a few questions I wanted to ask you."

"Well, uh . . . now's a bad time. I'm putting my baby down for a nap."

"This won't take long."

Pursing her lips, she nodded. "All right." Pulling her sweater around her, she stepped out of the door.

"I was told you just moved here from Kansas. Is that why you work for an agency instead of having a regular job with benefits?"

She nodded stiffly. "I'm a single parent. I take what I can get."

Jay nodded. "That's right, you have a newborn son. Congratulations."

"Thanks, but he's already a month."

"Where's the baby's father?"

"He . . . he left me."

Jay tried to keep the rage from overcoming him while he stalled, waiting for the police to arrive. They were slow as usual.

"Well, if there isn't anything else, I've got a hundred things to do while Tyler is asleep," she said, backing into the house.

"Sure thing. Thank you for your time, Mrs. J.W. Price."

Jay saw her expression change, then she shrugged. "You know my name. So what? I'm just tryin' to get on with my life."

"I almost didn't recognize you with the weave."

When he last saw her, she was standing over her husband's dead body sporting a short black bob.

Cries came from inside, and they sounded so familiar they ripped at his heart. He placed a hand on the door before Ledora could shut it. "Why, Mrs. Price, that sounds just like my son, J.J."

"All babies sound the same. Now if you please, I've got to go—"

Before she could say anything else, Jay pushed past her and raced into the tiny house, following the cries. Ledora was right behind him and, knowing which room the baby was in, she beat him there. Holding the baby close to her chest, she hissed, "Get out! Whatcha tryin' to do, steal my son?"

"I don't believe he's your son," Jay challenged, fighting to stay calm.

While she backed into a corner Jay quickly scanned the room, seeing toys and stenciled walls. The room smelled of baby powder—and something more. The smell reminded him of that too-brief time in the hospital, holding his son.

For the first time in days, Jay felt a sense of relief that his prayers had been answered. He was still uncertain as to why she had taken him, but it was reassuring to know that his son had been well taken care of.

"I'm calling the police," she warned, eyes large, lips trembling.

Jay lowered himself into a nearby rocking chair. "No need. They're already on their way."

Several minutes later, Officer Holman was leaning against his car shaking his head. "Jay, you can't go barging into people's homes. You know that."

"That's my son," Jay said.

He lifted a brow. "How can you be so sure?"

Jay took a deep breath and said, "Because I know how my son sounds. I know how he smells."

The officer laughed. "All babies sound and smell alike."

At one time, Jay would have believed the same thing, but now that he'd had a chance to hold a life he had created in his hands, he knew better. "No, they don't," he told the officer. "When you have kids of your own, you'll understand." He then walked back to the house, where two officers were helping Ledora and the baby into a patrol car. She shot him an anger-filled glance just before her head disappeared into the back.

One of the officers moved forward when he saw Jay approach. "Mrs. Price has agreed to bring the baby to the hospital so we can compare footprints and take some DNA samples."

Jay was surprised at her cooperation, and for a brief moment thought that maybe he could be wrong. But then he shook his head.

Not a chance.

Soft jazz poured from the speakers as Honey glanced around the room, pleased at the turnout for the grand opening of her new full-service salon. Thanks to MAJIC 105 announcing the event every couple of hours, the place was packed. There had to be just about every last one of their customers in attendance, as well as several potential new customers.

Looking to her left, Honey watched Mrs. Doyle, who had arrived earlier with Collins, her new beau.

Honey smiled. Apparently, the class reunion her favorite customer had been so nervous about was a success. Collins had his arm draped possessively across Mrs. Doyle's shoulders, and Honey was pleased at his quite obvious affection.

Out the corner of her eye, she saw Shaquil and Tequila at the buffet table sampling the buffalo wings, probably trying to find out if they were as good as theirs. She chuckled at Marcus, who was sitting in the corner eating his second piece of cake.

Honey was dressed in gray wool slacks and a black turtleneck sweater, and she, as well as the rest of her staff, sported new burgundy smocks with their names embroidered on the left breast pockets. All the new staff members were in the back, already adding appointments to their schedules.

She frowned when she saw Mercedes at the buffet table filling the half-empty punch bowl. Once again, she had dropped all the charges against Dean and had let him back in her apartment just yesterday. With a sigh, Honey wished there was something she could do, but knew nothing could be done other than continuing to be her friend. Hopefully, Mercedes would come to her senses before something unthinkable happened.

"Everything looks great," George said, strolling up from behind with Helen at his side. "It looks like Rashad knows his stuff."

Glancing over at her brother, who had his arm draped around Candy's waist, Honey chuckled proudly. "Yes, he does." *What's up with those two?*

Turning to her mom, she smiled. The couple had been inseparable since their trip to Las Vegas, and were even considering moving in together.

Helen glanced around and then faced Honey. "This is beautiful. I'm so proud of you." She clasped her daughter's hands and leaned in to kiss her cheek.

"Thanks, Mom," Honey said when they pulled apart.

Sasha, Terraine, and Roxaner, who was carrying Ciarra, moved over to join them. Honey reached up to stroke her goddaughter's tender chin, then looked up at Terraine. "Have you heard anything yet?" she asked softly.

Terraine studied her face and saw the crinkles of worry around her eyes, but had to shake his head. He'd been paging Jay for the past several hours without any answer. When it rains it pours, and the Andrews family had seen more than their fair share. He hoped to God all that was about to change.

Honey nibbled nervously on her lips. The party had been underway for over an hour. "Maybe I should try his office again."

"I just did." Terraine caught her fingers in his, then said, "He'll show up. Jay knows how important today is for you."

"I'm more concerned about J.J. I pray that he found him."

Terraine gave her a lingering glance and held her hand tighter. "You really care about him?"

Honey inclined her head and met his eyes. "I love him." She sighed. "When he hurts, I hurt."

Terraine's eyes sparkled with affection at the woman who had taught his brother a powerful lesson in love.

"Speak of the devil!"

At the sound of Roxaner's voice, Honey's head whipped around to find Jay walking through the door. She inhaled sharply. Still dressed as he was in faded jeans and a hooded sweatshirt, she knew he didn't intend to stay. She stared wordlessly across at him, her heart pounding. His expression was so still she trembled, afraid of what it meant. As he moved through the crowd, she searched his brown eyes for a sign. To her relief, just as he neared, Jay's lips curled upward. She reached out and grasped his hands, her eyes never leaving his.

"You found him," she said softly, hoping she was correct.

He nodded, tugging her close. The group cheered, and Terraine patted his brother on the back.

Honey draped an arm around his waist and hugged him. "I'm so happy for you," she said, her voice choking.

He planted a kiss on her forehead, thankful for her support and wishing he'd had more faith in her from the beginning.

Everyone started asking questions all at once. A chuckle started deep in Jay's throat and came out in a burst of laughter. His usual warm and relaxed manner had returned. "J.J. is doing just fine," he said, loud enough for those nearby to hear. "However, his doctor is keeping him in the hospital overnight for observation." He looked over at his brother, who was smiling at him, and winked. "The police are questioning the woman who took him. So I'll be able to answer your questions later." He looked down at Honey. Her hair was pulled back in a ponytail, the way he liked it, and his eyes grew pensive. "I can't stay. I just dropped by to get something."

Scooping Honey into his arms, he moved toward the door. One arm around his neck, she used the other to wave as they pushed through the crowd. The room burst into applause so loud that Honey and Jay could barely hear as the family promised to meet them at the hospital.

Resting her head against his chest, Honey tried to catch her breath, but her heart raced with excitement and joy. She lifted her head and stared into his beautiful eyes as he stepped out into the cool wind. "Where are we going?" she asked.

"I'm taking you to meet someone who's gonna be a very important part of your life," he murmured against her lips, then lowered his mouth to settle on hers.

Terraine couldn't contain his smile as he watched them pull out of the driveway. "About time my brother came to his senses."

Sasha nudged her husband in the ribs and said teasingly, "I told you so."

Shaking his head, he turned to his wife with a wide grin. "Yes, you did."

Twenty-six

Honey carried the slumbering baby boy to his crib and carefully lowered him onto the mattress, then pulled the blanket around him. Staring down at the precious darling, she stroked his soft, shiny black curls with the back of her hand. He was beautiful. J.J. Andrews lay at peace, without a worry in the world. He would never know how scared his father had been.

According to the police, Ledora's son had died of SIDS only a week before the abduction. Made irrational by the double loss, she had blamed Jay for both her husband's and son's deaths, and had come to St. Louis seeking revenge without the slightest idea how she would exact it. Ledora had just started a position with the temporary nursing pool when Kendra went into labor. The rest was pure luck.

Hearing footsteps behind her, Honey anticipated his warm breath at the back of her neck.

"I see he's finally asleep."

She looked over her shoulder at Jay, put a fingertip to

her lips, and signaled for him to lower his voice. Speaking softly, she asked, "How'd things go with Kendra?"

He smiled. "Piece of cake. After that stunt she pulled, she didn't have much choice. The judge awarded me full custody."

Honey returned his smile and said, "That's wonderful."

"I'm so glad this shit is finally over. Now we can get on with our lives." Jay nuzzled her neck and found that Honey smelled like baby powder—and his son's sweet scent. Now he was certain he couldn't have a better woman in his life.

He wrapped his arms around her waist, and they both stared down into the crib. After a brief silence he said, "There's only one problem."

Honey swung around in his arms, her eyes wide with concern. "What's wrong?"

His dark eyes twinkled. "J.J. is now without a mother."

She playfully slugged him in the arm for scaring her. "He doesn't need a mother with a wonderful father like you."

He dropped his head and kissed her, then said, "Then his father needs a wife. Will you marry me?"

She searched his face. Something in his gaze told her he was serious. The laughter was gone. His eyes were solemn.

Honey loved her some Jay. He was her soul mate. If Walter and Kendra had never stepped into their lives, if things had been so very different, she would have shouted *hell yeah* at his proposal of marriage. However, she couldn't hide her rape and infertility any more than Jay could pretend Kendra and J.J. didn't exist. Both occurrences would always be a part of their lives. Each would come to the other with excess bag-gage. Honey knew she wasn't ready yet for marriage and a part of her didn't believe Jay was either.

Her sessions with her therapist were going well and hopefully in time she would discover her true self. But that was still a long way coming. Besides, she and Jay needed time. Time to love. Time to learn to trust. They needed to strengthen their relationship before she could even consider the package deal. Because she knew that package would include not only J.J. but Kendra as well.

"I love you, Jay, but I don't think we're ready to take that big step."

Jay reached up to cup her chin, his eyes determined. "Boo, I wouldn't have asked if I wasn't ready."

"And you're only asking now because of J.J., but I'm okay with that. I just need more time to finish discover-ing who I am and all I ask is that you try to do the same."

Jay was quiet for a long moment and even though her rejection hurt, he realized she was probably right. They had both been through quite a bit. He loved Honey and wanted her to be a permanent part of his life, but deep down he knew he still had issues to work out between him and Kendra. She was J.J.'s mother, and even though he had sole custody, she would always be a part of their lives. Part of him wanted the bitch to stay as far away from him as possible, while the other half, mainly his dick, was pleased she would still be around.

While sitting in the courtroom, he had watched Kendra sitting with her lawyer on the other side of the room. Each time she ran her tongue across her juicy red lips, his dick jerked. Instead of listening to the judge, his mind had wandered off with visions of her down on all fours with her head bobbing up and down at his crotch. Honey he had yet to school in the art of giving good head, while Kendra already had a master's in the subject. Would he ever be free of his sexual attraction to her? If the situation presented itself, would he be able to resist? He was a man and his dick, his weakness. *After all the bullshit she's put you through, are you ever going to learn?* That was something he couldn't answer yet.

Lifting Honey into his arms, he whispered against her cheek, "Everything is gonna work out. 'Cause I love you and there ain't no way in hell I'm ever lettin' your fine ass go."

"Good, 'cause I plan to stick around for the long haul." Honey gave her man a long, wet kiss, then wrapped her arms around his neck and pulled him close.

Staring out the window, Honey saw the sun peeking out behind a cloud and she smiled. It had been raining on her world for far too long, but she had a strong suspicion all that was about to change.

Want more Angie Daniels?
Turn the page for a preview of
IN THE COMPANY OF MY SISTAHS,
TROUBLE LOVES COMPANY, and
CAREFUL OF THE COMPANY YOU KEEP

Available now wherever books are sold.

In the Company of
My Sistahs

One

Renee

"What the hell do you mean you can't find your birth certificate?"

"I thought it was in my desk drawer, but when I looked a few minutes ago, it wasn't there."

I took a deep breath, drawing on the lessons bestowed upon me. *Patience is a virtue* is right up there with *do unto others as you want done unto you*. Shit, I've been flunking both for years.

"Why the hell did you wait until it's time to leave to look for your damn birth certificate?"

"I thought I had it," Nadine mumbled.

See, this is a prime example as to why I have very few female friends—because they are either catty or doing some stupid shit, like losing a damn birth certificate.

I told my sister Lisa this wasn't going to work, but she refused to hear me. So listen to what I am about to tell you. Four women can't spend a week in Jamaica together.

Nadine, who I'm on the phone with now, is a notori-

ous procrastinator. I've been telling her big titty behind
for almost three months that she needed a birth certificate. I even went as far as to instruct her to put the
damn thing in her suitcase so she wouldn't forget it.
Now she wants to call me just as we're getting ready to
roll down to St. Louis to say she can't find the damn
thing.

"Renee, what am I going to do?" I heard her say.

"I don't know what you're going to do, 'cause I told
your ass!" What she needed was a miracle and my
name sho' in the hell wasn't Helen Keller.

Glancing over at the digital clock on my nightstand,
I noticed it was already after five and rolled my eyes.
"If you had taken the time to look for it an hour ago
you could've ran downtown to Vital Statistics and
picked up another copy."

"What time they close?"

"They closed five minutes ago! See, that's why I
don't fool with you." Breathing heavily into the receiver, I tried counting to five but that shit wasn't working. I had problems of my own. My ex-husband was
supposed to have picked up his kids at one o'clock.
As usual his tired ass was late.

You know what? I ain't got time for this shit.

"My advice to you is to keep looking and call me
back." Without bothering to say good-bye, I punched
END on the cordless phone, then tossed it onto my bed.
I wasn't even about to worry about her right now.

Besides, Nadine ain't even my friend. She's my sister Lisa's homegirl.

It doesn't matter that Nadine and I used to blow spit
bubbles together or the fact that her funky-ass feet used
to be in my face when she slept at the bottom of my

bed. So what if I used to fart and pin her ass to the mattress so she had no choice but to smell it. None of that shit counts. She's still Lisa's friend, not mine. I just hang with Nadine from time to time 'cause she doesn't have too many friends. After my sister moved to Texas her ass was acting all lonely and shit, so I felt sorry for her. But regardless of how you want to look at it, Nadine ain't my friend. She's Lisa's homegirl.

With her dilemma still fresh on the brain, I reached under my bed, pulled out my suitcase and decided that after all that ranting and raving I better make sure my passport hadn't expired. I believe it's good for ten years. My second husband was in the Army, and we lived overseas, but that's another story.

I found it between my vibrator and a box of magnum-size condoms (hey, a sistah's gotta be prepared) and just as I thought, my passport was still good for another two years. I tossed it into my purse and reached for my deodorant on the dresser.

Hearing footsteps coming down the hall, I looked up to find my thirteen-year-old daughter, Tamara, entering my room, followed by our schnauzer, Nikki.

"Mom, you need some help?" she asked me as she took a seat on my bed.

I shook my head. "No, Princess. Are you all packed?"

"Yes, Mom."

"You got your toothbrush?"

"Yes, Mom."

"Plenty of clean underwear?"

"Mom," she groaned, "you already asked me that this morning!"

"And I'm going to keep on asking, smart-ass," I retorted. Who the hell does she think she's talking to? I don't know what's wrong with kids today. If I had spoken to my mother that way she would've knocked my ass clear into next week.

Nikki jumped on top of my open suitcase. Spoiled-ass dog. "Get down, Nikki," I ordered. Luckily, she obeyed and jumped down, taking a seat near my daughter's feet; otherwise I would've thrown my shoe at her. Don't get me wrong. I love my dog. We all do. She's been in our family for almost nine years, and I consider her part of the family. Nevertheless, her ass is spoiled. Have you ever heard of a dog that sleeps in the bed under the covers with her head on a pillow? *Rotten.*

I looked over in time to see Tamara reach into my suitcase and pull out a size-ten bikini I found on clearance at Wal-Mart.

She turned up her nose. "Mom, I hope you ain't wearing this."

"Shoot! I don't know why not."

"'Cause, your stomach is too big."

"Whatever," I mumbled as I snatched it from her hand. I don't care how big my stomach is, not this week, anyway.

All four of us agreed that whatever happens in Jamaica, stays in Jamaica. So if I want to wear a bikini and show my childbearing stretch marks, then that's my damn business. I will never see any of those people again. Besides, my stomach ain't that bad. I'm the stomach-crunch queen. I just have a little pooch, nothing more . . . well, maybe a little more, but not that much. Nevertheless, after two kids, I still look good. Smooth caramel skin, hazel eyes, small firm breasts (my shit don't sag), big legs, and a phat ass—*ssshittt,* you better ask somebody.

I put the bikini back in my suitcase and took a quick

inventory of its contents. I had a swimsuit for all five days with flip-flops and butt wraps to match. There were also sundresses, tops, and shorts. Yes, you better believe this sistah was prepared. "Princess, can you go get my blue-jean shorts out the dryer?"

"Aw'ight." She slid off the bed. "Come on, Nikki." On command, her dog rose and happily followed her down the hall.

Before she got too far, I called after her. "Before you do that, go call your dad." The sorry bastard.

I'm sorry. I'm probably coming off as a bitch and I apologize. I just have a lot on my mind these days. A great deal of stress. When I get back from Jamaica, I have to make what I consider one of the biggest decisions of my life. I have been putting it off for months and time has finally run out.

By the time I inventoried my suitcase, my phone rang. I looked down at my caller ID and saw it was my girl Kayla Sparks.

"Whassup," I greeted.

She smacked her lips as she spoke. "Gurl, Nadine says she can't find her birth certificate."

"I know, she already called and told me."

"What's she going to do?"

"I don't know what she's gonna do. I've been telling her the same damn thing for weeks and it went in one ear and out the other."

"She's ridiculous."

I clicked my tongue. "Tell me something I don't already know."

Obviously there wasn't shit else she could tell me that I didn't already know, because she changed the subject.

"I've already dropped Kenya and Asia off at my mom's. My bags are packed and I'm ready to go."

"So am I. That is, as soon as Mario's sorry ass gets here."

"How much spending money you taking?" Kayla asked.

"Not much. My car insurance was due. I got enough to cover my half of the room and buy everyone a gift."

Kayla paused a second too long. "I thought you were paying for our rooms with your credit card," she finally said.

"Excuse me? I *reserved* our rooms on my credit card. You need to *pay* for your half of the room when you get there." My statement was followed by another long pause. *Uh-oh, not another one.* I lowered onto the bed. "You do have money for your room, right?"

"No-o-o. I thought you were paying for them and we were paying you back later."

"Y'all are fucked up! I'm not First National Bank. I specifically said I would hold the rooms on my card. I never said shit about paying for them."

"You're silly." Kayla had the nerve to sound appalled.

"No, y'all bitches are crazy," I spat. My other line beeped. "Hold on." I clicked over. My older sister Lisa was calling me from her cell phone. She and her husband Michael arrived from Texas last week and have been staying with his parents.

"Hey, you ready?" she asked.

"Almost. I got Kayla on the other line, but check this shit out. Nadine called; she can't find her birth certificate."

"What?" Lisa screamed. "Just the other day she told me she had it."

"Well, she lost it. The way her house looks I ain't the least bit surprised." It was no secret Nadine's house was a damn pig sty. She saves every doggone thing she gets her hands on because she's afraid to throw anything away. I tried once to help her organize her shit. Even brought over a paper shredder, but she refused to part with anything. Which was fine with me because I don't have to sleep there. However, I did tell her nasty ass not to even think about inviting me over again until she cleaned her damn house.

"Man, this is unbelievable," I heard Lisa say.

"You right. She called right after Vital Statistics closed."

"If she had bothered to look yesterday, she could have gone down with me."

"I know. To top it off, Kayla thought I was paying for both rooms with my credit card and y'all were paying me back at a later date."

"Damn, both my girls are trippin'."

"Hell yeah, they're trippin'." Especially since my credit card was maxed out. Shit, I couldn't even use it to pay for my own half of the room. "You ready to roll?"

Lisa cleared her throat. "Actually, I was calling 'cause Michael wants me to spend the evening with him. I'ma go to the boat tonight."

"Bitch, whatever! You gonna end up missing the plane."

"No, I won't. You know I get up that early anyway."

"Uh-huh," I returned with straight attitude. My sister owns a bakery in San Antonio and yeah, she does get up early, but that's beside the point. The four of us had made plans for the evening that obviously now had changed. Leave it to some damn man to rain on my parade. "Yeah, whatever."

"What's wrong with you?" Lisa asked.

"I need some dick. I'll call you back." I clicked back over to the other line in time to hear Kayla's pissed-off sigh through the receiver. "Ho, don't even try to get no attitude, 'cause you're always putting me on hold." Returning to the problem at hand, I asked, "So, do you have money or what?"

She sighed again. "Yeah, I just got paid. I was going to put my house note in the mail before we left but I guess it can wait until I get back."

"It's gonna have to. I'll have a check waiting for me when I get back. So, if you need me to spot you a few bucks then, I can help you out. I just don't have it this week."

"Cool." Kayla sounded pleased by my offer. I don't have a problem loaning her money as long as her broke ass remembers to pay me back.

I heard my kids fighting in the other room. "Girl, I'll call you when I'm on my way. In the meantime, see if you can help Nadine."

I hung up and made it down the hall and into the living room in time to catch my sixteen-year-old son hitting his sister upside the head with a pillow. "Y'all are trippin'! You know this room is off limits."

"Mom, Quinton started it!" Tamara screamed.

"No, I didn't!" he countered.

"I don't care who started it. Just get out of my living room. Now!" My kids know when I ain't playing, because they scrambled down the hall to their rooms. I picked the throw pillows off the floor and put them back on my cream-colored Italian leather couch.

I love my living room set. It took every dime of my income tax return but it was worth it. With beige carpeting on the floor and runners to protect it, my children knew the living room was for company only.

I was checking my plants to make sure they had enough water, when I heard a car pull up in my driveway. Peeking through taupe mini blinds, I saw my ex-husband Mario's raggedy blue Cavalier. About damn time.

"Mama, Daddy's here!" Tamara screamed from her room.

"I know," I returned. I waited until he knocked before I opened the door and gave him my best negro-you're-late stare.

"Sorry, I had car trouble." He was dressed in his faded blue jeans and a white t-shirt, smelling like motor oil.

I stepped aside so he could enter. He moved over to the couch I just fluffed, and—*oh no he didn't*—dropped his funky ass onto my cushions.

His eyes traveled around the room. "I see you've been decorating."

"Always."

He draped his arm across the back of my couch. "Yeah, I miss this old house. We should still be doin' all this together."

Oh, Lord, here we go again. Mario and I have been divorced for almost twelve years but every time he comes around he wants to talk about what we coulda, shoulda been if we had stayed together. I don't feel like hearing that shit today.

"Hey, Dad." My daughter came bouncing into the living room, flopped down on my couch next to him, and planted a kiss on his cheek.

"Hey, girl." He smiled down at her.

Tamara's a daddy's girl. She sees him only one weekend a month but to her, he does no wrong. They look just alike. They have the same dark eyes covered by thick bushy eyebrows and long black lashes. Mario was a tenderoni back in the day. He's just short as hell. I don't know why I used to have a thing for short men.

Quinton came into the living room, carrying a tote bag over his shoulder. I smiled because my son is handsome and destined to be a heartbreaker. Already six feet, he got his height from my side of the family. He is always dressed nicely. If it doesn't have a designer label, he ain't wearing it, which is why I made his spoiled ass get a job this summer. As I said before, my name ain't First National Bank.

"Look at them gym shoes." My ex-husband was referring to my son's one-hundred-dollar Nikes.

"We put your child support to good use," I snorted.

"Must be nice. I can only afford Wal-Mart. I ain't got it like that."

"Whatever," I mumbled under my breath. He was about to go into his long spiel about how poor he was.

"Shoot, I ain't got a pot to piss in or a window to throw it out of."

What did I tell you? Mario's got my daughter feeling so sorry for him she asked me to give him back his child support. Has she lost her damn mind?

Mario rose. "Let's go, kids. Renee, make sure you bring me back some of that Jamaican rum."

Yeah, whatever. I gave both of my kids a hug and a kiss, made sure Mario had the number to the hotel in case of an emergency, then pushed them and Nikki out the door.

I straightened the couch again, then moved to the bathroom. After a quick shower, I was ready to get my vacation started. Tamara never did bring me my shorts. I went down to the basement and pulled them out the dryer. I double checked the doors and windows to make sure they were secure, then raced back up the steps to grab the phone.

It was Nadine.

"Did you find it?" I asked.

"No. I must have thrown it away when I cleaned my room last week." She sounded frustrated, but I didn't have time to be feeling sorry for her. Nadine ain't never bothered to clean her house before, so why start now?

"I don't know what to tell you," I said with probably a little less feeling than I should have. Hey, it's been a long day and my ass is horny.

"I think I might have one at my parents' house."

"In Kansas City?" That was almost a two-hour drive.

"Yeah, I'm waiting for them to call me back. If so, I guess I'll drive there and back tonight and leave for St Louis in the morning."

"That's fine. Lisa and Michael are spending the night at the boat. She's getting dicked tonight, so I won't see her until the morning either. Just meet us at the Waffle House." I hung up and went to my room to get dressed. Getting some dick didn't sound like a bad idea.

I have a hook-up in St. Louis that I visit whenever I'm in town. Vince is a real kind of brotha. What you see is what you get. He lives in one of those old historical homes in the city that is in such bad shape, it needs to be either restored or torn down. He drives on the back of a garbage truck and is broke, but what the hell. I don't want his money. Just his dick. We met at a nightclub six months ago and just by the way he gyrated his hips I knew he could fuck. Maybe I'll call him when I get to St. Louis. Maybe I won't. He knows I'm coming tonight so maybe I'll wait and see if he calls first.

Thirty minutes later, I was rolling down the road in my black Camry with Mariah's new CD blasting through my speakers. I rolled down my window, allowing the warm July breeze to toss my braids. I needed a drink.

My cell phone rang. I reached for it and noticed that the number had been blocked. When I'm at home I ignore blocked or anonymous callers because nine times out of ten, it's either a telemarketer or a damn bill collector. Now my cell phone, that's a different story altogether. The first thing that comes to mind is somebody is playing on my dime.

"Hello?"

"Yeah, is this Renee Moore?"

"Who wants to know?" I asked with straight sistah girl attitude.

"Ricky Johnson's wife, that's who."

Uh-uh. No the bitch didn't. She doesn't know my ass from the damn man on the moon. So how the hell she gonna call me talking crazy?

"*Excuse me?* I know you ain't calling my phone talking slick." The tone of my voice told her whatever my words didn't, because she didn't say shit. "What can I do for you?"

Finally, she sucked her teeth. "I want to know why my man's been calling you."

"Why don't you ask your man?"

"I did and he says y'all been discussing business."

You know, one thing that burns me up is a lying-ass nigga. First off, I met Ricky's ass last week at this club that ain't no more than a juke joint. Now, I ain't gonna lie. The brotha is fine. Berry black skin, wavy hair, tall, and one helluva dresser. I didn't waste any time getting his attention and before the end of the night, we had exchanged cell phone numbers. Now I might not remember everything that slick mothafucka told me, but one thing I do know, he told me his ass wasn't married.

I rudely laughed in her ear. "Okay, so if he already gave you an answer, then why the hell you calling me?"

"Because I don't believe him."

"Then that sounds like a personal problem."

"No, it ain't no problem 'cause all I need to know is what the hell y'all were talking about; then I'm gonna whoop somebody's ass."

I thought the shit was funny so I started laughing again. "Bitch, you know what? First off, you must be hard up for a man because there ain't no way in hell I would be calling some female's number I found on my man's caller ID, trying to find out what he's been up to. Secondly, the only ass you're gonna whoop tonight is his. So unless you want me to hang the fuck up, I advise you to come correct."

She then had the nerve to laugh. "Damn, girl, your ass is hard. You have to excuse me 'cause right now I'm feeling some kind of way. Me and Ricky been together ten years so I have a lot of time invested in this relationship."

"Yeah, and it's obvious you make a habit of checking his phone."

"Shit, I pay the damn bill."

Stupid wench. "Girlfriend, let me school you. You need to check Ricky's punk ass instead of wasting my damn time. 'Cause by you calling me all you're doing is letting me know the dick is good. I mean why else would you be checking his every move? Now, first off, one sistah to another, your man told me he wasn't married. And one thing I don't do is mess with another sistah's husband. Secondly, the only business he and I had to discuss was me getting some dick. However, since I am in such a good mood, I'll do you a favor, and leave his ass alone. In return, do me a favor . . . both y'all mothafuckas lose my damn number." I clicked END and lowered the phone onto my lap. That bitch had to be ugly—why else would she be running after some trifling negro. Or maybe as I said before, Ricky's got some good dick.

I reached for my cell phone again and called Kayla to tell her I was on my way, then I stopped by the ATM and withdrew enough cash to last me a week. Five minutes later, I pulled into her driveway.

Kayla was standing on the porch, with her suitcase in front of her feet, waiting. She was dressed in her usual black pants and white t-shirt. She is a big woman with a really pretty face, and tall enough to be a model if she was a dozen dress sizes smaller. She has a cute up-turned nose, big green eyes, and a dazzling white smile. Her skin is so beige she could almost pass for white if it wasn't for her nappy-ass hair.

We met during college. I was attending night classes and she was in several of them. Somehow, like oil and vinegar, we mixed. I'm wild as hell, while Kayla is one of those who travels the straight and narrow, living her life according to the good book. She is the type of woman to be married. Instead, she has two girls with different baby's daddies that she has to track down every six months for child support payments.

"Hey, girl," she greeted. She put her suitcase in my backseat. As she climbed onto the seat beside me, I complimented her on the ten straight-back cornrows she had secured with a hair tie.

"Your hair looks good."

"So does yours." Kayla reached out and fingered one of my braids. "I can't believe she was able to braid your hair."

"I didn't even." Her cousin Danita did my hair. You can't go to Jamaica with a curling iron. The humidity is a bitch. I have always worn one of those Halle Berry haircuts, so my hair is only *that* long. But I've been growing it out for almost four months for this occasion. Danita had to pinch, and damn that shit hurt. My hair was so tight that I had fucking Chinese eyes. But I refused to take them out. I just took the pain and two days of severe headaches. It's a shame the things women have to go through to look beautiful.

"Where's Lisa?" Kayla asked as I was pulling out of the driveway.

"She's at the casino with Michael. We'll see her in the morning."

"This is ridiculous! We were supposed to go to St. Louis, get a room, and hang out at the club before leaving for Jamaica in the morning."

"So, what's the problem?" I asked even though I knew good and damn well what she was getting at.

"There ain't no one but us. How are we gonna kick it if it's just us?"

I glanced over at her holy ass wondering why she was tripping. Kayla wouldn't have done anything but sat in a corner all night sipping on a virgin daiquiri, telling every brotha who tried to step to her that they needed Jesus in their life.

"You know what," I finally said as I made a U-turn in the middle of the road. "We are going to Tropical Liquors. I'm gettin' me a frozen Long Island Tea, and you a daiquiri, then we're rollin' out. When we get to St. Louis, I'm droppin' your ass off at the hotel."

"Where're you going?" Kayla asked.

"I'm going to get me some dick."

Trouble Loves Company

One

Renee

If I had known my girl Danielle was going to call and spend the last half hour whining about her sorry-ass boyfriend, I wouldn't have answered the phone.

"Whaddaya think I should do?" she asked in a low whisper, as if someone else might be listening.

I clicked my tongue and answered, "You already know what I would do."

"Yeah, but I ain't like you."

See, that's one thing I've never understood. Why ask for advice when you really don't want it? I have never been able to figure that out, especially when the answer is obvious. Kick his ass to the curb! As my grandmother always said, "Can't nobody tell a woman to leave her man. She has to decide on her own when she's had enough." I understand what Big Mama was trying to say, really I do. But it's a shame how much shit a woman is willing to take before she finally decides enough is enough.

Take my girl Danielle, for instance. Her ex-boyfriend

Deon fucked around on her for years. Not only did he fuck around, but he brought home the kind of shit you have to take a trip to the free clinic to get rid of. Yet and still, she forgave his trifling ass. It wasn't until one of his baby mamas clocked her upside her peanut head, while he stood by and watched, that she finally decided enough was enough.

Now Ron, the latest thug in her life, is never home, can't keep a job, and has bitches calling her house at all hours of the night bold enough to ask for him, yet she's determined to stick by him.

I love my girl, really I do. We talk on the phone at least five times a week and I know if I ever needed her, she'd have my back. Her brain is short a couple of screws, though. There ain't no way, at thirty-six, I would be putting up with that kind of shit. But unlike me, Danielle loves a thug, and will go crazy without daily drama in her life. And that's why her ass is always getting dogged.

"That muthafucker got off work three hours ago, and I ain't seen his ass yet. He ain't got no respect for me," she complained.

I couldn't help but laugh in her ear. "What do you expect? He's only twenty-four. I doubt he respects his own mama."

"Yeah, right!" she laughed. "But that's ai'ight 'cause he's got the shit twisted. I'm gonna get all in that ass when he gets home."

Ooh! Like that's gonna make a world of difference. "It's been a year. He's not gonna change. What you need to do is put his lazy ass out."

While Danielle tried to justify why she wasn't ready to end the relationship, I rose from the couch, turned the light off, then moved up to my bedroom and changed into a nightgown. It was late and a school night, so my kids, Quinton and Tamara, were in their rooms, probably pretending to be asleep. That's okay with me just as long as they're in bed by ten.

As Danielle rattled on I half-listened, because she really didn't want to hear what I had to say. If it was me, Ron would never have moved into my house. So, instead of giving advice, I pretended to be paying attention and said, "Uh-huh" on cue. I really think she just likes for someone to listen. Shit, I ain't mad, because I do the same thing. Nevertheless, it's late and I am tired. I yawned rudely in the mouthpiece, hoping she'd get the hint.

She didn't.

Okay, she's got ten more minutes, then I'll come up with some kind of excuse and hang up

I had just stepped into the adjoining bathroom and dropped my clothes in the hamper when I heard the garage door rising. "Oh shit!" I exclaimed as I dashed back into the bedroom.

Danielle gasped. "What?"

Leaning over, I turned out the Tiffany lamp on the nightstand. "John's home."

"Already? I thought he didn't get off work until midnight."

"He doesn't, but I guess he decided to get off early." I glared at the clock—it was barely eleven.

"It must be nice being the boss." I heard the envy in her voice.

"Look, I'll holla at you tomorrow." I hung up the phone, then slipped beneath the covers as quickly and quietly as possible, and waited. As soon as I heard heavy footsteps coming up the stairs, my stomach felt all tied up in knots. Damn! I can't deal with him tonight. I was irritated, because if John got off early from work, it was for one reason and one reason only—he wanted some booty. *Girl, quit trippin'! Everything ain't always got to be about you. Maybe he's tired,* I thought to myself. Okay, maybe I'm being silly. Maybe I'm wrong.

When John entered the room and turned the lock behind him, I knew my luck had run out.

Shit!

While he undressed, I lay perfectly still on my back and breathed deeply, praying he'd think I was asleep and would leave me the hell alone. From the corner of my eyes, I watched him move about the room in the dark. Then he stepped into the bathroom, took a leak, passed gas, and flushed the toilet. I turned up my nose, totally disgusted, but relieved when I heard the water running. At least he washed his hands. A few minutes later, the mattress beside me sagged from the impact of his weight, and within seconds he was underneath the covers with his large arm pressed against mine. My nose began to itch, but there was no way in hell I was going to scratch it, because the slightest movement and John would spring into action.

The clock on the dresser ticked and seconds became minutes and finally I began to relax. Yes! He's not going to touch me tonight. Then, just as I started to really fall asleep, I felt his hand creeping up my thigh. I tensed because I knew that in the next five seconds he was going to ask me that same stupid-ass question.

"Can I have some?"

I wanted to yell, "Hell nah, you can't have none!" No, what I really wanted to say was, "If I wanted to give yo' fat ass some, I would've been lying in the bed butt-naked instead of in a long gown and a pair of grandma draws." Instead, I remained stone-faced and tried to pretend I hadn't heard him, but at this point it was obvious he wasn't falling for it.

"Hey, Renee, you hear me?"

I gave a long, exasperated sigh because for once I wished my husband would just get the hint and leave me the fuck alone. "Not tonight," I said as nicely as I could manage, then rolled onto my side. I even threw a little sleep in my voice since I hadn't quite given up on that trick yet.

"Aw, come on," he begged. "I'll be quick. I promise."

I know his *quick*. Thirty minutes of him playing with my left titty, then he'll want me to play with his dick before he'd finally climb on top of me for another half hour of torture. I blew out another angry breath, then rolled over onto my back and looked up at him. "Why can't you wait until I want you sometimes? I mean . . . I can't understand why you always want some when I'm not in the mood."

There was a long moment of silence and one would have thought I had hurt his feelings, but not John. He gave me this sad, pleading look. "So you gonna give your husband a little bit or what?"

I couldn't help it. I tossed my arms in the air and gave a frustrated laugh. He was obviously not going to let up until I gave him some coochie. And as usual, I felt guilty as shit for depriving him of what he felt he was entitled to have on an "ass-needed basis." "I'm not in the mood," I snapped with attitude. "I don't want no dick! But if you want it, if you really, *really* want it, then go ahead and do the damn thang!"

Now any other brotha would have said, "Fuck you,

bitch," and rolled over. Not John. He rose long enough to shrug out of his t-shirt and tighty-whities, then eagerly climbed back in the bed. The moment I felt his limp dick on my thigh, I sighed because I knew I was in for a long night.

Lord, why me?

Now, I could have refused, but Big Mama taught me never to bite the hand that feeds you, so as usual I gave in, and let him have his way. Within seconds, I felt his hand slide underneath my gown. I cringed as his fingers grabbed my nipple, tweaking it like he was trying to tune a transistor radio. I have discovered in the five years of our marriage that playing with my breasts for five to ten minutes is one of the only ways John can get an erection. The other is me going down on him, but that shit's not about to happen. John lifted the gown over my head while I lay there like a stiff board. He suckled one nipple between his dry, cracked lips while he twisted and pulled at the other with his fingertips.

The entire time, I stared at the ceiling fan twirling above while tears ran from the corners of my eyes and onto the pillow. I'm so sick of this shit, I don't know what to do. Every time he touches me I feel like I'm being violated. I've never been raped, but it can't be too far from what I'm feeling. As he slid my panties down to my ankles, I allowed my mind to disappear to another time in my life. A time when I was free to do what I wanted with whomever I wanted. I then traveled back even further to happier times when I was in grade school before all the madness in my life had begun. My sister Lisa and I used to lie in our bunk beds, laughing and creating make-believe worlds. I bit my lip and forced myself not to cry. Even after a year, thinking about my sister still brought tears to my eyes. At thirty-eight, Lisa had lost her battle with ovarian cancer. I didn't even know she had it until it was too late. One of her last wishes was for me to give my marriage an honest try, and because of her I was still trying to hang in there with John. As much as I loved my sister and tried to be a woman who stood by her word, I wasn't sure how much more I could endure.

"Play with it," John instructed as he reached for my hand and moved it over to his limp dick.

I was so pissed off, I lashed out at him. "I don't understand this shit! If your dick ain't hard, why're you bothering me? Why can't you wait until it wants to work?"

My voice cracked but he didn't seem to notice because he gave an impatient sigh and said, "Just play with it a minute."

I practically yanked at his shit because I just don't get it anymore. For the last year his dick has only half worked. Not that it has mattered to me. Even when it was still fully functional, the sex between us had been bad. I just didn't think it was important. Seriously! It may sound crazy but I really thought that what I was getting out of the marriage far outweighed what I had to give in return. That shit sounds crazy as hell now. When he met me I was a broke bitch trying to rub two nickels together and when he asked me to marry him I jumped at the chance, thinking that life could only get better. Now I wasn't so sure.

By the time my hand was about to fall asleep, John's dick finally rose to the occasion. Quickly, before it grew soft, he climbed between my legs and searched for the hole. "Help me find it."

I don't understand why John can't find my coochie!

Damn! We've been fucking for over five years but he still aims for the wrong hole. What the hell is up with that shit? Reaching over into the top drawer of my nightstand, I pulled out a tube of KY Jelly because my coochie was as dry as the desert. I squeezed a little in my hand and lubed the head of his dick. Damn! He was starting to get soft already.

"Mmm, baby, that feels good. Rub some more on me," he crooned.

I closed my eyes and prayed for strength, then squeezed another dab in the palm of my hand and jacked him off some more. By the time he was hard again, I quickly guided him to my hole and he entered me.

I sighed while he pumped his little dick in and out like he was hurting some damn body. He was moaning so loud, you would have thought it was me. As he thrust, his fingers tweaked my nipples. And tweaked and tweaked and tweaked some more.

"Dammit, would you stop before they fall the fuck off!" I yelled, then slapped his hand away. I've told him I don't know how many times to stop playing with them so much, but that shit goes in one ear and out the other. I don't even think plastering a note across my chest that read, "leave them the hell alone," would have made a difference.

John sighed, then slid me down to the middle of the bed and entered me, again pumping and pumping like he was doing some damage. I could have lain there and gone to sleep if he wasn't dropping balls of sweat all over me. I put a pillow over my face to stop the next droplet that was sure to fall in my damn eye. Thank goodness he paused long enough to wipe his face off on the sheets. He then tossed my pillow aside.

"Is that better?"

"Yeah, just hurry up," I managed through gritted teeth.

Draping my legs over his shoulders, John began to plunge all three hundred pounds into me. I couldn't feel shit, but I knew if I wanted this ordeal to end I had to pretend that I did, so I started to moan. As usual, the sound of my voice excited him.

"That's it, baby. Come with me," he said as he reached for my nipple. Instinctively, I slapped his hand away, then rocked my hips and met him stroke for stroke. "Yeah, that's it. I'm about to come."

I was so happy to hear that, I started moving my hips faster, moaning even louder, and urged him on. "Come on, big daddy, you can do it. Come all inside this pussy!"

"Okay," he said like a good little boy. "Okay." He pumped faster.

I reached up and stroked his nipples, since he seems to get off on that shit. "Come on, Daddy. I want to feel you nut inside of me. Wet that pussy!"

"Yeaaah! I'm getting ready to come!"

"Me, too!" I lied.

While he was howling like a hound dog during a full moon, I felt that wet, warm feeling as he squirted inside of me. The bed rocked. John was slamming the headboard against the wall so hard, I know the kids heard it, until finally, he collapsed on top of me. Thank you, Jesus! I lay there waiting for him to get off of me. He finally rolled over and within seconds he was snoring. Overcome with relief, I eased out of bed and went into the adjoining bathroom and cleaned myself up. Catching a glimpse of myself in the mirror, the tears began to fall again. What has my life become?

I'm miserable, but nobody seems to believe me. Especially not the big muthafucka who happens to share my bed. I feel trapped. Being trapped in a bad marriage is bad enough, but being trapped in a marriage with a good man who you don't love makes you want to stand in the corner and bang your head against a cement wall. Don't get it twisted. If it wasn't that John was an excellent provider and that my kids adored him, I would have left a long time ago.

John and I have been married five years and I've been miserable for three. A one-night stand I met at a club. I was horny and after a night of no other prospects, I went home with him. I was too drunk to remember the specifics of his performance. The only reason why I know we fucked was because I woke up naked and spotted the used condom wrapper on the nightstand beside me. We dated a couple of times after that. None—to his disappointment—ended with sex. I found John to be a kind, generous man, but too damn nice and touchy-feely for my taste. He was also dull, very lonely, and needy. Not to mention he wasn't much to look at—dark, five-eleven, over three hundred pounds, with a waist I couldn't even wrap my arms around, and a face that resembled Shrek. What's even worse, the brotha can't dress! And even when I try, it's no use. Phat Farm on John just looks like the fat farm. But despite his appearance, he had a six-figure salary, which meant he took me to the finest restaurants in town, his company had box seats to all the sporting events, and he drove a Lexus. I know my reasons for dating him were purely selfish, but hey, it isn't every day a girl from the streets gets the opportunity to sample the finer things in life. After a while, though, even those weren't enough to make me want to keep seeing him.

The second time I gave him some was because I

couldn't bring myself to say no after he had spent over two hundred dollars on a lobster dinner. As soon as we were in the bed, he was all over me, touching, feeling, sucking, and, of course, tweaking. When I reached down and felt what he was working with, I almost laughed in his face. Good Lord, my thirteen-year-old son had more than he did! Nevertheless, I endured the hour-long session, and when I finally left his place, I had every intention of ending the relationship. Unfortunately, the next day at work I got fired, and who did I call? John. He let me cry on his shoulder. Back then, I didn't know what I was going to do. I was already behind on my house payment. After a month of hitting the pavement hard, I panicked—then John offered a solution.

"Let's get married."

"What?" I looked at him like he had lost his damn mind.

He simply shrugged. "Why not? You need help and I want to help you."

I tried to think of every reason I could why that wasn't even a possibility and ended up stating the obvious. "We've barely known each other three months."

He shrugged and smiled. "It wouldn't matter to me if it had been two years. In the short time we've been together, I have fallen in love with you and your children."

I was at a loss for words because although he was starting to grow on me, love wasn't even a factor, not to mention that the sex had gotten worse instead of better, and I was ready to move on to the next guy.

John noticed my hesitation, because he added, "Listen, I know you don't love me and that's okay. You can learn to love me later. Let's try it out for a year and if it doesn't work out, then we can go our separate ways."

If I hadn't known it before, I definitely knew it then—his ass was desperate. Why else would someone ask a woman he barely knew to marry him? With two kids, and a foreclosure notice from the bank, I did the only thing any desperate single mother would do. I accepted.

His face lit up like a Christmas tree. "You just made me a happy man."

John then gave me one of those kisses that lacked passion, as well as tongue, then moved into the kitchen. I was about to yell, "Wait! I changed my mind," When I saw him grab the stack of bills I'd left lying on the kitchen table. When he removed his checkbook from his back pocket and took a seat, I didn't say a damn thing. That night I lay in his arms, trying to imagine a life with him, and all I saw was boredom and lousy sex. Still, I kept my mouth shut. Three days later, John got down on one knee in front of my kids, holding a one-carat solitaire. I didn't even feel my lips move but I definitely heard myself accept. Within the next two weeks, we were standing in front of the justice of the peace with my sister Lisa and her husband as our witnesses.

After that I tried to make the best of it, even though I knew I didn't love him. John was so good to me, I thought nothing else mattered, and that in time I could surely learn to love him. Making him happy was easy. I fucked him when he wanted to be fucked and told him what he wanted to hear.

A year passed with me trying to convince myself that I had made the right choice. With his six-figure salary, I made myself believe that I loved him and everything that he was able to do for me. I was financially secure. I didn't have to work. I was home when the school bus arrived. I attended PTA meetings and made brownies, things that so many mothers wished they could do. I started getting into that Suzie Home-maker shit and began planning meals. I even learned how to crochet.

John loved me to death and showered me with so much affection that I tried to tell myself this was the best thing that could have ever happened to me. I even tried to enjoy sex with him. I would fondle and play with him and for hours we would lie in the bed, kissing and hugging between rounds one and two. I convinced myself that I had a lot to be thankful for. Sex was a small price to pay for the lifestyle I was living.

John built a four-bedroom home for me and my kids and I got the joy of decorating it myself. Then, when I had nothing left to do, I started looking for a job. I applied for every management position I could find, and after a year, I still hadn't found a job. Every rejection was proof that marrying John had been the right deci-sion. However, at the end of the first year, I thought I was going to lose my damn mind. I had too much time on my hands and all I did was sit around and think.

"Why don't you write?" John suggested after I started complaining about being bored. "You said you always wanted to write a book."

It had always been a dream of mine to become a fa-mous author someday. So, I decided to give it a try. John bought me a computer. Before long, the words began to flow and I got so wrapped up in my writing that I discovered a way to fill the void in my life for the next year. After that, every time I thought about leaving him, a voice in my head would say, *Bitch, look at all you have accomplished with this man. You'd be a fool to let him go.* Then I would glance over at his kind face sitting in a chair like a damn puppy just waiting for me to scratch his head, and I would feel guilty for even thinking about leaving him. But still, even after I had published three erotic romance novels, I realized with a sinking feeling in the pit of my stomach that no matter how much I tried to hide behind the stories I was writing, my marriage wasn't going to change. I realized that after three years, I still wasn't in love with him. I liked him and loved how good he had been to me and my kids, but I didn't love him.

I mean, come on. To this day, I'm embarrassed to be seen in public together. With our fifteen-year age difference and his old-school spirits, it's like having my daddy on my arm. I dread going out alone, just the two of us, because we have nothing to talk about. Vacations are a bust because we never have any fun unless I create it. I didn't realize until we were married that John had no friends, no hobbies. Anything I do, he wants to do. He has become so needy that his entire life revolves around me and my kids, and it is driving me crazy. I'm not kidding you. I do almost anything to get away from him. Book-signing tours, vacations with my girlfriends, any excuse to put some distance between him and the boring life he wants me to continue to share with him. The only reason we have lasted this long is because of financial stability, and after my divorce I wanted to offer my children a stable home. Something I never had.

I never knew my real daddy. He died in a car accident when I was barely four. Growing up with my stepfather was pure hell. Paul Perry made it no secret he didn't like me. No matter how hard I tried, it was never good enough. To hide my pain, I rebelled and generally gave him a hard time. My mother, Bernice, was and still is a crackhead. Talking to her was a waste of time. A week after my sixteenth birthday, she left and didn't bother to come back. During that time, I had already met my first husband. High-school romances seldom work, and my marriage to Mario was just that. By the time I received my diploma, I was already pregnant with Quinton. Tamara came three years later. After Mario put his hands on me one time too many, I took a bat to his head, and filed for divorce.

Now you're probably wondering, after all that drama, how I could even think about leaving a man like John. Believe me, I hear it a lot, and I've been asking myself the same question for years. Only I can't come up with one good excuse except to say, I am unhappy. I just wished I felt the same way he does. I've tried so hard, but I've got needs and wants that he just can't meet.

The thought of him touching me turns my stomach. His kisses make me want to run to the bathroom and throw up. I can't help the way I feel. I love John for who he is, but I am not in love with him. There is a difference. I didn't believe that at first, but I know it now. I just can't take it anymore. I know now he isn't my soul mate. That I can't spend the next fifty years with him because, in the process, I'll be losing a piece of myself. I need a man who challenges my mind, body, and soul, who I look forward to sharing my evening with, talking about our day. I want a man who holds me in his arms through the night after making me come.

With John, if you give him a hug he wants sex. If you kiss him, he gropes your breasts. Any form of affection results in sex, so eventually I've stopped touching him altogether. Also, with John I can't initiate sex, because if I do, I kid you not, his dick won't work. He has to be the aggressor and even then he asks for permission. What brotha do you know asks for the coochie? I want a man to flip my ass over and bury all ten inches in before I can take a breath. John is so kind and obedient that if I ordered him to bark like a dog, he would respond like that princess in *Coming to America.*

After the first two years, I couldn't take it any longer. I started hanging out on the weekend and messing around with one man after another, trying to find what I was missing at home. John never once complained about me being in the streets as long as I gave him some whenever he asked. I didn't mind at first, but now that his dick only works half the time and I have to spend the majority of it whacking him off, I'm fed up and can't take too much more. I am dying inside. I just wish I could get him to understand.

During our marriage, I have suggested splitting up at least four times. And every time he has talked me out of it. I just don't understand it. I remember what he said the last time I tried to tell him I was unhappy.

"What do I need to do to make Renee happy?"

I shrugged. "I don't know anymore."

"I'll do anything you want, but you've got to give me a hint."

After a moment of hesitation, I said, "Time away from each other."

I saw the flash of panic in his eyes before he pulled me in his arms. "I don't want you to leave. We can work this out if you tell me what I've got to do." His chest began to heave and his tears stained the side of my neck. "I love you so much."

I was overcome with guilt. This man had given me

everything and here I was, trying to bail out on him. I held him in my arms and promised to try harder. But I continued to mess around and the months passed with me stepping out on my husband every chance I got. Then, two years ago, he accepted a position hundreds of miles away. I stayed behind with no intention of joining him until my sister made me promise only minutes before she had gone into surgery to pray to God for answers, and to give my marriage one last chance. Then, only days after agreeing to try harder, my sister died from a blood clot to the heart. Overwhelmed with grief, I stayed true to my word, and gave John another year of my life. I've prayed regularly and have given up all the other relationships. I can honestly say that I haven't messed around on my husband, not once, in a year. Okay . . . make that nine months. Damn . . . all right, in the last six months. And that is a record for me. But my ass is so horny that I don't know how much longer I'm gonna be able to hold out. Why do you think I write all those erotic novels? Because I need some real dick, and not that cracker-box shit I'm getting at home. That's why it's time for me to start building another life. It's time for me to get a job teaching. I already have a bachelor's degree in Journalism and a master's in English. Teaching would allow me to get back into the workforce again so I can support myself. Writing pays well but not as good as everyone thinks. I have a fat savings account but how long will that last without John's help? I love to shop and have gotten used to living an upper-class lifestyle. Change is not going to be easy. Okay, so all I need is a job—then I can save up enough to move and buy my own house. One more year, that's all I have to survive, then I can pack my bags and get the hell up out of here. It sounds easy enough, but somehow I know that leaving him won't be that easy. Freedom will come at a price. I just hope I can afford it.

Careful of the Company You Keep

One

Renee

There are a lot of things I expected to face in my life. Walking in on my husband with his dick stuck in another man's ass was not one of them.

Shock was an understatement. I couldn't think. I couldn't breathe and damn near choked. All I could do was stand there and watch John and another man racing to the finish line in *my* bed. They were so busy fucking neither of them heard the bedroom door open or noticed me standing there.

Think, bitch, think!

Inhale. Exhale. I knew I had to do something quick, fast, and in a hurry because any second now and the moment would be lost. I reached down to my waist, removed the cell phone from my hip, and aimed it in their direction.

"Cheese, mothafuckas!"

As soon as both of them fags looked my way, I pressed the camera button on my phone.

Priceless.

John jumped back so fast, he tripped over a shoe and fell flat on his ass. "Renee! What the hell?"

"My words exactly. You should have taken that booty bandit shit to a hotel." I moved in for a close-up and pressed the button again.

John held up his hands in a panic. "Hold up, baby! I can explain."

I glared at his fat ass. "Save it for someone who cares, because I don't give a fuck."

At a loss for words, John just sat there breathing heavily while Shemar scrambled for his pants. I looked at him and rolled my eyes in disgust. To think, I've been fucking his faggot ass for the last couple of weeks. Angrily, I snatched the first thing I could get my hands on— a bottle of scented lotion—and tossed it across the room and got pretty boy on the side of his head.

"What's wrong with you?" Shemar shouted, then ducked out of the way before my hairbrush got him in the forearm.

"What's wrong with me?" *Oh no, he didn't just ask me that.* "What's wrong is finding you . . . bent over . . . like some bitch . . . with my husband fucking you!" I tossed John's aftershave, and it hit the wall and shattered. "What's wrong is knowing my husband . . . *my husband* . . . fucked you in the bed that *I* bought!" I kept on screaming and throwing shit at the two of them.

John's eyes grew wide with guilt. "Renee, please, let's talk about this," he pleaded.

"We ain't got shit to talk about!" I screamed. Was he smoking crack? What could he possibly have to explain? I moved over to my dresser and started throwing everything in reach. I snatched up a bottle of Diamonds perfume and was about to toss it when I remembered how much I paid for it. I put it down and grabbed the cheap shit instead. By now I was throwing anything I could get my hands on in their direction, including a pair of three-pound dumbbells I kept on the floor in the corner. Both of those bitches were bobbing and weaving and trying to cover their heads. "As soon as you get dressed, get the fuck outta here!"

"We ain't going nowhere!" Shemar screamed like a little bitch. "Tell her, John. Tell her you're my man now and this is . . . this is *your* house!"

John looked over at Shemar and cut his eyes. "Shemar, this is not the time."

Shemar propped a hand at his waist. "The hell it ain't. What have we been talking about for the last several months? You promised we'd be together, and I'm tired of waiting. Dammit, John, you belong to me!"

What the fuck? I couldn't believe this gay shit. The longer I looked and listened, the angrier I got. I reached for a pair of scissors and lunged at Shemar, who saw me coming and hurried into the adjoining bathroom and slammed the door. I was moving so fast the blades stabbed the wood. I yanked the scissors free and headed toward John, who ducked, then grabbed my wrist and wrestled the scissors out of my hand.

"Let me go!" I screamed. I balled up my fist and started beating him across his face and chest. And just like a bitch, he let me tear his ass up.

"Go ahead, Renee. Do what you have to do, but it's not going to change anything."

"Fuck you!" I shouted, then swung hard and got him in the nose. Finally he grabbed my hands and I jerked away from him. I was breathing so hard I was hyperventilating. Leaning over, I placed my hands on my knees and tried counting to ten to catch my breath. "How . . . could . . . you . . . do this to me?"

John moved and took a seat on the end of the bed, holding a T-shirt up to his nose. It was bleeding. *Good.*

"As soon as you calm down, we can sit down like two adults and talk." I could tell by the tone of his voice that he never expected me to find out this way.

"I said we ain't got shit to talk about! I've been tolerating your itty-bitty limp-dick ass for the last five years, and this is how you treat me?" No wonder his dick half worked when we made love. Part of me felt like laughing—and probably would later, because this was the excuse I'd been waiting for to finally get out of my marriage—but right now, it was too humiliating for words.

"I can no longer hide how I feel."

"You sick bastard." I was so mad I didn't realize until I saw John holding the side of his head that I had hurled my wooden jewelry box at him.

"Quit it, Renee!" he ordered and tried to reach for me, but I jumped out of the way.

"Fuck you, John!"

I was too through. I had to bite my tongue to stop from telling him how I really felt about the last five years of our marriage. Big Mama taught me a long time ago not to bite the hand that feeds you, and I needed John to keep supporting me until I could figure out a plan. The best way was to play on his sympathy by making him think I was hurt to discover our marriage was over. No, I wasn't hurt. I was pissed the fuck off. "How could you do this to me?" I forced myself not to blink so my eyes would become misty, and tears eventually appeared.

"I . . . I never expected you to find out this way. I'm really sorry. How—"

I cut him off before he could finish.

"Sorry, my ass!" I screeched. "Both of y'all get out of my house!"

"Bitch, this is my man's house!" Shemar screamed from the other side of the bathroom door.

"Faggot, shut the hell up!" I ran over and kicked the door and hurt my damn toe. I screamed at the top of my lungs, then started pacing the length of the room.

John just continued to sit there holding his head with one hand and applying pressure to his nose with the other. I removed my cell phone from my hip and went ahead and sent those pictures to my e-mail address just in case one of those gay mothafuckas decided to get bold and try to snatch the phone. My hands were trembling with anger.

"What're you planning to do with those pictures?"

I rolled my eyes in John's direction. "Nothing just yet, but if you *fuck* with me, I'm going to send them to everybody, including your uppity-ass mama."

I expected him to lunge from the bed and snatch the phone from my hands, because the last thing John wanted was to tarnish his image. Lenore never did think I was good enough for her son. Shit, if she only knew.

However, instead of wrestling me to the floor, John just sat there like a bitch with his hands on his lap, looking at me like what I saw happening never really happened. As if it had been my imagination. "Quit trippin'," he finally said.

"Trippin'? Trippin'!"

He gave me a dismissive laugh. "Yes, Renee, trippin'. It's not that big a deal."

"Oh, it's not? Okay, then let me show you how big a deal it is!" I ran across the room to the large walk-in closet we shared and started fumbling on the top shelf. John must have heard me loading his gun because he hurried into the bathroom with Shemar and shut and locked the door just in time. I aimed, and a bullet pierced the wall only inches from the door.

"Renee, what the hell are you doing?" John screamed. "Put that gun down!"

"Shut the hell up!" I yelled and shot at the door again. Shemar was screaming at John to "control that crazy bitch." I pulled the trigger again and screamed, "Shut up, punk, before I give you something to cry about." He must have realized I was serious because everything got quiet. "That's more like it. Now listen and listen good. I want both of you gay mothafuckas out of *my* house by the time I get back. Otherwise, I'm shooting y'all fags for real!" I decided it was time for me to bounce before one of the neighbors called the police.

I couldn't get out of that house fast enough. I took the stairs two at a time and grabbed my purse from the table. A retired couple who lived across the street was standing on the porch. As soon as they saw me coming out the door with a gun in my hand, they raced back in the house.

I climbed into my Lexus and peeled down the driveway and onto the street. A mile up the road, the tears began to fall and I angrily wiped them away. "Don't you dare cry over that gay bastard."

I was driving, thinking over everything that had happened, and trying to figure out how in the hell I missed the warning signs. I hear women all the time talking about how they had no idea their man was on the DL, and I always say to myself, "what the fuck ever." The signs were there. Hell, most of the time I could spend five minutes with a man and could tell he was gay. Yet I had no idea about my own husband. But then ours was a weird relationship from the start.

Our marriage was a one-night stand that turned into a five-year commitment. We'd barely dated a month before he proposed. My ass was unemployed and about to be homeless. With two little kids, that was not an option. So when John proposed, "marry me now and love me later," I jumped at the opportunity.

And that's what your stupid ass gets.

Yep, I should have left him years ago. Quit talking about it and be about it, that's the shit I say to my friends all the time, yet I didn't follow my own advice.

I was ten miles from home, speeding down the highway, when my cell phone rang. I looked down and saw I had a private call. *I bet you five dollars and a Long Island iced tea it's John's gay ass.*

"What?"

"I'd appreciate it if you'd not share those pictures." He said the words so slowly that it gave me an eerie feeling.

"That depends," I stated calmly.

"Depends on what?"

"On how much you plan to pay, mothafucka!" Even with the windows down and the wind whipping across my face, I could hear Shemar yelling something in the background. "Tell that fag to shut the hell up!"

John covered the mouthpiece and mumbled something, then came back. "Sorry, he's upset, too."

"Who give a fuck how that fag feels?" I screamed. This was some straight-up soap opera shit.

"Don't be like that," he scolded.

"Don't tell me what the fuck to do before I come back over, shoot both y'all gay asses, and then plead temporary insanity."

"Listen, Renee, we can work this out if you'd give us a chance. I love you, Renee, but I'm not going to lie to you, I love Shemar as well. You didn't mind sharing me before, so what's different about now?"

"It was *your* idea to start swinging with other couples, and it was *you* who thought you weren't satisfying me sexually, so you invited Shemar to fuck me while you were in the room watching. Nowhere in that conversation did you say you would be fucking him as well. Huh? Tell me, John, because not once in the five years that we've been married did you mention anything about being gay."

"I'm not gay," he barked defensively.

"Then what the fuck would you call it?"

There was a brief pause before he answered, "I would call it . . . liking variety."

"And I call it liking dick!" I was screaming so hard the lady in the next car was staring nervously at me. I flipped her off for not minding her own business. "I'm divorcing yo gay ass. And according to our prenuptial agreement, if either of us catches the other in a compromising position, the other gets paid. And I'm getting ready to milk yo ass!"

"And what about the men you've been with? Remember, I have home videos," he reminded me.

"Yeah, and your bitch ass is in every one!" I was no fool. From the first day we started trying to add a little flavor to our marriage, I made sure every time John pulled out the camcorder, he was in that home movie as well. All the things that we had done with Shemar and the others started racing through my head. Hell, I even sucked Shemar's dick. *Oh my goodness! I'm going to be sick.* I was so nauseous my dinner tried to come up. I choked, then pushed that shit back down.

"Are you okay?"

"Hell nah! What the fuck? I just walked in on you fucking another mothafucka in his ass and *you have the nerve to ask me if I'm okay?*"

My response was met by a wave of silence.

"Renee, I don't know what else to say other than I'm sorry and hope we can work this out."

"What the hell is there left to work out?" This shit was so unbelievable I didn't know what to think or how to react, and that's rare for me. Never in a million years would I have expected to walk in on my husband, or any man for that matter, banging another one in his ass. I don't even watch boy/boy adult videos. I got sick watching *Brokeback Mountain.* "I want my monthly allotment doubled and don't even think about canceling my insurance benefits. You got one hour to pack yo shit and get the fuck out of my house. Oh yeah . . . and take them sheets with you!" I screamed, then ended the call.

Tears were running down my face. I don't know why I was crying over that fool.

John had never been good in bed. His thing is too little and he spends more time tweaking my damn nipples like they were knobs to a transistor radio than anything else. Nevertheless, he was rich and I told myself it was a small consequence for everything he had given me. Big-ass house. New ride. Private schools for the kids, and money in my own personal bank account. In exchange, all I had to do was give him some pussy three times a week. It was easier in the beginning, but the last three years, I started feeling like it was too much damn work. Hell, if I wanted a job, I would have gone out and applied for one. So to escape, I started writing and was now a published best-selling author of erotic romance. What I wasn't getting in my bed, I was getting in my books, and plenty of it. And when that was no longer enough, I started fucking around with every Tom, Dick, and Jerry I came in contact with. But after a while, I still wasn't happy.

Somehow, John sensed my misery, and two months ago, he invited Shemar to our bed for a ménage à trois. I thought *cha-ching*, I had hit the jackpot. Shemar and I would fuck while John sat back, beating his meat and watching. Then John and I started swinging with other couples. The husband was banging me while John was poking the man's wife. I thought I was getting the best of both worlds. Only the joke was on my black ass.

I guess I can't blame anyone but myself. I should have known that it was too good to be true. That's what I get for thinking I was getting something for nothing. I'd been talking about leaving John for years, and now that the time had come I had to quit talking about it and be about it. Starting right now, my life was beginning anew. A tear streamed down my cheek because I wasn't sure if I even knew where to begin.